P9-AOA-822

VESTAL PUBLIC LIBRARY
0 00 10 0269149 9

Under *the* Skin

Other works by

James Carlos Blake

• •

A World of Thieves

Wildwood Boys

The Pistoleer

The Friends of Pancho Villa

In the Rogue Blood

Red Grass River

Borderlands: Short Fictions

Under the Skin

a novel

James Carlos Blake

wm

William Morrow

An Imprint of HarperCollins*Publishers*

HarperCollins books may be purchased for educational, business, or sales promotional use. For information please write: Special Markets Department, HarperCollins Publishers Inc., 10 East 53rd Street, New York, NY 10022.

FIRST EDITION

DESIGNED BY DEBORAH KERNER/DANCING BEARS DESIGN

Library of Congress Cataloging-in-Publication Data

Blake, James Carlos.

Under the skin : a novel / James Carlos Blake.—1st ed.

p. cm.

ISBN 0-380-97751-6

1. Galveston (Tex.)—Fiction. 2. Organized crime—Fiction. 3. Bodyguards—Fiction.

4. Generals—Fiction. I. Title.

PS3552.L3483 U54 2003

813'.54—dc21 2002023892

03 04 05 06 07 JTC/QW 10 9 8 7 6 5 4 3 2 1

Everyone's skin is so particular and we are so largely unimaginable to one another.

—JIM HARRISON, *Legends of the Fall*

The heart has reasons that reason cannot understand.

—BLAISE PASCAL, *Pensées*

Si el mundo es ilusión la perdida del mundo es ilusión también.

—CORMAC MCCARTHY, *The Crossing*

UNDER *the* SKIN

A chill desert night of wind and rain. The trade at Mrs. O'Malley's house has been kept meager by the inclement weather and the loss of the neighborhood's electrical power since earlier in the day. Rumor has it that a stray bullet struck dead a transformer. For the past two days errant rounds have carried over the Rio Grande—glancing off buildings, popping through windowpanes, hitting random spectators among the rooftop crowds seeking to be entertained by the warfare across the river. Even through the closed windows and the pattering of the rain, gunfire remains audible at this late hour, though the latest word is that the rebels have taken Juárez and the shooting is now all in celebration and the exercise of firing squads.

The house is alight with oil lamps. Its eight resident whores huddled into their housecoats and carping of boredom. Now comes a loud rapping of the front door's iron knocker and they all sit up as alert as cats.

The houseman peers through a peephole, then turns to the madam and shrugs. Mrs. O'Malley bustles to the door and puts her eye to the peeper.

"Well Jesus Mary and Joseph."

She works the bolt and tugs open the door. The lamp flames dip and swirl in their glass and shadows waver on the walls as a cold rush of air brings in the mingled scents of creosote and wet dust.

Mrs. O'Malley trills in Spanish at the two men who enter the dim foyer and shuts the door behind them. The maid Concha takes their overcoats and they shake the rainwater off their hats and stamp their boots on the foyer rugs.

"Pasen, caballeros, pasen," Mrs. O'Malley says, ushering them into the parlor.

They come into the brighter light and the girls see that they are Mexicans in Montana hats and suits of good cut. One of the men has appeared in photographs in the local newspapers almost every day for the past week, but few of these girls ever give attention to a newspaper and so most of them do not recognize him.

"Attention, ladies," Mrs. O'Malley says, as the girls assemble themselves for inspection. "Just look who's honoring us with a visit." She extends her arms toward one of the men as if presenting a star performer on a theater stage. "My dear old friend—"

"Pancho!" one of the girls calls out—Kate, whom the others call Schoolgirl for her claim of having attended college for a time before her fortunes turned. Only she and two of the other girls in the house—a small brunette they call Pony and a fleshy girl named Irish Red—were working at Mrs. O'Malley's last winter when this man regularly patronized the place. The three waggle their fingers in greeting and the man grins at them and nods.

"General Francisco Villa," the madam enunciates, fixing the Schoolgirl with a correcting look and poorly concealing her irritation at being usurped of the introduction.

The girls have of course all heard of him and they make a murmuring big-eyed show of being impressed. He is tall for a Mexican, big-chested and thick-bellied without conveying an impression of fatness. His eyes are hidden in the squint of his smile. The madam hugs him sideways around the waist and says how happy she is to see him again. He fondly pats her ample bottom and repositions her arm away from the holstered pistol under his coatflap.

"Hace siete o ocho meses que no te veo, verdad?" the madam says. "Que tanto ha occurido en ese tiempo."

Villa agrees that much has happened in the eight months since he was last in El Paso, living as an exile in the Mexican quarter with only eight men in his bunch. Now he commands the mighty Division of the North. He is one of the most celebrated chieftains of the Mexican Revolution and a favored subject of American reporters covering the war.

Would he and his friend like a drink, the madam asks. Some music on the hand-cranked phonograph?

Villa flicks his hand in rejection of the offer and returns his attention to the women, a man come to take his pleasure but with no time for parlor amenities. The girls have thrown open their housecoats to afford the visitors a franker view of their charms in negligee or camisole, but Villa already knows what he wants. He has come with the express hope of finding the Irish girl still here, and now beckons her. He much admires her bright red hair and lushly freckled skin as pale as cream—traits not common among the women he usually enjoys. She beams and hastens to him.

Mrs. O'Malley pats his arm and says she just knew he'd pick Megan again.

"Y cual prefiere tu amigo?" she says, and turns to the other man.

"Pues?" Villa says to him.

He is taller than Villa, leaner of waist but as wide of chest, his mustache thicker, his eyes so black the pupils are lost in their darkness.

"Esa larguirucha," he says, jutting his chin at a tall lean girl with honey-colored hair and eyes the blue of gas flames. The only one of them able to hold his gaze, her small smile a reflection of his own.

"Ava," Mrs. O'Malley says. "Our newest." She turns from the man to the girl and back to the man, remarking the intensity of the look between them. "My," she says to Villa. "Parece que tu cuate se encontró una novia."

"Otra novia mas," Villa says with a laugh. Then says to the redhead, "Vente, mi rojita," and hugs her against his side and they head for the stairway. The Ava girl takes the other man by the hand and they follow Villa and Irish Red up to the bedrooms.

The rest of the girls resettle themselves, some of them casting envious glances after the couples ascending the stairs, chiefly at the Ava girl, who has been with them but a week, the one they call the Spook for her inclination to keep her own company and her manner of seeming to be elsewhere even when she's in their midst.

• •

At dawn the rain has departed. So too the men. The few remaining clouds are ragged red scraps on a pink horizon. The light of the ascending day eases down the Franklins and into the city streets.

By late morning Mrs. O'Malley is away to her daily mass at Our Lady of Perpetual Sorrows. The girls rouse themselves from their beds and descend to the sunbright kitchen for coffee and the pastries Concha has fetched from the corner panadería. They sit at a long table under a row of windows open to the late-November coolness and the croonings of Inca doves in the patio trees. The gunfire across the river has abated to faint sporadic fusillades, each volley prompting Concha to a quick sign of the cross.

As usual at the breakfast table most of the girls are closemouthed and drawn into themselves, absorbed in the ruminations that come with the light of each newrisen day. Only Kate the Schoolgirl, reading a newspaper, and Irish Red and Juliet—called Lovergirl—who are engaged in antic whisperings about Megan's night with Pancho

Villa, seem unaffected by the rueful mood that daily haunts this hour of the whore life.

Now the Lovergirl's giggles rise keenly and Betty the Mule, long-faced and bucktoothed, says, "Why don't you two take your snickering somewhere else? You sound like a couple of moron kids, for shit's sake."

"Why don't you mind your own business?" the Lovergirl says. "Nobody's anyway talking to you."

"She's just jealous," Irish Red says.

"Jealous?" the Mule says. "Of *what*? Some greaser who probably left you a case of clap and a furpatch full of crabs?"

Lightfoot Gwen chuckles without looking up from her coffee, but the Pony says, "Hey," and gives Betty a look of reprimand and nods toward Concha standing at the stove with her back to them. The Mule glances at the maid and makes a face of indifference.

"Not much you aint jealous," Irish Red says.

"Jesus," the Schoolgirl says, gawking into her newspaper. She will sometimes share with the table an item she finds of particular interest, sometimes even read it aloud in spite of their inattention and feigned yawns. But now the timbre of her voice is such that few of them can ignore it. She glances from one item on the page to another and then back again, as if confirming some correspondence between them. "Sweet Jesus."

"What now?" says Jenny the Joker.

"He killed *three hundred* men," the Schoolgirl says. "Prisoners. Just yesterday."

"Who did?" the Pony says.

"Hell, they're always shooting them by the trainload over there," the Mule says. "They're shooting them right now, just listen."

"It's not the same," the Schoolgirl says. She looks down at the paper and puts a finger to it. "They were in a corral and there was this wall and he said any man who could get over it could go free. He let them try it ten at a time. And he killed them all. He shot men for *three hours*." She looks up from the paper. "And then he came here."

"Pancho?" Irish Red says. "*He* shot—"

"No, the other. There's a picture."

Some of them gather around the Schoolgirl to look over her shoulder at the newspaper photograph. It shows Villa and a white-haired American general standing together on a bridge between Juárez and El Paso, smiling at the camera and flanked by their aides. The man directly next to Villa is the one who came with him to the house last night. The Schoolgirl puts her finger on the caption, on the name identifying him, then moves her finger to the small report about the three hundred federal prisoners and taps her nail on the name of their executioner.

"Be goddamn," the Lovergirl says.

They turn their attention to the Spook, who was with this man last night. She sits at the far end of the table where she has been drinking coffee and staring out the window toward the sounds of the firing squads. None of them can read her face.

"It says here his name's . . ." The Schoolgirl looks down at the paper again and in Anglicized fashion enunciates: "Fierro."

"Padre, hijo, espiritú santo," Concha says as she blesses herself.

The Spook turns to them and scans their faces, their big-eyed show of shock mingled with wet-lipped curiosity.

"I know," she says.

And leaves the room.

• •

She had been with other men of seemingly insatiable desire but their lust had no object beyond her naked flesh. This one's hunger was of a different breed. He took obvious pleasure in her body, but it seemed to her that his urgent effort was toward something more than sexual release, toward something beyond the pulse and throb of their carnal flexions, as if what he sought after lay in some unreachably distant region of the soul itself. But whether the soul he strove toward was hers or his own she could not say. She could not have given words to any of this, she could but sense it, know it only by way of her skin.

On completion of their first coupling he sat with his back to the headboard and drank from a bottle he'd brought with him. She recognized the uncorked smell as the same one she'd tasted with their first kiss and it occurred to her that he might be a little drunk. He lit a cigarillo and offered her both the packet of smokes and the bottle and she accepted only the cigarillo. He lit it for her and she said, "Thank you," the first words between them. In the dim light from the lantern turned down low on the dresser he looked to be carved of copper.

"Como te llamas?" he said.

The query was among the rudimentary Spanish locutions she had thus far learned from Concha. "Ava," she said.

He chuckled low and repeated the name in its Spanish pronunciation, watching her eyes in the low light. Then said, "Es una mentira. Dime la verdad."

"I don't hablo español too very . . . bueno. Sorry."

"No te llamas Ava. No es . . . is no true."

She wondered how he'd known she was lying, and why she was not surprised that he'd known. His eyes on her were as black as the night of rain at the window and utterly unfathomable, but she felt as if they saw directly to the truth of her, whatever that might be.

"Ella," she said. "Ella Marlene Malone."

"El-la-marleeen-malooone," he said in singsong. "Como una cancionita."

"You're making fun," she said, and put her fingers to his mouth. He held her hand there and kissed each fingertip in turn. And then he was on her again.

This time he afterward got out of bed and paced about the small room, stretching, flexing, rolling his head like a pugilist, briefly massaging one hand and then the other. He drained the last of the bottle and set it on the dresser. The light was behind him and she could not see his face.

"Hoy mismo maté trescientos pinches Colorados." He turned his gaze to the dark window. "Pues, puede ser que los maté ayer. Los días pasan." He looked at her again. "Pasan a la memoria y la historia, los más enormes museos de mentiras."

She stared at him in utter incomprehension. He stepped to the chair where his clothes were draped and from them extracted a pair of revolvers. She'd had no notion of their presence.

"Los maté con éstas." He twirled the pistols on his fingers like a shooter in a Wild West show, then put one of them back into the coat. He held up three fingers of his free hand. "Tres*cientos*. Los maté todos." He struck his chest. "*Yo,* Fierro!"

She understood of this only the number three and what might be his name and that whatever he was telling her was attached to a ferocious pride.

"Your name . . . tu . . . llama . . . is Fierro?"

He laughed low in his throat and made a slight bow. "Rodolfo Fierro, a su servicio, mi angelita."

"Rodolfo," she said, testing the name on her tongue.

"Para algunos mi nombre es una canción tambien, como tuyo. Pero el mió es una canción de muerte."

"Muerte," she said. "I know that one. Death."

"Si—death." He laughed low. "Tienes miedo de la muerte? Tienes . . . cómo se dice? . . . *fear?*"

He stepped up beside the bed and raised the revolver so that the muzzle was within inches of her face. He slowly cocked the hammer and she heard the ratchet action as the cylinder rotated and even in the weak light she could see the bluntly indifferent bulletheads riding in their chambers.

Her breath caught. Her nipples tightened. Her blood sped.

She reached up and gingerly fingered the barrel. Then drew it closer, breathing its masculine smells of oiled gunmetal and burnt powder. And put her tonguetip to the muzzle and tasted of its taint. She could hear her own hard breathing.

His teeth showed. "Otra loca brava."

She tried to disengage the pistol from his hand, which felt as much of iron as the weapon itself. He uncocked it and released it to her.

The metal frame was impressed with the Colt symbol and the grips were pale yellow and each was embossed with an eagle holding a snake in its beak.

"I want it."

"La quieres?"

He seized her mouth in his hard fingers. She was unsure if he meant to kiss her or hit her or do something she could not begin to imagine. With an instinct she hadn't known she possessed she pressed the Colt against his stomach and cocked the hammer.

He chuckled—then kissed her deeply. She slid the gun down his belly to his phallus and found it standing rigid and they broke the kiss in laughter.

"Christ Jesus, I aint the only one loco," she said. She eased down the hammer as she had seen him do.

He made an expansive gesture of relinquishment. "Te la doy, güerita. Como un . . . pressen."

"A *present?*" She giggled happily and slipped the gun under the pillow as he got on the bed and positioned himself above her, his grin white, black eyes glowing.

"Wait," she said. "Momento."

She could not have said then or ever after why she did what she next did. It was as if something of the man's blood was calling to hers—some atavistic urge as primitive as a wolf howl—and she could not deny its pull, her own blood's yearn to join with his. In that moment of primal impulse, she probed into herself and extracted her pessary and slung it away.

He chuckled as at some comic mummery. "Y mas loca todavía."

And entered her.

• •

Dr. Marceau is a bespectacled man with a neatly trimmed gray beard and the polite but reserved manner of a distant uncle. The most lucrative portion of his practice comes from clients who share the need of his discretion and his willingness to help women beset by an age-old trouble consequent of reckless passion.

He regards the girl seated across the desk from him and shows her a small practiced smile bespeaking sympathetic understanding. His long experience has taught him to recognize the demimondaines even when they do not honestly identify themselves but assume some tired guise to preserve an illusion of dignity. Besides, the fallen ones of good family rarely come to him unaccompanied. It's almost always some young pony, green and given to mistakes, who arrives at his door all alone. Like this one.

"Well, ah . . . Mrs. Sullivan," he says, consulting his record sheet. "It's definite. The stork is on the wing. And has been for about three months, as nearly as I can determine."

She turns to stare out the window, her face revealing nothing of what she might be thinking. The doctor's office building is set on a mountainside overlooking the two cities flanking the river. On this chilly winter morning the vantage affords a vista beyond a low blue haze of woodsmoke and past the near sierras and broad Mexican plain to a jagged line of long dark ranges deep in the distant south.

The doctor removes his eyeglasses and cleans them with a handkerchief, permitting her a moment to ponder the verdict. The situation is worse for these soiled doves, he has come to believe, than for the innocent ones whose sin was to love too dearly some charming rogue who then abandoned them to the fates. He knows how abruptly some of these young cyprians can collapse into tears, their circumstance all at once an irrefutable testament to their ruined lives, to their far remove from the world's respect, from the future they had envisioned in a childhood only a few years past but seeming as distant as ancient history. The doctor prides himself on a certain finesse on these occasions. He has found that the whole matter was usually somewhat mitigated if he was the one to broach the solution to the problem rather than oblige them to tender the request. He sets the spectacles back on his face and rests his elbows on the desk and stares at the laced fingers of his hands like someone who has forgotten everything of prayer but its posture.

The girl continues to stare out the window.

"Ah, Mrs. . . . Sullivan. I know very well that in some instances—more prevalent than one might think, I assure you—such news as this is not especially gladsome. There are, after all, any number of reasons why a young woman might not be fully prepared for, ah, such a medical condition. Perfectly understandable reasons. Reasons she need not feel compelled to explain to anyone. And because the, ah, condition may be remedied by a rather simple procedure, a procedure in which I am very well—"

He is startled by the sudden look she fixes on him, blue eyes sparking, her aspect bright.

"I'm sorry," she says—and it takes him a second to understand that she is apologizing for her distraction. "I only came to be sure."

She rises from her chair. "Maybe I'll be back. Maybe not."

She goes to the door and stands there until he overcomes his befuddlement and hastens forward to open it for her. She smiles and bids him good day.

• •

"Bullshit," Frank Hartung says.

Cullen Youngblood's smile is small.

"Be damn if I don't about believe you're serious."

"That I am," Youngblood says. He sips of his drink.

"I damn well can't believe it."

"If you believe it or not doesn't change a hair on the fact of it," Youngblood says. He catches the bartender's attention and signals for another round.

"Christ sake, bud."

"I know," Youngblood says.

"Bad enough to want to get married, but . . . well, goddam, aint there no decent women?"

"She's plenty decent."

"Hell, man, she's a whore is what she is."

"Not anymore. Come next week she'll be Mrs. Cullen Youngblood, so don't go saying anything ungentlemanly about her or I'll be obliged to kick your ass."

"Shit. There's no end to your pitiful illusions."

"You might try congratulating me like a friend ought."

"I ought have you locked up in the crazyhouse till you get your right sense back, what I ought."

The bartender brings the fresh drinks to the end of the bar where they stand. Double bourbons with branch. Hartung picks up his and drinks half of it at a gulp.

"Christ sake, bud."

"I aint the first to do it. I known others to do it."

"Me too. Larry McGuane married one used to work in that house in Fort Stockton. They weren't married a month when he caught her at it with a neighbor boy."

"That one of McGuane's—"

"He whipped her ass bloody and she swore to him she'd never again. Thought he'd straightened her right out. Coupla days after, she cooks him a big fine dinner to show what a good wife she's gonna be. Half hour later he's near to dying of the poison. He just did get himself to Doc Wesson in time. Meanwhile she's burning down his house and emptying the jar of greenbacks he kept buried behind the stable and thought she didn't know nothing about. Took her leave on the midnight train. That was what, five, six years ago. You seen him lately? Looks like a old man. Living with his aunt and uncle. His stomach aint never been right since. Yeah, I known some to do it."

"That one was crazy to begin with and everybody knew it. McGuane knew what she was like, he just didn't have no caution nor a lick of sense. He always was a damn fool with women."

"I wouldn't be calling nobody crazy nor a damn fool neither, I was you," Hartung says. "Forty-five-year-old man."

"They aint all like McGuane's. Jessup Jerome married his Louisa out of Miss Hattie's in San Angelo. Been twenty-some years and a dozen kids. A man couldn't ask for a better wife."

"One in a damn thousand," Hartung says. He drains the rest of his drink.

"It aint that uncommon. I had a old uncle used to say they make the best wives because it means more to them after working in the trade. They got a better appreciation, he said."

"That uncle sounds loony as you. Must run in the family."

Hartung catches the bartender's eye and makes a circular motion with his finger over the bartop.

"Everybody thought it was a joke," he says. "You asking and asking and her steady saying no. Even Miz O'Malley thought you were only funning."

They have been friends, these two, since their boyhood in Presidio County, whose westernmost corner lies 150 miles downriver of the saloon where they now stand. Youngblood has owned the YB Ranch in Presidio since shortly after his father suffered a severe stroke fifteen years ago. Unable to walk or get on a horse or speak a coherent word, reduced to communicating by means of a small slateboard he wore around his neck, the old man endured his crippled state for four months before writing DAMN THIS! on his slate and shooting himself through the head. Youngblood couldn't blame him, but the loss was the last one left to him in the family. His elder brother Teddy had been killed at age eighteen in an alley fight in Alpine, and his little brother James, whose birth their mother had not survived, was twelve when he drowned in the Rio Grande.

Hartung's daddy had died two years prior to Youngblood's. The man was badly given to drink and one night on his way home from the saloon he stood up to piss from the moving wagon and lost his balance and fell out and broke his neck. He left the family so deeply in debt they'd had to sell their ranch, which neighbored the Youngblood place. Frank's mother and sister moved to Amarillo to live with relatives, but Frank chose to go work on his uncle's ranch near Las Cruces, New Mexico, some forty miles north of El Paso. The uncle was a childless widower and happy to take him in. When he died not long after, he left the place to Frank.

For more than ten years now Hartung and Youngblood have been getting together in El Paso once a month or so for a Saturday-night romp. Their usual procedure on these rendezvous is to take rooms at the Sheldon Hotel, dine at a fine restaurant, do a bit of drinking in various of the livelier saloons, and then cap the evening with a visit to Mrs. O'Malley's. They have on occasion arrived at her door in battered disarray, having obliged hardcases spoiling for a barroom fight, and she has in every such instance refused them admission until they first went to the pump shed at the rear of the house to wash the blood off their faces and tidy themselves somewhat. They can still get a laugh from each other with the recollection of the time she said they were too disorderly to be allowed to come in, and Hartung said, "Too *disorderly*? Hellfire, this is a disorderly house, aint it?"

One Saturday night just three days into the year of 1914 they met the darkly blond Ava, the "new girl" as Mrs. O'Malley called her, though by then she had been with the house nearly two months. Youngblood went upstairs with her and was so thoroughly smitten that he gladly paid the steeply higher price of staying with her all night. For the next two weeks he had frequent thoughts of her as he worked at the ranch, as he tried to read after supper, as he lay in bed and waited for sleep. The following Saturday he was back in El Paso and again bought her for the night—and he had returned every weekend thereafter.

His enjoyment of her went beyond the carnal, was of a sort that had been absent from his life since age twenty when Connie Duderstadt of Alpine threw him over for a boy of more prosperous family. In the years since, he has gained much experience with whores and believes himself no fool about them. This Ava's interest in his life—in his descriptions of the YB Ranch and the ruggedly beautiful country surrounding it, in the tales of his adventurous youth and of the last wild Indians that roamed the region in those days and the Mexican bandits that still did—seemed to him fully genuine. It soon became clear that she knew something of horses and rivers and weather, that she took as much pleasure in the natural world as he did. When he asked if Ava was her true name, she said it was, and on his promise to keep it to himself told him her full name was Ava Jane Harrison. She shared in the smile he showed on receiving such intimate information.

He had of course early on asked the ineluctable question of how she'd come to be in this business, but her mute stare in response had carried such chill he did not ask again. Although she steadfastly refused to reveal anything of her own history, he formed an impression that she'd grown up a solitary child. Her accent carried the softer resonances of the South, though he could place it no more precisely than that. For all her guardedness, she did let slip a small hint of her past on the night she asked if he'd ever read Edgar Allan Poe. He had—and he was delighted to know that she too was a reader. They talked and talked about Poe's poetry and such of his stories as "The Fall of the House of Usher" and "The Tell-Tale Heart." Her favorite tale was "The Imp of the Perverse," which he had not read. She was fond as well of Stephen Crane, especially his poetry, though she liked *The Red Badge of Courage* for its glorious renditions of battle and tormenting self-doubt. Had she also read *Maggie: A Girl of the Streets,* he wanted to know. She said she had, but she would not be drawn into a discussion of it—and he reasoned that its subject lay too close to home. She then asked who had taught him to enjoy books and he said his mother. "Me too," she said. And left it at that.

It was in the course of these postcoital conversations that he grew aware of just how lonely he had been for many years now, and that he did not want to continue that way.

By the time he and Hartung got together for their next monthly lark in El Paso, Youngblood had begun coming into town on Fridays so he could spend both nights of the weekend with Ava. Over supper he told Hartung of his interim trips into El Paso. His friend chuckled and said it sounded like he'd caught himself an expensive case of poontang fever and ought to try and get over it before he went broke.

Youngblood told him he had already twice asked her to marry him and had both times been turned down. Hartung looked stunned for a moment—and then broke out laughing and slapped him on the shoulder, taking it for a grand joke. On their arrival at Mrs. O'Malley's that evening, Hartung jovially asked the madam if she knew of his friend's quest to marry one of her girls. Mrs. O'Malley had known a number of working girls who'd married men they'd met professionally, but the idea of a confirmed bachelor and funlover such as Youngblood wanting to marry a girl like the Spook—and even more, the idea of the Spook turning him down—well, it had to be their little jape on everybody, and she joined in Hartung's laughter. The other girls suspected that the Spook had enlisted Youngblood's help to make sly fun of their own hopes for marriage some day, and they indignantly ignored the matter altogether.

For his part, Youngblood didn't care whether anyone except Ava believed his sincerity. He continued to catch the train from Marfa every Friday to be with her. On the past two Saturdays he had taken her to an early supper at a nice restaurant and then they had gone for a walk along the riverside before returning to the house at sundown, at which time she was officially back on the job. He then paid Mrs. O'Malley and they ascended the stairs to Ava's room.

He every weekend asked for her hand and she every time turned him down. The first time she'd refused him he'd been too stunned to even ask why not, but after the second rebuff he did. She'd given him an exasperated look and said, "What difference does it make?"—an answer so baffling he didn't know how to pursue his argument. He had settled for asking if it were possible she might change her mind one day.

"They say you ought never say never," she said.

He chose to interpret her smile as encouragement. He secretly believed her refusal was more a matter of inexplicable willfulness than solid conviction, but he was not without strong will of his own.

"In that case," he said, "I guess I'll go on asking."

And he had. And she had continued to say no. Until this morning.

The bartender brings the fresh drinks and retreats.

"If it wasn't no joke," Hartung says, "why'd she keep saying no?"

Youngblood shrugs.

"It's a shitload about her you don't know."

"I won't argue that. But what more you need to know than how you feel?"

"Miz O'Malley says maybe you just figure it's cheaper to marry it than keep spending as much on it as you been. She says you'd be dead wrong if that's what you think."

"O'Malley's no fool, but I wouldn't lay too big a bet on her knowing everything."

They sip their drinks.

"So how come she changed her mind?"

"That's something I do know," Youngblood says. He looks sidelong at his friend, then stares down into his drink. "Fact is, she's in the family way. Only ones to know it are her and me. Now you."

Hartung stares at him. And then looks around the saloon at the scattering of other patrons engaged in low conversations spiked with sporadic laughter. He clears his throat and says, "Let's see if I got this straight. She says you knocked her up and so now she's willing? Now how in the purple hell can a whore even know *who*—"

"It's not like that," Youngblood says. "And I said to quit calling her that. She aint that no more."

Hartung leans and spits into the cuspidor at their feet and wipes his mouth with the back of his hand. He stares at Youngblood in the backbar mirror. "How's it like then?"

"She don't know whose it is except she's sure it aint mine. She wanted me to be real clear on that before I asked again."

"When she tell you?"

"Last night. Wanted me to know it's a chance it was a sixteen-year-old kid from Chihuahua City. Boy's daddy wanted to give him an American girl for his birthday."

"The daddy might be *Mexican*?"

"She recollects having a problem that night with her whatcha-callit . . . that thing they use to keep from having this kind of trouble."

Hartung sighs and stares into his glass. Then clears his throat. "Don't you think this whole thing calls for maybe a little more consideration?"

"It's all I did last night was consider it. The news didn't set too good with me, let me tell you, none of it, especially the part about it's probably Mexican. She said the first thing she thought to do was go see somebody . . . you know, somebody who could . . . eliminate the problem. But she rather not do it. Said it's hers, no matter what. Said she never knew before how much she wanted to be a momma, have her a normal life. Said if I was still wanting to get hitched she'd be willing to lay low someplace till it's born. Back home we can say it's her sister's, say she died borning him. Say the husband was a Mexican armyman and got killed in all that mess down there."

"Sweet Baby Jesus." Hartung shakes his head and studies his drink.

"She said she'd sure enough understand if I said no. Said she wouldn't have no choice then but to go see somebody about it."

"She'll get rid of it if you won't marry her, but she won't marry you unless she can have it?"

"That's it."

Hartung lets a long breath and stares at him in the mirror.

"I walked all over town and thought about it till sunup."

"Then went ahead on and asked her again."

"I'll rent a place in San Antone where she can stay. I'll go see her every weekend till it's born. Then I'll take them home and tell the neighbors meet the new wife and her baby nephew whose momma died. Or maybe niece, I guess."

"What about its name?"

"We talked about that. Decided it'd be better to let him be Youngblood than have a Mexican name. I mean, he'll be my nephew too. No harm he can have my name."

Hartung rubs his face and sighs. He takes off his hat and runs a hand through his hair and stares into the hat as if it might hold some sensible explanation for the ways of men and women and the whole damned world. Then puts the hat back on and looks at Youngblood in the mirror.

"I don't even know what to say anymore. I been standing here thinking you were crazy but this goes way past crazy. This takes crazy all the way to the end of the goddamn line."

Youngblood meets his friend's eyes in the mirror and sips his drink.

"Jesus, bud. I never knew anybody to have it so bad."

"I know. But that's the whole thing, don't you see? The plain and simple of it is I love her. Can't help it, I just do. And if it's the only way to have her for my wife, then it's how I aim to do it."

He turns from the mirror to look at Hartung. "I'm tired of how I been doing, Frank. And I aint getting any damn younger. Which by the way neither are you, but that's your business."

Hartung spits into the cuspidor. "I give up. There's no making sense with a crazy man."

He stares into his whiskey for a time, then sips of it. "Damn hopeless case."

Youngblood grins. "Guess so."

"No guess about it."

"She's really a sweet girl."

"I'm sure."

"Wait'll you meet her."

"I done met her."

"No you aint, you just seen her and said howdy. I already told her you're gonna visit us real often."

"I am?"

"You damn right. You're gonna have many a supper with us."

Hartung drains his drink and contemplates the empty glass. "Supper, huh?" Then steps back from the bar and gives Youngblood a look of alarm. "Whoa! Is *she* gonna do the cooking?"

It takes Youngblood a second to catch the allusion to the hapless McGuane—and they burst into loud barking laughter.

• •

If she is a mystery to others she is hardly less of one to herself, a fact that troubles her not at all. No one will ever learn anything of her life prior to her arrival at Mrs. O'Malley's. There were witnesses to that earlier life, of course, but none are known to anyone who now knows her or will come to know her. Only her own memory can bear testimony to her past, but not in all the years to come will she permit herself even a passing thought of where she's come from or who she's been, and thus will her previous history disappear to wherever the world's vast store of unrecorded past does vanish.

The last recall of it she allowed herself was when Youngblood returned to her after a full night of pondering her disclosure that she carried another man's child, returned to her with the morning light and held her hands and said it didn't matter. And asked her again to be his wife.

She had searched his eyes for any hint of uncertainty but saw nothing in them but love.

Love. The very thing in Cullen Youngblood she had wagered on. A love whose power she dared not test against the truth but which proved equal to the lie. And in the moment of staring into his eyes and marveling at the blazing force of that love, she had the final thought she will ever have that touches on her earlier self:

And they used to call me *crazy.*

We wore good suits and hats and freshly shined shoes. Brando and LQ carried briefcases stuffed with old newspapers. Anybody who checked us out as we came through the Jacinto's revolving door would've figured us for three more members of the East Texas Insurance Association attending the year-end convention.

The lobby was brightly lighted and well appointed with dark leather sofas and easy chairs and ottomans, embroidered carpeting and tall potted palms. Business types stood chatting in clusters and huddled around documents laid out on coffee tables. Most of the action at this hour was in the hotel dining room, which was jammed with conventioneers and other New Year's celebrants and pouring out music and laughter and the loud garble of shouted conversations. The smell of booze carried out from the room. Even though Prohibition was two years dead and done with, you still couldn't belly up to a bar in Texas and buy a hard drink, not legally, but you could bring in your own, and this bunch must've brought it in by the carload. Through the open double doors I caught a glimpse of the mob inside, and of a man and woman seated on a dais—the man grayhaired and wearing a white toga and a sash that read 1935, the woman young and good-looking in a white bathing suit with a 1936 sash.

A couple was embracing at the bank of elevators as we came up, the man holding the woman close and nuzzling her neck, running his hand over her ass. The woman glanced over at us and pushed his hand away and hissed, "Will you just hold your horses?"

The little arrow over one of the elevator doors glided past the arc of floor numbers to stop at number one. The doors dinged open and another loud bunch of conventioneers came surging out and headed for the dining room. We moved fast to get into the car ahead of the couple and LQ turned and raised a hand to them and said, "Houston police business, folks. Yall take the next one, please."

Brando smiled at the pretty blond operator and made a shutting gesture and she closed the doors on the couple standing there with their mouths open. She had nicelooking legs under her short skirt and wore her cap at a sassy tilt. Brando winked at her and said, "All the way up, honey." She got us moving and said, "Yall policemen?"

"Don't we look it?" LQ said.

"Yessir," she said. "I guess so."

LQ said he was Sergeant O'Brien and Brando and I were Detectives Ramos and Gallo. She wanted to know if we were going to arrest somebody. LQ said probably not, just ask some people some questions. She looked from one of us to the others. LQ was fairhaired and cleanshaven and spoke with an East Texas drawl, but Brando and I were darkskinned and had big mustaches, and I thought the girl might be wondering when the Houston PD had started hiring guys that looked like us.

At the top floor LQ set down his briefcase and he and I got out. Brando stayed with the elevator and kept the door open. I heard the girl say, "I wanna see," but Brando told her to keep back from the door.

We'd figured on the watchdog in the hallway. He got up from his chair and dropped his magazine on it, tugged his lapels into place and planted himself with hands on hips. He held his coat flaps back so we could see the shoulder holster he was wearing.

"Stop right there," he said.

We kept walking toward him. "Houston police," LQ said. "Here to see William Ragsdale."

The guy cut his eyes from one of us to the other. He was goodsized but so was I, and although LQ was on the lanky side, he had the height on us. The guy's hands dropped off his hips.

"Let's see some badges," he said. You could almost hear the gears turning in his skull, thinking what might happen if he pulled a gun and we were really cops. That was the trouble with dimwits—in the time they needed to think it over, they were had.

"Sure thing," LQ said, pulling the .380 out from under his coat and cocking it as he put the muzzle in the guy's face. "Have a good look."

I drew my revolver from under my arm and held it down against my leg. It was an old single-action .44 with high-power loads that could knock down a horse.

The guard looked heartbroken at being taken so easily. He held his hands away from his sides as LQ reached in his coat and stripped him of a bulldog.

"How many?" LQ said, jutting his chin at the door.

"Just him and Kersey, a pair of chippies."

"Kersey a gunner?" LQ said.

"Naw, shit. Owns a truck company, some strip clubs."

LQ told him what to say and warned him that if he said anything else he'd be the first to get it.

I stepped off to one side of the door and LQ stood on the other. LQ nodded and the guard gave the door two sharp raps, waited a second and then gave it one more.

A voice inside said, *"What?"*

"Got a package here for Mr. Ragsdale. The desk just sent it up. Didn't say who from."

We heard the dead bolt working and then the door opened a few inches on its chain. "Where's it—"

LQ yanked the guard aside and I stepped up to the door and gave it a hell of a kick, snapping the chain and knocking the guy on the other side backpedaling and down on his ass. I went in with the revolver raised. LQ shoved the guard staggering past me and hustled in behind me and closed the door.

Ragsdale was gawking at us from the sofa where he sat in his underwear and with a girl on his lap. I knew him from a photograph Rose showed me. Husky, paunchy, thick head of oily hair, fleshy drinker's nose. The girl scooted off him in a half-crouch, holding her shoulders in a shrug and her hands turned back at the wrist in a gesture that said she had nothing to do with this. You could see she wasn't wearing anything under her white slip.

"What the *hell*?" Ragsdale said. He started to reach for his pants but I pointed the Colt at his face and shook my head. He raised his hands chest-high and sat back. I picked up the pants to make sure they didn't have a gun in them and tossed them aside.

LQ ordered the other two guys to stand with their noses and palms against the wall and they were quick to do it. A girl in just bra and panties appeared at the bedroom door, looking scared but keeping her mouth shut. Another cool pony. I took a look in the bedroom to be sure there was no adjoining door, then waved both broads in there and shut them inside.

There was an open valise on the table against the wall and I sidestepped over to it and saw that it held a .380 semiautomatic and a few lean packets of greenbacks held together with rubber bands. One pack of hundreds, a couple of fifties, the rest all twenties and tens. Three, four grand at most was my guess.

"Listen, can I say something?" Ragsdale said. He was bouncing back fast from his surprise—and he'd figured who was running the show and was talking to me. Rose said they called him Willie Rags.

"Just let me say something, okay?" he said. I stood there and stared at him.

"Look, I know who sent you boys. Just tell me what them wops want. You aint wop, are you? Look Mex to me—no offense, hell, I *like* Mexes. Anyway, what they want? Money? Want to know whose slots I'm pushing? Well, all right, all right, we can discuss all that. We can straighten everything out, guys like us, right?"

He'd probably fast-talked his way out of plenty of jams before. Rose had spoken to him on the telephone once. "Talks like a guy on the radio," he said.

"Listen, I know you guys aren't gonna *shoot* me," he said. "Not *here*. Hotel fulla people. Shit, it's Houston but it aint Dodge City. They probably told you get the money I made off those slots, right? Plus a little interest on top? Probably said knock me around some, teach me a lesson. Okay, all right, won't be the first ass-kicking I ever took. But look, the money on the table's all I got on me. You want more than that you gotta wait till morning. I'm meeting a guy in the morning with lots more cash. But you don't want me all beat up when I meet him, right? Might make him suspicious, know what I mean? Would *you* hand over a bunch of money to a guy all beat to shit? What you oughta do, you oughta hold off on the ass-whipping till *after* I get the dough from this guy. That's good business sense, and you boys are businessmen, I can tell. So let's talk a little business while we wait for the man with the money, what do you say?"

I stared at him with an expression like I might be thinking it over.

"Listen," he said, "tell me what kinda deal you got with the Maceos. Maybe I can cut you something better, you know what I mean? I mean, no harm in talking, is there?" He pronounced their name MAY-cee-o, the same way the Maceos themselves said it, like Texans, which is what they considered themselves to be.

I looked at LQ. He pursed his lips and shrugged like What the hell.

Ragsdale caught LQ's expression and took encouragement from it. He patted the sofa and said to me, "Come on, pal, sit down. No harm done. Let's talk business."

I lowered the gun, and he chuckled and patted the sofa again. I uncocked the .44 and slipped it into my waistband under my coat as I started to step past him to the other side of the sofa. Then brought the ice pick out of my inside coat pocket and drove it into his heart.

If you can get them off guard like that you can do it quick and neat and fairly quiet. They give a little grunt and that's it. I yanked the pick out and he started to fall forward but I caught him and positioned him so he'd stay seated. A red spot the size of a quarter was all the blood there was. His head was slumped to one side and his eyes were open. He looked like he'd just been asked a stumper of a question. I closed his eyes and wiped the pick on his undershirt and put it back in my coat.

The other two still had their faces to the wall and looked like they were trying not to even breathe.

"Tell those Dallas assholes we know it's their machines Willie Rags was pushing," I said. "Tell them Rosario Maceo says don't cross the line again."

I picked up the valise and we hustled out of the room and over to the elevator. Brando patted the girl on the ass and said, "Let's go, honey."

She blushed and worked the levers and down we went. She looked a little disappointed we hadn't brought anyone out in handcuffs.

• •

It was normally an hour's drive between Houston and Galveston, but we went back by way of Kemah and League City, a pair of burgs just inside the Galveston County line. We had a list of all the places where Ragsdale had put in his Dallas machines and we stopped at each one to have a talk with the owner—a dozen or so cafés and about as many filling stations and pool halls.

Ragsdale must've thought he was being smart just because he stayed away from any joint that already had our machines in it. Maybe he thought the Maceo brothers wouldn't care that he was working in Galveston County so long as he dealt only with joints free of Maceo machines. Maybe he was so dumb he thought they wouldn't even hear about it. But Sam Maceo had friends everywhere and they had eyes and ears all over. They reported everything they heard that might mean some outsider was working this side of the county line. Sam would then pass the information to Rose and Rose would decide what to do about it.

What set Rose off about Ragsdale and the Dallas outfit wasn't just the money they were siphoning out of a few mainland joints. What galled him was their lack of respect. He couldn't blame outsiders for wanting to get in on Galveston's easy money, but he did blame them if they tried to get in on it without Maceo permission. Sometimes Rose would let an outside bunch work its game on the county mainland—never on the island—but only for a percentage of the gross. If the outside outfit thought the Maceo cut was too high, Rose would shrug and wish them luck and that was the end of the discussion. Only fools tried to work their game in Galveston County without Rose's blessing. Those who did try it could count on Rose taking swift measures to set things straight.

I was one of the measures he could take.

So were about two dozen other guys, the bunch of us known as "Rose's Ghosts." We saw to it that Maceo territory was defended and Maceo will was done. We were a fairly open secret—even the chief of police and the county sheriff knew about us—but you'd never see a word about us in the papers except as "person or persons unknown." Besides discouraging outside outfits from crossing the Galveston line, we protected the Maceo interests in neighboring counties. We collected the Maceos' money—the daily take from Maceo clubs, the cuts from places renting Maceo equipment, the loan payments from businesses staked with Maceo cash. We kept the grifters out of the Maceo casinos. Hell, we kept them off the island altogether. We came down hard on drunkrollers and room thieves, even harder on strongarms and stickup men. Although few of the good citizens ever said it out loud, most of them knew that the real law enforcement in Galveston wasn't the cops—it was us.

It was in the Maceo brothers' interest to keep their gambling rooms honest and make sure the hotels and the city streets were safe. The "Free State of Galveston," as everybody called it, was the most wide-open place in Texas, probably in the country, and what kept the highrollers and big spenders coming was the knowledge they wouldn't be cheated at the tables or robbed on the streets. Like the cathouse district that had been doing business on the island ever since the Civil War, the Maceos ensured the town a steady prosperity—even now, while the rest of the country was getting hammered by the Depression. It was a benefit not lost on the islanders, who knew a good thing when they had it.

Rose was a master of backroom business with the local politicians and the cops. One recent morning when I'd gone to Rose's office to deliver some cash I'd collected in Texas City, the secretary hustled me right in, even though Rose had the county sheriff in there with him.

I handed Rose the bag and he peeked in it and took out a half-inch pack of hundreds and dropped it on the desk in front of the sheriff.

"There you go, Frankie," he said. "A little contribution for the Lawmen's Association."

I'd seen the sheriff coming and going from Rose's office many a time and we had sometimes exchanged nods. But I doubted he'd ever accepted money from Rose in front of anybody, and he looked uneasy about it.

As the sheriff put the money in his coat, Rose pointed at me and said, "You know Jimmy here, don't you, Frank? Let me tell you, they don't come any better than this kid. A real whiz at taking care of business, you know what I mean? And he got a sharp eye. Don't miss a thing. He sees something and *click,* it's like his mind takes a picture of it."

The sheriff gave me a careful once-over and we exchanged one of our nods. We all sat there without saying anything for a long moment before the sheriff made a show of checking his watch and saying oh Christ he was late for an appointment. He said so long to Rose and let himself out. When the door shut behind him Rose and I turned to each other and laughed.

The look the sheriff gave me had been both wary and somewhat impressed. Like everybody else, he knew Rose wasn't one for openly praising anybody, not like Sam, who was always telling guys how swell they were, no matter if they were a crooked local judge or a visiting shoe salesman from Tulsa, some regular highroller from Houston or a whorehouse bouncer who came in once a week to drop ten bucks at the blackjack tables. It wasn't any wonder Sam handled the public-relations end of things. Most city officials from the mayor on down were personally acquainted with both brothers, but it was Big Sam, as everybody called him, who dealt with them in public. He was the happy glad-hander, the drinking buddy with a thousand jokes—or, when it was called for, the gracious host of impeccable manners. He was the one to hand over the big contributions to the latest charity drives and to help local politicians cut the big ribbons with the outsized scissors, to bring in big-time celebrity entertainers to perform for free at civic events, to serve as the sponsoring host at sporting competitions and bathing beauty contests. He paid for smart orphan kids to go to college and made large weekly contributions to all the local churches. Sam used charm and generosity to promote the Maceo interests, and Rose used the Ghosts to protect them. They were a perfect team. And I knew that under his goodbuddy exterior

Sam was no less serious than his big brother. Rose called the shots, but he always consulted with Sam first, always sought his advice. They were damn close brothers and partners to the bone.

Some of the Ghosts had been with the Maceos since back in the bootleg days. I'd been with them not quite two years—but I'd been Rose's main Ghost from the time I joined him. Whenever he had to go out of town on business, I went with him, and if it was just the two of us, I did the driving. The other Ghosts got their orders through various captains but I took mine directly from Rose and I answered to nobody but him. And after he'd agreed to let me have them as my regular partners, Brando and LQ answered only to me.

This had been a busy week. Just a few days before Rose sent us on the Ragsdale business, Brando and I had tracked down a pair of strongarms who'd been working the island for about two weeks. They'd been stalking big winners out of the Hollywood Dinner Club—the Maceos' biggest and fanciest place. They'd follow them back to their hotel and jump them in the parking lot, in one case even busting into the guy's room. A Ghost captain had put some boys on the problem but they hadn't been able to get a lead on the thugs, and Rose was fuming. By the time he put me on it, six customers had been robbed and two of them beat up. I collected Brando and we started hunting.

Two days later we found them on the mainland, in the Green Dolfin Motor Court just east of Hitchcock. They had a suitcase with twelve grand and were ready to cut for New Orleans. If they had settled for the eight thousand they got off the first few muggings, they would've made away clean, but they got greedy—just one more job, then just one more. It's how it was with smalltimers. No discipline. No sense of professionalism. An hour after we caught up to them they were on a freight train bound for Kansas City. We'd had to load them aboard the boxcar because their hands and knees didn't work anymore after Brando used a claw hammer on them.

As we started back to the office with the suitcase, Brando did his impersonation of Rose, adjusting and readjusting his necktie knot, eyes half-closed, mouth slightly pinched, saying in a heavy Sicilian accent: "Goddamn, but I hate a fucken thief." It made me grin every time.

At first Rose was angry when I told him the strongarms were still alive, but when I told him what we'd done to them he paced up and down for a minute, thinking about it, and then laughed.

"You see why I love this kid?" he said to Artie Goldman, his head bookkeeper. Artie just sat there and looked a little out of sorts. He never did like to hear about my end of the business. "Goddamn genius," Rose said. "Every time those two punks even think of how nice it'd be if they could walk into the kitchen for a glass of water, every time they need to blow their nose or wipe their ass, they're gonna remember how stupid they were to try thieving in Galveston." He adjusted my necktie and then his own and beamed at me.

The next day he saw to it that the money got back to the customers who'd been robbed. The strongarms had spent about three hundred of it but he made up the difference from his own pocket. That's how he was.

• •

LQ told the owner at each place where Ragsdale had put his slots that the machines now belonged to the Gulf Vending Company and the standard fee for their use was 50 percent of the take. A company representative would come by every night to collect. If the owner had any complaints, any trouble from the cops or anybody else, he was to contact the main office on the island and the company would deal with the problem.

None of this seemed to be news to the owners. Even the ones who didn't really want any machines in their joint weren't about to argue. They knew the score. What the hell—they got 50 percent of something as opposed to 100 percent of nothing, and they knew they could count on Maceo protection. What was there to complain about?

• •

By the time we were done making our visits it was close to ten o'clock. We stopped at a diner to buy beer for the rest of the drive to town.

The joint had a jukebox, and "Blue Moon" was playing when we came in. A Christmas tree in the corner was blinking with colored-glass electric candles, half of its needles already on the floor.

It wasn't the sort of place to pull them in on New Year's Eve. The only customers besides us were a mushy young couple at a back table. Brando and I went into the men's room to take a leak while LQ went to the counter and ordered the beer.

When we came out of the john, "Blue Moon" was playing again. The cooler beside the front counter was out of order but the guy had some beer on ice in the back room and had gone to get it. "Blue Moon" played out and the mushy guy went over to the juke and punched it up again. The girl stood up and they held each other close and swayed in place to the music.

"Goddamn," LQ said in a low voice, "I like the song myself, but there's such a thing as overdoing a good thing. There's bound to be other lovey stuff on that juke they can dance to. I bet 'I Only Have Eyes for You' is on there."

Brando said that was an all right love song but not nearly as good as "I've Got You Under My Skin."

LQ said that one sounded like a song about a bad disease. "I bet the guy who wrote it was thinking about some dame who gave him the worst case of clap he ever had."

"Jesus, it's no wonder your wives all left you," Brando said.

"At least they wanted to marry me," LQ said. "Only thing women want from *you* is as far away as they can get."

"You don't know a damn thing about me *or* women."

The counter guy came back with the beer and put it in a sack. While LQ was paying him I went over to the juke and scanned the titles, then put a nickel in the coinbox and pressed a number button. I stood there till "Blue Moon" finished playing and I watched the selector arm pick up the record and replace it in its slot, then swing over and pick up the one I'd punched and set it on the turntable. The record began to spin and the tone arm eased into the starting groove and the speakers started putting out "Tumbling Tumbleweeds."

The lovebirds turned to see what was going on. The girl looked confused and the guy was frowning. I nodded at them and touched my hatbrim.

LQ and Brando were waiting at the door. As we went out to the car LQ said, "That wasn't very nice."

"That's Jimmy's trouble," Brando said to LQ. "He's like you. Not a romantic bone in his body."

"What are you talking about?" I said. "That's the most romantic song I ever heard."

"Cowboy probably means it," LQ told Brando.

For a time after we first met, LQ had called me Cowboy because of my boots and the frontier Colt and the wide-brimmed hat I wore back then before I switched to a fedora—and because I'd grown up on a ranch, which was all I'd ever told him and Brando about my past. As he got to know me better he eased off on the nickname and it had been a long time since he'd used it. He was no cowboy himself—he came out of the East Texas piney woods, which made him closer kin to Southern good old boys than to any Texan raised west of Houston.

He slid behind the wheel and started up the Dodge. I sat up in front with him. Brando uncapped three beers with a church key and passed two of them up to me as LQ got us back on the road. I waited till LQ shifted into high, then handed him a beer.

"Salud, amor, y pesetas," I said, and we all raised our bottles in the toast.

A few minutes later we were on the causeway and looking at the low stretch of lights ahead of us that marked Galveston across the bay. Thirty miles long and some three miles across at its widest point, the island had long been a haven to pirates and smugglers, to gunrunners, gamblers, whores, to shady characters of every stripe. Geographically it was completely different from the place where I'd grown up, but I felt at ease with its character, which Rose had described pretty well as "Live and let live unless somebody fucks with you."

Near the middle of the bridge we had to halt behind a short line of cars while the lift span rose to let a large ketch go motoring through. Its sails were furled and it trailed a small wake in the light of the pale half-moon just above the water to the west. Even though the calendar said it was winter and we had recently had a brief cold snap, the evening was warm as spring. The breeze was gentle, the air moist and smelling of tidal marsh.

I'd never seen the ocean until I came to Galveston. The first time I stood on the beach and stared out at the gulf it struck me as beautiful, but also damn scary—and I detested the feeling of being afraid. I couldn't remember having been truly frightened before except for one time when I was fourteen. I'd been beating the brush for strays all morning when I stopped to eat the lunch our maid Carlotta had packed for me. It was a heavy meal and made me sleepy, so I lay down for a nap in the raggedy shade of a mesquite shrub at the bottom of a low sandrise. The shrilling of my horse woke me to the sight of a diamondback as thick as my arm and coiled up three feet from my face. The horse snatched the reins loose of the mesquite and bolted over the rise. If the damn jughead hadn't spooked so bad the snake probably would've slid on by with no trouble, but now it was scared too and ready to give somebody hell for it. I figured if I tried to roll away it would get me in the neck and that would be all she wrote. Its rattle was a buzzing blur and I could see its muscles flex as it coiled tighter. I knew it was going to strike me in the face any second—and I was suddenly afraid. And then in the next instant I was furious at myself and I thought, *To hell with it*—and made a grab for the snake. It hit my hand like a club and I rolled away hard as the rattler recoiled. I scrambled over the rise on all fours and whistled up my horse and got the Winchester out of the saddle scabbard. The snake had started slithering off but then coiled up buzzing again when I ran back to it. I admired its courage even as I blew its head off. The bastard had nailed me on the bottom edge of the hand, and I cut the wound bigger and sucked and spat for a while, then tied a bandanna tight around my wrist. I draped the snake over my neck—I later made a belt of the hide—and mounted up and headed for home. I was sick as hell for three days, but I promised myself if anything even came close to scaring me again, I'd go right up to whatever it was—man, beast, or bad weather—and kick it in the ass. But nothing had ever really spooked me again, not until I saw the Gulf of Mexico.

The day after my first look at the gulf, I bought a swimming suit and returned to the beach. I watched the swimmers carefully for a while and then started imitating their techniques in water no deeper than my hips. And I taught myself to swim. I practiced and practiced over the next few days until I could swim parallel to shore in shallow water for a steady hundred yards.

Then one bright noonday I swam straight out from shore until I was gasping and my arms were heavy and aching. I clumsily treaded water and looked back at the tiny figures of the people on the beach. I must've been out two hundred yards. The dark water under me seemed bottomless and I couldn't help thinking of all the shark stories I'd so recently heard. The most fearsome were about Black Tom, a hammerhead more than twenty feet long that they said had been prowling the waters around the island since before the World War. They said its top fin was as big as a car door and spotted with pale bullet holes.

I'd been terrified by the thought of being so far out in the water, which of course was why I did it. It would be better to drown, better to be eaten by sharks, than to be so afraid of the sea—or of anything else. So I'd made the long swim. And it worked. I was still a little scared, sure, but not as much as before, and I'd proved I could beat the fear, that was the thing. As I started stroking back toward the beach, I didn't know if I'd make it, but I was feeling great. When I finally tumbled up on the sand, I sprawled on my back, my chest heaving, and stared up at the dizzy blue depth of the sky—and the people sunning themselves around me must've thought I was a lunatic, the way I broke out laughing.

Ever since then, I'd made the same swim once every two weeks. And after I found out that sharks fed mostly at night, I'd always made the swim after dark. Always a little tight in the throat at the thought of what might be swimming close by.

The causeway melded into the island and became Broadway Avenue. We drove through the deep shadows of palm trees and live oaks lining a wide grassy esplanade that separated the opposing traffic lanes and held the tracks for the interurban, the electric passenger train that ran back and forth between Galveston and Houston.

We stopped at a red light, and a Model T sedan started laboring across the intersection, its motor rapping in the distinct Model T way. The old Ford was missing its left front fender and had received a splotchy handbrush coat of green paint as pale as lettuce.

"Look at that rattletrap," LQ said. "Thing could use a pair of crutches."

"I wouldn't be too sure," I said. "Some of those old T's don't look like much but they run like a Swiss watch."

In the glow of the streetlamps I saw that the driver of the heap was a Mexican with a drooping gray mustache and wearing a straw hat. A burly guy sat beside him but his face was obscured by the shadows. Another passenger sat in the darkness of the backseat.

As the Model T passed by directly in front of us, the

passenger at the near window leaned forward to look out and the lamplight fell full on the face of a girl. Blackhaired, darkskinned. Our eyes met—and for that brief instant I felt naked in some way that had nothing to do with clothes. Then the old car was clattering away down the shadowed street.

"Whooo," LQ said. "You see *that*?"

"What?" Brando said from the backseat. His attention had been elsewhere.

"That was some finelooking chiquita," LQ said.

I busied myself lighting a cigarette. I wasn't one to get caught off guard by things, including some dopey sensation I didn't understand, and it irked me that the girl's look had ambushed me like it did.

The light turned green and LQ got the Dodge rolling, looking to his left at the fading single taillight on the Model T. I took a look too—then told myself to cut the crap. The world was full of goodlooking girls.

"You shoulda hollered something at her in Mexican," LQ said to me. "Maybe get a little something going."

"It's Spanish, not *Mexican,* you peckerwood," Brando said. "How many times I got to tell you?"

"And how many times I got to tell *you,*" LQ said. "Spanish is what they talk in *Spain.* Let me ask you something: what do they talk in Germany? German, aint it? And in France? I do believe they call it French. In China they talk Chinese. Get the picture? Anybody's a peckerwood in this car it's you."

"You are one ignorant hillbilly," Brando said. "What do you call what we talk in America, for Christ's sake—*American*?"

"Goddam right," LQ said. He gave me a sidelong wink.

"Jesus Christ," Brando said.

"You shoulda seen her, Ramon," LQ said, grinning at Brando in the rearview. "*Fine*looking thing. I always heard them young beaner girls prefer doing it with Americans on account of we know how to treat their hairy little tacos so much better than you boys."

"Go to hell," Brando said. He kicked the back of my seat and said, "Why do you put up with that kinda talk?"

I always got a kick out of how easily LQ could rile Brando with some crack about Mexicans, or even by calling him Ramon. It was funny because, despite his Mexican looks, Brando was a naturalborn American. He couldn't even speak Spanish except for a few phrases of profanity, and he spoke those with a gringo accent. At twenty-four he was three years older than me, born and raised on a dairy farm just east of Austin, where his wetback parents had worked. They were the only Mexicans on the place, and because they'd wanted their son to be a good Yankee citizen they named him Raymond and encouraged him to speak English from the time he learned to talk. They'd made it a point to converse with him only in English, like everyone else on the farm, even though they themselves could barely get by in it, and so even though he never learned Spanish, his English had a touch of their accent, which only added to the impression that he was Mexican.

People usually took me for Mexican too, until they got up close enough to see my eyes. Then they knew I was even more of a breed than most Mexicans—most of them being mestizos, of Spanish-Indian mix. There were Spaniards with blue eyes, of course, and some of their kids by Indian women had the same eyes as daddy. But more often than not, when you saw blue eyes in a brown face they came from Yankee blood. Unlike Brando, however, I could speak Spanish pretty well, and my only accent in either language was a touch of border twang.

We turned off Broadway onto 23rd and drove toward the neon blaze of the Turf Club a few blocks ahead at Market Street. The Club did good business late into the evening every night of the week, but tonight being New Year's it was even busier than usual.

LQ honked his horn at the traffic crawling along ahead of us. He'd started to worry that he was running late for his date with a redhead named Zelda. She worked as a hostess at the Hollywood Dinner Club and he'd already taken her out once but hadn't been able to score. She was impressed that he was one of Rose's Ghosts, but she'd been around some and she made it clear to LQ she wasn't any pushover, that she expected to be wooed. She was pretty enough that LQ thought she was worth the effort. She came off her shift at ten-thirty and he was taking her for Chinese at a Maceo place called the Sui Jen that was on a pier jutting out into the gulf. Then down the street to the Crystal Palace to ring in the New Year with some dancing and champagne. Then to her place for a nightcap. He was sure tonight would be the night.

Brando had a hot date too. He was going to a party with a long-legged thing he'd met at a dance the week before. She'd told him her name was Brigitte and she was French. He said she spoke with a slight accent but he suspected she was really just some bullshitting hustler out of New Orleans. Of course he had been bullshitting her too, claiming he was a partner in the Big Trinity Oil Company, which was about to be bought by Texaco.

"With golddiggers," he said, "the idea you got money works better than Spanish fly."

"Too bad Mexican flies don't work as good," LQ had said. "You always got plenty enough of them on you."

"Go fuck yourself," Brando said.

"If I only could," LQ said with a sigh. "I'd finally be doing it with the best there is and somebody I truly love."

He stopped the car in front of the Club and Brando and I got out. I carried Ragsdale's valise and one of the briefcases, in which I was carrying my revolver and the .380 I took from Ragsdale. LQ waved so long and drove off.

Brando punched me on the arm and asked if I was sure I didn't want to go to the party with him. "Frenchy can prob'ly get a friend."

"Thanks, anyway," I said. "I'll find my own fun."

"Suit yourself, bud," he said, and walked off to the parking lot in back where he'd left his car.

• •

The Turf Club was a three-story building where the Maceos kept their headquarters. Everybody just called it the Club. On the ground floor was a restaurant called the Turf Grill, and as restaurants go it was fairly flashy and the food was always good. On this night the place was packed and there was a line of diners out on the sidewalk, waiting to be seated. A hostess named Sally gave me a wink when I went in, and some of the harried waitresses smiled at me in recognition as I made my way across the room to a doorway leading to the real attraction on the lower floor—a large betting room where you could lay money on any horse race at any track in the country. The day's major races were broadcast over the parlor's wall speakers and the hollering in there could get pretty intense when a race was in progress.

Anybody could get into the betting room, but the upper floors were exclusive. The elevator and the narrow stairway were in a hallway at the rear of the room. The stairway doors on every floor locked automatically from the inside, and there was always a palooka posted at the elevator to make sure nobody but special customers or friends of the Maceos got on it. Rose and Sam had their offices on the second floor, which also contained a billiards room and the Studio Lounge—a small restaurant with a dance floor and a long bar and a backroom gambling hall for big-money card and dice action. The third floor was a health club equipped with a boxing ring and all kinds of exercise equipment.

The only raids the local cops ever pulled were of course just for show. They always let the Maceos know they were coming and they never hit anything but the ground-floor betting parlor. Whatever equipment they confiscated they returned on the Q.T. a few days later. Every now and then, however, the Texas Rangers would come calling. That's when the elevator man would push a hidden button to buzz a warning to the upper floors. The band in the Studio Lounge would strike up a blaring rendition of "The Eyes of Texas," which everybody knew was the signal of a Ranger raid. The staff in the gambling room would fly into action, covering the gaming tables with expensive tablecloths and setting them with dinnerware and platters of food. The back bars would swivel around to hide the booze racks and display nothing but seltzer bottles and tea sets and urns of fresh coffee. The elevator was also equipped with a secret switch that turned it into the slowest mechanical conveyance in Texas. By the time the Rangers arrived at the second floor the only booze they'd find was what the customers had brought in—which was legal to do—and there wouldn't be so much as a poker chip in sight.

At this hour the day's races were long over, and the betting parlor was pretty quiet. A few guys sat around with bottles of beer, gabbing and telling each other how close they'd come to winning big today in the first or the fifth or the last race at such and such a track.

Guarding the elevator tonight was an ex-pug named Otis Wilcox who'd once lasted six rounds with Tunney before the Gentleman Marine coldcocked him. Otis said he couldn't remember his own name for an hour after he came to. He worked as both a Turf Club guard and a trainer in the gym. He gave boxing lessons to health club members and still liked to spar, but he wasn't one to pull all his punches, so regular partners were hard for him to come by. I was his favorite sparring buddy because I could take it. Besides, I was a fast learner and had gotten good enough to make it interesting for him. The lumps I took were worth it to me for the chance to box against somebody who knew what he was doing. We rarely got a chance to work out with each other, though, because of our different schedules, and we hadn't been in the ring together in a month. We'd gone three rounds the last time, and we got pretty serious in the third. With about a half minute left in the round he'd got careless and I nearly knocked him down with a right. For the rest of the round he went at me with everything he had. By the time the bell rang, my headgear was in a lopsided twist and my ribs felt like he'd used a ball bat on them. But Otis took a lot of kidding from some of the boys about the right hook I'd hung on him, and I knew he couldn't wait for our next session so he could get back at me.

As I walked up to the elevator he feinted a left at my ribs and popped a lazy right into the valise I threw up to block the punch.

"Christ, kid, you getting too quick. You'll knock me on my ass next time."

"Count on it."

"Name the day," he said.

"Been out of town a lot. I'll let you know."

"Do that, kid."

The old guy working the elevator nodded hello and took me up.

The Studio Lounge was loud and smoky and dimly lit, jammed with revelers, the band hammering out "Let's Fall in Love," the dance floor swirling with couples. The Maceo offices were in a hallway on the other side of the room and I made my way through the crowd between the dance floor and the bar. A lot of the customers knew who I was, and they pulled each other out of my way. No telling what kind of stories they'd heard about me except that all of them were scary and probably half of them bullshit, but that was all right with me. The more such stories got around, the easier it sometimes made my job.

As I entered the hallway, a door at the far end opened and Big Sam came out, adjusting a gardenia in his lapel. A blond cigarette girl I'd never seen before was with him, holding to her tray and straightening her pillbox hat over her slightly disheveled hair. She had the right body for the little shorts and low-cut vest of her uniform.

She'd missed a button on the side of her shorts and Sam pointed it out to her. Then he saw me and said, "Hey now . . . Jimmy the Kid!"

He'd started calling me that from the time we'd first been introduced and he heard how Rose and I had met in San Antonio. "You should've *seen* this guy in action, Sammy," Rose told him. "Like fucken Billy the Kid or somebody."

"Only this one's *Jimmy* the Kid," Sam said with a big grin—and that was his name for me from then on, though he usually just called me Kid. Then Rose took up the name, and Brando and LQ sometimes used it, sometimes Goldman the bookkeeper. But nobody else. Even people who knew me well enough to say hello—and there weren't many—rarely called me by any name at all, but when they did, it was just Jimmy.

Sam gave the girl a smack on the ass and she hurried past me with a fetching blush. She gave off a sweet warm smell with a tinge of sex in it. I watched her disappear into the crowd, then arched my brow at Sam.

He laughed and said, "Just getting a happy start on the new year, Kid."

Sam and Rose were both married, but you never saw their wives and children, and the brothers rarely spoke of them. Their business lives and their home lives were completely separate worlds—except that their families and luxurious homes were protected around the clock by a crew of Ghosts and special police patrols.

Sam put a hand on my shoulder and stood with his back to the lounge so no one who looked down the hall could see his face.

"So?" he said, his aspect serious. "Okay?"

"Okay," I said.

His face brightened again and he patted me on the arm. "You always do good work, Kid."

He pointed with his thumb over his shoulder into the lounge behind him and said, "Listen, do yourself a favor and take a spin with that doxy was just here. New girl. Suzie Somebody, from . . . I don't know, Hick City, Nebraska. She's a regular carnival ride, I swear."

"I'll keep it in mind," I said.

Sam liked to hire small-town girls who'd been brought up so straitlaced they couldn't wait to run off on their own. Girls who'd been hit over the head with religion all their life, who'd been told over and over that if they let a boy so much as touch their tit they were no better than whores. But the girls would see broads like Harlow and Crawford having all that slutty fun in the movies, and some of them wanted to have that kind of fun too, wanted it *bad*. When they finally couldn't take any more preaching, they'd run off to some big city and dive into sin headfirst.

"It's like they wish Mommy and Daddy could get a load of them with a mouth full of cock," Sam once told me. "Like they'd love nothing better than to give everybody back home a heart attack." I'd heard a few Galveston madams say pretty much the same thing about a lot of the girls who worked for them.

Sam was husky and handsome and always impeccably groomed, every curly hair in place even now, just minutes after a roll in the hay. His teeth were as bright as a movie star's. Hell, he could've been a movie star if he'd wanted. I'd never seen him in need of a shave or a haircut, and he always smelled of just the right touch of cologne. Nobody could make a suit look better. His usual good spirits were so contagious you couldn't help getting caught up in them.

I accepted the Chesterfield he offered, then the flame of his gold lighter, and then he lit his own.

He told me Rose was up in the gym, and as he walked me back to the elevator he said, "Hey, you hear about the suicidal twin who killed his brother by mistake?"

I smiled politely.

"Yeah, yeah, okay. How about the nun and the oyster shucker? Sister Mary Antonia goes into this oyster bar, see . . ."

• •

Rose was punching the heavy bag when I pushed through the frosted-glass door to the gym. You could tell on sight he was Sam's brother. The same curly hair and beaked nose, the same dimpled and slightly double chin. At forty-nine, Rose was seven years older than Sam and he looked it, at least in the face. He almost always had blue half-moons under his eyes and his hair was already half gray. He was a little shorter than Sam and not as husky, but in truth he was in pretty good shape and he tried to stay that way with workouts in the gym. Sam was naturally strong and built like a halfback, but his only exercise was in humping the chippies.

A hulking, bushy-bearded health club worker named Watkins was bracing the bag with his shoulder as Rose threw hooks and crosses, bobbing and shuffling, showing good footwork, glaring at the bag like it was a flesh-and-blood opponent. He popped a few sharp jabs, cut loose with a roundhouse right, ducked and hopped back like he was dodging a counterpunch. Sweat ran off his face, and his sweater was dark around the neck and armpits. He saw me watching from the door and beckoned me over. Then pivoted and drove a right-hand lead into the bag like he'd caught his opponent off guard. He followed up with a pounding combination of steady lefts and rights before finally stepping back and dropping his arms, blowing hard breaths.

"Okay . . . thanks, Billy," he said to Watkins. "That'll do."

"Good work, chief," Watkins said. He exchanged nods with me and headed for the elevator.

Rose stripped off the bag gloves and tossed them on the table, then wiped his face and neck with a towel. He draped the towel around his neck and stepped over to the open locker where his white suit was hanging and reached into a coat pocket and fished out a pack of Lucky Strike. He put one in his mouth and I took out my lighter and lit it for him.

"Jab's looking snappy," I said.

"You think? How about that right lead?"

"You try it against somebody knows what he's doing and he'll take your head off with a counterpunch."

"That's what Otis says. He also tells me you landed a stinger on him the last time you guys sparred. Says he's gonna tap you a good one next time, remind you who's who."

"I always expect him to try tapping me a good one."

"I think he's right—you're getting too goddamn cocky." He softly spat a shred of tobacco off the tip of his tongue and took a casual look around. We were the only ones in the gym. "So?" he said.

"Everything's jake," I said. I put the valise on the table and worked the snaps and opened it and he looked inside.

"It's all he had with him," I said. "Said he could get more from the bank tomorrow, but you said let it go, so I—"

"Fuck the money," Rose said. "He down?"

"He's down."

"I don't mean are his hands and knees busted. Not for a bastard I warned."

"He's *down,*" I said. "Two other guys were there. I gave them the word for Dallas."

He nodded and smiled. His best smile couldn't hold a candle to Sam's, but then Rose rarely smiled with the intention of making someone feel warmly regarded. His usual smile was the one he showed now. The smile he wore when he won.

"There was a piece in the money bag too," I said. "I took it."

"Let's see."

I unzipped the briefcase and took out the .380 and laid it on the table. He picked it up and thumbed off the safety and pulled the slide back just far enough to see the round snugged in the chamber, then eased the slide forward again and reset the safety. He turned it over this way and that, regarding it from every angle. A .380 was the second kind of pistol I'd ever fired and I liked the model a lot. It didn't have the punch of the army .45 automatic but was generally more accurate. Still, everybody knew an automatic could jam on you and a revolver never would. This piece was in mint condition, though, and I couldn't resist it.

"Nice," Rose said. He set it on the table and pushed it back to me. "Had supper?"

"I was about to."

"Good." He dropped the butt on the floor and stepped on it, then picked up a fresh towel and slung it over his shoulder. "I'll take a shower and we'll go for clams."

"Don't you have a party or something?"

"Because New Year's? Hell, Kid, it don't mean nothing but another year closer to the grave. What's to celebrate?"

• •

Forty minutes later we were in his private corner booth in Mama Carmela's, a small Italian place on Seawall Boulevard. A picture window looked out on the gulf. The faint lights of shrimp trawlers moved slowly across the black horizon. I'd brought the briefcase with me, both pistols in it, so I wouldn't have a gun digging into my belly while I ate.

The grayhaired waiter brought a basket of breadsticks and poured glasses of Chianti. Rose waved off his suggestion of minestrone and salad and ordered clams in pesto over capellini for both of us.

"Molto bene, Don Rosario," the waiter said with a bow, and retreated to the kitchen. A Victrola behind the front counter was softly playing Italian songs.

As always, Rose wanted every detail, so I told him exactly how it had gone in Houston. And as always, he listened intently and without interruption.

When I was finished, he raised his glass and said, "Salute."

The clams and pasta arrived and Rose ordered another bottle of Chianti. We tucked our napkins over our shirtfronts and dug in, twirling pasta on our forks, spearing fat clams dripping with pesto, sopping up sauce with chunks of warm buttered bread. Rose wasn't one for conversation while he dined. He broke the silence only to ask how my clams were. "Damn good," I said. He nodded and refilled our glasses and gave his attention back to his food.

When we were done and the waiter cleared away the dishware and poured coffee and bowed at Rose's dismissal of dessert and left us again, Rose said he wanted me to stick around town for the next week or so.

It took me by surprise. He knew I liked making out-of-town collection runs, that I hated hanging around the Club with nothing to do.

"I'm supposed to make the pickups in Victoria tomorrow," I said. "Then there's the pickups across the bay in a couple of days."

"I already put another man on the Victoria run. And your partners can handle the eastern collections. I want you close by for a little while."

"How come?"

"I got a hunch about those Dallas guys. They might just be dumb enough to try something. If they do, they'll probably try it pretty soon, and I want you here to deal with it."

He read the question on my face. "I got a phone call," he said. "One of the other two guys must've called Dallas as soon as you left the hotel room. Then Dallas called me, some guy named Healy—fucken mick. Says he represents the organization that owns the machines Ragsdale was pushing on this side of the line. *Organization*—like he's talking about Standard Oil. Says he wanted me to know his *organization* had nothing to do with Ragsdale putting the slots in Galveston County, that it was strictly Ragsdale's doing.

Says the organization only contracted the machines to him. Says Ragsdale deserved what we gave him."

"So what's the problem?" I said. "Sounds like he was saying they got your message and they want no trouble."

"That's what I thought. He's telling me it was all Ragsdale, his outfit's hands are clean, right? So I tell the harp no hard feelings, Ragsdale crossed the line but the account's all settled."

"*So?* What's the problem?"

"I'm getting to that. You know, that's *your* problem, Kid, I told you before—you get in too big a hurry. The man in a big hurry is the man who misses something important. Always be sure you know what's what *before* you make a move. You listening to me?"

"Yes, Daddy. So . . . what's the problem?"

He gave me a look of mock reprimand and pointed a warning finger at me. A lot of people referred to him as "Papa Rose," though never to his face—they didn't dare get that familiar with him. The truth was, he didn't mind the "Papa Rose" at all. He took it as a show of respect toward him as the head of a sort of business family. Calling him "Daddy" was my sarcastic way of ribbing him about it, especially when he'd lecture me like I was some schoolkid. I didn't do it often, and rarely in front of anybody else, but one day I'd called him Daddy when Artie the bookkeeper was in the room, and Artie's eyes got big as cue balls. He must've expected Rose to blow his top at my insolence. But all Rose did was roll his eyes and shake his head and say to Artie, "Young people today got no respect. My old man woulda taken a belt to my ass if I'd been so disrespectful, believe you me, no matter how old I was."

LQ heard me one time too, and later that night when we were in a waterfront beer bar he said I was the only guy he knew besides Sam who could chivvy Rose like that. LQ was thirty years old and had been Rose's main Ghost until I came along, but he swore he wasn't jealous about me replacing him.

"I never was all that much at ease around the man," he said. "Truth to tell, I never seen nobody at ease around him but you and Big Sam. I figure it's on account of you and him are two peas in a pod."

The idea that Rose and I were alike had never crossed my mind. "How so?" I said.

"Well, lots of ways. Like how the both you sometimes look at somebody you know like you never seen him before in your whole entire life and you aint decided yet whether you even like him or not. There's never no telling what's going on in you-all's head, either of you. You and him both got this way of . . . aw, hell, you both can be creepy as a graveyard is how so."

I gave him the two-fingered "up yours" sign, and he just laughed.

"The problem," Rose said, "is this Healy guy said his organization wants fifty percent of what their slots in Galveston County bring in." He signaled the waiter for a refill on our coffee.

"So," Rose said after the waiter withdrew, "I told him that far as I'm concerned, his *organization* can have a hundred percent of what their machines take in."

"Really?" I said. I knew a punch line was coming. "Bet he didn't expect to hear that."

"The only thing is, I says to him, his organization aint *got* no machines in Galveston County. The only slots in Galveston County are *my* slots. I said if his company was a little short of machines, I'd be happy to sell him some at bottom dollar, help them out, one businessman to another. Just be sure and don't put them in Galveston County, I told him."

"Well hell," I said, "that's a very generous offer. I hope he appreciated it."

"Every mick I ever met got a potato for a brain. They don't understand nothing, don't appreciate nothing. Here I'm giving them a chance to buy back the slots at a bargain and all the guy says is they're willing to *negotiate* the percent. I said to him he still didn't get it, there's nothing to negotiate. And *he* says, well then, I can just give the machines back. Said he could send his boys around to pick them up."

"Give them *back*? He said that?"

"My hand to God. So I tell him again: any machine in Galveston is *my* machine, so there's nothing for me to pay a percent on and nothing to give back to nobody. *And,* I tell him . . . anybody who tries to take any machine out of Galveston would be trying to steal from me. Know what that fucker said then?"

I arched my brow. I always got a kick out of his outrage at the rest of the world's inability to understand things as clearly as he did.

"Said if I wanted my own machines in those joints I shoulda had them in there already. Then Ragsdale wouldn'ta had no place in Galveston County to put theirs. Like *I'm* to blame for them cutting in on me."

"Brass balls, I'll give him that."

"Brass fucken brains. I told him it was none of his business how I run mine. He tells me I oughta think it over. I tell him I just did—and hung up. Fucken guy."

"So? Now what?"

"Who knows? They might be stupid enough to think they got to get even somehow, and stupid people are the hardest to predict. They don't think logical and they don't plan careful."

He shook out another cigarette and lit it. "So you stick around," he said. "You don't have to be at the Club, just stay in town and check in with the office every now and then. Let Bianco know where you are in case I gotta get you in a hurry." Mrs. Bianco was his office secretary.

"You talk like I'm the only one on the payroll. There's two dozen Ghosts in town every day, a half dozen always right there at the Club."

"I only got one the best."

"Oh, Christ, spare me the charming con, Don Rosario."

"I'm just telling the truth, Kid, like always." And we both laughed.

Then Caruso started singing about the clown who laughs to hide his sorrow, and Rose leaned out of the booth and gestured for somebody at the register to turn up the volume. I lit a cigarette and looked out at the distant trawler lights. Rose sat back and stared out at the gulf too, and softly sang along with the great tenor.

Before Prohibition came along and changed their lives the Maceo brothers had been barbers for years, and Sam told me they often harmonized with opera recordings on the Victrola while they cut hair. Sam's favorite was *The Barber of Seville,* which I'd never heard until he played some of it for me one night. He said he'd work his scissors in quick, jumpy time to the music and laugh at the way the customer in the chair would cringe in fear of getting an ear snipped off.

They started out in the barbershop of the Galvez Hotel and then opened a little shop of their own downtown. They'd learned the haircut trade from their father, who brought them from Palermo to New Orleans when Rose and Sam were still children. Sam once told me that on the ship coming over from Sicily he'd gotten beat up and had his pocket watch stolen by an older boy, a big dark bully from Naples. The watch had been a present from his grandfather and he didn't want to tell his daddy what happened. But he told Rose. They hunted all through the steerage sections but didn't find the guy until Sam finally spotted him on the topside deck and pointed him out. The boy was about fifteen, Sam said, a couple of years older than Rose and much bigger, but Rose lit into him like a bulldog and got him down and beat the hell out of him while a crowd of kids cheered him on. He banged the bully's head on the deck till he was almost unconscious, then dug through his pockets and found the watch, then started dragging him to the rail to shove him overboard, but a deckhand intervened.

Another thing the brothers learned from their daddy in the early

Louisiana days was how to make wine. When they moved to Galveston they made it in tubs in a shed behind their rented house. At first they made it just for themselves and a few close friends, then they started selling jugs of it to some of their regular barbershop customers. When Prohibition became the law, they produced the stuff in greater quantity and sold it under the counter to anybody who wanted it. Pretty soon they became partners with one of the two main gangs fighting for control of the island's bootleg business. Over the next few years there were gunfights in the streets and killings in broad daylight, but the Maceos were able to stay legally clear of the worst of it. Once the top dogs of the two gangs were all in prison or the graveyard, Sam and Rose brought the factions together and took over the whole operation. By then they were also in the gambling business, which swiftly became their most lucrative enterprise.

Most of the Maceo stories you heard were about Rose, of course, and no telling how many were true. That's always how it is—the guy nobody really knows is the guy who gets the most tales told about him. Like the story about his first wife, who'd been murdered way back when the Maceos were just starting in the bootleg business. I heard it from LQ, who'd heard it from somebody else, who'd heard it from who-knows-who. The way the story went, one evening Rose invited three friends home for dinner on the spur of the moment—although he'd never invited anybody to his house before—and when the four of them got there, they found his wife in bed with another man, both of them naked and both of them dead.

"You could say they died of natural causes," LQ said, "since it's pretty natural to die when somebody shoots you in the brainpan."

According to the witnesses, Rose wept like a baby, but there was a lot of secret curiosity about the true cause of his tears—whether he was crying because his wife was dead or because she'd put the horns on him. The police investigated but the killings were never solved.

"Way I heard it," LQ said with a sly look, "the cops had *no* idea who mighta done it. About the only thing they knew for sure was that it wasn't suicide. The old boy who told me the story did say real quiet-like that it was *sorta* like suicide, since a woman who'd cheat on Rose Maceo might as well wear a big 'Kill Me' sign on her back."

Caruso finished wailing about the tragic clown. Rose dabbed at his eyes with his napkin, then blew his nose.

"Fucken guinea," he said. "Voice like an angel."

The waiter came and topped off our coffee. A moment later the window abruptly brightened with an explosion of light and sparkling skyrocket trails arcing over the gulf. There was a muted staccato popping of firecrackers, an outburst of car horns. Somebody in the kitchen began banging pots and shouted "Happy New Year!"

Rose raised his coffee cup and I clinked mine against it.

I drove Rose back to the Club and parked the Lincoln in the reserved spot by the back door of the building. The moon was down now, the stars larger and brighter. Rose said he had to take care of a few things before he went home. He slapped me on the back and said goodnight, then went into the Club.

I walked up the alley and into the bright lights of 23rd Street. The haze and smell of spent fireworks were still on the air. The theaters had let out and the line of people waiting outside the Turf Grill was even longer than before. I'd been vaguely edgy all through supper and wasn't sure why—but as I stood there, watching the passing traffic in its clamor of klaxons and clattering motors, what I hankered for was to get laid.

I usually took my pleasure with one or another of the hostesses or waitresses who worked at the Maceo clubs, but then I'd have to wait for the girl to get off work, and I didn't feel like waiting. Besides, I was in no mood for the banter and kidding around that was required for a free one. I just wanted to get to it.

It was an urge you could satisfy more easily in this town

than probably anywhere else in the country and I was already in the neighborhood for it. Post Office Street—the heart of the red-light district—was right around the corner. With my balls feeling heavy as plums I headed on over there.

For a span of five or six blocks, Post Office—and portions of Market and Church, the two streets north and south of it—was mostly one cathouse after another. Most of the houses were narrow two-story buildings with latticework screens in front of the porches to give a little privacy to guys who didn't want to be seen going in or out. I always wondered who they were afraid might see them, since anybody who was in the neighborhood sure as hell wasn't shopping for shoes.

The houses were owned by a variety of different people but they were all managed by women. The madams paid rents that were practically robbery, but the district was so well established they didn't have to pay off the cops to leave them alone—at least not as long as there was no bad trouble in the place. Most houses turned a nice profit by simply staying honest and clean. The madams wouldn't stand for their girls getting drunk or fighting on the job, and they made them get regular medical checkups. A man might have to pay a house price of fifty cents for a dime's worth of booze or a quarter for a nickel glass of beer, but he could be pretty sure he wouldn't catch a dose from his three-dollar hump. And if he gave the madam his money to hold while he had his fun upstairs, he knew none of it would be missing when he got it back.

Tonight the district was as raucous as I'd ever heard it. Every house had a jukebox, and a crazy tangle of oldtime rags and recent big-band instrumentals streamed from the parlors to mix with the racket outside. Cars honking and jarring over the uneven brick pavement, the sidewalks full of soldiers and sailors and college boys, dockwallopers, businessmen off the leash from home, laughing and looking damn happy. Bad fights were uncommon in the houses—guys eager to get laid or who'd just had their ashes hauled weren't usually in a fighting mood. There'd be some hothead every now and then, or some guy too drunk to know better, but every house had its bouncer to take care of them.

The best thing about the Galveston houses—and the most surprising to me when I first arrived on the island—was that so many of the whores were actually pretty. Where I'd grown up, there had been only two whorehouses inside a hundred miles, and of the handful of women who worked in them only one looked to be under thirty years old, and only if you'd had enough to drink would you call her fair of face. It was a widespread joke that most of the girls at both those houses were so ugly *they* ought to pay the guys who humped them. But it was also a common saying that you always paid for it with any woman, one way or another, and a whore was the only one honest enough about it to charge you a specific dollar price and give you what you paid for and leave the complications out of it. The steepest price for it was marriage, of course, and lots of men paid it. "The full freight," LQ called it, and he'd already paid it twice. But he still preferred trying to woo a woman into bed rather than giving her cash.

"A man needs to feel like he's getting it because the woman thinks he's handsome or charming or can make her laugh," LQ said. "Like he's getting it for *some* goddamn reason other than he's got three bucks in his pocket. A man's got to at least *feel* that way every now and then, no matter it aint true."

Not even Brando argued the point with him. But we all knew that sometimes a man wanted it the other way, too—straight and simple and without the bullshit. Here's the money, honey, let's get to it. Which is how I was wanting it just then.

I had intended to go into the first house I came to, but as soon as I turned onto Post Office Street I remembered a Mexican girl who'd been working at Mrs. Lang's the last time I'd been there, about three months before. She wasn't really Mex—she'd told me she was born in Colorado and that her grandparents had been the last real Mexicans in her family—and I knew she didn't speak Spanish any better than Brando. But she *looked* every bit Mexican, and tonight that was what I wanted.

A skinny Negro maid with sullen eyes greeted me at the door. A loud jazzy version of "Sweet Georgia Brown" was playing on the juke, and the parlor was hazed with cigarette smoke. About nine or ten guys were in there, waiting their turn to go upstairs. They sat on sofas along the walls or stood at the small bar at the rear of the room, where they were served by a little gray man with a hangdog face. Some of the younger guys were talking low and snickering among themselves, but the older ones just sat and smoked and stared at the nude paintings on the wall or down at their own shoes. Even through the smoke and the scent of incense candles, you could detect the faint odor of disinfectant and a musky hint of sex.

Mrs. Lang came toward me with a bright red smile, blond hair braided in a bun at the back of her neck, gold hoops dangling from her ears. She gave me a quick hug and said happy new year and been so long and so forth. She had bright green eyes and a wide sexy mouth and looked pretty good for a woman in her forties. She gave my briefcase a curious look—not a lot of guys carried a briefcase into a whorehouse—but said nothing about it. As she led me toward the bar with her arm hooked around mine I asked if Felicia still worked there.

"She surely does, honey. She just this minute went upstairs. But sweetie, we're just *so* busy tonight, you're going to have to wait a bit. Another fella's already waiting specially for her too."

I wasn't disposed to wait. I slid a twenty out of my pocket and slipped it to her.

"My, we *are* in a hurry, aren't we?" She slid the bill up her sleeve. "But you know, baby, the other fella waiting on her is in a hurry too. It'll be awful hard to explain things to him just right."

I gave her another ten and said she ought to at least have the decency to pull a gun on me.

She laughed and patted my arm and discreetly tucked the money in a side pocket of her skirt. Then looked across the room at a big guy leaning against the wall with his thumbs hooked in his pockets. The bouncer, a different one from the last time I'd been here. A young guy wearing an open coat over a black T-shirt stretched tight across his chest. He caught Mrs. Lang's look and straightened up, made a little nod and began cracking his knuckles.

Mrs. Lang fitted a cigarette to the end of a long holder and I lit it for her, then bought her a glass of sherry and had a beer for myself while we waited for Felicia to finish up with whoever she had upstairs. Over the next few minutes three guys, almost one right after the other, came out of the upper hallway and down the stairs and only one of them waved so long at Mrs. Lang before scooting out the door. Each time a guy came down, she nodded at another one in the parlor and he'd go up to the girl waiting at the top of the staircase. Most whores couldn't remember your name from one minute to the next, but they had damn good memories for faces, and madams had the best memories of all, never losing track of their customers' order of turns even on the busiest nights.

The girls wore short little camisoles, and one of the whores on the upper landing grinned down at everybody in the parlor and flicked up the front of hers to give us a glimpse of her trim brown bush, then busted out laughing and retreated into the hall with her next trick.

"That Carolyn is such a slut," Mrs. Lang said, but she was smiling. Girls like Carolyn were great for business.

Now another guy came out of the upper hall, still adjusting his tie, and started down the stairs. And Felicia stood up there, her skin dark against the pale yellow camisole.

Mrs. Lang took me by the hand and hurried me to the stairs and gave me a little push up the first few steps. "*Move* it, honey," she hissed at me. "You're the one in such a rush."

Somebody said, *"Hey!"* and I stopped on the stairs and turned.

A burly redfaced guy in a derby hat who'd been sitting on a sofa was coming toward us. But the bouncer cut in front of him, saying something I couldn't hear over the loud volume of "Let's Fall in Love" coming from the jukebox. I knew he was hoping the derby man would try something, if only to break the monotony. I'd been a bouncer in San Antonio for a time and knew how boring the job could get.

Mrs. Lang flapped her hands at me like she was shooing something, and then Felicia had me by the hand and was tugging me the rest of the way up the stairs, saying, "Come on, baby, come on—long time no see."

As we got up to the landing, I looked back and saw the madam speaking in earnest fashion to the derby man, the bouncer standing with them and looking disappointed. Then we were in the hallway and out of view of the parlor.

We went into her little room and she shut the door and glanced at a bedside chair holding a small stack of fresh hand towels. I set the briefcase down next to the bed and hung my hat on a bedpost and took off my coat and draped it on the chairback. She pulled off her camisole and tossed it on the chair, then stood naked in front of me and helped me unbutton my shirt, talking all the while, saying she'd been wondering what had become of me, had I got married or moved away or what, trying to sound casual but doing a poor job of concealing her eagerness to move things along and serve as many tricks as she could on this most lucrative night of the year. Then I was naked too and we got in bed and went at it.

I was surprised at how worked up I was. She said, "Oh yeah, honey, yeah," as I hammered away at her. The whole thing didn't take but a minute. Then she was squirming out from under me, saying "That was great, baby—wooo, yeah."

She wiped herself with a towel and handed me one, then slipped her camisole back on and shook my foot by the big toe. "Hate to rush you, sweetie, but gosh, tonight it's just busy-busy, you know?"

I put my pants and shirt on, then sat on the bed to tug on my boots, sensing a familiar sadness. I'd heard or read somewhere that the French called sexual climax "the little death," which was a pretty good description for the way it always felt to me. I wasn't sure what it was that died each time, but I'd often wondered if the strange sadness that came afterward might be some form of grief for it, some special sort of sorrow rooted so deep inside of us that we didn't even have a name for it. This time, for some reason, the melancholy was more insistent than usual.

"Dream a Little Dream" was on the juke when we went out to the landing. Felicia gave me a so-long peck on the cheek, then turned to smile down at the guy in the derby hat who'd gotten up from the sofa and was heading for the stairs as I started down. Mrs. Lang was at the bar and looking at us. She cut her eyes to the bouncer, who was over by the juke, pointing out selections to a guy feeding coins into it.

The derby man's face was as easy to read as a fist. I figured him for a sailorman treating himself to a New Year's Eve on the town in his best suit and hat, and he'd obviously been sitting there seething about me buying a turn ahead of him. Maybe he was drunk or maybe he was one of those guys who took everything personally, or maybe it was something else, I didn't give a damn. But everything about the way he was carrying himself as he came up the narrow stairway said he'd worked himself up for a scrap.

Mrs. Lang must've seen it too. She called out, "Hollis!" I caught a glimpse of her directing the bouncer's attention to us, of other guys looking up to see what was going on.

We were in the middle of the staircase and almost abreast when the derby man pointed his finger in my face and said, "Lemme tell you something, you mongrel sonofa—"

I grabbed the finger and pushed it back so hard my knuckles touched his wrist, and even over the music the whole room probably heard the bone snap.

He screamed and fell to his knees. I gave him a knee to the chin that cracked his jaws together and his derby twirled off and he went tumbling down the stairs, his head banging the steps. He landed in a heap at the foot of the stairway and didn't move.

Everybody in the parlor was on his feet. Some were gawking at me, some were clearing out fast. The bouncer hopped over the derby man and came up at me with his fists ready, happy for the chance at some action and in no mood to talk things over. Fine with me. But the fool should've waited for me to come down rather than give me the advantage of the higher stairs.

I raised the briefcase like I was going to throw it at him—and as his hands rose to defend against it I kicked him in the chest. He sailed down the stairs and on his ass and his momentum carried him in a complete somersault over the derby man and he slammed the floor on his back so hard the vibrations came up through my feet. He lay spread-eagled with his eyes and mouth open wide, one leg twitching slightly like it had an electrical short in it.

As I came down the stairs the only two guys still in the room sped for the front door. The derby man was on his belly and out cold. Blood was seeping from his nose and open mouth, and his broken finger jutted awkwardly on a knuckle that looked like a purple walnut.

The bouncer's eyes were terrified. His mouth was working without sound and he probably thought he was going to die for lack of air. And then it came to him, a deep hissing inhalation, and he closed his eyes and gave himself over to the luxury of breath.

I stepped around them and went to the bar. Mrs. Lang was enraged but I knew she wouldn't call the police. A fracas like this didn't happen often and was anyway a hazard of the trade, an inconvenience that would cut into the evening's profits but wasn't as much of a problem for her as the cops would be.

"Beer," I said to the old bartender. His morose expression hadn't changed a bit. He drew a glass and put it in front of me and said, "Two bits."

I grinned at Mrs. Lang as I dug a quarter out of my pocket. "Jesus, I pay enough for ten turns *and* I entertain the joint, and I don't even get a beer on the house?"

Her mouth pinched tighter. Her good humor had fled with her customers. I flipped the coin to the old guy and he made a neat catch.

"That stupid man was spoiling for a fight," Mrs. Lang said. "And that damned Hollis didn't give you much choice, I know. But I can't have fighting here, it's terrible for business. I'm afraid you're not welcome here anymore. Neither is he."

I drained most of the glass in a swallow. One of the girls and her trick came slowly down the stairs. The man stepped carefully around the two guys on the floor and hustled on outside. The girl knelt beside the bouncer and helped him to sit up.

I finished the beer and wiped my mouth. "Well," I said, "all right. I just hope to hell I can find me another whorehouse somewhere around here."

The crack didn't raise a smile from anybody but the skinny maid. I exchanged winks with her as I went out the door.

• •

When I'd first arrived in Galveston I lived in an apartment on Seawall Boulevard. Sam had gotten it for me on the day after I arrived in town. I liked the gulf view from the front windows and the sea breeze that came through them. I liked the nearby dance halls with their swell bands, the restaurants, the entertainment joints with their indoor swimming pools and penny arcades and shooting galleries. During my first few weeks on the island I explored the rest of the city little by little. I grew acquainted with the downtown streets—I especially liked the Strand, with its large buildings and old-time architecture. I went to the theaters and moviehouses, patronized all the cafés to see which ones I liked best. I took my ease on benches in the city parks and the German beer gardens. I wandered along the railyards, the ship port, the shrimp docks. I bellied up to the bar in waterfront saloons full of sailors speaking a dozen different languages.

The main Negro quarter was just south of the red-light district, and in those early weeks I sometimes went there for barbecue and to listen to the blues and watch the couples dance to jazz. It was dancing to beat any I'd ever seen. One night I was in a place called the Toot Sweet Jazz Hall and a lean smoky girl with bloodred lipstick and an ass as round as a medicine ball asked me to dance. When I said I didn't know how, not that way, she laughed and pulled me out on the floor and taught me.

A little while later we were in her apartment and going at it. But then while we were resting up and having a cigarette the door crashed open and a guy big as a gorilla came charging in, cursing her for a no-good bitch and holding a straight razor. I rolled to the floor so he'd have to stoop to try to cut me, but the fool only kicked me in the head and then went for the screaming girl—which gave me the chance to drive my foot into the side of his knee, breaking the joint and bringing him down with a pretty good holler of his own. I grabbed his blade hand and bit it, crunching bone and tasting blood, and he let the razor drop. I slapped it away under the bed and punched him in the neck and got to my feet and stomped my heel into his crotch. His eyes bugged out and he rolled onto his side and threw up.

She was sitting on the bed and pressing a hand to her cheek, blood running from between her fingers and down her arm and dripping on the sheets. *"Kill him!"* she said. "Kill that lowdown nigger!"

But since the lowdown nigger in question already had a busted knee and a chewed hand that would infect worse than a dog bite, not to mention a pair of swollen balls that would be hurting him for days, I didn't see the need. I started getting my clothes on fast.

She said I didn't have to worry about the cops, they never came to Niggertown unless a white person called them in. I wasn't worried about cops—but if the gorilla had pals close by I didn't want to fight them bare-assed too. She pressed a towel to her cheek with one hand and held her dress with the other and stepped into it and clumsily tugged it up over her hips.

The guy had quit puking but he wasn't about to stand up on that knee, not for a long time. He was holding his balls and glaring at me in a painful rage. "Kill you, mothafucker. Come back in Niggertown, man, I *kill* your ass."

It wasn't a good time to talk to me that way—the knot he'd raised over my eye was starting to ache. I fetched him a bootkick to the ear that shut him up except for the moaning.

As I went out the door she was cursing him and stamping on his head with her bare foot, still only half-dressed, her pretty tits jiggling as she let him have it.

I returned to the Toot Sweet Club a few nights later. I didn't see the girl or the gorilla anywhere, but hadn't expected to, considering their condition. Some of the spades gave me pretty hard looks, and I supposed the story had got around. One girl finally sidled up to me and said if I was looking for Corella—I hadn't even known her name, it had all been "baby" and "sugar" between us—she'd gone home to Lake Charles where she had a childhood sweetie who'd probably take her back, cut face and all. As for Zachary, the fella who cut her, his leg was in a cast and his hand looked like a boxing glove and all he could do was stay home drunk. I bought her a drink, but before she could take the first sip some guy in dark glasses and with a gold front tooth came over and whispered in her ear. She gave me an "I'm sorry" look and moved off with the guy, leaving the drink on the bar. I hung around long enough to let any of them who wanted to try me have the chance, but nobody made a move.

Over the next few weeks I went to some of the other Negro clubs, but it was obvious the word was out. The guys never took their eyes off me, and for all their looking, the women kept their distance. No fun in that, so I quit going.

Rough as it was, the Negro quarter wasn't any rougher than the streets and alleys between Post Office and the railroad tracks. The area's rundown tenements were home to Galveston's poorest and most troublesome whites, and the town's meanest coloreds lived in its alleyway shacks. On a section of Market Street called Little China, a Chinese family with a dozen or so members lived in the single back room of a laundry, and another Chinese bunch lived in a tiny restaurant down the street. Rumor had it that the two families had belonged to different tongs in China and brought their ancient feud with them to America. Which probably explained why every now and then somebody'd find a dead Chinaman stuffed in an alley garbage can with his throat cut, or floating in the channel with a wire garrote still around his neck. But they were only Chinamen, so you never read about them in the papers except now and then as a little filler on a back page, saying something like FOREIGNER FOUND DROWNED IN BAY.

In this part of town too was an isolated street of a half-dozen houses and some three dozen residents, all of them Mexican. Though the residents called it La Colonia, the street had no sign and did not appear on the city maps. It was too small of an enclave to qualify as a quarter, but there weren't all that many Mexes on the island to begin with, and this was one of the few neighborhoods of them.

I'd been in Galveston about three months when I stumbled onto it. I was wandering the streets north of the redlight district one humid night and caught the peppery scent of Mexican cooking. I followed the smell to a dirt lane branching from Mechanic Street near a hazy amber streetlamp. The lane cut through a scrubby vacant lot before passing through a dark hollow of mossy oaks and magnolias to dead-end at the railtracks. In the shadows of the overhanging trees the little frame houses stood in a ragged row along the left side of the lane. Their porchlights were on and their windows were brightly yellow. Light also showed against the underbranches of the trees in a backyard about midway down the street and I heard music coming from behind the house. Accordion and fiddle and guitar playing "Tu, Solo Tu." I'd heard the tune a hundred times but now it reminded me of a moment less than three years past that seemed like ancient history, reminded me of a packed-dirt dance floor under a desert night-sky blasting with stars, of dancing close with a pretty Mexican girl to this same song as my cousin Reuben and my friend Chente danced with a pair of blond sisters. . . .

The roast-pepper aroma had grown stronger, and mingling into it were the smells of maize tortillas and refried beans. I went around to the lit-up backyard and found a small party going on.

Couples were dancing on a wide patch of bare dirt, kicking and swirling and spinning each other around in the cast of light from lanterns hung on tree branches. A kid spotted me and told the people gathered at a long picnic table loaded with bowls of food, and they looked over at me. One of the men approached me, removing his hat, and I took mine off too.

The lantern light was full on my face and I could tell by his look that he could see the color of my eyes. I'd seen such inquisitive stares more times than I could count.

"Buenas noches," he said, and added, "Good evening," in deference to the possibility that I spoke only English.

In Spanish I apologized for intruding and told him I'd smelled the food and heard the music and wanted to see what was going on.

His face brightened and he beckoned me to join them, saying, "Pase, caballero, por favor. Nuestra casa es su casa."

His name was Arturo Alcanzas and he was host of the party. The others also welcomed me warmly, everyone speaking in Spanish. They introduced themselves all around and made room for me at the table bench. They admired my suit and boots, the briefcase I kept at my side. They tried not to stare too obviously at my eyes. The musicians finished the number and came over to the table and Arturo introduced them too, three brothers named Gutierrez. They called themselves Los Tres Payasos, and though they modestly professed not to be very good, Alcanzas said they were good enough to get hired to play at small fiestas and quinceañeras from Port Arthur to Bay City.

Someone fetched me a bottle of Carta Blanca from a tub packed with ice. A bowl of fried jalapeños was set close to me on one side and a platter of chicharrones on the other. While I munched on the chiles and pork rinds some of the women passed around a plate for me, filling it with red rice, beans, spiced shredded pork. A young girl placed a wicker basket of corn tortillas within my reach.

I told them my name and their faces showed curiosity about it, but their natural politeness restrained them from asking how I had come by it. One who spoke English told the others that James meant Santiago, and everyone was pleased by this and addressed me by that name from then on. When one of the men remarked that I spoke with the accent of the western frontera, some of the others made faces of reprimand for his breach of manners with such familiarity. He looked chastened and assured me he'd meant no disrespect. I assured him I'd perceived none. I told them I'd grown up along the Chihuahua and Texas border, and they said "Ah, pues," and nodded at each other around the table as though I had clarified a great deal.

They told me all about themselves. The first of them to settle here had named the little street La Colonia Tamaulipas, in honor of their home state, but over time it simply became La Colonia. Many of them were related by blood or marriage and were from Matamoros, just the other side of the Rio Grande. Others were from Victoria, Monterrey, Tampico. "Pero todos venimos con espaldas mojadas," one of them said with a smile, joking about the wetback fashion in which they'd all crossed the river. Some of the men had found work on the docks, some in the railyard, some on the shrimp boats. A pair of brothers named Lopez talked excitedly of their plan to own their own shrimper one day.

In the group was a whitehaired old man named Gregorio who owned a small boardinghouse. I asked if he had a vacancy, and he did, and after we were done eating and had another beer, he took me over there to see it. The building was the only two-story on the street, a rundown clapboard at the end of the lane, its front yard bordered by a weathered picket fence. He called the house the Casa Verde because of its moldy-green roof shingles and the thick growth of vines on the outer walls and around the porch columns.

Inside, the place smelled old but the parlor and hallway and kitchen were neatly kept. Gregorio himself occupied the only bedroom on the ground floor and rented out the three bedrooms upstairs. The vacancy was on a front corner, with one window overlooking the lane and another facing the traintracks. A light bulb dangling from the ceiling illuminated a battered wardrobe, a narrow bed, a small wooden table and a straightback chair. Columns of numbers had been scratched into the tabletop. The old man saw me fingering them and said the previous tenant had been a gambler. I asked what had become of him, and Gregorio turned up his hands. One day the man had been there, he said, and one day he had not, as had always been the case with men and would be the case with us as well.

"Casero y filósofo tambien," I said, and he showed a yellow grin and said all men became philosophers if they lived long enough.

The bath was at the end of the hallway. An old telephone—the only phone in the colonia, Gregorio said—was mounted on the wall at the foot of the stairs. I asked for its number and wrote it on a piece of paper to give to Rose. I moved in the next day and had been living there ever since.

LQ and Brando had thought it was a smart move on my part because wetback neighbors weren't the nosy sort. Among the few things

LQ and Ray agreed on was that a guy—especially one in our business—shouldn't own anything more than he could carry in a single suitcase and should never live anyplace where the neighbors didn't mind their own business.

Sam couldn't understand why I'd leave a beachside apartment with new furnishings and appliances to move into a ramshackle place in one of the worst sections of town. I didn't even try to explain, and he finally just shook his head and quit ragging me about it.

Rose didn't say anything about the move. Except maybe he did, a few days later, in a sort of roundabout way. I was driving him back from some Houston business, and as we went over the causeway he said the look of the water in the afternoon sunlight always reminded him of a little lagoon in Palermo where his father had taught him to swim.

"It's funny," he said, staring out at the bay and the island on the other side. "This place is so different, but there's things about it that remind me of Palermo when I was a boy. I tell you, if there was some part of town called Little Sicily—Little Italy, even—I'd move in there in a minute. I wouldn't give a shit how beat-up it was. It'd be nice hearing the language, you know, people talking to each other in it. And the music. And smelling the food. I'd like . . . Ah hell."

He made a dismissive gesture and changed the subject.

• •

The fight at Mrs. Lang's had boosted my spirits more than Felicia had. I stopped in a place on Market Street and drank a beer and then had another in a joint on Mechanic. But by the time I got to La Colonia, I was feeling the same undefinable irritation that had been nagging me earlier in the evening.

It was after two in the morning. Clouds were bunching over the gulf, blocking out the stars. The slight wind had kicked up and was gently stirring the treetops. The evening's earlier warmth was giving way to a rising chill. It smelled like it might rain.

Other than the Casa Verde at the far end of the lane, only the Avila house showed light—a dim yellow glow against the pulled shade of a front window. The Morales family had hosted a neighborhood party earlier in the evening and I could make out the dark shapes of several cars parked in the deeper shadows between the Morales and the Avila houses. Overnight visitors, I figured.

A cloud of bugs was swarming around the Casa Verde porchlight. I didn't need a key because Gregorio had stopped locking the door shortly after I'd moved in. I'd never told him or anyone else in La Colonia what I did for a living, but before I'd been there a month everybody on the block seemed to know who I worked for. I was pouring a cup of coffee in the kitchen one morning when I heard Señora Ortega, the next-door neighbor, talking to Gregorio in the sideyard, telling him how her daughter had warned a coworker at the oystersheds that if he didn't stop pestering her she would complain to her neighbor, Don Santiago, who was a bodyguard for Rosario Maceo. The man, the señora told Gregorio, had not bothered her girl since.

Gregorio had mounted a small slateboard with a chalk holder next to the hallway telephone, but the only messages I'd ever seen on it were rare ones for me to call the Club. I'd never seen either of the other two tenants use the phone or known them to receive a call. One of them, Moises, was older than Gregorio and almost deaf. Even though he had one of those old-time ear horns, you still had to shout into it. The other resident was Sergio, a nervous little man who worked as the night clerk for a motor hotel on the beach. He kept to his room all day and was said to have no friends at all.

Tonight the slateboard was blank, as usual. At the far end of the hall the kitchen door shone brightly. I wasn't surprised to find Gregorio in there, sitting at the table, sipping a bottle of beer and reading a movie magazine, his wire-rim glasses low on his nose. It was his habit to stay up all night and go to bed at dawn and sleep till noon.

He said he had not been able to sleep at night for the past thirty-two years. He'd never said why and I'd never asked.

The kitchen was big and high-ceilinged and a large heavy dining table stood in its center. I helped myself to a beer from the icebox and pried off the cap with an opener hung on the door handle by a wire hook and sat across the table from him. I took a pack of Camels from my coat and shook one out for myself and then slid the pack across the table to him and we both lit up. He looked tired and a little glass-eyed. There had probably been plenty to drink at the Morales party.

He tapped a hand on the article he'd been reading. He could speak and read English much better than the rest of the residents of La Colonia, not counting the kids. "Do you know what those Hollywood assholes said after they gave Fred Astaire his screen test?"

Fred Astaire was Gregorio's favorite movie star. The old man had seen *Top Hat* three times already.

He looked down at the article. "They said he couldn't act very good and the women wouldn't like him because he was 'slightly bald.' But they said he could at least 'dance a little.' "

He peered at me over the rim of his glasses. "That's like saying Jack Dempsey could punch a little, no?" He shook his head. "Assholes."

I drank my beer and leafed through a magazine from the stack on the table. Gregorio said I'd missed a good party. They roasted a kid on a spit in Morales' backyard and there were platters of every kind of dish and enough beer and tequila for everybody to get as drunk as he wanted. He'd never seen so many visitors to a Colonia party as this time. Morales' brother had come down from Beaumont. Ortega's brother and sister-in-law up from Lake Jackson. Avila's uncle and cousin and the uncle's goddaughter, who was pretty but didn't talk much, had come all the way from Brownsville. And a cousin of the Gutierrez brothers, a car mechanic from Victoria, had come too. Turned out he was a hell of a singer and guitar player and he'd been the hit of the party.

"Sorry I missed it," I said. The wind was blowing a little harder now, and tree branches scraped the side of the building. I finished the beer and dropped the bottle in the garbage can.

"Happy new year, viejo," I said, and headed for the stairs.

"Feliz año nuevo, kid," the old man said.

My room was chilly, so I took the extra blanket out of the wardrobe and spread it over the one already on the bed. I got undressed, then opened the briefcase and took out the guns. I put the .380 on the bedside stand. The Mexican revolver went under the pillow. I turned off the light and got in bed and listened to the wind and rasping branches for a while before I fell asleep.

• •

I woke in darkness to a sound I thought I recognized but I couldn't immediately place it. The wind had ceased. For a moment I thought maybe I'd been dreaming—and then realized I still heard it. A car motor. Down in the lane and beginning to move away.

A Model T.

I swung out of bed and went to the window, released the shade to go fluttering up on its spindle, raised the window sash and pushed open the screen frame and stuck my head out into a chilly drizzle.

In the light of the streetlamp, a lettuce-green Model T sedan without a left front fender was turning onto Mechanic Street. I saw the dark form of the driver but I couldn't tell if there was anyone else in the car. The T rattled down the street and then its single taillight went out of sight.

I stood at the open window a moment longer before I pictured what I must look like—gawking out at an empty street, shivering in my underwear, getting my head wet. I cursed and let the screen frame down and closed the window. My wristwatch was on the table and I struck a match to read the time. Almost six. From the time I was old enough to do chores on the ranch until the day I left there in the hurry I did, I had always been up well before this hour.

But I wasn't on the ranch now, and what I wanted was more sleep. I ran a towel through my hair and got back in bed.

And couldn't get the green Ford out of my mind.

Bullshit, the Ford . . . I was thinking about the girl.

I wondered if she'd been in the car just now. I remembered her look under the traffic light, how it caught me flatfooted for one big heartbeat and got me rankled for some damn reason. Which, it occurred to me, probably had something to do with my edginess the rest of the evening.

The realization agitated me all the more because I hadn't been able to put my finger on it earlier. Not much ever got under my skin, but when something did I damn well knew what and why and I knew how to get rid of it.

Little chippy. What'd she think she was trying to pull?

She had to be the one Gregorio had mentioned, the one at the party, the goddaughter of Avila's aunt and uncle. All the way from Brownsville, Gregorio said. Had they just now been getting an early start on the long drive back? They sure as hell weren't going to the movies at five in the morning or to a picnic on the beach. How far to Brownsville? Way more than three hundred miles, probably closer to four. All-day drive and then some—especially in that old T.

Christ's sake, I told myself, who *cared*?

Some face on her, though.

Yeah, right—but there were pretty faces everywhere, hundreds in this town alone.

Not like that one.

Bullshit. It wasn't *that* special. Besides, I didn't see anything except her face. For all I knew she had an ass like an Oldsmobile.

Not likely.

For all I knew she was married.

A married woman came to Morales' party with her *godfather*? How much sense did that make?

What's sense got to do with anything? Besides, the old man said Avila's cousin had come too. For all I knew he was her beau . . .

So it went, while I lay there staring at the ceiling and the New Year slowly dawned.

On the second-floor balcony of the casa grande of the Hacienda de Las Cadenas, César Calveras Dogal is taking his noon brandy and awaiting the arrival of his foreman, El Segundo.

The great house stands on a long low bluff, and the balcony affords a vista beyond the mesquite woods along the north wall of the hacienda compound. To the northeast Don César can see the meander of the shallow Río Cadenas whose origin is high in the dark sierras and whose flow through a venous array of irrigation ditches nurtures the estate's tenacious pasturelands and its meager gardens. He can see all the way to the Ciénaga de las Palmas, glinting like a little glass sliver five miles away. In truth the ciénaga has no palms at all and is but a muddy marsh where the river drains and quits. Almost forty miles beyond the ciénaga, in the blue-hazed distance, lies the hard road from Escalón to Monclova. The surrounding country is dense with cactus and thickets of mesquite, and the mountains at the horizons are long and blue.

The years have not lessened Don César's admiration of the natural beauty of this estate set on the border between the states of Durango and Chihuahua, a beauty the more remarkable for being at the southern edge of a vast desertland that includes a portion of the Bolson de Mapimí, perhaps the meanest desert of the earth's western side. The hacienda's beauty is as remarkable as the fact of its having survived the rage of the Revolution.

The bastard Revolution! A year before its outbreak, Don César had been a thirty-five-year-old captain in command of a company of Guardia Rural—the fearsome national mounted police of President Porfirio Díaz—and he had earned the lasting personal gratitude of Don Porfirio for his company's heroic rescue of the president's niece and her party of travelers besieged at a desolate Durango outpost by a band of Yaqui marauders. Captain Calveras and his men had killed a dozen of the savages and captured ten, including their chief. But one of the travelers had received a fatal wound and a pregnant woman among them had miscarried. Hence, rather than send the captives to the henequen plantations in the Yucatán as was customary, Captain Calveras hanged them in the nearest village square—all but the chief, whom he executed by tying one of the Indian's legs to one horse and the other leg to another and then lashing the horses into a sprint in opposite directions. He telegraphed his report to the headquarters office at Hermosillo and by day's end he received notice of Don Porfirio's appreciation and of an immediate promotion to the rank of comandante.

Two months later, in still another battle with still other Yaquis, Comandante Calveras took an arrow through a thigh and up into the hip. It was three days before he could present himself to a surgeon and by then the infection was so deeply rooted that the surgeon spoke of amputation of the entire leg. The comandante rejected that procedure with a promise that if he should awaken from the surgery without his leg he would hang the doctor. He survived the operation with the leg intact but the hip was in permanent ruin. He would evermore walk with a limp and he could no longer sit a horse for more than a few minutes before the pain became excruciating. He was offered the command of a regional rurales headquarters but he disdained desk jobs and instead chose to retire. Though the decision delighted his wife and children, it was a difficult one, for he had been in the rurales since the age of sixteen, when he had turned his back on his father's patrimony—a hacienda and vast cattle ranch in Zacatecas state—and enlisted in the national police.

On the day of his retirement he was received in the National Palace by Don Porfirio himself, who presented him with an unexpected prize—the title to La Hacienda de Las Cadenas, an estate which until recently had belonged to a political rival of the Porfiriato. The president slid the ornately embossed paper across the polished desktop and told Comandante Calveras to consider it a spoil of war, the sweetest of life's possessions. But a man with title to a hacienda, Don Porfirio said, should of course have the means to maintain the place, and so he also awarded the comandante a trunk filled with silver specie, a prize of such weight that it required three strong men to load it onto the transport wagon. Comandante Calveras had by then already amassed a considerable sum of money by means of the rurales' right to confiscate the assets of fugitives and of killed or convicted criminals—a sum which, together with el presidente's cash award, now amounted to a small fortune.

But eight months after Don César's retirement, there came the Revolution—and before another year passed, Porfirio Díaz was exiled in Paris, never to return.

The memory of the Revolution taints Don César's tongue with the taste of blood. The name of "Revolution" was entirely undeserved by that lunatic decade of national riot and rampage by misbegotten Indian brutes and primitive bastard half-castes. The shit-blooded whoresons had razed his father's hacienda and crucified the man on the front door of the casa grande before setting the house aflame. A few months afterward they murdered Don César's own family as well.

By means of an exorbitant bribe, Don César had secured passage for his wife and three children (his angelic trio of blond daughters!) aboard a federal troop-and-munitions train bound for Juárez, from where his beloveds were to cross the river to refuge in El Paso. But just south of Samalayuca, a bare forty miles from the border, the track under the train was dynamited.

The handful of survivors told of the slew and crash and tumble of the railcars one upon the other, the hellish screams, the great screeching and sparkings of iron, the explosions of the munitions that the rebels had desired for themselves but in their incompetence destroyed along with the train. ("Viva Villa!" they shouted—"Viva Villa!"—even as they looted the wreckage and the dead and robbed the survivors.) Don César had traveled to Samalayuca and was able to identify his daughters' remains by their diminutive forms and take them back for burial at Las Cadenas, but his wife was unrecognizable among the array of charred and mutilated corpses and she was interred with the others in a mass grave.

In the years to follow he had endured the loss of his family as he endured the abuses and indignations of one raiding pack of mongrels after another, each calling itself an army of the Revolution and each claiming the sanctioning ideal of liberty—a word not one in every hundred of them owned the literacy to recognize in print. He had withstood the sudden emptiness in his life as he had withstood the degradations to his estate, his great house, his fields, his person, the spit in his face, the ridicule of his crippled leg. He endured their insults, their laughter, the ceaseless threats to shoot him, hang him, quarter him, burn him alive, endured it all with indifference. How could their threats of death make him afraid? Only a man with desire to live could be made afraid of death.

But one of them had perceived the truth of his lack of fear—the leader of one of the first gangs of invaders to arrive at Las Cadenas, the one they called El Carnicero and whose revolver muzzle had pressed to Don César's forehead as the man asked if he had a last word. A large man whom he would hear described by some as handsome in spite of his dusky mestizo hide, his face hard but smooth-featured, his eyes black as open graves and untouched by his mustached smile. Don César stared hard into those eyes and waited for the blast to end his misery. But then the brute laughed and took the gun from his head.

You're not afraid, the man said. You're only miserable. You *want* to die, don't you, patrón? Why is that, I wonder.

The man put a hand on Don César's shoulder and leaned close to him in the fashion of a commiserating intimate. They tell me you were a comandante of rurales, patrón. Is that how your leg came to be maimed? Ay, what a hard life that must have been, the rurales. Tell me, patrón, has life been *cruel* to you? Have you been robbed of your possessions, of your comforts? Have you lost *loved ones*? Does your fine hidalgo mind hold memories too horrible to bear? Ay, don't tell me, patrón . . . have you suffered *injustice*?

Some among the mob of onlooking peons snickered and some laughed outright and some called out to El Carnicero to shoot the gachupín son of a bitch. They who an hour before would have cowered in Don César's presence, who would have obeyed his every command without hesitation and were ever in fear of displeasing him, they now laughed at him oh so bravely. How they had hastened to show their whip and branding scars—as if they hadn't deserved them!—to this murderer, this notorious executioner and infamous right hand of Pancho Villa the bandit, Villa the mad dog, the king of all half-caste whoresons. Yet some few of the spectators wept in their witness of Don César's ordeal.

Yes, you have suffered much, patrón, El Carnicero said, holstering the revolver. He slid his hand behind Don César's neck and held him gently and smiled at him. Then the hand clamped tight and Don César saw but an instant's gleam of the knife before all in a single motion its point pierced the corner of his eye and the blade slid around the curve of the socket to core the eyeball from its mooring.

Don César screamed and clapped a hand to the emptied socket and flexed into a half-crouch of agony, biting his lip hard against further outcry. His remaining eye saw blood pocking the dust at his feet and staining his boots. Some in the mob laughed, some cried out, some blessed themselves and turned away.

El Carnicero grabbed him by the hair and pulled his head up to face him. He had the bloody eye in his palm and held it for Don César to see. This thing, the man said, bobbing his palm as if assaying the worth of what it contained, has always been blind to justice, to the truth. He dropped the eye to the ground and made Don César look down at it and then ground it under his bootheel.

Maybe the other eye will now serve you better, El Carnicero said. If it does not, I will come back and remove it too.

He told the mob not to kill Don César, that killing would be too swift a punishment and kinder than he deserved. Then he wished Don César a long remaining life full of unpleasant memories and rode away with his gang of devils.

Still more thieves and scavengers fell upon the hacienda over the following years. Sometimes they came almost on each other's heels, sometimes there were no raiders for months, but always they had come, pack after pack, each finding less remaining to pillage on Las Cadenas. But each had heard the story of how the patrón—the former rurales comandante—had come to wear the eyepatch. They had all heard of El Carnicero and knew better than to kill a man he had deigned to leave alive. What if the Butcher should come back to pleasure himself further with this gachupín once more and learn that someone had killed him? What if he should learn who had done it?

And so Don César lived and endured. It might be that the man who cut out his eye never knew that he had protected the patrón of Las Cadenas from other rebel bands, or that he had given Don César a reason to live. Don César withstood the remaining years of the Revolution in anticipation of the deaths of his tormentors—and of rebuilding the hacienda as best he could, if for no other purpose than to show that it could not be destroyed by such rabble as his tormentors.

Two years after the loss of his eye, he received word of El Carnicero's death. The man had drowned in a horseback crossing of a lake in northern Chihuahua. Don César sang at the news, he did a little dance. But his celebrant joy was checked by the knowledge that Pancho Villa—the man who had unloosed El Carnicero on Mexican civilization—was yet alive. And the bastard managed to stay alive all through the Revolution. In 1920, when the government made its separate peace with Villa and granted him a hacienda, Don César's rage was apoplectic. Then three years later came the news of Villa's assassination by persons unknown—and Don César declared a three-day fiesta to commemorate the grand occasion.

Every year since then, he had made an annual hundred-mile trip to Hidalgo de Parral, the town where Villa had been killed and was buried, and there Don César had pissed on the monster's grave. Three years after Villa's death, unknown persons broke into his tomb and made away with his head, and Don César had been torn in his emotions—elated by the desecration to Villa's remains, but dismayed not to have thought to commit the act himself. He fancied he would have used the skull as a dish to feed his dog. The headless cadaver had been reburied and the grave fortified, but even a concrete grave can be pissed upon, and so Don César continued to make his yearly visits to Parral.

The Revolution had reduced the breadth of his patronage and robbed the estate of an opulence it would never recover—not to speak of the caches of money the bastards had rooted out. Yet the hacienda had survived. Unlike his father's estate, whose ownership had been usurped by a decree of the revolutionary government, Las Cadenas remained Don César's property by prevailing legal title. The casa grande stood intact, and most of its outbuildings. Nor had all of Don César's hidden strongboxes been discovered.

For all their plundering, the savages had been unable to thieve the beauty of the land nor drive away all of the hacienda's peon population, who after all had nowhere else to go. Even many of those who had fled the estate during the years of greatest violence had begun to come back to Las Cadenas' guardian walls, their hats in their hands, to ask Don César if they might serve him as before. And he had taken them back. And if some among them had returned with errant notions that the strict discipline of Las Cadenas had been ameliorated by the riot called the Revolution, well, his whips and branding irons were at hand to prove them wrong, and he again made routine use of those instruments of moral and political instruction. Occasionally he invented punishment on the moment, as when he unleashed one of his hunting dogs on a twelve-year-old boy who had flung a pebble at the beast for barking at him. The boy's face was horribly disfigured and his left arm forever crippled, and well into his adulthood mothers would point him out to their children as an example of the consequence of transgression against Don César, or El Comandante, as he was commonly known among the peons.

His surviving gold and silver amounted to a fraction of his former wealth but it was sumptuous in comparison with what remained to so many of his caste. Many had seen their great houses reduced to rubble, their estates razed to charred earth. Many had lost every peso. Many had lost their lives. With his remnant money Don César was able to restore Las Cadenas to a semblance of its former splendor. He repaired the casa grande, re-tiled its roofs, re-landscaped its patios, refurbished its rooms. He put his peons to work on the estate's damaged earth until portions of the fields again began to produce maize. He acquired some few horses of passable worth and the herd slowly grew to respectable size.

But without his family to inhabit it, the casa grande, for all its revived beauty, was like an empty husk, and his sense of isolation increased over the years. His sleep was ever fitful, visited nightly by frightful dreams. He was consumed by horrid spells of melancholy. His loneliness swelled to smothering size. Vaguely insidious yearnings stirred in him like a nest of vipers. He of course had his pick of the prettiest mestizo girls on the estate, but their gratifications were strictly of the flesh and left him in progressively greater despond for reasons he could not name. His heart itself felt like a house abandoned, a dwelling for none but creatures of the dark.

And then one day of the preceding summer, when he was on the Gulf Coast on business, he caught sight of the girl for the first time.

He saw her as she dashed across the beach road, the blue skirt of her school uniform swirling around her brown legs. He could not take his eyes off her as she strode down the streets of the city, a straw bag over her shoulder, her black hair wet from her swim and swinging to her hips. Men turned and stared as she passed them by.

Don César directed his driver to follow her. She made her way deep into an increasingly squalid neighborhood of stinks and strident voices and at last entered a courtyard containing two tiers of hovels. She vanished through the doorway of one on the lower floor.

He ordered his men to make discreet but thorough inquiries. By the following evening he knew that she was sixteen years old and lived in that dismal place with her mother and father and was their only surviving child. The father was a street cleaner for the city and given to drink, the mother did seamstress work at home and was herself drunk every night. The couple frequently and violently quarreled, common behavior in that shabby barrio. They were the girl's only living kin. She'd had an uncle, a fisherman, whom she had clearly favored over her parents, but he had drowned in the gulf the year before. Despite her family's poverty, she was enrolled in an excellent Catholic academy, attending on a scholarship she had won at age twelve in a statewide essay contest. She was required to maintain superior grades in order to renew the scholarship from year to year, and so far she had done so, despite, as her school record phrased it, "unconventional attitudes," a proclivity for asking "mischievous questions" of the faculty nuns, and a reputation for occasionally "prankish behavior."

Don César could not sleep that night but only lay in bed with the smell of the sea carrying into his hotel room and moonlight slanting through the open balcony doors. He was enraptured—feeling more alive than he had in more than two decades. A bat swooped into the room and circled it thrice and flew out again, and he, a lifelong disparager of all superstition, took it for an omen. At dawn he rang down for coffee and was sipping his second cup on the balcony when the edge of the sun broke red as blood at the far rim of the gulf. And he was decided.

He had first thought to buy her outright—to offer the parents a sum greater than they could conjure in their dreams, and he was certain they would greedily accept it. But then, on reflection, he was not so sure. One could not trust to the practicality of primitives, could not trust them to know what was best for themselves. Never whisper to the deaf or wink at the blind—an old adage and a wise one. They might in their stupidity reject his money and thus make the matter altogether more difficult. But even if they should accept the offer, only a fool would trust in brutes to honor their side of a bargain. The word of a brute was worthless. The rabble were slaves to their emotions, notorious for sentimental shifts of mind. The parents might sooner or later choose to create complications for him by way of protest to the authorities, a turn of events that would at the least oblige him to make an additional round of payoffs to a wider circle of hands. No! Despite his inclination to be fair, to pay a just price for what he desired, he knew it was folly to expect the girl's parents to understand even the most fundamental notions of fairness and honor.

And so, later that day, after the girl was out of school and had taken her swim in the gulf and was making her way home through the rundown back streets, they drove up alongside her and one of Don César's men asked if she could give them directions to an address they were unable to find. As she stepped up to the Cadillac the man jumped out and clapped a hand on her mouth and pulled her into the backseat and the vehicle gunned away. In seconds the car was around the block and out of sight. Whoever might have witnessed the kidnapping could not have noted very much, the whole thing happened so swiftly.

She was terrified of course—her eyes wild above the hand that stifled her efforts to scream, curse, plead, whatever she might have done. Don César leaned against the other back door and watched her. By the time they were out of town and on the open road she had ceased to struggle, but her eyes were streaming tears and she was snorting hard for breath through her runny nose. Don César gestured for his man to unhand her. She pulled away from the man but was careful not to come into contact with either of them—sobbing hard now, her arms crossed over her breasts, her knees together, her hand wiping at her eyes and nose. Don César held his silk handkerchief to her and she glanced at it and looked away. Don César shook the hankie gently and after another moment's hesitation she snatched it from his hand and blew her nose and wiped her eyes.

He asked if she felt better now—and her face was suddenly as tight with anger as with fear. Who was *he,* she demanded to know. Where was he *taking* her? What did he *want*? As if she already knew the answer to that last question, she hugged herself even more tightly and drew her pressed knees still farther from him.

Don César said everything would soon be clear to her, and asked that she not agitate herself further. He promised she would not be harmed.

She wiped at her eyes and stared down at her lap.

He could hardly believe his grand fortune—she was even more beautiful up close than she had appeared from a distance.

They arrived at an isolated landing strip just north of the city and boarded a small chartered plane. He'd been afraid she might resist going aboard and would have to be carried bodily, but her awe of the aircraft was obvious—and her excitement, it amused him to note, was sufficient to distract her from her fears. When the engine roared and the craft began to move she clutched tight to the arms of her seat. She stared out the window at the landscape speeding past and he made soothing sounds at her as he would to a skittish horse. The plane lifted off and she gasped—and then gaped at the sinking, tilting view of the gulf. And then the sea was behind them and the dark green hill country appeared below, and then the sudden mountains like enormous heaps of crushed copper gleaming in the day's dying light. Then they were in clouds and there was nothing more to see.

He told her his name, told her where he was from, told her of his past. When he told her he'd been an officer of the Guardia Rural her eyes widened. He told her of his heroic rescue of the president's niece some thirty-six years ago and of the wounds he had suffered, of the honors he had been given by Don Porfirio, told her of La Hacienda de Las Cadenas and described its magnificence, told her of the barbarities inflicted upon it by the Revolution. He told her—his throat going hot and tight with the recollection—of the tragic loss of his family, and told how he had lost his eye.

Through the latter portions of his narrative, her attention had begun to wane, and she several times turned to the window, perhaps checking to see if the clouds had cleared. But when he described the life she would have at Las Cadenas she listened with greater heed. At Las Cadenas, he told her, she would lead a more wonderful life than she could ever have envisioned for herself. She would live like a princess, she would have servants, beautiful clothes. She would never again know want.

He saw his words touch her, saw in her eyes a sudden spark of imagination. Though her aspect was still uncertain, he could see that she was envisioning the life he had pictured. And that the vision excited her.

She asked again what he wanted with her.

He wanted her to live with him at Las Cadenas.

As what, she wanted to know. His *whore?*

No. As his wife.

She stared at him for a long moment as if he were some intricate message written in a difficult scrawl. Then asked why her.

Because she was so beautiful, he said. Because she possessed a wonderful spirit. Because he loved her.

Loved her? But how, she wanted to know, could that *be?*

He admitted he did not know. But then who, he said, can explain love?

She blushed and covered her mouth with her hand and turned to the window and the dark clouds sweeping by.

When she looked at him again her face was changed. There was no fear or wariness in it now, only a mien of careful calculation, as if she were assessing odds at a gaming table. He could not imagine what she was thinking.

And then she accepted his proposal. She said it as if she were agreeing to some irrefutable practicality.

He laughed with a mix of delight and relief and briefly touched her hand. She smiled and said she had heard of less dramatic and somewhat more extended courtships—and this time they laughed together.

His two men in the seats ahead of them never said a word and never turned around.

They landed at Torreón, where his car was waiting, and late that night arrived at the casa grande. He spoke with the head housemaid and then told the girl to go with her, that she would be fed and bathed and shown to her bedchamber. The girl trailed after the maid, casting looks everywhere as she went.

The following day he had a team of seamstresses from Torreón fit her for a silk wedding gown and a silver crown inlaid with three small rubies. A priest was fetched and that early evening they were wed in the garden alongside the casa grande. Some hours later, following a celebration party in the patio, the maids brought her to his open chamber door and knocked timidly. The girl wore a satin nightgown the color of pearl. Her unpinned black hair shone in the candlelight. Her eyes were uncertain. He dismissed the maids and beckoned the girl. From the pocket of his dressing gown he took out a necklace, a fine gold chain holding a small diamond pendant. He gestured for her to turn around and told her to raise the hair off her neck. She was facing a full-length wall mirror and their eyes met as he clasped the necklace at her nape and then tenderly kissed her bare shoulder. Her eyes widened and her lips parted, and whether she was looking at the diamond at her throat or his lips on her neck he could not have said. He held her breasts from behind, their nipples hard against his palms.

He turned her around and kissed her. He slid the straps of the gown from her shoulders and the garment streamed to a pale puddle at her feet. Whatever she might have been feeling, shame in her nakedness was no part of it. She was more beautiful than he had imagined. Lean, sleek, brown. He took her hand and led her to the bed. She was eager for it. Her mouth received his with a hunger the more arousing to him for its obvious lack of practice, her touches more exciting for their tentativeness. She was virgin—the bloodspot on the sheets would testify to it. Had she not been, he was prepared to annul the marriage in the morning. She cried at his entry but then was soon gasping from effect other than pain, writhing unartfully but urgently beneath him, digging her fingers into his back, inspiring him to heroic effort.

They made love on each of the first few nights of the marriage before he flagged utterly. He had not risen to such occasion with such frequency since his youth, and his expended vigor was slow to recoup. Thereafter he rarely visited her bedchamber more often than once a week. He desired her constantly in his imagination and the sight of her naked body never failed to excite his lust, but his aged flesh was recalcitrant and he was deeply humiliated by his frequent failures as a lover. He had secretly hoped that she might bear him a son, a successor to Las Cadenas—but if she were never to conceive he knew the fault would more likely lie in his old and sapless seed than within her young womb. Still, he believed he could endure the disappointment of a barren marriage as long as he could touch her.

But by the time they had been together two months she was wearying of the accounts of his youthful adventures and of his ordeals under the Revolution. She had grown bored with his talk of people she did not know, many of them long dead. For his part, he could but feign interest in her redundant schoolgirl memories and descriptions of the beach where she always went swimming and tales of the times when she went to sea with her uncle the fisherman. Unlike her, he had no interest in books other than ledgers. But he didn't care. He derived unremitting pleasure from simply staring at her, from the knowledge that she was there and would still be there the next day and the day after that.

He lavished her with gifts, with everything he thought might please her—jewelry, clothes, a beautiful black stallion and custom-made saddle, the newest model phonograph, affectionate pet dogs, a parrot that spoke her name. He sent a man to Jiménez to buy whatever recordings she asked for. He filled the house with her favorite flowers. He replanted the patio garden to suit her tastes.

She told him she missed the sea and asked if they might go to the coast for a holiday so she could swim. He said he could not leave the hacienda, that there were many duties he must personally attend to, that he never traveled except when he absolutely must on essential business. The truth was that he was afraid she might desert him if they went to a town—any town, but especially one on the seacoast. He did not know how to swim, and he had never told anyone of his recurrent bad dream in which they were at the seashore and she fled him by swimming away. He built a spacious pool for her in the west-side patio and for a time she took pleasure in it. She tried to teach him to swim but his efforts had been comically inept and she had laughed at him. He came close to losing his temper but was able to restrain it. He would not, however, enter the pool again. She swam in it every day—and made daily complaint that it was not the same thing as the sea.

The months passed. He was aware of her increased discontent. She turned moody. She rarely laughed anymore and never with him. He felt hopeless in his attempts to please her. One evening he caught her staring at him across the length of the dinner table and could see that she was beholding him as an old man. He was more deeply pained than he could say.

And then barely three weeks ago she asked if she might ride her stallion beyond the walled confines of the casa grande grounds. She was bored with the round-and-round of the riding track and with the horsetrail through the mesquite thickets at the rear portion of the compound. He refused. He said the countryside was too dangerous for a woman alone. He could send a rider with her, she said, one of his pistoleros, if he was so concerned for her safety. No, he said—and knew instantly that she had perceived his mistrust of her, his fear that she might cuckold him with a younger and more virile man. You could send two of them, she said, to keep an eye on each other as well as on me. She retreated to her bedchamber and remained there the rest of the day.

When he went to her door that evening he found it bolted and she refused to admit him. He might have walked away except he caught sight of a housemaid passing at the end of the hall and glancing at him. How many of the staff, he suddenly wondered, had heard him pleading with her like a whining boy? He tore the drapery off the hall window and piled it at the foot of her door and set it afire. In minutes the door was ablaze. There was no other door to the room and her windows were forty feet above the patio but she made no call for help or cry of fear. Servants appeared at the end of the hall and went racing away again, yelling at each other to bring buckets of water. When the door was a sheet of crackling flames he kicked at it until a portion fell away in a shower of sparks and then he covered his head with his arms and crashed through the burning wood and into the room. He slapped away smoking cinders from his clothes and hair, saw her staring huge-eyed at him. He took off his thick leather belt and doubled it and threw her facedown across the bed and stripped away her robe and pinned her with a knee between her shoulders. She was strong and kicking wildly but he was furiously determined and tore off her silk underpants and whipped her bare buttocks with the belt. He was elated by her shrieks and the servants' arrival at the door to fling hissing bucketfuls of water on the fire and witness his punishment of her. She managed to break free after he'd laid on a dozen strokes. Her bottom was striped with red welts and she was crying in pain and outrage. She called him a bullying old bastard, she shouted that she hated him. He warned her that if she ever again bolted a door against him he would tie her to a tree in the patio and strip her naked to the waist and use a horse quirt on her back while everyone of the hacienda looked on. But he feared her will to resist and told the carpenter that the new door to her chamber should have no bolt.

They saw little of each other over the following days. Whenever they came in sight of each other they did not speak. Their suppers were silent affairs but for the clink of dishware and the serving staff's footfalls on the hardwood floors.

His temper was now in constant confusion, a mix of anger, injured pride, and despair. He pined for her affections even as he refused to lower himself to apology. He yearned to touch her even as he refused to speak or even look directly at her. He was meting harsh punishments to his peons for the smallest infractions, ordering the whipping of a stableman for being slow to saddle a horse, of a pair of kitchen-boys for dicing in the pantry. He had a woman branded on the cheek on her husband's charge of infidelity, though there was no proof of it and she swore it was not true.

He was drinking heavily every night, pacing himself to exhaustion in his chambers, trying to understand how things had come to such a pass—his mind in a mad muddle, his emotions in chaotic tangle. When he thought of her naked beauty he had to bite his tongue against howling in desire for her. He thought he might be going mad.

And then one night, less than a week ago, he could bear it no longer. He smashed a brandy bottle against the wall and stalked to her chambers with a lamp in his hand and banged open her door, waking her in a fright. He set down the lamp and shrugged off his robe and flung himself on her. She resisted for only a moment before letting herself go limp and shutting her eyes, refusing him even her sight, refusing him everything but unresponsive flesh. He could not help but proceed, though it was like coupling with the newly dead. When he was finished and realized he was crying, he cursed her and struck her with his open hand. She flinched but did not open her eyes. He stormed from the room in a weeping rage.

He kept to his chambers for most of the following day, heartsickened by his brute behavior, frantic with fear that her affections were forever lost to him. The next day was Christmas, and hoping to begin a process of amends and reconciliation, he presented her with an exquisite emerald brooch. He laid it before her on the supper table and she stared at it without expression and then ignored it. He asked if he might pin the brooch on her to see how it looked, and she picked it up and put it in her dress pocket. He'd had to restrain himself from striking her—and from bursting into tears.

The next days passed like a time of mourning. He would see her from his window as she set out on her stallion onto the riding trail in the mesquite woods. On her return she would linger within the stable, no doubt seeing to it that the horse was properly tended, perhaps feeding it apples as she liked to do. Then she'd go for a walk in the garden and he'd lose sight of her. She would not return to the house until dusk. Sometimes she would take another wordless supper with him in the dining hall, sometimes she would retire for the night without eating, and he would dine alone at the head of the huge empty table.

And then that morning, four days before the new year, she was gone. Her bed had not been slept in. She was not in her bath, on her balcony, in any of the reading or music parlors, not in the dining room nor the kitchen. The maids said la doña had not come down for her morning cup of chocolate. The household staff was called to assembly in the main parlor and it was discovered that her personal maid was also absent. None of the staff had seen either of them since the evening prior. Before he could send for his segundo, the foreman himself appeared with the news that the stableman in charge of caring for la doña's stallion had departed the hacienda last night in one of the trucks and had not returned. The man told the gate guard he was being sent to Torreón to pick up a new saddle for la doña. The women must have been hiding in the vehicle.

Don César dispatched teams of searchers to the nearest towns, more than a hundred miles south to Gomez Palacio, to Torreón, to San Pedro de las Colonias, seventy-five miles north to Jiménez. But there was no need—they found the truck twenty miles away, where the hacienda road met the highway at the small railstation pueblo of Escalón, found it parked behind the depot. They roused the night clerk from his bed—a man they called El Manco Feo for his ruined arm and the ugly dogbite scars on his face—and learned that yes, a man and two women, all strangers to him, had boarded the night train to Monclova. His description of them was accurate. The clerk was taken to Las Cadenas to give his report to Don César in person, to tell him that the train had arrived in Monclova hours ago. Don César knocked him down and kicked him repeatedly before ordering him out of his sight.

He had no notion at all whether she was still in Monclova or where she might have gone from there. He sent men to that city to seek her. He interrogated every member of the house staff, questioned all of his vaqueros. The missing stableman was Luis Arroyo, who had been on the payroll less than six months. None of the other hands knew where he was from, knew anything of his past.

And then a short while ago it had been learned that the maid who fled with the party, one Maria Ramirez, had been born and raised in a village called Apodaca, just outside of Monterrey, and that her father was a baker there. . . .

El Segundo arrives on the balcony as Don César finishes his brandy. Segundo is a tall lean man of middle years and wears his black beard in a sharply pointed goatee of the grandee style, his long hair in a ponytail. His dress is impeccable and his manners courtly, but his dark hands are scarred from ropeburns and branding irons, with knife cuts, its knuckles large and prominent and scarred as well.

"A sus órdenes, patrón," Segundo says.

Don César instructs him to send their best retrievers to the family home of this Maria Ramirez and question her about his missing wife. If the Ramirez girl should not be there, then the family must be questioned about *her*. The retrievers are to be given ample expense money and are to act upon whatever information they get that might lead them to his wife. If they are unable to find her, then that will be the end of it and he will be shed of the bitch.

Segundo says he understands completely. He will dispatch Angel and Gustavo—and then softly inquires what Don César desires them to do if they should find her.

"Quiere que se la traigan? O prefiere que . . . se desaparesca?"

Don César considers the question as he stares out at the great desert beyond the hacienda.

And finally says that they should bring her back, of course.

In the hours after the wind and drizzle quit, a thin fog rolled in off the gulf and the windows glowed pale gray in the morning light of New Year's Day. I got dressed and tucked the Mexican Colt under my coat at the small of my back and went downstairs.

As always, Gregorio had set out the makings of breakfast for his tenants before he went to bed. A big kettle of coffee was lightly steaming on the stove, next to a warm pot of refried beans and a large and ready frying pan. On the counter stood a wire basket of eggs, a fresh loaf of bread on a cutting board, a can of lard, some bulbs of garlic, a string of dried chiles, and a large roll of chorizo sausage. A gourd covered with a warm damp cloth held a stack of fresh corn tortillas. On the table were bowls of butter, sugar, grape jam, shakers of salt, red pepper, ground cinnamon.

By this hour Sergio had already come in from his night clerk job and had eaten and cleaned up after himself and gone up to his room. I usually took breakfast at a café across the street from the train station but I wanted a word with old Moises this morning, so I figured I might as well eat while I waited for him to come down.

I lit the gas burner under the big frying pan and cut off a chunk of chorizo and put it in the pan and ground it with a fork. Then broke off a clove of garlic and peeled it smooth and dropped it in with the chorizo and used the fork to crush it up good. I chopped a big chile to fine bits and stirred it in with the sausage and garlic. The chorizo sizzled and darkened and the fragments of garlic and chile turned brown in the oozing grease. The sharp aromas mingled with the fragrance of coffee and refried beans. I turned down the burner a little and cracked three eggs into the pan and scrambled them with the chorizo and seasonings. When the eggs were almost done I pushed them with the spatula to one side of the pan and took two tortillas from the gourd and quickly heated them in the cleared side of the greasy pan. I laid the tortillas on a plate and scraped the chorizo-and-eggs onto them, then added some beans on the side and poured a cup of coffee and stirred in plenty of sugar. Then sat at the table to eat.

Gregorio had taken his magazines to his room with him but the morning paper was on the table. I was leafing through it and having my second cup of coffee when old Moises came down and looked surprised to find me there. "Buen año nuevo, joven!" he said.

I waited till he sat himself with a cup of coffee, then gestured for him to put the tin horn to his ear. He did, and I asked if he had been to the party at the Morales place last night.

"Como?" he said, pressing the horn harder to his ear. "Qué?"

I leaned over the table and asked the question louder.

"La fiesta de Morales? Sí, yo fui, claro que sí. Era muy buena fiesta."

Had he met Avila's relatives from Brownsville?

"Que?" he bellowed, twisting the horn like he meant to screw it into his skull.

With my mouth right at the ear horn, I loudly and slowly repeated my question. He listened hard, then said that there had been many people at the party, a few he had never seen before, but with the music and laughter and his bad ears he hadn't caught their names.

Was there a pretty girl he hadn't seen before?

"Ay, hijo!" But of course there had been pretty girls! Every woman in the world was a pretty girl in her own way, did I not know that? As a man ages he gains wisdom and comes to see the eternal beauty of all womanhood. Why, if he were only ten years younger . . .

I patted his shoulder and cursed myself for a fool to have thought he might be of any help, then took my plate and cup to the sink and washed them while he rambled on about all the women he'd known, large and small, darkskinned and fair, all of them lovely, all of them a wonderful mystery, although of course there had been a special one, a girl back in Michoacán whom he'd known for less than a month, when they were both nineteen, one whom Death the Bastard took from him but whom he had not failed to think about every day since . . .

He was still going on and on when I said goodbye and went out the door.

• •

The holiday street traffic was of course much lighter than usual for a Wednesday. Most businesses were closed and a lot of people were still in bed with aching heads and new regrets.

The air was cool and heavy with the smell of the sea, but the wet and littered streets still carried tinges of the town's hangover, the faint odors of booze and tobacco ash and rank bedsheets. A sickly yellow seadog still arced through the light mist over the Offatt Bayou.

But holidays were good for the gambling business. Even at this midmorning hour I found the betting room behind the Turf Grill already half-full and loud with talk of the day's favorites and longshots at the Florida and California tracks. The Juárez and Tijuana races would get a lot of play too. The parlor betting would be heavy all day long.

Up on the second floor I went into Rose's outer office and spoke with his secretary, Mrs. Bianco. A lot of the guys called her Momma Mia, and she seemed to enjoy it, but to me she was always Mrs. Bianco. She had a pronounced Italian accent and a motherly manner and could have been on an advertising poster for pasta or tomato paste. Portly and beginning to gray, always dressed in neat and matronly fashion. She lived alone in a boardinghouse down the street from the Club. Not many knew it but she was one of Rose's highest-paid employees and among the handful of people he truly trusted, and there was no aspect of Maceo business she wasn't privy to. She knew how I stood with Rose too and tended to be more direct with me than she was with others—and I'd caught glimpses of the .38 bulldog she kept in the bottom righthand drawer of her desk. I once asked Rose if she knew how to use it and he smiled and winked and left it at that.

She told me Signore Maceo had sent LQ and Brando and one of his slot machine mechanics to the Red Shoes Cabaret near Alvin. I knew the place. It was in Brazoria County, just west of the Galveston line, and it rented its machines from the Gulf Vending Company. The place had changed hands a few months before and the new guys had been consistently slow about toting up the daily take from the slots and handing over the Maceos' cut. Artie Goldman suspected they were shaving their revenue reports, and Artie's suspicions were good enough for Rose.

The Red Shoes guys would be surprised when the mechanic showed up that morning to check their machines. Each of the slots had been geared to keep a tally of the money it took in—a running tally that wasn't erased each time the machine was emptied, as many of the joint owners had been led to believe was the case. LQ and Brando would ensure that nobody interfered with the mechanic's inspection of the slots—and they would take the necessary measures if the machine tallies didn't match the ones on the Red Shoes reports. It was a job I normally would've been tending to.

I told Mrs. Bianco I'd be in the gym if Rose wanted me, then went up to the third floor.

• •

The health club was always open to members—weekends and holidays included—and there were already a dozen guys there, the usual bunch who always showed up early. Club rats, Watkins the trainer called them. As the morning wore on, still more members would come in for their regular workouts or just to sweat last night's booze out of their system.

The large room echoed with the huffing and grunting of hard effort, with the slapping of jump ropes and the clanking of barbells, punches smacking the heavy bags. The daily reek of sweat and liniment was already starting to build.

It had been a good while since my schedule let me have a morning workout, and Otis was glad to see me come in during his shift. I figured he'd want to go a few rounds and I was ready to oblige him. But he was booked solid with his club rat boxing lessons for the next two days.

"I got a ten o'clock open on Saturday," he said. "Don't tell me you'll be out of town."

I said I had to hang around town all week, so Saturday was fine.

"I'm locking us in at ten," he said, writing "lesson to hotshot" in ink on his big desktop calendar.

I took the pen from his hand and drew a line through the word "to" in his notation and wrote "from" above it.

"Cocky sumbuck," he said. "We'll see. Three three-minute, no headgear, Watkins refs?"

"You're on," I said.

I went to my locker and got into my shorts and T-shirt and ring shoes. I'd never been in a gym before I got to Galveston, never fought with gloves or according to any rules. I'd known how to fight—not box, *fight*—since I was a boy. Nobody had taught me how, I just knew. And I learned early that a real fight had no rules. And nobody stopped it. A real fight wasn't over until one of the fighters couldn't fight anymore, and even then it sometimes wasn't over. Boxing wasn't real fighting, it was an exercise of skill and endurance, a test of your self-control. It required you to hold to the rules no matter if you were losing, no matter how hurt or angry you might be, no matter how sure you were you could kill the other guy if you just said to hell with the rules. Fighting in the ring exercised your discipline. It's what I liked about it.

I did a few sets of sit-ups on the slantboard, then skipped rope for a while, breathing deep and easy. After that I put on the bag gloves and pounded the heavy bag till my T-shirt was pasted to me. Then I moved over to the speed bag.

I started slowly, building a smooth rhythm of alternating lefts and rights. Little by little I increased the tempo until I had the bag ricocheting in a steady racketing blur that sounded like a train highballing by. I was aware of the attention I'd attracted, the guys gathered behind me. Even Otis couldn't work the light bag better than I could. I kept at it until my arms felt packed with burning concrete, then gave the bag a hard overhand that shook the boards and I stepped away and gestured to the others that the bag was all theirs.

A few of the guys applauded and somebody let out a whistle.

Otis had interrupted his boxing lesson to lean on the ropes and watch me work the speed bag. I grinned at him and stripped off the gloves, then mopped my face with a towel. He smiled and shook his head and then went back to showing some husky guy in the ring how to slip a punch.

After I showered and dressed I checked in at Rose's office again. Mrs. Bianco said he'd been dealing chiefly with phone business all morning. He'd received a few visitors, none of them strangers to her. He'd given her no messages for me. I told her I'd be out for a while and come back later.

• •

I took a trolley over to the Strand, downtown's main street. The clouds had broken and scattered and the sun was high and warm and had done away with last night's threat of a cold spell.

Unlike the stores, most of the cafés were open for business. I went into De Jean's and had a T-bone and a bottle of beer. I finished up with coffee and a cigarette as I watched the sparse pedestrian traffic pass by the sidewalk window.

It was strange to be so idle. My days usually consisted of going here and there to take care of this or that. The other Ghosts tended to the routine jobs around the island, including the daily cash pick-ups, but the Maceos had dealings all over this region of Texas, and sometimes Rose would hand me a list of jobs that took me out of town for days or even a couple of weeks at a time. I frequently went up to Houston, sometimes out to San Antone, now and then down to Corpus. More often than not I took LQ or Brando with me, usually both.

Among my assignments were visits to guys who'd been slow to make loan repayments or turn over the daily slot cuts. They usually got their accounts up to date real quick after I gave them a warning. Everybody knew one warning was all Rose ever gave, and few of them were late with the money again. Now and then somebody would require a second visit but nobody ever needed a third.

The ones who'd been doctoring their books were another matter. They never failed to correct themselves, either, but their transgression was more serious than a late payment, and it had to be punished, even as a first offense. A broken hand would usually do, but sometimes a foot was also called for, maybe an arm or a leg, sometimes something worse. It depended on how long they'd been at it and how much they'd skimmed.

Then there were the robbers. The island clubs never got robbed—they were much too well protected—but now and then some little joint on the mainland or in a neighboring county would get hit, some club or café or filling station with Maceo machines in it, and although the stickups were rarely for more than peanuts, they included Maceo peanuts. Only the dumbest stickup guys would ever hit a place without first making sure it had no Maceo connection. Next to an outsider who tried to cut in on Galveston, nobody got Rose as hot under the collar as a robber. Any business that had even one Maceo machine in it was guaranteed protection, and Rose took his guarantees seriously.

Most of the stickup men were such dopes they didn't even leave the local area after pulling their heist. They'd hole up with a relative or a friend or a sweetheart. But the Maceos had a standing reward offer for information about robberies—the reward sometimes more than what was taken in a holdup—and the information always came, as often as not from the people the robbers were hiding with. It never took me long to track them down, and when I did, there was nothing to discuss. If they had the money with them, fine, and if they didn't, the hell with it. Not only was the money rarely very much, its recovery wasn't the point, not to Rose. As he once put it, "What I want is those bastards removed from the living"—which made me chuckle and say he sometimes had a touch of the poet in him. Which made him give me a look and say he sometimes thought I was fucking touched. In any case, once the thieves were removed from the living, he made sure the news got around.

Few robbers ever skipped the state, but if we got a sure tip on one that did, we went after him—no matter how little he'd made off with, no matter how far he'd gone. But reliable information about a guy who lammed the state was hard to come by, and even when Rose thought the tip was solid he was reluctant to send more than one man on the job. He believed one man had a better chance of getting around unnoticed in unfamiliar territory and a better chance of getting back out if the job went bad. I agreed. The only two times he sent me out of Texas I went alone.

I ran down the first guy in a rooming house in a rundown section of St. Joseph, Missouri, exactly where the rat had said he'd be. I slipped in after midnight. The stairs creaked but if any of the other tenants woke up they stayed put and minded their own business, lucky for them. The guy's doorlock was even easier to jimmy than the one in the kitchen. He didn't wake up till I cut his throat. I'd killed with a knife before but never cut a throat—although I'd come close one time, when I was still a kid—but I'd seen Brando do it and knew they didn't make much noise that way, just a kind of gargle like water going down a partly clogged drain. I thought I'd be able to avoid the mess better than Brando had, but I wasn't. I had to trade my bloody shirt for a clean one of the guy's, and I went out with my ruined coat rolled under my arm. He'd made off with about five hundred dollars but I found less than fifty in the place.

After that job I started using an ice pick for the close work. You had to be more exact with a pick but it was a hell of a lot neater.

In the other case, the robber hit a Texas City club for three grand and then went to hide at his brother's house on the Pearl River, a few miles south of Jackson, Mississippi. The place was so isolated I didn't have to be very clever about it. I waited till dark and then left the car in among the pines and walked back up the road to the house. I found his car parked around in back where it couldn't be seen from the road. I peeked in all the windows and saw that there was nobody in the place except him and a girl. He was in his undershorts, the girl in T-shirt and panties. I couldn't spot a gun anywhere.

I kicked open the door to the kitchen where they were having supper and shot him through his open mouth before he could even stand up. The back of his head splattered the wall behind him and he drained off his chair.

The girl shrieked and jumped away from the table and then clapped her hands over her mouth like she wasn't all that new to situations suddenly gone bad and knew that rule number one was shut up. But her eyes were huge with fear. She was a slim bob-haired blonde with freckles and nice legs. She looked about seventeen. One of her cheeks had a pale purple bruise.

"Where's the guns?" I said.

"He aint got but the one." She nodded at the kitchen counter behind me. I picked it up—a snubnose five-shot .38—and dropped it in my coat pocket. Then I stepped out the kitchen door to see if any lights had come on anywhere, some nearby cabin, some neighbor in the woods who maybe heard the .44's blast, but there was nothing. I went back in and shut the door.

"The money?" I said. And was pleasantly surprised when she led me into the bedroom—being careful to keep from stepping in any of the blood spreading from the guy's head—and pulled a valise out of the closet. She put it on the bed and opened it to show the cash.

"I knew it had to be somebody's," she said. "I knew he didn't win it in no card game." Her accent was swamp rat to the bone.

I riffled through the money. It looked to be almost all there.

"I don't know how much all he spent of it," she said. "I got about four dollars in my shirt yonder. You want I should get it?"

"Never mind," I said.

"You gonna hurt me?" She looked all set for a bad answer.

"You help him steal it?"

"No sir, I never did any such."

"Then I've got no reason to hurt you."

"Truth to tell, I didn't never expect to see him again. Then he shows up in Port Allen a coupla weeks ago and says he's hit the jack-pot and to come on if I was coming. Momma said he was no-count and I was a harebrained fool to go with him and she was right both times."

"You the one to rat on him?"

She shook her head. "Probably his brother Carl. He was all the time beating on Carl and finally run him off from his own house—can you imagine? I wouldn't blame Carl a bit if he told on him."

She glanced toward the kitchen and her mouth tightened. "I told him he hit *me* again I'd stick him with a butcher knife. I meant it too. Momma always said they got to sleep sometime."

I knew her story without having to hear it. I knew a dozen just like it: sweet girl takes up with some mean bastard who mistreats her till she goes sour and sometimes gets pretty mean herself. Some of them might deserve a slap now and then—some of them needed it—but none of them deserved to be made mean. This one was headed that way but might still take a lucky turn.

"What's your name, girl?"

"Sally. It's Sally May Ritter."

"Can you drive that car out there, Sally?"

"Yessir. I kinda can."

I took about three hundred from the valise and gave it to her. I told her to go to the second nearest depot, not the nearest one. "Park a few blocks away and then walk to the station. Get yourself a ticket to anywhere else."

She stared at the money and then at me.

"And try to be more careful about the company you keep," I said.

She said she aimed to be. Then said, "Where you from, anyway?"

"Someplace else. Now get a move on."

She was packing a bag fast as I went out the door.

When we didn't know where a robber had lammed, Rose would

put out the word on him. If the bastard ever showed his face in Texas again, we'd hear about it.

Next thing the guy knew, there I'd be.

There were times, of course, when everything was running smoothly, when nothing was out of order and Brando and LQ and I didn't have much to do but exercise in the gym or play cards or go to the police range and take a little target practice. Times when the only duty to come our way was to drive Rose to Houston or Corpus Christi to tend to some matter in person like he sometimes had to do.

But such times were pretty rare and never lasted more than a few days—praise Jesus, as LQ was prone to say in moments of gratitude.

• •

After lunch I wandered along the Strand for a while, then went into a movie house showing *A Night at the Opera.* The Marx Brothers could always get a laugh out of me.

When I got back to the Club, Mrs. Bianco said to go on into the office. Rose was on the phone and Big Sam was in an easy chair, puffing a cigar and sipping a glass of wine. Sam gestured for me to sit in the chair beside his. I took a Chesterfield from the case on the desk. Rose did too and I leaned over and lit it for him. I sat down and Sam punched me lightly on the arm and said, "Jimmy the Kid."

"Right," Rose said into the phone. "Louisiana Street. They're expecting you this afternoon. Just fill in the forms and get the signatures. I told them if they signed today the machines would be there tomorrow afternoon."

He listened for a moment. "Yeah . . . Yeah . . . Right. Railyard warehouse got plenty in stock. Soon as they sign, let the warehouse know and they'll get the shipment out to Houston . . . Okay. Yeah."

He hung up and scribbled something on a sheet of paper, then leaned back and looked at me and Sam and gave a tired sigh that struck me as a touch theatrical.

"I swear to Christ, there's times I wish I was still a barber," he said. "A barber can whistle while he works, know what I mean? Can sing while he does his job. Shoot the shit with the customers. Talk about sports, pussy, stuff in the papers. *This* . . ." He gestured vaguely at the big desk in front of him. "Nothing but fucken *deals* all day. Phone calls. Arrangements. Nothing but *business*."

Sam looked at me and winked. It wasn't the first time we'd heard this complaint from Rose—but it was sentimental bullshit. He wouldn't last two days back in a barber shop before he'd be scheming at how to outfox the big-time crooks at their own games, both the legal and the illegal ones, just like he and Sam had been doing all these years.

He saw how Big Sam and I were smiling. "Go to hell, both you."

He poured me a glass of wine and refilled his own. Then held his glass across the desk and said, "Salute," and Sam and I clinked ours against it.

He wanted to know if I'd picked up on anything today that might connect to the Dallas guys. I said I hadn't.

"I keep telling you," Sam said to him, "you're worrying for nothing. I was on the phone with our ears in Dallas ten minutes ago. None of them have heard anything."

"Everybody knows we got ears all over," Rose said. "If they're planning a move they're keeping a tight lid on it."

"They got no reason to make a move on us," Sam said. "Ragsdale lost their machines to us, we didn't steal them. They made a bet on Willie Rags and they lost."

"Could be they're sore losers," Rose said. "Could be they don't give a rat's ass it's Ragsdale's fault."

"What can they *do,* come get the machines back?" Sam said. "As soon as they tried it we'd hear about it and be there before they got the first slot loaded on the truck. They can't do anything except forget the slots or buy them back. You got them over a barrel, Rosie."

Rose arched his brow at me in question.

"I'm with Sam," I said.

He nodded but didn't look convinced. "Well . . . keep a close tab with the ears," he said to Sam.

"And you," he said to me, "just keep close."

Lucio Ramirez is about to close his bakery for the day when the little bell jingles over the door and two men enter. One of them flips the sign hanging inside the glass door to the side that says CERRADO and then turns the doorlock.

Angel Lozano and Gustavo Mendez are large men in finely tailored suits and snapbrim fedoras. They could pass for brothers, their chief distinction in their mustaches—Angel's thick and droopy, Gustavo's thin and straight—and in Angel's left eye, which is held in a permanent half-squint by a pinched white scar at its outer corner.

Apodaca is a small pueblo and these men in smart city clothes are obvious outsiders. Even as Ramirez asks how he may serve them, his apprehension is stark on his face.

Angel asks if he is related to Maria Ramirez, who until recently was in the employ of La Hacienda de Las Cadenas.

The baker can see that the man already knows the true answer—and sees as well that he is not a man to lie to—and so he admits that Maria is his daughter and asks what they wish with her.

At that moment his rotund wife emerges from a curtained

doorway to the living quarters in the rear part of the bakery and stops short at the sight of the strangers.

Ramirez tells her who they are and she turns back toward the curtain but Gustavo catches her by the arm and yanks her to him and claps a hand over her mouth. Ramirez starts toward them but Angel grabs him by the hair and rams his forehead against the wall and lets the baker fall to the floor unconscious, his forehead webbed with blood.

Angel passes through the curtain and sees the girl sitting on the edge of her bed, her sewing sliding off her lap, her eyes large. Before she can scream, Angel is on her, pinning her down, a hand on her mouth and a knife blade at her neck.

He tells her he will ask her only once—where is the wife of Don César?—and tells her that if she lies he will see the lie in her eyes and he will cut her throat to the neckbone.

He eases his hand from the girl's mouth but she is terrified to incoherence. He tells her to calm down, for Christ's sake, and she tries, but as she talks she continues to weep and partially choke on her mucus and he permits her to sit up so she can speak more clearly.

She is at last able to tell him that la doña paid the stableman Luis Arroyo with jewelry to escort her to the border town of Matamoros. At the Monclova station, Maria Ramirez took leave of them and caught a train to Monterrey and from there took a bus to Apodaca.

She doesn't know—she *swears* she doesn't—where in Matamoros la doña was going or why. She knows nothing more to tell except that, on the train trip to Monclova, Arroyo had spoken of a brother who owns a cantina in Matamoros, a place called La Perla.

I left Rose and Sam talking business in the office and went into the lounge and ordered a bottle of beer. At that hour, there were only a few guys at the bar, a few couples at the tables. The place would start filling fast by suppertime and would as always be packed at midnight.

"Say, Kid!"

At the rear of the lounge, LQ stood in the doorway to the billiards room, a cue stick in one hand. He waved me over. Brando leaned into view around the door jamb and gave me a high sign, then stepped out of sight again.

I went to join them. They were shooting eight ball, best of three for five bucks, and had split the first two games.

"Got winners," I said, and started searching the wall holder for my favorite cue.

"Why not just say you want to play me next?" LQ said. He was in good spirits. Brando had a fresh shiner under one eye.

"Quit the bullshit and shoot," Brando said.

"Hard to tell who's winning, aint it?" LQ said to me.

I found the cue I wanted and dusted my hands with talc and slicked up the stick.

The table was showing all of the stripes and only two solids other than the eight ball. LQ laid his cigarette aside and leaned into the light under the Tiffany tableshade and set himself to try banking the six ball into the side. He squinted in the shadow of his hatbrim, sighting and resighting on the six as intently as a surveyor peering through a transit.

He missed by half a foot. The six caromed off the cushion and went banging into several other balls and smacked the eight into a corner pocket.

Brando hooted and said, "Pay up, sucker."

For all their bluster with a cue stick, neither of them could play worth a damn. I'd seen them knock the balls all over the table for more than half an hour before somebody finally scratched, which was the way most of their games were decided. It was rarely a matter of which of them would win, but who'd be the first to lose.

LQ peeled a five from a wad of greenbacks and flung it fluttering to the table. "Lucky bastard," he said.

Brando laughed and tucked away the bill. "Like the man said, talent makes its own luck." He turned to me and said, "Next!"

I fished the balls out of the pockets and racked them, then eased the wooden rack off the balls and returned it to its hook at the foot of the table. There had been a pool table at the ranch and over the years I'd become a fair hand with a cue. I was no match for the hustlers, but Brando and LQ wouldn't play me for money anymore unless I gave three-to-one odds.

The strong point of Brando's game was his break. As usual, he broke the balls with a crack like a sledgehammer. They ricocheted in a wild clatter, the seven falling in a corner, the four dropping in a side.

"Yes *sir*!" Brando said.

He called the two in the corner, straight and easy, and made it. Then cut the five into another corner. Then tapped the three in the side. He grinned at me and blew across the tip of his cue like he was clearing smoke from a rifle muzzle.

LQ groaned in his chair behind me and said, "Shooting out his ass."

"One in the corner," Brando called. It was a clear shot but he stroked it way harder than necessary and the yellow ball spasmed in the rim of the pocket before it dropped in.

Brando laughed and banged the heel of his cue on the floor. "Somebody stop me before I kill again."

The only shot he had with the six was a cross-corner bank. He came close, but it didn't fall.

"Son of a bitch," he said.

"Finally back to your normal game," LQ said.

I sank seven in a row—bank shots, rail shots, combinations—and just like that, there was nothing left standing but Brando's six and the eight ball.

But I hadn't played the last shot well. The eight was positioned at one end of the table, near the center of the rail and an inch off the cushion, while the cue ball had ended up at the other end of the table and up against the rail.

"Got too cocky, hotshot," Brando said. "Left yourself hard."

"Five-buck side bet, two to one, says I sink it." I tapped the corner pocket to my left. "Here."

"Too much green and a bad angle," Brando said. "You're on."

I formed a thumb bridge for the stick and set myself, then laid into the cue ball. It zoomed toward the eight and caught it just right and the black ball jumped off the cushion at an angle and came barreling down the table like it had eyes and vanished into the corner pocket.

"Whooo!" LQ hollered.

"Shit!" Brando said. He dug two fives out of his pocket and tossed them on the table. "That's it. I aint playing you anymore. I don't need this kind of humiliation."

"Kind you usually get's plenty enough, huh?" LQ said.

"Kiss my ass," Brando said. "Let's see *you* take him."

I arched my brow at LQ and gestured toward the table.

"No thanks," he said. "I'm short enough at the moment. I can just about make it to payday tomorrow."

"Well hell," I said, "if nobody's going to play, let's go park our asses in the bar and have a few."

"Winners buy," Brando said.

"It's how come you always drink for free," LQ said.

Out in the lounge I got us a pitcher of beer and we took a table in the corner. I filled the three glasses and we touched them in a toast and drank.

"Kinda surprised this morning when Momma Mia said we'd just us two be going to Alvin with a slot man," LQ said. "I asked where you were and she just shrugs like she always does. Like she don't know the time of day."

"Poppa got you on a secret mission?" Brando said.

"Wish he did," I said. I told them all about Rose's talk with the Dallas guys and his suspicion that they might try to retaliate.

"You got to hang around all week?" Brando said. "Man, I like the Club, but I'd go crazy if I had to be here all the time for a *week*."

"I agree with you and Sam," LQ said. "Them Dallas peckerwoods aint gonna do a damn thing, not after how we done Willie Rags. They'd have to be the biggest dopes in Texas, and that's saying plenty. Shit, let 'em try something. I could use the action."

"Looks like you-all maybe got some action today," I said, pointing at the bruise on Brando's face.

"Oh man, the Shoes place," LQ said. He cut a look at Brando. "Some fun, huh, Ramon?"

Brando shrugged and lit a cigarette.

LQ said that when they got to the Red Shoes Cabaret that morning, along with a slot mechanic named Freddie, the place was closed, of course, but there was an armed security guard at the door. LQ told him what they were there for and the guard said he couldn't let anyone go in without permission from Mr. Dunlop or Mr. Garr, the partners who owned the place, and neither one of them was there at the moment. He expected them to show up sometime later but didn't know exactly when.

"Jesus, what's *that*?" LQ said, looking over the guard's shoulder into the club. When the guard turned to look, LQ snatched the guy's pistol from its holster and shoved him inside.

Brando took a quick look around the premises but there wasn't anybody else around except a grayhaired Negro janitor. LQ made him and the guard sit down out of the way.

Freddie was almost through with his inspection of the machines when they heard a car drive into the lot. LQ pulled the guard up to the window and drew the blind aside just enough for them to peek out and see a Cadillac stop beside the Dodge. There were two men in the Caddy, and the guard said it was Dunlop and Garr.

The car doors opened and the men got out. They stood there looking at the Dodge a minute and then headed toward the cabaret's front door. LQ told the guard to sit back down at the table and he and Brando took positions on opposite sides of the door with their guns ready.

The one named Garr came in first and stopped short when he saw Freddie standing at the bar with a toolbox beside a dismantled slot machine and the guard and janitor sitting there with their thumbs up their ass. He said "What the fuck you think—" and then shut up when LQ's gun pressed against the side of his head.

The Dunlop guy had been a few steps behind Garr and stopped at the door when he saw what was happening. Before he could haul ass,

Brando snatched him by the coat and pulled him inside. But the guy was no slouch—he grabbed Brando's piece and tried to take it away from him.

"Son of a bitch snatched onto it like a damn bulldog on a bone," Brando said. "We went banging against the tables and the bar, knocking over stools, both of us cussing a blue streak. He's trying to get the piece and I'm mainly trying to keep it pointed away from me. Bastard was *strong*."

"Ray finally jerks the gun away from the guy—but he was pulling straight back and hit hisself in the face with it," LQ said, demonstrating the move. "About knocked hisself on his own ass. I've got the other fella by the collar with my piece to his ear and it's a damn wonder I didn't shoot him by accident I was laughing so hard."

"Real funny," Brando said.

"I gotta say, the old boy paid for it," LQ said. "Ray just *whaled* on him with that gun—whap! whap! I expect the fella swallowed them top teeth he lost. I never did see them come out his mouth. When Ray got done with him the guy looked like he'd tried to stop a train with his face."

"Son of a bitch," Brando said softly, fingering his shiner.

But Dunlop's troubles—and Garr's too—had only just begun. When Freddie was done checking the machines, he handed LQ a piece of paper with a tally of the money the slots had taken in since they'd been rented by the Red Shoes Cabaret. LQ compared it to the slip of paper Rose had given him that showed the total slot receipts Dunlop and Garr had reported. The Red Shoes tally was way short.

"I told them fellas what the problem was," LQ said, "and they started talking a mile a minute to try and explain things. The one with the busted mouth sounded like a retard, it was so hard for him to talk. I never did understand how these old boys who get caught with their hand in the jar figure they can say something that's gonna make any damn difference."

They made Dunlop hug one of the thick floor-to-ceiling support beams and made Garr hug another and they tied their hands around the posts with their own belts and gagged the men with their own neckties. Then Brando told the janitor to get him a hammer.

"Would've settled it for just a hand," Brando said, "but that Dunlop bastard made me mad, so I did his foot too."

"What about the Garr guy?" I said.

"Well hell, same thing," Brando said. "They're partners, aint they?"

"Share the profit," LQ said, "share the loss."

• •

We all got nicely buzzed on another three pitchers while the afternoon dwindled away and the lounge windows turned pink with the sunset. When Brando asked what I'd done to celebrate the night before, I told them about having supper with Rose and then going to a cathouse, but I didn't feel like talking about the fight, so I left that part out.

Brando said he would've been better off going to a cathouse too, considering the way things turned out for him with the French girl. When he'd arrived at Brigitte's to pick her up for the party, she was already gone. She left a note saying she'd got tired of waiting and that the party was at such and such an address and she'd meet him there. So he went on over to the place, an apartment house by the wharves.

He said you could hear the shindig from three blocks away. The party took up the whole building, all eight apartments, with a different kind of music blasting in each one.

"Sounded like a goddam loony bin," Brando said.

He searched through five apartments before he found her. She was dancing with two guys at once, one holding her from the front and one from the rear, and all three of them so drunk they weren't really dancing as much as staggering around together.

Before Brando could make up his mind what to do—grab her away or start punching or what—the guy hugging her from behind suddenly puked a gusher over her shoulder, getting it all over her and the other guy both. That broke up the three-way dance in a hurry, Brando said. The puking guy backpedaled into the end of a sofa and fell over on a pair of necking couples who shoved him off on the floor and started kicking hell out of him. The other guy stood there staring down at his puked-on shirt and cussing. The Brigitte girl stumbled over to the wall and leaned against it and started doing some puking of her own.

"I have to say she pretty much lost all her glamour right there," Brando said. "I left her to her fun and went on home, had a beer and hit the hay. Some New Year's."

"It's what you get fooling around with them trashy women," LQ said. "You got to find yourself a woman you can respect."

"Oh man, if I have to hear about that Zelda again," Brando said. "It's all I've heard from this guy today—Zelda this, Zelda that."

And of course he did have to hear it again, since LQ had to tell me all about her. His New Year's Eve with the redhaired Hollywood Dinner Club hostess had been everything he'd hoped, although it had gotten off to a shaky start because she'd been miffed that he was late in picking her up. She'd heard enough about the Ghosts to accept his explanation that there was never any telling how long a job would take, but all the same she let him know she hated to be kept waiting. If a fellow were going to be tardy in arriving for a date, she told him, the least he could do was to call and let the lady know—it was the gentlemanly thing to do. LQ told her he agreed 100 percent and apologized for not having done the gentlemanly thing.

"From there on it was all smooth sailing," LQ said. "Best time I've had in a while. Good dinner, nice dancing, a walk on the beach in our bare feet. Then over to her place for a little brandy and soft music. Then into the bedroom and off to the promised land." He winked big. "She was worth the wait, I'll tell you that much. Got a supper date with her again tonight."

"Holy shit," Brando said, looking alarmed. He leaned over the table to stare closely at LQ's face. "What's that in your eyes?"

"What?" LQ said, rubbing at his eyes and then checking his fingers.

"Oh . . . I see," Brando said. "It's only stardust."

"Real funny," LQ said. "I already told you, I'm just banging the woman, I aint courting her."

"I bet that's what he said both times before," Brando said to me. "Dollar to a doughnut he marries her. Disaster number three, coming right up."

"I don't know if I should take that bet," I said.

"Piss on both you," LQ said. "I'll bet you a hundred dollars apiece I *never* marry her. I'll give you five to one I never."

"What the hell kind of bet is that, you'll *never* marry her?" I said. "Only way we can be sure you'll *never* marry her is wait till you or her dies."

"That's right," Brando said. "What if you wait to marry her when you're sixty years old? You expect *us* to wait that long to collect? We got to have a time limit, none of this *never* bullshit."

"Well, what about *me*?" LQ said, portioning out the remaining beer in the pitcher. "If I die before I marry her, I win the bet but I can't even collect on it." He paused in his pouring for a moment, frowning like somebody not real sure what he'd just said.

"Christ almighty," Brando said. "Only some East Texas peckerwood would come up with a stupid-ass bet nobody can collect on."

"Well now, he could collect if *she* died first," I said. "He couldn't marry a dead woman even if he wanted. I don't believe it's legal."

"Can't be, not in no civilized country," Brando said. "So if she dies first, that settles it—he'll never marry her and he can collect. But now hold on . . . what's to keep him from *killing* her the minute he's in need of two hundred bucks?"

I shrugged.

"You dickheads are drunk," LQ said.

"Bet's off," Brando said. "I aint putting up a hundred bucks he can win by just shooting the bitch."

"I knew you'd chicken," LQ said.

"Chicken *this,*" Brando said, giving him the jack-off gesture.

While they were going at it I signaled the waitress for another pitcher. She brought it over as we were finishing the last of what we had on the table.

LQ squinted at his watch. "Goddamn, I'm supposed to be there already. I gotta get rolling."

"Ah hell, have another beer," Brando said. "You got plenty time."

"Yeah," I said. "She had such fun with you last night she won't mind if you're a few minutes late, not this time."

"I aint gonna have no more such fun if she gets all out of sorts with me," LQ said, collecting his cigarettes and lighter and putting them in his pocket.

"Christ sake, he gets it off her one time and already she's got him pussywhipped," Brando said.

That got LQ's attention. "My *ass,*" he said. "You aint seen the day I been pussywhipped and you never will."

"Here he comes again with *never,*" Brando said. He took a sip of his beer and turned so LQ couldn't see his face and gave me a wink. He knew how to rile LQ as well as LQ knew how to rile him.

"Come on, pardner," I said to LQ, pouring him another glassful. "Help us put a dent in this pitcher before you go."

"Maybe you best give her a call," Brando said. "Ask if it's okay you have another beer."

"Up yours," LQ said.

I pushed the full glass over to him. "Here you go, bud. One for the road."

"Pussywhipped," LQ muttered, picking up his beer and giving

Brando another hard look. "Every woman tried to pussywhip me I got my hat and gone. I've walked out on better pussy than you'll ever see, pussy you'd beg for on your knees. I've turned my back on better pussy than you beat off to in your dreams."

One for the road turned into two more pitchers before he finally left. Brando and I ordered steak sandwiches and stayed put.

• •

The following evening, after I spent another boring day in town while Brando and LQ made collections around Pearland and Katy, we got together for supper again. Brando threatened to go sit at another table if LQ got started on the subject of his fiasco with Zelda the night before, but he only muttered "Here we go again" and rolled his eyes as LQ went ahead and told me about it.

Zelda had been so furious with him for being more than two hours late she wouldn't even open her door to talk to him. She said she'd call the cops if he didn't quit all his hollering and banging on the door and go away, and so he finally did.

"I keep telling you," Brando said, "it's what you get for fooling around with them snooty hostess types."

"Goddammit, I don't see why she couldn't even let me explain."

"Explain what?" Brando said. "How we put a gun to your head and made you get drunk on your ass?"

"Maybe I'll go see her at the Hollywood. She can't hide from me there."

"Swell idea," I said. "Rose and Sam always get a kick out of employees arguing in front of the customers, especially at their fanciest place. Make a big enough scene and Rose'll probably give you both a bonus for being so entertaining."

"Goddamn it," LQ said.

"Hell with her, man," Brando said. "Kick the bitch out of your mind."

A few more beers into the evening LQ decided on the age-old cure for getting a woman out of your mind—namely, by replacing her with another one. He and Brando had to make a collection run the next day, first to Baytown and then over to Port Arthur, a few miles south of Orange, where LQ had once had a girlfriend named Sheila. He hadn't seen her in about six months, not since they'd had a bad argument about something, he couldn't remember what.

"You reckon she's still living there?" he said. "I wonder if she's still red-assed at me. Could be she's married, huh?"

"I know how you can find out all that," Brando said. He nodded at a telephone booth in an alcove across the room.

So LQ gave Sheila a call. And discovered that she still lived in the same place and she wasn't married. Yes, she was glad to hear from him, and yes, she would like to see him again too. Yes, tomorrow night would be just dandy—just be sure and bring a little something to drink because she was running low and payday was a long way off. And yes, she remembered his friend Ray Brando, and yes, she could get a friend for him.

"I aint heard so much of yes in a coon's age," LQ told us back at the table. His spirits were vastly improved.

Brando was as pleased about the phone call as LQ. "You think she'll be goodlooking, the friend?" he said.

"She'd have to be a goddamn calendar girl to be any better looking than Sheila," LQ said.

"I wouldn't object any to a calendar girl," Brando said.

"You know, if things go good tomorrow night," LQ said, "we ought make a damn weekend of it."

"Be all right with the office if we don't turn in the pickup money till Monday?" Brando asked me.

"I'll square it with Mrs. Bianco. Just leave me this Sheila's phone number and don't wander off from her place for too long."

"Shitfire, man—if things go right, we won't leave her place at all for the whole two days."

"Things go right I aint even leaving the bed," Brando said. "I aint coming up for air."

"Better days," I said, raising my glass.

"With no damn memories of Zelda," Brando said to LQ as our three glasses came together.

"Zelda who?" LQ said.

Friday crawled by even more slowly than the previous two days. None of the Maceo informants had heard so much as a hint that the Dallas guys were planning any kind of move on us. Rose was starting to think Sam and I were probably right—they weren't going to try anything. "Guess I'm getting jumpy in my old age," he said.

I spent the rest of the morning in the gym. While I was going through my workout, Otis reminded me of our sparring session for ten o'clock the next morning.

"I could use that ten o'clock slot to make me some lessons money if you can't make it for some reason," he said.

"I'll be here, Otis."

He grinned big. "Well all right then." He couldn't wait to get me back in that ring.

I had lunch on the Strand again, then took in another movie, *The Bride of Frankenstein,* which mostly made me laugh. Then I went over to the beach and took off my coat and shoes and walked along the edge of the water for a while. It was about time for my twice-a-month swim. In winter the gulf usually got damn chilly, but I always made my swim anyway, even though I had to muster as much grit just to bear the coldness of the water as to swim way out and back in the dark. But the early part of this winter had so far been generally mild and the light surf on my feet felt only a little cooler than usual.

I took supper at a seafood joint across the street from the shrimp docks. They made the best red snapper in town, basting it with a sauce of garlic and lime. While it was being prepared I had a frosted schooner of beer and a platter of raw oysters on the half shell, dabbing each one with horseradish before slurping it down, then I finished off a mess of cold boiled shrimps the size of my thumb.

I checked in with Rose at the Club again, then ran into Sam at the bar and we had a drink together.

"Say, Jimmy. What do you call a girl who's always got the clap, the syph, and a bush full of crabs?"

"I give."

"An incurable romantic."

He checked his watch and said with a wink that he had an appointment to keep and took off. I finished my drink and called it a night and headed for La Colonia.

• •

On the past two nights, the whole neighborhood had been dark and asleep by the time I got in, but at this earlier hour the Avila house were still showing light in some of its windows when I came walking down the lane.

As I passed by the Avila place I sensed a movement in the shadows alongside the house. I stopped and pretended to be trying to read my wristwatch by the Mechanic Street lamppost's weak glow of light through the trees, turning my wrist this way and that, all the while checking out the shadows across the street from under my hatbrim.

A dark shape moved by the bushes beside the house, and then I lost sight of it. It couldn't be Avila or anybody in his family. What would they be doing out there in the dark? Even if it had been one of them, they would've seen me in the lane and recognized me and said something. A prowler, I figured, some passing tramp just in on a freight car and looking for an easy grab. The neighborhood had been without a watchdog ever since the Gutierrez brothers' mutt had chased a stray cat out into the railyard and been run over by a train.

I strolled on down the lane until I came abreast of the hedge between the Ortega and Morales properties where a fat oak momentarily blocked my silhouette from the Casa Verde porch light—and then I ducked behind the hedge and ran in a crouch till I was out of the line of sight of the Avila house. I cut over into the Morales backyard through a break in the hedge where the kids always crossed, then paused low to the ground and listened hard, but I heard only the brief groan of a ship's horn from the docks across the tracks. It was another cloudy night and the moon was a dim glow hard to spot through the trees. The darkness behind the houses was deep as a well.

I advanced slowly across the Morales yard to the shrubbery bordering the Avila sideyard, where I'd seen the prowler. I pulled the .44 from its shoulder holster and held it uncocked down against my leg.

I stood in a half-crouch and listened. Nothing. Maybe the guy had seen me duck behind the hedge and figured that I'd be doubling back. He could've hustled out of the Colonia while I was crossing the Morales yard. On the other hand, he would've had time to set himself for me. I stared through the shrubbery without trying too hard to fix on anything, letting my lax focus catch whatever movement it might.

Nothing.

I slowly stepped through the shrubs and into the Avila sideyard, the damp leaves brushing my hand, my face. I paused and listened again. I thought I heard something in the backyard. I eased over toward the rear of the house, then stopped at the corner and leaned around to look. Nothing but unmoving shadowy forms. I knew that the large bulky shape toward the rear of the yard was a toolshed. Could be he was hiding in its deeper shadow, looking my way as hard as I was looking his, having as much trouble making anything out clearly. I figured I'd cross the yard at an angle, then come around behind the shed.

Midway across the yard, I saw a low dark form ahead of me. Was that him? Crouching in wait for me to get closer so he could make out my shape a little better? See where my head was so he could take a swipe at it with a club? Take a slash at my throat?

I put my thumb on the Colt's hammer and kept my eyes on the shape and edged up to it, ready to cock and shoot the instant it came at me. But it didn't move. When I got up to it I could see it wasn't a man but still couldn't tell what it was. I crouched and touched it. A wheelbarrow.

I should have been watching the toolshed. He came out from behind it and said, "No te mueves, carajo."

I stared up at his vague dark shape and froze in my crouch.

And then he was suddenly and starkly illuminated in a flood of light from behind me—thick-bellied, large-headed, and hatless, heavy-jowled, the muzzle of his double-barreled twelve-gauge a foot from my face. In the instant that he gaped blindly into the glare, I lunged up and snatched the shotgun barrel aside and both barrels discharged, the muzzles flaring yellow.

I hit him on the head with the Colt and he wavered but clung to the shotgun and I hit him again and he lost his grip and fell to all fours. I couldn't believe he was still conscious. I was about to whack him once more but voices were hollering in Spanish, yelling my name and saying stop, stop, don't hit him, he's a friend.

I squinted into the blaze of the open kitchen door and saw Avila and his wife standing there. Then Avila ran down and started helping the guy to his feet. I tucked away the Colt and gave him a hand, still holding to the shotgun. The señora was urging us from the kitchen doorway to hurry because someone surely heard the gunblast and might be calling the police, but I wasn't too worried about that. Nobody in La Colonia was going to report a shot, and even if somebody out on Mechanic had heard it, it was unlikely they'd notify the cops either. In this part of town people knew to mind their own business. The neighbors' usual reaction to the sound of gunshots was to turn up their radios.

We got the guy upright and helped him over to the steps and up into the kitchen. Avila kicked the door shut. I propped the shotgun against the wall.

And there, standing beside Señora Avila, was the girl.

• •

Her name was Daniela Zarate. Avila said she was the goddaughter of his aunt and uncle. Up close she was even prettier than she'd looked in the passing Ford, and my face went warm for a moment with the same inexplicable sensation I'd had the first time our eyes met.

I bowed slightly and said, "Encantado, señorita."

I thought she was about to smile, but she didn't. She nodded at me without saying anything. I guessed her age at about twenty. She seemed not to recognize me, though I'd been sure she had seen my face as clearly as I'd seen hers.

The guy I'd clobbered, Avila said, was his cousin, Felipe Rocha, who was visiting from Brownsville. Avila invited me to have a cup of coffee and I sat at the dining table with him and Rocha. He offered to take my hat, but I said that was all right and held it on my lap. It was all I could do to keep from turning around to watch the girl in the kitchen as she brewed the coffee.

Señora Avila had bundled some ice cubes in a dishcloth to make a clumsy ice pack for Rocha. He accepted it in place of the wadded towel he'd been pressing to his crown. I had hit him in almost the same spot both times and you could see the raw swelling through his hair. It was surprising there wasn't more blood. Even minor scalp wounds usually bled so much they looked a lot worse than they were. The guy had a brick head. His nose was offset and he was missing the lobe on his left ear and a wormy white scar curved along the outer edge of his right eye socket and ended on his cheekbone. He'd been in some serious disagreements. Holding the ice pack like a man keeping his cap from blowing off in the wind, he scowled at me across the table. I gave him a look right back.

Avila repeatedly apologized to us both—to me for being accosted by Rocha's shotgun, to Rocha for the knocks on the head.

"What were you doing out there, anyway?" I asked Rocha.

"Qué?" he said. He looked like he wanted to leap over the table at me.

"Felipe, he doesn't understand English so good," Avila said.

So I asked Rocha in Spanish.

What the hell was *I* doing sneaking up on the house, Rocha wanted to know.

I said I thought he was a prowler.

He said he thought I was one.

Felipe was a man of precautions, Avila said, and had insisted on checking around the outside of the house every evening before going to bed.

A guy who didn't know everybody in the neighborhood, I said, had no business assuming that somebody was a prowler just because he didn't recognize him. And a man should be damn careful about who he pointed a gun at.

Rocha said a man ought to be goddamn careful about who he hit with a gun too.

Señora Avila brought out more ice for Rocha's pack and said for us to stop speaking so meanly to each other, for the love of God. Could we not be grateful that no one had been badly hurt?

Rocha cut a look at her as if to dispute her notion that no one had been badly hurt, and Avila narrowed his eyes in rebuke of her for intruding into men's business. She made a face at her husband and retreated to the kitchen.

Daniela, Avila said, would be living with his family for a while. He told me her father had been a fisherman in Veracruz, where she'd been born and had lived all her life, but a year ago his boat had foundered in a bad storm in the gulf and he and his crewman drowned. And then some months later an outbreak of yellow fever took her mother among its victims. An orphan at seventeen and with no other living kin, the poor girl had made her way to Brownsville to live with her godparents—Avila's aunt and uncle—who were now naturalized American citizens. They had become her godparents in Veracruz, where they'd lived for many years and had been best friends to Daniela's mother and father before moving to Brownsville ten years ago to care for their only daughter, a young and childless widow in frail health who died the year before last.

Daniela was a fine seamstress, Avila said, and could have easily found work in some Matamoros or Brownsville dress shop, but she didn't much like the border country and who could blame her? She and her godfather—and her godfather's nephew, Felipe—had come to Galveston to celebrate the New Year with the Avilas. As soon as they arrived on the island Daniela decided that she preferred it to the Rio Grande Valley. When the Avilas learned of her situation they offered to let her live with them until she found work and could afford quarters of her own, and with her godfather's permission she'd accepted. They had but one bedroom in their house, so she would sleep on their sofa.

There was something strained in the way Avila told all this, like somebody who'd memorized the words to a song but still hadn't got the tune quite right. It didn't make any sense for them to lie to me. I wasn't somebody from outside La Colonia, somebody to whom there was good reason to lie—such as immigration agents or the police or any stranger at all.

Then again, maybe I was reacting out of professional habit, sensing untruth where there was nothing more than nervousness. Maybe the Avilas were simply rattled by the scrap I'd had with Rocha and still afraid cops might come around to investigate the shotgun blast. Whatever the case, I didn't give their nervousness much attention, not with the girl so close by. Even as I listened to Avila and exchanged hard looks with Rocha, I wasn't unaware of her for a second.

While Avila had been talking, his wife set out cups, saucers and spoons, a bowl of sugar. Now Daniela went around the table and poured coffee for us. As she leaned beside me to fill my cup I caught the smell of her, a faint scent like a mix of sea wind and grass. Her fingers looked strong. She appeared uninterested in what Avila had been saying, as if he were talking about somebody besides her. She finished serving and took the coffeepot back to the kitchen.

"What about this guy?" I said, nodding at Rocha.

"Qué?" Rocha said, glowering.

Felipe would soon be taking the train back to Brownsville, Avila said. The poor fellow had been sleeping on the floor. He had only stayed here in case Daniela changed her mind about living in Galveston after a few days and needed someone to accompany her back to the border.

And would Señorita Daniela, I asked Avila, be seeking a job as a seamstress?

I looked over my shoulder into the kitchen. She stood with her back to us, helping Avila's wife do the dishes at the sink. If she'd heard my mention of her name she gave no sign of it. Her calves flexed as she went up on her toes to replace a dish in the overhead cabinet. Her hips were roundly smooth and slim. Her blouse was slightly scooped in the rear to expose a portion of her brown back and the play of muscle as she hung a cup on its hook on the wall. She dropped a dishcloth and bent to retrieve it and the light gleamed along the upper ridge of her spine. She'd knotted her hair up behind her head but a few black tendrils dangled on her neck.

I turned back around and saw Rocha staring at her too.

Most probably the girl would find work in a dress shop, Avila said. But he and his wife had told her she should rest herself for a few days more before she started looking for employment.

I took out my cigarettes and offered one to Avila, who politely accepted it, then shook up another one in the pack and extended it to Rocha. He hesitated a moment and then took the smoke with his free hand and gave me a grudging nod of thanks. Avila struck a match and lit us up.

We smoked and sipped at our coffee in an awkwardly growing silence. I was hoping Daniela would join us—but of course she would not, nor would Señora Avila. It wasn't a social gathering at the table but an affair of men. After another minute, I snuffed my cigarette in the ashtray and stood up, saying I had to be on my way.

She was still at the sink with her back to the door, folding a dishtowel. Señora Avila came out of the kitchen, her expression somewhat uncertain. I thanked her for the coffee and apologized for any distress I may have caused her. Then I called to the girl in the kitchen, "Buenas noches, señorita. Mucho gusto de conocerle."

She turned to look at me. "Buenas noches, señor."

Avila escorted me to the front door. I put my hat on and looked back and saw her watching me from beside the dining table.

From the moment we'd been introduced I'd been wondering how I might go about seeing her again. And now, before I knew I was going to do it, I said, "Con permiso, señorita. Me gustaría invitarle a—"

"I speak English," she said, with only a mild accent. And smiled at me for the first time.

I was so surprised, I said, "Yes, you do"—and felt like a moron.

Everyone was looking from me to her, her to me.

"Well," I said, "I was wondering . . . there's a café just a few blocks from here, over by the train station—the Steam Whistle, it's called—and, ah, they serve a pretty good breakfast, and . . . I was wondering if you might want to go with me tomorrow. For breakfast."

Smooth, I thought, really slick. You babbling jackass—what the hell's *with* you?

"Qué le dijo?" Rocha said. He was looking from Avila to his wife, but they were both staring at me and ignored him.

"I would be pleased to accompany you to the café," she said. "What time should I expect you?"

"Well, is . . . seven o'clock? That okay? I mean if that's too early . . ."

"Seven o'clock is . . . o-kay," she said, sounding the word like she hadn't used it before and like she found it fun to say. "I shall be ready."

I was tickled by the "shall" and grinned like a fool.

"Okay then," I said. "Seven it is."

Rocha looked angry. The Avilas seemed confused. I tipped my hat and said, "Buenas noches a todos," returned her smile across the room, and took my leave.

I skipped down the front steps and practically danced all the way to the Casa Verde.

They find La Perla cantina on a muddy street in a ramshackle neighborhood on the swampy east side of Matamoros. A windless rain falls steadily from a black sky. They step out of the taxi and Gustavo curses the mud on his new shoes and the cuffs of his tan trousers, the rainwater spotting his Stetson. The air is heavy with the smells of muck and rotted vegetation. Angel tells the driver to wait for them and gives him the slightly smaller half of a torn bill of large denomination.

The place is dimly lighted and roughly furnished. A radio on the backbar plays ranchero music. There are only three customers on this miserable night, two of them at a table and a solitary drinker at the end of the bar. The bartender is reading a newspaper spread open on the bartop. He has a fresh black eye swollen half-shut and his lips are bruised and bloated. He doesn't look up from the paper until they are at the bar—and then his battered face comes alert. La Perla receives few patrons so well dressed as these two.

He puts aside the paper and spreads his hands on the bar and asks their pleasure. Gustavo pulls open his coat just enough to let him see the pistol in its holster and tells him in a low voice not to move his hands from the bar or he will shoot him where he stands.

Angel turns to look at the three drinkers, who all cut their eyes away. "Oigan!" he says, and they return their attention to him. He tells them he and his partner are policemen and the bar is being closed for improprieties. Anyone still in the place in one minute will be arrested. The three men bolt out the door and Angel goes over and locks it.

Gustavo asks the bartender if he has a gun hidden anywhere on the premises and the man says no. He says that if this is a holdup they're going to be disappointed with the take.

Gustavo tells him they are collectors for the Monterrey gambling house called La Llorona and they have been searching for him all over the states of Nuevo León and Tamaulipas. And now, thanks to a tip, they've finally found him.

Angel asks if he really thought he could get away with owing La Llorona ten thousand pesos.

The bartender's face is pinched in fearful incomprehension. He swears he doesn't know what they're talking about, that he's never been in La Llorona.

"Ah, Victor," Gustavo says, "no me digas mentiras."

Victor? the bartender says. Who the hell's Victor? They've got the wrong guy. *His* name's Luis. His brother Guillermo owns this place and maybe *he* knows this Victor son of a bitch. They can ask him when he comes in later in the evening.

Angel laughs and asks Gustavo if he can believe the nerve of this guy, denying he's Victor Montoya.

"Pero yo no soy Victor Montoya," the bartender says. He swears it on the Holy Mother. "Me llamo Arroyo, Luis Arroyo."

Angel and Gustavo smile at him. And only now does Luis Arroyo begin to understand that he has been tricked—and to sense that he has seen these men before. And then he remembers. Yes. At Las Cadenas.

They were driving up to the casa grande in a convertible with a dead man tied across the hood. He feels a sudden urge to urinate.

Gustavo goes around the counter and Luis Arroyo tries to turn to face him without moving his hands from the bartop. Gustavo hits him hard in the kidney and Arroyo collapses into a whimpering heap. Gustavo takes off his coat and hands it to Angel who drapes it over a barstool. Then Gustavo squats down behind the bar to interrogate Luis Arroyo.

The thing is done in less than ten minutes. Cursing softly, Gustavo stands up and wets a portion of a bar towel with water and dabs at a small bloodstain on his shirt. Angel gestures for a bottle of tequila and Gustavo sets it and a couple of shot glasses on the bar. Angel pours them both a drink and they toss them back and Angel refills both glasses.

They have learned that Arroyo agreed to help la señora effect her getaway and get over the border in exchange for several pieces of jewelry that she assured him would fetch a sizable price. She had given him part of his payment before they set out and the rest when he delivered her to a certain house in Brownsville, Texas, which he accomplished with the help of a smuggler acquaintance who showed them where to ford the river upstream of the international bridge. When he crossed back to Matamoros, however, Arroyo had been set upon by robbers who beat him up and stole his jewelry. He cursed the meanness of this goddamned world and the brute injustice of life until Gustavo painfully brought him back to the matter at hand and such germane details as the address of the Brownsville house.

He described it as a yellow house on Levee Street, just off the main boulevard, with a short fat palm in the middle of the yard. La señora said the place belonged to friends of hers, but she had not told anything about them, not even their names.

Now Angel leans over the bar and looks down at Luis Arroyo. He says for Luis to have a drink and pours a stream of tequila into Arroyo's upturned bloody face and open unseeing eyes, onto his head, comically angled on the broken neck.

A deep-orange sun was breaking over the trees and rooftops when I returned to the Avila's front door. I'd shined up my boots and I was wearing a white suit fresh from the cleaners and a brand-new fedora. It had taken me a long while to fall asleep the night before, but it hadn't occurred to me till I awakened that I should've gotten up earlier and gone to the Club to get a car. If Rose was already there he would've let me use the Lincoln.

She answered the door herself, and good as her word she was ready.

"Good morning," she said. The sight of her set a butterfly loose under my ribs.

Señora Avila stood behind her, looking pleased. Whatever had been worrying her the night before, she was over it. Avila rose from his chair at the dining table and called hello. He was in visibly better spirits also. He invited me in for a cup of coffee but I said I had an appointment this morning and had just enough time for breakfast.

Rocha was still sullen, staring hard at me from the sofa where he sat with a cup of coffee. A white pad bandage on top of his head was held in place with a cloth strip knotted under his chin so it looked like he was wearing some kind of ridiculous bonnet. He knew what I was smiling at and gave me a rude hand gesture, which only made me chuckle.

It was another unseasonably warm morning. The only clouds were to the south, far over the gulf. She was dressed for the weather in a light yellow blouse much like the one she had worn the night before—without sleeves and with small scoops in front and back—a white skirt, open-toed leather sandals. As we started up the lane I apologized for not having a car, but she said she wouldn't have wanted to ride anyway, she liked to walk, especially on such a lovely day. Her black hair hung long and loose and she swept it back over her shoulders.

I had spoken in Spanish, but she had answered in her slightly stilted English. I asked which language she preferred we use.

"In what country are we?" she said, giving me a sidewise look that made me laugh.

"Okay, girl. Whatever lingo you want."

"Lingo?" she said. Then brightened and said, "Ah, lengua . . . *lingo*. Yes."

We went along Mechanic and then turned toward the rail station, chatting all the while about what a pretty day it was and how the smell of the sea was especially sweet in the early morning. She said she loved the sea. She had grown up breathing its scent in Veracruz and she missed it when she went to Matamoros, which was more than twenty miles inland.

"In Matamoros the smell was always of dead things and the river mud," she said.

In daylight her hair looked even blacker than it had the night before and it gleamed dark blue when the sun struck it at a certain angle. Her eyes seemed darker, brighter. Her skin was the color of caramel. I took her hand to cross the street to The Steam Whistle, which stood opposite the train station. She had a strong cool grip and she laughed as we scooted through a break in the traffic.

The café was small—a half-dozen tables, a row of stools along a short counter, four booths in the rear. Except for the rare mornings when I ate at the Casa Verde, this was where I always came for breakfast. I liked the place so much that I paid the owner, a balding guy named Albert Moss, fifteen dollars a month to reserve a particular table for me every morning from six to nine o'clock, in the corner by the big front window. All the regular customers knew whose table it was.

I hadn't been in for the past few days, and when Albert saw us he raised his spatula in greeting from the grill behind the counter. I gave him a nod and held Daniela's chair and then sat across from her. The table's little hand-printed RESERVED sign couldn't have looked more out of place except in front of a barstool but it was necessary for warding off strangers who stopped in. I turned it facedown. She didn't remark on it—or on all of the sidelong attention we'd attracted from the other patrons. She was the first one I'd ever brought in here.

The café was a family business run by Albert and his wife, and on Saturdays their teenage daughter Lynette came in to lend a hand. The girl brought us coffee and checked-cloth napkins and sets of silverware. She said, "Hi, Jimmy," but couldn't keep her eyes off Daniela. I introduced them and they beamed at each other.

I knew the little menu by heart but Lynette had brought one to the table for Daniela in case she wanted to look at it. Daniela asked what I was going to eat. I said the fried tomatoes were pretty good—they were coated with bread crumbs seasoned with garlic and pepper—and I was going to have them with scrambled eggs and toast. "I'm eating light this morning but I recommend the smoked sausage to you," I said.

"Then that's what I will have," Daniela told Lynette. The girl gave her another radiant smile and took our order to her father.

"Why do you eat . . . light . . . this morning?" she said.

"Gotta be quick on my feet today," I said, and made a little running motion with two fingers along the tabletop.

She was about to say something to that, then checked herself. I asked where she'd learned to speak English and she said in a Catholic school called Escuela de Los Tres Reyes. She had practiced every day with her teachers and classmates, and with store owners along her route between home and school who spoke English well.

I asked if she'd mind if I smoked and she said no, then shook her head when I offered a cigarette. We looked out the window at the people passing on the sidewalk, the cluster of traffic in front of the train station, then turned to each other and started to speak at the same time—and both laughed.

I said, "You first," but she said, "No, *you,*" and insisted on it.

"I only wanted to say I'm sorry about the loss of your parents," I said. "Your mother . . . I mean, having lost your mother so recently must be hard for you."

"Yes," she said, with no tone at all.

It was obvious she didn't care to talk about it, so I said, "Why did you leave Veracruz? Since you liked it so much, I mean. Didn't you have kinfolk there, relatives you could've stayed with?"

"No, there was no one." She looked out the window and then back at me. "I am happy to be here."

"I can understand why. Galveston's an interesting place."

"Yes, I like Galveston, but I mean I am happy to be *here.*" She patted the tabletop.

"Oh. Well, I'm glad." More Mr. Smooth.

"This town reminds me of Veracruz. Where we lived, you could see . . . el malecón?—the sea*wall?*"

"Yes. *Sea*wall."

"The *sea*wall," she said. "You could see the seawall from the window of our house. You could see the beach. I went swimming every day, from the time I was a little girl. Do you swim?"

I told her of never having seen the ocean until two years ago and how I had learned to swim, and of my habit of going for a long swim every two weeks. I left out the part about how much the gulf had scared me when I first saw it.

She was awed by the idea that I'd not looked on the sea until I was grown, and was impressed that I had taught myself to swim. But she couldn't understand why I didn't go swimming more often.

"Every day since I have been here," she said, "I have felt such . . . gana. Como se dice gana?"

"Urge," I said. "Hankering. Desire . . ."

"*Desire,* yes. I have felt such desire to go swimming. I asked the señor and Señora Avila if they would escort me to the beach tomorrow when they do not have to go to work, and the señora said yes but the señor said no. He believes the women's bathing suits are indecent. His face became red when the señora said he enjoys to look at the other girls on the beach but could not bear the shame if a woman in his company exposed her legs to the world."

She turned her palms up and made a face of incomprehension.

The thought of her exposed legs deepened my breath. I cleared my throat. "What about Rocha? Why doesn't he take you to the beach?"

"*That* one." She rolled her eyes. "He will not go to the beach. He does not say why but I think he is afraid. I think he fears even the sight of the sea. Can you imagine?"

I shook my head and made a puzzled face to convey inability to imagine a man afraid of the sea.

"I suppose I will have to go to the beach by myself, if no one will accompany me."

She gave me a look I'd seen from other women. From them it had been a clear invitation to an invitation, but with this one I couldn't be sure.

"Well," I said. "Maybe I shouldn't ask, but . . . I mean, we just met and I don't want to offend . . ."

She gave my shin a light kick under the table and said in a low voice, "Be brave!" She covered her smile with her hands but it was still in her eyes.

I had to laugh at her boldness. "All right, then. Would you like to go swimming with me?"

"I should very much like to go swimming with you," she said. "When?"

"Well, I've been going at night, but I can arrange for—"

She said she loved to swim in the sea at night. "It's so beautiful at night," she said. "I have done it only one time but it was wonderful. It was like . . . like all the sea belonged to me."

"Actually," I said, "I was thinking of taking a swim tonight."

She leaned over the table and said in a whisper of mock conspiracy: "And I may join you in swimming in the darkness?"

"Yes you may," I said. "But I'm warning you, the water can be pretty chilly this time of year."

She did a little bounce in her chair like an excited child. "I don't care. I am very brave."

Lynette came to the table with a platter in each hand and set down our breakfasts.

"It all looks very good," Daniela said, examining the oozing sausage and the fried tomato slices, the eggs thoroughly scrambled the way Albert knew I liked them. She watched me pick up a crisp slice of tomato with my fingers and bite into it, and then she did the same.

"Oh this is delicious," she said, and took a bigger bite.

Lynette grinned at Daniela's pleasure and then went back to the counter and fetched a stack of thick-sliced toast moist with melted butter. She refilled our cups and said, "Yall enjoy your breakfast. I'll keep an eye on your coffee, make sure you don't go dry."

Daniela thanked her and the girl went to tend to other patrons.

"Yall?" Daniela said.

"All of you. You all—yall."

Daniela mouthed the word silently and looked over at Lynette who was at a back booth, taking an order. The other customers had quit eyeballing us and gone back to minding their own business.

She liked the sausage but thought the eggs needed more spice and sprinkled them with cayenne sauce. "So," she said as we ate, "now you have learned everything of me. Tell me of yourself."

"Not much to tell," I said. "I grew up on a ranch in West Texas, then came here a couple of years ago and here I still am."

"That is a very short story," she said.

"What do you want to know?"

"Everything," she said. "Are you American or Mexican? Why do you have blue eyes? Tell me everything."

I was born in San Antonio, I said. My mother was a blue-eyed American named Alice Harrison. Her parents managed a hotel in Laredo. My father was Mexican, a federal cavalry officer named Benito Torres. He met my mother at a fiesta, when he was on leave and visiting relatives on the American side. They married a week later.

"Oh my," she said. "It must have been love at first sight."

"Must've been," I said. "But a few days after their wedding he had to go back to his troops in Mexico. About a month before I was born he was killed at a place called Zacatecas."

Her face fell. "Ay, that is so sad. I am sure it broke your mother's heart."

"I guess so." I told her that my mother's heart had already been bruised pretty hard a few months before. There had been a cholera epidemic moving along the border, and because she was frail in her pregnancy with me, her parents wanted her away from the threat of the disease, so they sent her to live with family friends in San Antonio. Shortly afterward she got the hard news that both of them had been killed in a fire that destroyed the hotel.

"Dios mio," Daniela said. "She lost so much in such little time."

"Yeah, she didn't have much luck and it didn't get any better. She died giving birth to me."

Daniela stared at me.

"It's all right," I said. "It's not like I ever knew her or anything."

"But still, she was your *mother*. Who took care of you?"

My aunt, I said, my mother's sister. She was something of a black sheep and had run away at an early age but she and my mother had always kept in touch. When my mother wrote and told her what happened to their parents, my aunt came to San Antonio all the way from El Paso to stay with her and be of help until I was born. She'd only recently gotten married herself. When my mother died, my aunt and uncle took me to live with them on their ranch in West Texas. That's where I grew up. My uncle—whose name was Cullen Youngblood—gave me his family name, agreeing with my aunt that I'd be better off with an American name than with my father's Mexican one. They christened me James in honor of one of Uncle Cullen's dead brothers.

"James Youngblood." She said the name like she was testing it in her mouth. "Do you have a middle name?"

"Rudolph," I said. "I've never told it to anybody else, and if you repeat it I'll call you a liar. My aunt gave it to me for no reason except *she* liked it."

When I was two years old, I told Daniela, my aunt gave birth to a son, the only child she and Uncle Cullen ever had. He had blue eyes too, but darker than mine and my aunt's. They named him Reuben, after my uncle Cullen's father. We grew up like brothers. We learned to ride about as soon as we could walk and we worked as hands on the YB Ranch from the time we were boys. The only mornings we didn't work were when we were at school.

"And that's pretty much the story," I said.

"Was it difficult for you in your childhood," she said, "to be an American but to look so much Mexican? Did the other children, the

American children—the Anglos, I mean—did they . . . make funny of you?"

"Make *fun,*" I said. "Oh, a few of the peckerwood kids made some cracks when I first started school—called me half-breed, blue-eyed greaser, things like that. I shut them up pretty fast."

"The macho hombre was a macho boy."

I scowled fiercely and put my fists up like a boxer—and she chuckled.

"There have only been one or two fools to say anything like that in the years since," I said. "But hell, I wasn't the only Mexican-looking American around there, you know. And around there the Anglos and Mexicans were pretty used to each other anyway. They pretty much got along okay."

"Who taught you to speak Spanish? Your aunt?"

"No. She never knew more than a few words, and my uncle knew even less. I picked it up from the Mexican kids. It came to me pretty easy."

"Well, you speak it very well," she said, "for a gringo." She was able to hold a straight face for about two seconds before breaking into giggles.

"Listen to you," I said. "Your back's still sopping wet and you've got the nerve to show that sort of disrespect to a naturalborn citizen of the United States."

"Oh, you are so cruel to speak of wet backs," she said, affecting a look of injury. She glanced around the room at the other diners busy with their own breakfasts and conversations, then turned sideways in her chair and said, "Does this back appear wet? Does it *feel* wet?"

I reached across the table and placed my palm on the exposed top of her back. Her skin was warm and wonderfully smooth.

She gave me a sidelong look. *"Well?"*

I withdrew my hand. "Your back is very cleverly disguised as dry."

"You *see?*" she said in a tone of triumph.

As she finished her eggs she said she was even more impressed by my English, which she thought I spoke better than most Americans she had heard. She said I must have attended a good school.

I had to chuckle at that. I told her how Reuben and I had ridden horseback to a two-room regional schoolhouse six miles from the ranch. Each room had its own teacher, one for the kids in first through the sixth grade, the other for the smaller number of kids in grades seven to twelve. Only a handful of students ever made it to the tenth grade or above. None of the first-graders—except for me and then Reuben—could read at the time they started school. My aunt had taught me to read and letter by the time I was five, then did the same for Reuben.

"So you and your cousin had a . . . how do you say ventaja? No, wait . . . *advantage*. That is correct? You had an advantage upon the other students. You must have achieved easily to grade twelve."

"Not exactly," I said—and immediately gave myself a mental kick in the ass. It would've been easier to say sure we did, and let it go at that. But now I'd roused her curiosity and had to explain.

"My aunt didn't think the teachers at the school were educating us very well," I said, "so she took over the job of teaching me and Reuben herself. Truth to tell, she was a better teacher than they were. She'd drill us in arithmetic every morning. She'd give us grammar tests. She'd make us read a few pages aloud from some book she'd pick at random from the shelf, and every time we came to a word we didn't know, she'd make us look it up in the dictionary. Every week she assigned a different book to each of us and we had to write a report on it."

"She deserves praise. What is her name?"

"Ava."

Lynette came to the table to replenish our coffee and clear away our dishware. She complimented Daniela on her outfit, saying she really liked her sandals. Daniela thanked her and said she had been admiring Lynette's auburn hair and asked if she ever wore it in a French braid, which she thought would look very attractive on her. Lynette said she didn't know what kind of braid that was, and so Daniela showed her how to plait it, demonstrating the technique with her own long hair.

I was glad for Lynette's interruption—it got us off the subject of my school days. I'd told the truth about my aunt Ava's decision to assume our education herself. I just hadn't told the full reason for it . . .

I was fourteen, Reuben was twelve, and for weeks he'd been getting teased every day by a husky fifteen-year-old named Larry Rogerson. I'd kept out of it because Rogerson hadn't laid a hand on him; his teasing was all verbal. Besides, a bully was something every kid had to deal with at one time or another, and Reuben knew as well as I did that he had to handle it himself. Then one day Reuben took a peppermint stick to school and at recess Rogerson snatched it away from him. I didn't see that—I was tossing a football with some of the other boys—and I didn't see Reuben try to kick Rogerson in the balls and only get him in the leg. But a lot of the other kids saw what was going on and their sudden shouting made me look over there to see Larry Rogerson holding Reuben in a headlock with one arm and beating him in the face with his other fist. Reuben was always on the skinny side but he never did lack for sand, and even as Rogerson was pounding his face he kept trying to kick him.

I ran up and punched Rogerson on the side of the head so hard I thought I broke my hand. He went sprawling but scrambled to his feet and came up with a buckknife, open and ready. He managed to cut me on the upper arm before I caught him by the wrist and tripped him to the ground and got the knife away from him. I straddled his chest and pinned his arms under my knees and held the tip of the blade to the base of his neck. My hand hurt like hell and blood was running down my arm and the sight of it had me in a fury.

"I oughta kill you," I said. "I could do it easy."

As soon as I said it I knew it was true. It *would've* been easy. It was one of those moments when you realize something about yourself that you hadn't known just a second earlier, something as true as it can be and that changes the way you see yourself from then on, the way you see the whole damn world.

Rogerson knew I could do it too—it was in his eyes. That's what saved his life. If I had detected the smallest doubt on his face I would've shoved the blade in his neck to the hilt and he would've died learning the truth. But he already knew it. He lay there staring at me in big-eyed terror, too afraid to even breathe. Maybe he was thinking how different a knife could be when it was in somebody else's hand and at your own throat.

I became aware of the silence around us and looked up to see the other students gawking, and I saw that they all knew the truth too. Even the two teachers standing there with their mouths open. They knew.

I cocked my arm like I was getting ready to stab the blade into him. He made a half-whimper and turned his face to the side and I jabbed the blade into the ground next to his neck, close enough for the handle to press against his skin. I left it there.

I got up and stared around at the others and every pair of eyes cut away from mine, including the teachers'. My sleeve was sopped with blood. Rogerson kept his eyes on me and didn't move. Reuben stepped up beside me and gave him the two-finger horns sign—fuck you.

Nobody said anything as we walked over to the open shed where our horses were tethered and I got a bandanna out of the saddlebag and ripped open my sleeve and Reuben tied the bandanna around my gashed arm. Then we mounted up and rode for the ranch.

Neither of us spoke till we were halfway home, and then Reuben said, "You'da damn sure done it too."

I looked at him but didn't say anything.

"You'da done it," he said. Grinning.

When we got to the house and Aunt Ava saw our condition, she took us to the kitchen and told us to sit down, then fetched her small shoebox of medical supplies. She gave Reuben a handmirror and a bottle of iodine to treat the cuts on his face himself, and while she sewed up my arm I told her what happened.

She'd never been one to make a display of her feelings. She rarely smiled or frowned, never raised her voice, never openly fretted about anything. I'd never heard her laugh and I couldn't even imagine her in tears. She listened to our accounts of the fight without comment or any kind of look I could read—except when I was telling how I threatened to cut Rogerson's throat, and for a flickering moment she looked like she might smile. I didn't tell her the part about how I'd known I could do it as easily as I'd ever done anything, but I had a hunch she knew it. All my life I'd had a strange sense about her, a feeling that she knew things having to do with me that I didn't know myself, like some gypsy fortune-teller who's reading the cards she dealt you. It was like she could see through my flesh and bones and down into some part of me so deeply hidden I couldn't even tell what it was.

Reuben told me once that he loved his mother very much but she always seemed like a stranger in some ways and he couldn't help being a little afraid of her. He thought his father was kind of scared of her too. I didn't know about that, but I was never afraid of her—I was only mystified. And always would be.

She'd baked a sweet potato pie that morning and she let us have a big slice of it with a glass of milk, which had us gawking at each other, since it was almost dinnertime. When my uncle came in from the range at noon and she told him what happened he was enraged. He wanted to ride over to the Rogerson place and kick the elder Rogerson's ass for raising a boy who'd pull a knife in a schoolyard fight. My aunt dissuaded him. No real harm had been done, she said, and Reuben and I would not be going back to the school anyway. She said she didn't believe we were learning very much from the teachers and she had been thinking of tutoring us herself, and now she was decided on it.

Uncle Cullen grumbled a while longer during dinner about those Rogerson hillbillies out of Missouri, but the episode was closed. He was boss of the YB crews and range, but my aunt ruled the family and all matters in it . . .

"You see?" Daniela said, her hands braiding her hair behind her head, her breasts pushing tightly against her blouse. Lynette was watching Daniela's hands and trying to do the same with her own hair. Albert called to the girl to quit pestering us and come get a ready order. Lynette made a face but Daniela told her she should get back to her duties, that she'd help her braid her hair some other time, when the café wasn't so busy.

"Promise?" Lynette said. Daniela nodded and patted the girl's hand. The girl poured more coffee for us and took up our plates and hustled off to take care of the waiting orders.

"Looks like you have an admirer," I said.

"She's nice," Daniela said, undoing the braided length of her hair and shaking it free. "So. Tell me, why did you leave the ranch?"

"Oh, things changed. There was one of those epidemics that hit the border every so often, one disease or another. I don't even remember what this one was, exactly, but both Reuben and Uncle Cullen got hit with it. They got sicker and sicker for almost a week and then died within a day of each other. It all happened pretty fast. Aunt Ava couldn't bear to stay on at the ranch without them, so she sold the place and moved away to Denver. She had kinfolk there. She asked me to go with her, but a vaquero buddy of mine knew of a ranch just outside San Antone where we could hire on, so we did. A few months later I got a notion to come to Galveston, get a look at the sea. And here I am."

I thought it was a pretty good lie. Up to now the only lie I'd told her was about my father—but hell, what did *that* matter? I had believed the same lie myself for most of my life and so what? But I hadn't wanted to complicate things with her, and the truth about my leaving the ranch would've required a lot of explaining and maybe even confused her. So I'd lied. Not because I wanted to deceive her or because I was afraid of the truth—the reasons most people lie—but only to keep things simple.

"I am sorry for you," she said. "There has been so much terrible misfortune in your family."

"Hell, there's probably not a family anywhere that hasn't had its share of rough luck."

"Do you and your aunt write letters to one another?"

"Not as often as we used to. She's got a pretty busy life. I'm glad for her."

She nodded, then looked out the window and sipped at her coffee. I lit a cigarette.

We sat in silence for a minute. Then she turned to face me and said, "I have seen you before. Four nights ago. You were in a car on the street when we went by. You looked directly at me. But when Señor Avila introduced us, you didn't remember."

"Yes I did. But I thought *you* didn't remember, so I didn't say anything."

"Truly?"

"Yeah," I said. "Truly."

She stared down into her coffee cup for a moment. "After you departed last night, Señor Avila spoke about you."

"Oh?" I'd figured he would have.

"He said you work for a powerful man named Don Rosario."

I waited.

She looked up. "He believes you are a pistolero for this man."

I looked out the window at people passing by on the way to the next part of their lives. Then turned back to her and shrugged and said, "People who gossip like to dramatize things. I collect money for my employers. I drive here and there and collect account payments and bring them back to the office. To tell the truth, it's pretty dull work."

"Do you always have with you the pistol you had last night?"

"I sometimes collect a lot of money in a day's work, and the world's full of thieves. I've gotten used to carrying it."

All true.

She studied my eyes like she was trying to see behind them. "Señor Avila says everyone of La Colonia is pleased that you live among them. They feel protected by the nearness of you."

I didn't know what to say to that so I just shrugged.

Lynette delivered breakfast to a nearby table and then asked if we were ready for more coffee. I checked my watch and shook my head. "We have to get." I left the money for the bill on the table, including a bigger tip than usual.

I took her hand again to cross the busy street and we didn't let go of each other till we were back at La Colonia.

At the Avila front door I said I'd come by for her just after dark, about six-thirty. I told her to wear her bathing suit under her dress and bring a towel.

She said she'd be ready, then waggled her fingers at me and went inside.

I headed for the Club.

As he had told his wife he would do on his way back from Galveston, Oscar Picacho stopped off in Corpus Christi to visit with his cousin Ernesto. They went fishing in the bay in Ernesto's boat and caught snapper and dorado and they filleted and grilled the fish in Ernesto's backyard. They smoked cigars and got happily half-drunk and told funny stories of their boyhood days in Reynosa. It had been an altogether fine time. And now, on this late Saturday morning more than three days after leaving the Avila house, Oscar Picacho steers his trusty green Model T onto the narrow dirt driveway alongside his Brownsville home.

He calls to his wife as he comes through the front door and into his small living room and catches only a glimpse of Teresa where she sits on the sofa—her eyes large and terrified, her hands gripping her knees—before Angel Lozano's pistol barrel crashes into the side of his head and the room tilts and he hears Teresa's scream as something distant and cut off almost as soon as it begins and he is only vaguely aware of hitting the floor on his face.

He regains consciousness to find himself beside his wife

on the sofa, his hands tied behind him, his face and mustache dripping with water flung on him to bring him to his senses, his shirt soaked. The right side of his head feels misshapen and pains him from crown to jaw. Teresa now with her hands bound before her and a gag in her mouth, her face bright with tears.

Angel Lozano and Gustavo Mendez loom over them, their foul mood in their faces, a mood made worse by their having been cloistered in this little house for more than two days while they awaited Oscar's return. In that time they have learned much from Señora Picacho: that the Picachos had known the girl as a child in Veracruz and always loved her and despised her parents for their miserable neglect of her, and in their letters to her over the years they constantly reminded her that she was always welcome in their home, which was why she had come to them on fleeing Las Cadenas; that the girl—Daniela, as the woman called her—had told the Picachos of her abduction from Veracruz by a rich but evil one-eyed man named César Calveras who had put her through a terrible ordeal over the following months at Las Cadenas before she was able to effect her escape, but she had not told them of her marriage; that the Picachos had offered to let her live with them for as long as she wished and that she had accepted—and accepted as well Oscar Picacho's invitation to accompany him to Galveston Island on his annual trip to celebrate New Year's Eve at a party with his favorite nephew, Roberto Avila; that they had departed for Galveston on the day before Angel and Gustavo showed up, and that with them had gone another Picacho nephew, Felipe Rocha, who had been a Brownsville policeman until he was fired last year for stealing several pistols from the station arms room and, though it was never proved, selling them across the river; that Señora Picacho herself had not gone with them because she did not like car trips, that she had never been to Galveston, and that she had no idea where in that town Roberto Avila lived.

Angel and Gustavo had had no choice but to wait for the trio to return. When they finally heard the rattle of the Model T as it pulled into the driveway, they told Señora Picacho to sit on the sofa and make no sound of warning or the last thing she would see in this life would be the deaths of her husband and nephew and dear friend Daniela. But the only one to come through the door had been Oscar Picacho.

Now Angel Lozano grabs Oscar by his wet hair and yanks his head around so he can see Gustavo holding a knife to the señora's throat. The woman is close to hysteria.

Angel demands to know exactly where the girl is—and without hesitation Oscar tells him.

Shortly thereafter Angel and Gustavo slip out of the house and casually make away along the tree-shadowed sidewalks of the quiet neighborhood. At a Ford dealership a few blocks farther on they pay cash for a new sedan.

It is almost noon when they reach the main highway and turn north, Gustavo driving, being careful not to exceed the speed limit, Angel studying the open road map on his lap and calculating mileage and driving time. Allowing for reduced speeds in most of the towns they will pass through, he estimates they will get to Galveston around midnight.

It will be more than a week before neighbors become sufficiently concerned about the Picachos—having seen neither of them in that time and their car unmoved from the driveway—to call the police. An officer will investigate and discover the bodies in the house, both of them with drapery cords tight around the neck.

Had I told her the truth about my life on the ranch and how I came to leave the place, I would've had to tell at least a little about Frank Hartung. He was Uncle Cullen's oldest friend. He had a ranch in New Mexico and had a good foreman he could trust to run things in his absence when every so often he'd come see us for a few days' visit. We'd meet him at the Marfa station—Uncle Cullen and Aunt Ava, me and Reuben—and then take supper at a café before making the long drive back down to the YB in Uncle Cullen's old Studebaker truck.

Frank had a funny habit whenever he sat down to a meal with us at the house. He'd never take the first bite of his food until Uncle Cullen had eaten a mouthful of his own. He'd watch Uncle Cullen chew and swallow, then they'd stare at each other for a moment, then Uncle Cullen would shrug at him and they'd both grin and Frank would start digging into his own plate. It was some kind of private joke between them that always made me and Reuben chuckle—even though we didn't know why it was so funny. But Aunt Ava didn't much appreciate their comedy.

She always gave the two of them a tightmouth look and sometimes shook her head like she couldn't understand how grown men could act so silly. I don't recall that she ever said anything about it except one time when I was about eight years old. "For God's sake, Frank," she'd said, "do you think I'm out to *poison* the bunch of you?"

The remark set Frank and Uncle Cullen to laughing so hard they almost choked on their beef—and Reuben thought *that* was so funny his milk came out his nose.

In some ways Frank Hartung was more of an uncle to me than Uncle Cullen was. Maybe because no matter how hard Uncle Cullen tried to treat us the same, Reuben was his flesh and blood and it was only natural that he'd be the favored one. But Frank never had any children, was never even married, and since he was so close to Uncle Cullen I guess he probably saw me like a nephew, maybe even a little like a son. Whenever the four of us shot pool together at the house, it was always Uncle Cullen and Reuben against me and Frank, and we almost always won. Uncle Cullen taught me how to ride, but Frank Hartung taught me the most important things I came to know about horses and riding them well. Even when the four of us were out riding the backcountry together, Frank would be instructing me about reading the land and sky, about tracking a rider or a man afoot, about the proper way to make a camp or build a fire or dress game. He was always teaching me something. As often as not, Reuben would drift over to join us too and learn what he could. Uncle Cullen seemed content enough to let Frank provide most of our education in the ways of the natural world.

The first guns I ever fired were Uncle Cullen's twelve-gauge double-barrel and his Winchester carbine, both of which he let me shoot as soon as I was big enough to steady them on a target. He did the same with Reuben. For my thirteenth birthday he gave me a .30–30 carbine of my own—then gave one to Reuben when he turned twelve. But it was Frank who really taught us how to shoot. He taught us which shooting positions allowed for the steadiest aim with a rifle. Taught us to get a spot weld and to let out half a breath and hold it as we took a bead. Taught us to squeeze the trigger not jerk it. He taught us about sight adjustment, about Kentucky windage and Tennessee elevation, about shooting uphill and down.

Actually, he taught all these things to Reuben—I already knew them, although I had no idea how I did. I was a deadeye from the start and I could tell that Frank knew he wasn't teaching me anything. He called me a naturalborn shooter and I supposed that was all the explanation for it.

As good as I was with a rifle, my real talent was with handguns. I was fifteen the first time I held one—Frank's .38 Smith & Wesson top-break revolver—and it was like handling some tool I'd used all my life. It was a strange but comforting sensation. I busted a beer bottle at forty paces with each of the first six shots I took. Reuben yelled "Yow!" with every hit. It was like I didn't really have to aim, just point the gun like my finger at whichever bottle I wanted to hit—and *pow,* I'd hit it. Frank then let me shoot his .380 Savage and I did just as well with it. I loved its semiautomatic action, the thrill of firing one round after another in rapid sequence, shattering a bottle with each shot. When I squeezed off the tenth and last round in the magazine, Frank stared at the litter of glass on the ground, then looked at me kind of curious but didn't say anything.

When I turned seventeen Frank gave me a rifle that once upon a time had belonged to his grandfather—an 1874 Buffalo Sharps. It weighed twelve pounds and fired a .50-caliber round that could carry over a mile. It had double-set triggers and a folding vernier peep sight mounted on the tang. Frank said his granddad had used it when he was an army scout hunting Apaches. The rifle came with a protective buckskin boot fitted with a rawhide loop so it could be hung on a saddle horn.

A month after he gave me that present Frank was killed in El Paso.

Two men tried to rob him when he came out of a whorehouse. He was sixty years old and half-drunk but still managed to bust one guy's head against a rock fence before the other one stabbed him from behind. The one with the fractured skull survived and got sentenced to forty years. The killer was executed in the electric chair.

Frank was buried in the Concordia Cemetery in El Paso. Reuben and I accompanied Uncle Cullen to the funeral. It was our first train ride and we stared out the window the whole trip, not seeing much of anything except more of the desert country we knew so well and marveling at how big West Texas truly was. Aunt Ava had come down with a bad stomachache that morning and stayed home.

There were about two dozen people at the graveside service, half of them from Frank's ranch, including his foreman, Plutarco Suárez. Frank had bequeathed the place to him. And left his Mexican saddle to Reuben, who had always admired it. To me he left his .38 top-break.

Everybody knew what close friends Uncle Cullen and Frank had been, and when the service was over they came up to offer their condolences. He introduced me and Reuben to several of them, including a wrinkled orangehaired woman who reeked of perfume and was red-eyed with crying, a longtime acquaintance, Uncle Cullen called her, named Mrs. O'Malley.

• •

About a year later—and just a few days after I'd turned eighteen—we were hit by rustlers. Early one morning Reuben and I were saddling our mounts when the vaquero foreman Esteban came riding hard with the news that a dozen of our horses had been stolen in the night. Uncle Cullen was away on business and so Esteban had come to me with the report.

He had followed the tracks from the south range where the thieves had cut the horses out of a larger herd to a ford where the stock was driven across the river. The tracks told him that two thieves had done the work on this side, and when he crossed over to study the prints on the other bank he saw that there were two more men in the band. Judging by the droppings, he figured they'd made off about three or four hours earlier.

The YB Ranch was in Presidio County, a rugged region of desert country busted up with bald mountains and mesas and buttes—and with scattered scrubland holding enough grass to graze our herds. Uncle Cullen raised cattle and horses both, marketing beeves and horsehair and saddle ponies. A portion of the Rio Grande formed the ranch's eastern boundary. Although rustling had been a constant problem all along the border in the old days, there hadn't been trouble with stock thieves around this part of the river in years. Lately, though, we'd been hearing stories of a small Mexican gang stealing from both Mex and American herds along a stretch of border down below El Paso. We figured that maybe things had got too hot for them up there and they'd decided to move farther south.

Esteban said he'd heard that a buyer of stolen horses was operating at a pueblo called Agua Dura, just west of the Sierra Grande, a Mexican range visible to the south of us and running roughly parallel to the Rio Grande. Each time the Agua Dura dealer accumulated a worthwhile herd he drove it down the Conchos and over to Chihuahua City, where nobody gave a damn about U.S. brands. Esteban figured Agua Dura was where our horses were headed.

The only one of us familiar with that country was a vaquero named Chente Castillo, who'd grown up in a pueblo called Placer Guadalupe, about sixty miles south of the border and within view of the Rio Conchos. He was a breed—more like a three-quarter than a half-breed, since he had a Mexican daddy and Apache mother—and there was no telling from his looks how old he was. He might've been thirty years old or fifty. He didn't speak much English but he seemed to understand it well enough. He anyway didn't need a lot of English with the other hands, most of whom were Mexican, and even the American hands could speak a little Spanish. He was a damn good rider and liked to work with me and Reuben because we didn't like cows any more than he did and we worked only with the horses. When Esteban mentioned Agua Dura, Chente said he'd been there and said it lay about forty miles to the south and the way there was through a pass in the Grandes. There was plenty of water and grass along the Grandes foothills to nourish the animals on the way to the pass, he said, and the forage was just as adequate on the other side of the mountains.

The way I saw it, the thieves wouldn't be driving the horses hard—they'd want the stock to be in good shape and fetch the best price. They'd anyway probably think they were safe now they were back in Mexico. If they were feeling cocky enough, they might take a couple of days about getting them to Agua Dura.

The sky behind the Chinatis was turning red as fire but the sun hadn't shown itself yet. If I started after them right away I thought I might catch up to them by noon. My black could do it. The only horse on the YB with greater endurance was Reuben's appaloosa.

I knew Uncle Cullen would raise hell with me when he found out. He'd warned me and Reuben never to cross the border for any reason, and I had never set foot in Mexico. Uncle Cullen had repeatedly told us it was a whole different world down there.

"There's nothing the other side of that river but meaner trouble than you can imagine. You get yourself in any of it and you'll play hell getting out again." He'd known two Americans who'd gone down there and were never heard from again. "Life aint worth spit to them people," he said, and slid his eyes away from me.

One time when he was going on and on about what a murderous

place Mexico was, Esteban was sitting within earshot on a corral rail behind him. The foreman widened his eyes and held his hands out and shook them in mock fright and it was all Reuben and I could do to keep from laughing. Uncle Cullen saw our faces and whirled around on his saddle to catch Esteban studying a buzzard way up in the sky like it was the most interesting creature he'd ever seen.

But Uncle Cullen was away in Fort Stockton and wasn't due back till late in the day—and I couldn't stand by and do nothing about a bunch of rustlers who thought they could help themselves to our stock as easy as you please.

I patted the black and waited for him to let out his breath and then I cinched the saddle tight. I mounted up and told Chente to pick out the best horse in the remuda for himself and get his rifle and meet me at the front gate.

As I heeled the black off toward the house, Reuben hupped his Jack horse up beside me.

"Where you think you're going?" I said.

"With you." He patted the Winchester he always carried in a saddle boot.

"Your daddy wouldn't care for it."

"We bring them horses back, I don't guess he'll be too awful red-assed with us."

He wouldn't quit his grin. What the hell, I thought—then smiled back at him and kicked the black into a lope and Reuben stuck right beside me.

I dismounted at the front porch and ran up to our room and took the Smith & Wesson from a dresser drawer and checked the loads and tucked it inside my shirt and under my waistband. I retrieved the Sharps in its buckskin boot from the closet and a box of cartridges off the shelf.

When I got back downstairs my aunt was standing just inside the open front door, her arms crossed, her face as impossible to read as always. Reuben was standing beside her, looking like somebody under arrest.

I'd wanted to avoid her, but there was nothing to do now except tell it to her straight, and so I did. I was hoping she wouldn't forbid me to go because I was going to do it anyway.

She looked out the door in the direction of the river. "And you think you can overtake them?"

"Yes, mam."

"And then what?"

"I'll get the horses back."

"How do you propose to do that, James Rudolph?" She was the only one who ever used my middle name.

"I just will."

"You know Mr. Youngblood doesn't want you crossing the river." She always referred to him as Mr. Youngblood, even addressed him that way, when she addressed him by any name at all. He seemed pretty used to it.

"I know it, but . . . goddammit, they got our *horses*. Pardon, mam."

She glanced down at the sheathed rifle in my hand, at the cartridges in my other, then looked at me for a long moment with those eyes that always made me feel like I was staring into my own.

"I'll have Carlotta wrap food for you," she said.

"Thank you, mam, but I can't wait. Those fellas are farther away every minute I'm standing here."

She placed a palm to my cheek for just a second and then folded her arms again. I couldn't remember another time when she'd made such a gesture. I knew Reuben was thinking the same thing by the way his mouth hung open.

I went out and slipped the loop of the rifle sheath over the saddle horn and stuck the packet of bullets into my saddlebag. Then

I swung up on the black and started off—hearing Reuben saying that he wanted to go with me, her saying something I couldn't make out.

And then I was riding out the gate with Chente alongside me and we headed down the road and toward the ford.

• •

About two hours later we were reined up on a low rise, letting the horses blow, studying the Mexican downcountry and seeing a faint hint of raised dust miles ahead and just about where Chente figured the pass cut through the Grandes.

"Allí están," he said.

I nodded—and cursed myself for having been in such a hurry I hadn't thought to bring field glasses.

Chente rolled a cigarette and passed it to me and then rolled one for himself. I struck a match on my belt buckle and cupped the flame and lit us up.

As soon as we'd crossed the Rio Grande I'd felt strangely different in some way I couldn't put my finger on. Even though I'd never set foot in Mexico before—this country Uncle Cullen called wild and dangerous and had so often warned us about—it somehow felt almost familiar. I wondered if some aspect of my father's Mexican blood carried in my own, something that recognized . . . what? . . . the character of the country, maybe. The soul of it. Something.

Our shadows were pulling in toward us. To our right the Grandes stood starkly red. The upland was thick with cactus—nopal, barrel, maguey. To the east the scrubland sloped away under the orange sun and toward the Rio Grande and the Chinati peaks were jagged and purple. The sky was hugely cloudless, its blue slowly bleaching. A hawk circled the bottoms. A pair of ragged buzzards sailed high and far over Texas.

The rustlers had been easy enough to track until they drove the herd over onto the rockier ground closer to the foothills and I lost the trail. But Chente didn't. They were moving the horses faster than I'd figured but Chente had been sure we were closing on them anyway, and now the thin cloud of dust ahead proved him right. He regarded the sun and figured we'd be through the pass and have them in sight by noon. "O poco antes."

Then he looked rearward and said, "Mira."

A horseman had come in view out of the rocky peppercorn breaks and was heading our way, riding hard as he started up the gradual slope of the higher ground.

We sat our horses and watched him come. There was something familiar about the animal's gait and the way the rider was leaned forward on him.

"Tú hermanito," Chente said. "Se escapó de la mamá."

He was right. Reuben on his Appaloosa, the tireless Jack.

I looked at the thin dust cloud along the Grandes again. It was moving into the mountains.

We each rolled another cigarette and smoked them slowly and were finished with them before Reuben got close enough for us to hear the clacking of Jack's shoes. Then we could see Reuben's white grin and hear him laughing. And then he was reining up beside us, the Appaloosa blowing but not all that hard.

"You must've had an hour's start on me," Reuben said. "You don't never want to bet good money against Jack in a distance race."

He hadn't snuck away—his mother had relented to the argument that if we were lucky enough to get back the stock, we could return to the YB a lot faster if there were three of us to drive the herd. She'd made him wait, though, while the maid packed a sack lunch for him to bring.

He had a pair of binoculars slung around his chest and I waggled my hand for them and he gave them over. I fixed the glasses on the dust cloud and then passed them to Chente.

Reuben stood up in his stirrups and studied the vague dust ahead. "That them?"

"It's them," I said.

He sat down again and looked all around. "Jesus, Jimmy—*Mexico!* Don't look all that different, but . . . hot damn, man! Feels like a thousand miles from home."

Chente gave him a look Reuben didn't see and said we'd catch sight of them for sure on the other side of the range.

"Well what the hell we sitting here for?" Reuben said. "Let's go."

• •

The sun was still shy of its meridian when we came out of the pass and onto a wide shelf. The trail swung around close to the mountain wall and dipped from view where it began its descent, but we reined over toward the cliff edge to have a look at the panorama of country below.

And there they were down on the plain. Hardly more than little dark figures against the pale ground. They'd stopped to make a noon camp at a narrow creek shining in the sun and running along a thin outcrop and a growth of scraggly mesquites. A long red mesa stood about a half-mile north of them.

It wasn't likely that they'd spot us against the shadowed mountain wall, not at this distance and not even with binoculars, but we reined the horses back and tethered them in the shade. We moved up in a crouch and lay on our bellies between a pair of boulders a few feet apart on the rim of the cliff. The Smith & Wesson was digging into my stomach, so I repositioned it at my side.

Chente checked the sun to make sure it wouldn't be reflecting off the lenses and then took a look through the glasses.

I asked how far off he thought they were.

"Pues . . . más de un kilómetro."

I thought so too—maybe close to 1,300 yards.

Chente passed me the glasses. Three of the thieves were at a small fire raising a thin smoke, roasting something on a spit. The fourth was about fifty yards downstream, mounted and watching over the stolen herd as it watered from the creek and cropped at a sparse growth of bank grass. There looked to be about three dozen head. Either Esteban had been wrong about how many we'd lost or the rustlers had hit one or two other ranches besides the YB.

I passed the binoculars to Reuben.

"Don't look too awful worried, do they?" he said. "Taking a leisurely dinner right out in the wide open."

"Guess they didn't figure anybody would come over the river after them."

He handed the binoculars to Chente, who had another long look through them and then looked at me and said, "Pues?"

Reuben was watching me too, the same question in his eyes. *Now what?*

I scrabbled backward out of the line of sight of the rustlers' camp and stood up and hustled over to the black and dug out the box of cartridges and took the Sharps off the saddle horn and unbuckled the heel of the buckskin sheath and slid the rifle out and tossed the sheath over the saddle and hustled back to the cliff edge.

Chente was grinning. He moved over to give me more room and flapped his hand at Reuben to do the same. I lay down between them, Reuben on my right, a little big-eyed.

I looked at him. "*What?* You think they'll give them back if we just go down and ask real nice?"

Chente snickered.

Reuben's face went red and he looked out at the rustlers on the plain. "No . . . shit no." He made a vague hand gesture. "It's just . . . they're a hell of a way is all."

He'd seen me hit watermelons with the Sharps at close to a half-mile on a downhill angle. But even though a man was a lot bigger than a watermelon, these guys were at half again that distance. And watermelons didn't move around. And maybe he was thinking that men anyway weren't watermelons.

"Can't get any closer except by going down the trail," I said. "If we do that they'll spot us sure before we get halfway down. Got to be from here."

"Soon as you shoot, they'll run, won't they? Even if you hit one, the others'll run off with the stock."

"No van a saber de donde viene el tiro," Chente said. "Es demasiado lejos."

"What?" Reuben said. "They won't hear it?"

"They'll hear it," I said. "But they won't know where it came from, not at this range."

I scanned the ground all around us and saw the rock I wanted. I pointed and Chente sidecrawled over to retrieve it. He snugged it into the dirt on the top lip of the slope in front of me. It was about the size of a football and almost flat along the top.

I dumped a handful of the huge cartridges on the ground between me and Reuben. "Every time I put out my hand," I said to Reuben, picking up one of the shells, "you put one of these in it. And don't keep me waiting."

He nodded, but his face was tight and pale. He must've read my eyes, because he said, "I'm okay—go on, do it." He scooped up several cartridges and held one up, showing me he was ready to hand it to me.

I squirmed around and set myself. Then levered the trigger guard forward to drop the block and open the breech. I inserted the cartridge in the chamber and pulled the trigger guard back in place and the breech slid closed.

Chente was watching the rustlers through the field glasses. I thought about hitting the rider first, since he was the readiest to make a getaway. But he'd probably fall somehow to spook his mount—jerk the reins or slump against the horse's head or get a foot caught in a stirrup, something—and then the herd would spook too. I didn't want to scatter the jugheads all over hell's half-acre if I could help it. So I started with the guys at the fire.

I didn't think about anything except making the shot. There was no wind at all. The tricky part was the downward angle of trajectory. I put my eye to the vernier and gingerly adjusted the sight. I took a bead on the guy squatting on his haunches who looked to be tending the fire. Then moved the sight over to the one sitting on the ground and facing my way. Then put the sight on the guy standing over them, the one in the best position to run for cover. I stayed on him. I rested the barrel on the rock for steadiness and lined the sight on his head and thumbed back the hammer and set the hair trigger.

The gunblast shook the air and rang up the mountain wall and flew out over the prairie. The man's hat jumped in the sunlight and he went down like his bones had unhinged.

"Jesus!" Reuben said.

That was my first one ever, and what I felt was proud—proud of my own precision. I hadn't expected to miss, but still it was a hell of a shot. Later on, when I had more time to think about it, I felt . . . I didn't know what it was . . . a sort of quiver . . . way down under my skin like something in my deepest blood. If there really was a God, this had to be a feeling He knew everything about.

Reuben slapped a bullet into my palm and I reloaded faster than I knew I could.

The herd by the creek was churning in a near spook. Not man nor beast down there knew where the shot had come from. The rider was reining his mount in circles and the other two guys at the fire were on their feet and looking all around. Both of them seemed to be holding a pistol, and one of them was turning and turning in a low crouch like he thought he might duck the next round, wherever it came from.

My next shot clubbed his head backward and took him off his feet and the report rolled away into the open plain.

"Hijo!" Chente said.

Half the herd bolted in our direction and the other lit out to westward. The rider didn't know where to go—he spurred his horse in one direction and then yanked it around and started in the other, then pulled up again and reined his mount around and round in tight close turns.

The last one afoot was running toward the outcrop with his arms covering his head like a man caught in the rain. I drilled him in the back and he flung forward and lay spread-eagled on his face, forming a small black X on the ground.

Now the horseman was galloping directly across my line of sight like a shooting-gallery target. I gauged a lead on him and fired—and both horse and rider went into a dusty rolling tumble. I'd meant to hit the mount anywhere just to bring it down, but either the shot killed it or the horse broke its neck because when it stopped rolling it lay stone still. The rider wasn't moving either.

"Ay, *Chihuahua*!" Chente said. He put down the glasses and looked at me. "Qué tirador!"

"Qué rifle magnífico," I said, patting the Sharps.

Reuben was gawking at the small dark figures littering the distant ground. Then he turned to me and said, "Jesus, Jimmy—*all* of them!"

"Not the rider," I said. "Hated shooting the horse but I didn't want to chance missing the guy and him getting out of range."

"Hellfire, he probably broke his neck in fifteen places, the way he went flying. *Jesus*."

"Or could be he's laying there thinking things over. Let's go see."

• •

We followed the winding trail down to the flats. I'd slipped the Sharps back into its sheath and moved the revolver to the front of my pants. The horses that had come our way had settled themselves and were feeding on the scrubgrass near the foot of the trail. Chente loose-herded them back toward the creek.

The rustlers were all Mexicans. The first one we came to was the first one I'd put down. He was on his side and we saw that a .50-caliber round treated a human head about the same way it did a watermelon—worse, actually, because a head was smaller and had less of itself to spare. The top part of the guy's skull was gone and ants were swarming over what was left of his head. The look on his face was suspicious—like he'd just heard something he couldn't believe.

Reuben leaned out from his saddle and puked. Chente glanced at him without expression and then headed off to the creek to round up the other horses still there. I thought the rustlers looked about how I had expected guys shot with a buffalo rifle to look. I'd seen other dead men, including one done in by a burst appendix and one drowned and one who'd passed out drunk on the tracks and got run over by a train, and the only difference among them was a matter of how neatly or how messily they'd died. Long before I ever pulled the trigger on these guys, I'd decided that dead was dead and there was no more reason to get sick at the sight of a messy dead man than there was in getting sick at the sight of a butchered beef. It was an opinion I pretty much kept to myself.

"I'm all right," Reuben said, wiping at his mouth with his shirt-sleeve. "Caught me by surprise is all."

"The others aint likely to look any better."

"I said I'm all right."

"Okay then."

The next one had caught it just under the eye and the bullet had stove in that side of his face and you couldn't see his eyes for the ants. He was lying faceup and the dirt under his head was a muddy red mess. Reuben made a good show of indifference to this one, leaning casually on his saddle horn and spitting off to the side.

The guy I shot in the back was lying on an even larger patch of bloody earth. He'd taken the round through a lung.

The horse I shot was dead too. The bullet had hit him just above the left ear and come out under its right eye.

The rider was still alive. He was on his back and his hat was mashed up under his head and his eyes were squinting against the overhead sun until my shadow fell over him and then they opened wider and fixed on me. He didn't look any older than Reuben.

"Mátame," he said in a low rasp. "No me puedo mover. Mátame, por amor de dios."

Reuben's Spanish was good enough to get the idea. "He say *kill* him?"

"He's paralyzed."

"Por favor . . . *mátame*."

Reuben looked all around like he might've been searching for somebody to ask for a better idea. Or like he was all of a sudden aware of just how right he'd been in feeling a lot farther from home than could be measured in miles.

It didn't seem too complicated to me. The kid had been a horse thief but now he was somebody who would cook to death under the sun unless somebody saw to it that he didn't.

I pulled the top-break from my pants and cocked it and aimed. The kid closed his eyes. Reuben said, "Jesus, Jimmy . . ."

I fired and the kid's head jerked and his right eye vanished in a dark red hole and the dirt under his hair went bloody. Our horses shrilled and spooked and I reined the black tight and talked to him and Reuben soothed the Appaloosa and the animals shuddered and blew and then were all right.

I put the revolver back in my pants. Chente sat his horse by the herd at the creek and was staring off at the mountains. Reuben was staring hard at the kid.

"Would *you* rather a bullet or a couple of days getting roasted?"

He turned to me. "I *know,*" he said. "It's just . . . ah hell, Jimmy, he wasn't but a damn *boy*."

So said Reuben Youngblood, not yet sixteen years old.

• •

We set out to round up the runaways, leaving Chente with the other horses at the creekside camp. We were at it for over an hour and still may have missed a few, no telling, since we didn't know exactly how many there'd been to start with. When we got them back to the camp and bunched them with the others and counted them up we had twenty-eight head, thirteen with the YB brand, the others wearing a brand that looked like a lopsided *A* with a flat top and one extralong leg. None of us had seen it before. They must've been stolen from somewhere north of the YB and been run farther than ours because they were the worse for wear.

Chente had searched the bodies and gone through the rustlers' saddlepacks and laid out their belongings. There were only three firearms—an old cap-and-ball Dance, a Colt double-action five-shot, and a single-barrel twelve-gauge with both the barrel and the stock cut down so that the thing looked more like a giant pistol than a shotgun. Every man of them had some sort of knife on him, one of them a fine switchblade with pearl grips on the haft and a spring so strong the blade popped out like a magic trick. Chente had put all their money in a small pile. There was seven dollars in paper and another dollar thirty in silver. The rest of the cash was in paper peso denominations and Mexican specie.

Reuben said he didn't want any of the money or anything else of theirs. I took the switchblade and gestured for Chente to help himself to the rest. He scooped up the money and stuck it in his pockets and picked up the cutdown and took it to his horse and wedged the short barrel into the saddle scabbard along with his rifle.

There was a skinny jackrabbit on the spit over the fire but it was charred beyond all possibility of being edible. Chente tried it anyway and chewed a mouthful for a while before spitting it out. I fetched the lunch sack Reuben had brought with him but Reuben didn't want any of that either, so Chente and I split the three beef sandwiches and the six flour tortillas folded up over refried beans. There were some apples too, and we gave them to our horses.

While Chente and I ate, Reuben kept glancing over at the dead men. I knew what was on his mind.

"It's gonna be slower going back, driving that bunch of jugheads," I said. "We spare the time to dig four graves and we'll never get back to the river before sundown. Your daddy's gonna have a shit fit as it is, but it'll be fifty times worse if we aint back by dark. *And* we'll play hell getting these animals across the river at night."

"It don't seem right, leaving them lay to rot."

Chente chuckled and said they wouldn't have much of a chance to rot. He jutted his chin upward, directing our attention to a pair of vultures circling way up high—and still others were coming at a distance out of the sierras to the west. I'd always marveled at the mysterious way they got the news so fast.

"Los zopilotes tienen que comer tambien," Chente said.

"Shit," Reuben said. "How'd you like them to feed on *you*?"

Chente said they might very well do that someday, whether he liked it or not. Then he put his head back and yelled at the vultures overhead that today wasn't the day.

And we all busted out laughing for no reason except the grandly certain feeling that today wasn't the day for any of us.

• •

Late in the day we got the herd across the river and onto YB land. By the time we arrived at the corrals the sun was almost set behind the sierras and the portion of it still visible was the color of melting gold. The western sky looked smeared with blood. The vaqueros had been at their supper but they all came out of the mess shack to watch us get the herd into the corral. Then we turned our mounts over to the stable boys for good rubs and a big feed.

When we came out of the stable, Uncle Cullen was at the corral, still in his traveling suit and tie, studying the recovered horses. Over at the house, Aunt Ava was watching us from the door with her arms crossed.

"Luego," Chente whispered to me, cutting his eyes at Uncle Cullen and sidling off to the cookhouse, his cutdown shotgun tucked under his arm.

We stood waiting for Uncle Cullen to say something. When he finally turned around to us, there was still enough light to see his face under his hat brim. He was sixty-three but had never looked his age until about eight months before, when he'd had a heart attack while he was working with some new horses. Since then he'd slowed down a hell of a lot and had acquired a slight stoop and had come to look every day of his years and then some. But his eyes still held some of their old fire.

"You disobeyed me," he said. "Both you."

"Yessir," I said. "It's all my fault."

"Oh? You force him to go with you?" he said, nodding at Reuben.

"No sir, but—"

"I can talk for myself," Reuben said. "I went on my own, Daddy. I disobeyed you too. We done it to get the horses back."

"I know why you done it." Then he said to me, "You know the brand on them others?"

"No sir. But I know they didn't belong to them thieves."

"So you figured we'd make them ours?"

"No sir. I figured you'd know what to do about them."

"So happens I know the brand. Arthur Falcone's, way up by the Vieja oxbows. I'll give him a call tonight. He'll probably want to come with some trailers."

He regarded the sheathed Sharps under my arm and the revolver under my belt and I wondered if he was remembering that I'd gotten both weapons from Frank Hartung.

"How many was it?"

"Four."

"Any of them like to steal again?"

"No sir."

He stared off at the purple eastern sky. Then looked at Reuben and I had a hunch what was on his mind, what he wanted to ask but was afraid of the answer to. So I told him.

"It was just me dealt with them."

"Just you all four?" He cut a look at Reuben.

"Yessir."

He nodded at the Sharps. "With that."

"Yessir."

Until that moment I hadn't really thought about how he might react to the news that I'd killed four men. I had probably assumed he would approve—after all, I'd only done what I had to do to get our horses back. Who could object to that? Not until I saw the way he looked at the Sharps did it occur to me how very differently he might see the whole thing—how differently most people would.

"You got any idea what could've happened to you-all down there? Not just from them thieves but from the police, from the goddamn rurales? From some bunch of bandits you might've come on?"

"I guess we could've had a little trouble, yessir."

"A little trouble. Yeah, you could call it that."

He'd never told me or Reuben very much about his younger days, but Frank Hartung had, and so I knew Uncle Cullen had never been a shrinking violet. Many a time when Uncle Cullen wasn't around, Frank had entertained us with stories of the bar fights they'd been in, tales of broken noses and lost teeth, blowed-up ears and black eyes and the different times they'd been tossed in the El Paso or the Las Cruces lockup till they sobered up and bailed out. But he'd never mentioned a knife or a gun in any of the fight stories. The only story Frank ever told us that involved a weapon was about Uncle Cullen's older brother, Teddy, who was found dead in an alley in Alpine one frosty morning. He was nineteen years old and had been stabbed a bunch of times. They knew it happened in a fight because his face was bruised and his knuckles all skinned. There were rumors of a girl and of a jealous boyfriend but nobody the local police questioned admitted to knowing anything about it, and whoever killed him was never found out. Teddy had been something of a loner, Frank told us. "A man friendless as Teddy," he said, "has got the least chance of all in this world."

If either Frank or Uncle Cullen ever killed a man, they did a good job of keeping it secret from us. But I really didn't think there was any such secret for either of them to keep.

In the last of the light before the closing gloom hid his face, Uncle Cullen looked at me in a way he never had before, like he was staring at somebody he wasn't real sure he recognized.

"I always did believe," he said, "that a fellow gets to be eighteen, he's old enough to make his own decisions, be he fool or be he wise. But Jimmy, I want you to promise me that as long as you continue living on the YB you won't never go across that river again without my permission."

I promised.

He turned to Reuben. "And you best promise me the same, leastways till you're a grown man too and decide for yourself what to do and where to do it."

Reuben promised.

"All right, then," Uncle Cullen said.

He jutted his chin toward the porch, where Aunt Ava's shadowy figure still stood. "You boys go on and get you some supper," he said. "Miss Ava told Carlotta keep yall a warm plate in case you got back tonight."

As we headed for the house, I still felt the look he'd given me. A look you give a stranger.

Aunt Ava stepped out of the shadows to meet us at the top of the porch steps. She gave Reuben a hug and told him to wash up before he sat at the table. He said yes mam and went inside. Then she took my free hand in both of hers and went up on her toes to kiss me quick on the mouth. I stood there in astonishment and watched her go into the house, and after a moment I went in too. It was the only kiss she ever gave me.

She never mentioned the rustlers even once, and Uncle Cullen never referred to them again. As far as I knew Reuben never spoke of them to anybody. When Falcone came with the trailers for his horses the next day, Uncle Cullen told him they had came splashing from across the river onto YB land and when he saw their mark he thought it damn strange that Falcone's stock was so far south and on the Mexican side. Falcone said he was sure the horses had been rustled. He figured the herd got loose of the thieves somehow. Uncle Cullen said that must be it and he told Falcone he should consider himself lucky. Falcone said if he was lucky the horses wouldn't have been stolen in the first place.

• •

Most of another year passed. Every day pretty much the same except as marked by the turning of the seasons. Yellowing days and chilly evenings turned into nights of frost and days of sharp blue air and coatings of snow on the mountains, and then slowly turned to days of wind and new warmth and foalings, then days of rising heat and dusty greenery along the river and the creeks.

We worked the roundups, Reuben and I, worked the brandings, worked at trimming manes and tails and bundling the hair for shipping. We tracked down strays and mended fences. If anyone had asked me what I expected to be doing in the years ahead I would've thought it was a fool question. What else would I be doing but living and working at the YB? Uncle Cullen had done it all his life and there was no reason to think Reuben and I wouldn't do the same.

But things can change pretty damn sudden, of course. And one night that summer they did.

Every year, the Veterans' Club held a Fourth of July Firecracker Dance at the old fairground just off the Marfa road, about halfway between the YB ranch and town, and that year Reuben and Chente and Uncle Cullen and I drove up there in our old truck. My uncle had been a devil of a dancer back before he had the heart attack and was forced to start taking it easy, but he still liked to go to dances and tap his foot to the music and watch everybody and criticize their dancing styles, and he liked to have a drink or two with neighbor ranchers and catch up on things. He tried to cajole Aunt Ava into going along with us, but she never was one to socialize and she said for us to all go ahead and have a good time.

It was the biggest turnout ever, at least two hundred people, lots of them families, both Mexican and Anglo, and there were plenty of high school girls from Marfa as well as girls from the local ranches. A pair of bands took turns providing the music—a string band from Alpine and a ranchera group from Marfa. The dance floor was a large patch of hard-packed dirt with rows of colored lightbulbs strung overhead. It was a moonless night and the sky was crammed with stars. There were bleachers and tables and benches, openfire pits smoking with slabs of ribs, a scattering of concession stands selling cold drinks and cotton candy and hot dogs. The air was rich with the aromas of it all—and with a taint of booze. Prohibition was on its last legs by then but was still in force and the bootleggers were still doing good business, especially since the sheriff didn't give a damn, being a drinking man himself. Almost every table had a jug or three on it and the only ones making a secret of their drinking were men who didn't want their wives to know and boys who'd been told by their daddies they were too young yet.

We'd brought a jug of hooch too—me and Reuben and Chente—and every once in a while we'd take a break from dancing and go out to the truck in the parking lot and have a snort. I'd slipped the jug behind the truck seat before Uncle Cullen came out of the house and got in. Not that he'd say anything to me about drinking—hell, I was only a month shy of nineteen—but he'd for sure climb all over me for letting Reuben drink, and he might yet have tried taking a belt to Reuben's ass if he caught him at it. Uncle Cullen of course had his own jug on hand—"to ward off the chill," he said, of the July night.

After about an hour of whirling around the floor with different girls, I settled on the one I wanted, a Mexican honey named Rosa Elena. She was in the country illegally and spoke just enough English to understand her duties as a housemaid for a prosperous Marfa family. They treated her well and had invited her to come with them to the dance. She was round-hipped and bright-eyed and a dozen guys were after her and had been cutting in on each other all through the early evening. We were just starting our second dance together when one of them came up to cut in on me, but she held to me and whispered that she wished we could stay partners. So I turned the guy down—and all the others who tried cutting in after him, and I refused to surrender her between numbers. One of the cowboys I shook my head at didn't take it too well, and for a moment I thought the fool might try to start something. But he didn't do anything more than give me a tough look and mutter under his breath before backing off. The word must've got around that we were paired for the evening, because we were left pretty much unbothered from then on.

At one point while I was dancing with Rosa, I saw Chente and Reuben sneaking off to the parking lot for another nip off the jug. Reuben glanced back toward Uncle Cullen, who was sitting at a table on the far side of the dance floor, sipping his hooch and talking to some rancher friends, all of them grinning at the high sheriff, who'd passed out with his head on the table. Reuben saw me and made a shooting gesture at me with his finger and thumb and then followed Chente into the crowd and out of sight.

I asked Rosa if she cared for a sip of whiskey but she said she'd better not. It wouldn't do for her employers to see her sneaking off to the parking lot or catching the smell of liquor on her breath. I wanted a drink myself but wasn't about to leave her unattended.

A little later, just as the string band finished up with a snappy two-step number that left us in a sweat, Reuben and Chente came shouldering through the mob of dancers to join us, Reuben with his arm around a strawberry blonde and Chente holding hands with a blonde of brighter shade. They introduced the girls as the Miller sisters, Laura Lee and Susan.

Their family owned a ranch up toward Fort Davis, the Susan one said, and they and their two brothers were visiting with family friends near Marfa. Did we know the Rogersons? She leaned back against Chente, who was standing sort of half turned to her so nobody but me and Rosa could see him stroking her bottom. All four of them had been hitting the hooch pretty hard—you could see it in their eyes and hear it in the silly way they laughed.

"We know them," I said. "We've never much socialized."

Reuben snickered and said, "Back in school one time Jimmy kicked Larry Rogerson's ass like a damn football."

"Next time you do it let me know so I can watch," the Susan one said.

"Susan don't much care for Larry all the time putting his hands on her," the Laura Lee one said.

Reuben hugged her tighter against him and she ran her tongue in his ear. Some of the dancers around us saw that and were amused and some were tight-faced with disapproval.

I'd never seen Reuben so close to drunk. I said excuse me to the Laura girl and pulled him aside and said he'd best lay off the stuff and sober up some before his daddy found him out. He said, "Right you are, Jimbo"—then took hold of me like a dance partner and tried to whirl me around. I cussed him softly and tugged his hat down over his eyes but couldn't help laughing along with Chente and the girls.

I lost sight of them during the next few dances as I spun Rosa around the floor, grazing against other dancers and them bumping into us and everybody saying "Sorry" and laughing about it.

And then, just as the Mexican band took over and began playing a loud rendition of "Tu, Solo Tu" and Rosa and I hugged close and started swaying to the music, I caught a glimpse of Chente in the center of the floor and saw the ready way he was standing and saw the two cowboys in front of him, one of them pointing a finger in his face and running his mouth in obvious anger. He was holding hard to the arm of the Susan girl and she was trying to break free of his grip. The other guy was holding a bottle of beer by the neck like a small club and glaring at Chente too. Even at this distance I could see the similarity between the cowboys and I knew they had to be the Miller brothers. And then Larry Rogerson stepped up beside them, giving Chente a hard look and saying something too. Then the crowd of dancers between us closed up and I lost sight of them all.

I stopped dancing and tried to spot them again through the swirl of couples. Rosa Elena clung to my neck and said, "What?"

I saw Chente giving the cowboys the horns sign with his index and little finger, then turning away and walking off through the crowd. The cowboy with the beer bottle started after him, followed by his brother and Rogerson. I yanked Rosa's arms off me and roughly shoved my way through the dancers, women protesting my rudeness, guys cussing me.

I came out at one corner of the dance floor and saw Chente emerging at the other—and saw the Miller guy behind him swing the beer bottle like he was throwing a baseball and hit Chente on the head. Chente's hat fell off and he staggered forward and fell to his hands and knees and the Miller guy kicked him in the ass and sent him sprawling in the dust.

A woman shrilled and people leaped up from the picnic tables and rammed into each other as some tried to back away from the fight and some tried to get closer. I was shouldering through the crowd and catching glimpses of the Millers and Rogerson kicking at Chente and even through all the yelling I heard one of the brothers shouting something about the greaser sonofabitch putting his hands on their sister. Then Chente had him by the leg and got him down and started punching him as the other brother and Rogerson kept on kicking and there was a haze of dust and women were shrieking and men cussing and bellowing to break them up, break them up. The lines of the overhead lights had been jostled somehow and the shadows were wavering and giving the whole scene an eerie look.

I shoved my way out of the crush of people and saw both Millers locked up with Chente on the ground and the three of them punching and rolling around while a half-dozen men were jumping all around them looking for an opening to grab one or another and pull them apart. Uncle Cullen was struggling to pry Reuben away from Larry Rogerson whose head was locked under Reuben's arm. Rogerson was worming around in Reuben's grip, and as I ran toward them I saw that he had a knife in his hand. And saw him stab Reuben in the stomach and in the chest.

Reuben's arms fell away from Rogerson and he sagged back against Uncle Cullen who was hugging him from behind. Uncle Cullen staggered under the sudden weight and fell to his knees with Reuben still in his arms. I ran up to them and Uncle Cullen was pressing a hand to the wound over Reuben's heart and croaking, "Son, son . . ." Reuben's eyes were open but they weren't seeing anything anymore.

Most of the people around us still had their attention on the fight between the Miller boys and Chente and some were cheering the fighters and some were still yelling to break it up and some were laughing at the attempts being made to stop them. Only the folk closest to us had seen what had happened to Reuben. Women were crying and somebody kept saying, "Oh my God oh my God . . ."

Rogerson was gawking down at us, still holding the knife. He looked at me and his eyes showed a lot of white and he flung the knife away and stepped back with his open hands up in front of him. All the blabber and shouting around me suddenly sounded very far away. I took the pearlhandled switchblade out of my pocket and snicked out the blade.

I had a vague sense of people drawing away from me as I walked up to Rogerson and he started to say something but I never heard a word of it. I grabbed him by the collar and jerked him toward me and stuck the blade in his belly all the way to the hilt. He made a sound like a small yawn and grabbed my shoulders as if he'd suddenly thought of something real important to tell me. I gave the knife a twist and jerked it sideways and blood gushed hot all over my lower arm. I pulled out the blade and stepped back and he put his hands to the wound and a bulge of blue gut showed between his fingers. His pants were dark with blood. I stabbed him again—in the chest, just like he'd stabbed Reuben—and he dropped to his knees and a bunch of women screamed at the same time as he fell on his face and lay still.

I stared around at the horrified faces, and the shouting and crying and confusion rose back to normal volume. Maybe the other fight had finally been stopped, I didn't know, but there were more people around us now, a lot of them yelling to know what happened and a bunch of others all telling them at once.

I retracted the blade into the haft and put the knife back in my pocket and turned to see about Uncle Cullen. He had let go of Reuben and was clutching at his own chest, his face twisted in pain. I helped him to his feet and asked if he thought he could make it out to the truck and he nodded but his face clenched even tighter. I pointed to his hat and somebody picked it up and handed it to me and I put it on my uncle's head and my fingers left smudges of Rogerson's blood on it. I heard somebody shouting that the sheriff was too drunk to stand up and others yelling to know where a goddam deputy was.

"Would some of you bring Reuben?" I said. There was a general hesitation and then three or four guys picked Reuben up and brought him along behind me as I half-dragged Uncle Cullen out to the parking lot, his grunting breath hot against my neck.

It might have been different if the sheriff had been sober or there had been any other lawmen around, but nobody said anything to me, nobody tried to stop me. They laid Reuben in the bed of the truck and I settled Uncle Cullen into the passenger side of the cab and then got behind the wheel. I pulled the truck into the flow of vehicles leaving the lot and a minute later we were rolling back toward the ranch.

• •

If I had any thoughts on the drive home I would never remember what they were. I must've known that the life I'd been living was done with. I must've expected to be arrested pretty damn quick. Arrested and jailed for the gutting of unarmed Larry Rogerson in front of dozens of witnesses. Then tried and convicted. Maybe I wondered what it was like to die in the electric chair. Maybe I didn't think about much of anything.

I could hear Uncle Cullen's wet breathing in the dark as the truck bounced along over the rough dirt road. And then I couldn't hear him anymore. He was slumped awkwardly against the door, his hat fallen off and down by his boots. I stopped the truck and pulled him upright and felt for a pulse on his neck but there wasn't one anymore. I eased him back against the door and put his hat on him and got the truck going again.

Pretty soon the house came into view and I saw that all the windows on the lower floor were lit up. For a minute I thought the law was already there and waiting for me. But there weren't any unfamiliar vehicles in sight.

Aunt Ava came out on the porch and watched me drive up. Over in front of the bunkhouse a few of the hands were gathered around a guitar player. I parked at the house and Aunt Ava came down the steps.

I got out of the cab, not knowing how to tell her what happened. She stepped around me and looked in the cab at Uncle Cullen for a minute, then stepped over and stared down at Reuben in the bed. She reached over the bed panel to brush his hair from his face.

"I'm so god-awful sorry, mam, but—"

"Helen Morgan telephoned a few minutes ago," she said, referring to a woman who ran a small bookstore in Marfa where Aunt Ava liked to browse. "She was there and saw it. She told me about the fight and . . . about Reuben. She said Mr. Youngblood was all right. Ailing, she said, but all right."

Her tone was almost as matter of fact as the one she'd use in asking if I'd gotten all the items on her grocery list whenever I came back from town. Almost. But there was something else in it this time. It sounded like it might be anger.

"He was, mam, but on the way home . . . well . . ."

"Yes," she said. "So I see."

I rubbed at my chin with the back of my hand and she stared at it and I saw that my whole hand was dark with dried blood and I stuck the hand in my back pocket.

"That's not all of it, mam. I believe I'm in trouble. I—"

"You *are* in trouble," she said. "Helen told me what you did." She looked off in the direction of the county road, then turned back to me. "You did what you had to, James Rudolph. Now you've got to get away from here—right now. You can't take the truck, they'll be watching the roads. Take Reuben's horse and ride the backcountry. Go saddle it—go. I'll get you some food."

I said I wanted to get my leather jacket and the top-break revolver from under my pillow and she said, "I'll get them. You hurry with that horse."

She rushed up the porch steps and into the house and called for Carlotta to put some food in a sack and I saw her go up the stairs.

All the vaqueros were outside the bunkhouse now and watching me as I headed for the stable. Esteban came over and fell in beside me and asked if there was anything he could do. I told him Chente was probably in the Marfa jail for fighting and would need someone to bail him out.

"Seguro que lo soltamos," he said. But what could he do for *me*?

I said for him to keep his eyes and ears open, that I would write to him to find out how things stood.

"Muy bien, jefecito," he said.

I was swift about saddling the Appaloosa. Jack could sense my tension and his ears twitched with excitement. I swung into the saddle and reached down to shake Esteban's hand and I saw his eyes take in the dry blood. Then I hupped the horse out of the stable and over to the house.

She was waiting with a small sack of food and my jacket and a cloth bundle shaped like a half-deflated football. She handed me the jacket and I put it on and then took the food sack from her and reached around and stuffed it into the rightside saddlebag while she put the bundle in the left one.

"What's that?"

"Something for you," she said, buckling down the flap. She took the top-break from her apron pocket and gave it to me. I opened the breech and checked the loads and closed it up again and slipped the revolver into my waistband. I told her to give my Sharps rifle to Esteban and let him know he could have my horse. I couldn't think of anything else I owned that I could bequeath to anybody.

She was standing with the light of the house behind her and it was hard to see her face clearly. She turned suddenly toward the distant road and I looked and saw two sets of headlights coming our way and then heard the rasping of the motors. She'd always had the senses of a cat.

"Go," she said. *"Go."*

I reined the Jack horse around and hupped off toward the back-country to the east.

When I turned to wave goodbye she was already out of sight.

• •

I rode steadily till a couple of hours before dawn, then reined up and tethered the Appaloosa in some scrub grass and rolled myself up in my bedroll and slept till sunrise, and then I got going again. I held to a course a half-mile or so south of the railroad. I rode through the day and into the night and stopped and made a fireless camp. Since riding off from the YB I had tried not to think about Reuben, but I finally couldn't help it and I let myself remember everything about him—and my throat got hot and tight, my chest hollow. He had been more brother to me than cousin and I'd never have a better friend. And Uncle Cullen—that damn good man. Aunt Ava would miss them both terribly but I doubted she would make any show of her grief, and people would gossip about her lack of proper sorrow. But the vaqueros held her in great respect and I knew she could manage the ranch on her own.

Toward the end of the second day I was a few miles south of Marathon. I watered the horse at a shady creek where a few kids were splashing and where I ate the last of the food Carlotta had packed for me. There was still about an hour of daylight left. When I finished the stale biscuit stuffed with a chunk of greasy ham I took the bundle out of the other bag to see what it held. It was tied with twine and was heavier than it looked.

I cut the twine with my switchblade. The cloth covering turned out to be a pillowcase wrapped around a revolver and a couple of tightly folded newspaper clippings. The gun was an old single-action .44-caliber Colt with grips of yellowed ivory carved with Mexican eagles.

I'd never seen her touch a gun, not even a rabbit rifle. Where had she gotten this? Her father? A brother, an uncle? I didn't know if she *had* any brothers or uncles. She had always refused to talk about her family, no matter how often Reuben had asked about it when we were younger. But it was all I could figure, that some man—probably one in her family—had given it to her, back when. And now she'd given it to me.

It fit my hand like it had been made for me, felt as familiar as my own skin. The embossed eagles were worn smooth and the burring at the top of the hammer had been thumbed dulled, but the Colt was in fine condition. How many hands had held it? I wondered. How many rounds had it fired in its time? How many men had it shot? It was fully loaded. I worked its action, cocked and uncocked it, put it on half-cock and spun the cylinder. I opened the gate and dropped a round into my hand and felt its weight, then put the bullet back into the chamber and thumbed the gate closed and eased the hammer down. I took the Smith & Wesson out of my pants and replaced it with the Colt and tucked the top-break into the saddlebag.

The larger of the two clippings was from a 1914 Mexico City newspaper and was a report on Pancho Villa's and Emiliano Zapata's takeover of the capital during the Revolution. It included a large photograph of about two dozen Mexicans crowding around Villa, who was seated in an ornate high-backed chair. He was in a military uniform but I recognized him immediately. There were a half-dozen photos of him on display in a Mexican café in Marfa, and the town's gun store had pictures of him on the wall too.

Everybody on the border knew Pancho Villa's story—how at the age of sixteen he'd killed the hacendado who raped his sister, how he was forced to hide in the mountains and become a bandit. Then in 1910 the Revolution changed his life. He became commander of the great Division of the North and one of Mexico's greatest heroes. The newspapers couldn't get enough of him. The American press flocked around him every time he visited the border. It was said he had a dozen wives and was a hell of a dancer. He was a fearless fighter, they said, a natural genius at military tactics—and a fearsome man, a merciless executioner of his prisoners. He could have been president of the country but he said he was not wise enough to be its leader. He captured Mexico City but couldn't hold it, and afterward, when his great army was beaten at last, he was forced to return to the mountains and once more live like a bandit. But then he did something that got the whole world's attention—he invaded the United States. He raided the town of Columbus, New Mexico, and shot up the army camp there. A massive U.S. Army force, including airplanes, was sent across the border to find him and kill him. They tried for a year and couldn't do it. The Yankee intrusion into Mexico only made him more of a hero to his countrymen. In 1920 he finally made peace with the Mexican government and—in a funny twist for a guy who had fought against hacendados all his life—he was given a hacienda as part of the deal. But even in retirement he was feared by many powerful men, and a few years later he was assassinated.

The caption under the photograph said Villa was sitting in the President's Chair in the National Palace. It identified the hawkish-looking man on his immediate left as Emiliano Zapata and the man at his right hand as Tomás Urbina. But the guy who really caught my attention was a large man standing at the very edge of the picture, holding his white Montana hat in a dark big-knuckled hand, his hair neatly combed, his shirt buttoned to the neck under his open coat, his watch fob dangling from the coat's breast pocket. His face had been circled in ink and he was looking at something or someone behind the photographer and off to the side. Judging by his expression, I'd have bet it was a woman.

He looked strangely familiar, but for a moment I didn't understand why. And then I did. If I'd worn my hair a little shorter, if I'd trimmed my mustache a little neater, if my eyes had been black instead of bright blue . . . I could've been looking at a picture of myself. The caption said he was Rodolfo Fierro.

I'd heard of him too, of course. Who hadn't? El Matador, they called him. El Señor Muerte. Manos de Sangre. El Carnicero—the Butcher. He had a dozen such names. He was Villa's chief executioner. The border Mexicans spoke of him in the same tone they used in speaking of Death itself. There were dozens of stories about him. They said he shot three hundred prisoners one afternoon in a big corral in Ciudad Juárez, that he gave them a chance, ten at a time, to run to a stone wall and climb over it, and he shot every one of them except the last, whom he deliberately let get away. But I'd never seen his picture, nor had anybody I knew. Until now.

The other clipping was a newspaper picture of Fierro by himself. It was taken from only a few feet away and had no caption. It showed him sitting in a chair at a sidewalk table, his face turned to the camera, his eyes shadowed by the brim of his Montana hat, his coatflap hanging away from the holster on his hip and exposing the butt of the Frontier Colt and its ivory grip carved with a Mexican eagle.

I stared and stared at that picture as the sky turned the color of fresh blood and the darkness slowly rose around me.

She sure as hell knew how to keep a secret, my mother.

The way I figured it, he'd either given her the Colt or she had stolen it from him. And she'd clipped these pictures. And before she died she'd shared the secret with her sister and given her the clippings and the gun. I wondered if Aunt Ava would ever have told me the truth if I hadn't had to run.

The light had gone so dim I could barely see his face in the photo. "Hey Daddy," I said.

• •

On a gray and windy afternoon two days later I sold both the Jack horse and my saddle to a rancher in Sanderson who knew a good mount when he saw one, even one that had been ridden as hard as I'd been riding this one. I kept the saddlebags and my blanket. He asked me no questions except if I'd sign a bill of sale, which I did. I patted the horse and said so long to it. I turned down the rancher's offer of a bed for the night but accepted a ride into town.

I hadn't eaten since the night before when I'd cooked a skinny jackrabbit over a low fire. So I went into a café and ordered a thick steak with gravy and fried potatoes, green beans and cornbread, a big glass of iced tea, and a slab of pecan pie for dessert. When I was done eating, the two plates looked freshly washed. The waitress gave me a wink and said, "Appetite's working just fine, hey?" I left her a half-dollar tip.

I went over to the railtracks and followed them eastward for about a hundred yards and then sat on my saddlebags in the meager shade of a mesquite and waited.

An hour later an eastbound train pulled into the Sanderson station for only as long as it took to load and unload mail, and then it started chugging on again. I had thought to wait till dark to jump a freight but I didn't see any sign of the railroad bulls I'd heard so much about from YB hands who'd ridden the rails, so I said the hell with it and jogged out to the track and picked out a boxcar with a partly open door as it came rolling up, slowly gaining speed.

I ran alongside the open door and pitched the saddlebags and blanketroll through it and then grabbed hold of the iron rung on the door with both hands and swung a foot up and hooked a heel on the car floor. I brought up my other leg and started wriggling myself in feetfirst—and somebody in there kicked me hard in the leg and said, "Ass off, wetback!"

He was a tramp with dirt-colored teeth and he kicked me twice more in the side before I worked myself far enough into the car to brace myself. On the next kick I snatched hold of his pant leg and pulled him off balance and he fell on top of me and almost rolled out of the car. He tried to scrabble back from the open door but I grabbed him by the collar and yanked hard and he went sailing out of the car with a yell.

The door on the other side of the car was shut and another guy was kneeling close to it and next to my opened saddlebags. He was grinning at me and holding the S&W top-break. He wore a baseball cap over a stringy growth of hair that hung down to his collar.

"Good goddamn riddance," he said. "I was awful tired of Weldon's company. Same dumbshit stories all the time, you know what I mean?" He turned the gun in his hand, examining it from different angles. "Aint this a pretty thing, though? Aint seen one of these in a coon's age."

"Yeah, it's an old one," I said, slowly sitting up and making a big show of the pain from the kicks I'd taken, probing my ribs gingerly and then easing a hand behind me and wincing big. "Christ almighty, he like to broke my back."

The tramp pointed the gun at me but hadn't cocked it. "Young fella like yourself don't need no gun to defend hisself as much as a old fella like me. Reckon I'll just hold on to it."

"Sure. Keep it."

"Well thankee, son. You real generous. Now do me just one more kindness and jump offa this train. I appreciate we're moving along right quick now but you hit the ground running and then roll just right you probly won't get busted up too bad."

"Can I at least have my bedroll," I said. "My last two dollars are in there."

He turned to look at the bedroll and I pulled the Mexican Colt from my waistband under the back of my jacket, cocking it as I brought it around. He heard the racheting hammer and snapped his attention back to me just in time to see me shoot him through the wishbone. The gunblast was loud but got swallowed almost instantly in the rumbling of the train. He flopped backward and against the closed door and fell over on his side with his legs in a twist.

I got up and stood over him with the .44 cocked and pointed at his head and he looked at me without expression as the light drained out of his eyes and he died. I took the top-break from his hand and put it back in the saddlebag. I snugged the .44 at the small of my back again and then opened the door a little way. There was nothing to see but passing desert. I sat and cooled myself in the rushing air and watched the country go clacking by.

• •

The sun had set and a dull orange twilight was closing around us when the train made a whistle stop at some nowhere station. I peeked out the door on the depot side and saw the engineer leaning out of the chugging locomotive and talking to a guy in shirtsleeves on the platform. The town consisted of fewer than a dozen buildings and even at that early hour of the evening there were more darkened windows than any with light showing in them. On the other side of the train there was only open country. I shoved the dead guy out the door on that side and then jumped down and positioned him so that his head was under the boxcar and his chest wound was centered on the rail. I tossed his cap under the car and then I got back inside and closed the door. A minute later the train got rolling again.

• •

We pulled up into Del Rio before dawn. I hunkered in the darkest corner of the boxcar and kept alert for the yard bulls, having heard stories about what rough old boys they were. I was ready to show them what rough was. But the only guys to peek into the car were a couple of kids about thirteen or fourteen who asked if anybody was in there and when I said yeah they asked if they could share the car with me. I told them to get in and keep quiet and they tossed their bindles in and helped each other aboard and then I eased the door to till it was almost closed. They said they were brothers, Charlie and Fred, and as we passed the miles together I came to learn that they'd had enough of their damn stepdaddy and were going to Houston to live with their uncle Stephen. The uncle didn't know they were coming but they were sure he would be glad to see them, him and Aunt Beulah both.

They each had a half-dozen peanut butter sandwiches in their bindles and they were quick to offer me one. I was so hungry I took it down in about four bites and they insisted I have another. I said it was a long way to Houston and they were going to need all the food they had but they said ah hell, we was hobo buddies, wasn't we. So I took the sandwich. I asked if they had any money and they said they sure did, they had four bits apiece. I gave them two dollars, which they refused until I convinced them I wasn't paying for the sandwiches, I was only helping out some hobo buddies who could use a little dough on their long trip. I said they could pay me back next time we ran into each other. "Well . . . in that case," Charlie the older one said, "all right then."

We went through Spofford, Uvalde, Hondo, the floor of the car vibrating so hard it was tough to get any sleep. When the train began to slow on its approach to the San Antonio yard, I shook hands with the boys and wished them luck. I secretly hoped they wouldn't get robbed and maybe worse by the first wolves they ran into.

The train didn't seem to be going all that fast now, but I didn't know how deceptive train speed could be.

"They say you supposed to try and hit the ground running," young Fred said.

"So I've been told," I said. "Thanks for reminding me."

I tossed out my saddlebags and bedroll, then crouched low at the edge of the car floor—and then jumped and tried to hit the ground running.

I went tumbling and flapping every which way and it was a wonder I didn't crack my skull. I gashed a cheek and banged up a knee and cut my elbows and pretty much felt like I'd been stomped by a herd of horses. I sat up and saw Fred and Charlie looking back at me from the boxcar. I waved like the landing had gone just perfect and they waved back.

The knee was bloody and hurt like a sonofabitch and at first I was afraid I'd broken it. But I could stand up and hobble around so I knew it was just badly bruised. I picked up my hat and went back and got my saddlebags and roll and then gimped on out to the nearest road and found a bus stop. About an hour later a bus came along with a sign saying DOWNTOWN. I got aboard and went into San Antonio, where I hadn't been since shortly after I was born.

• •

I'd picked San Antonio because it was far enough from Presidio County that I didn't think anybody would hunt me there and big enough to hide in if anybody did. I checked into a residential hotel called Los Nopales a few blocks over from the river. The room was on the second floor and the ancient elevator took forever, but at least I didn't have to take the stairs, which would've been hard labor on my bad knee. The carpeting was worn and the walls were water-stained and the room smelled of bug spray, but it was cheap and would do just fine. It was a good thing I had enough money from the sale of the horse to see me through for a while because I could hardly walk and I knew the knee would stiffen up and hurt even worse before it even began to get better. The place had one bellhop, a Mex kid, and I paid him to bring me a bottle of alcohol and bandages and, in the days to follow, to keep me in cigarettes and sandwiches and magazines.

I didn't do much of anything during the next two weeks except sleep and read and let the knee heal up. When I wasn't reading I'd sit in the tattered armchair by the window and smoke and watch the street and sidewalk traffic passing by. For exercise I'd do sitting pushups off the arms of the chair, raising and lowering myself till my arms were burning and about to cramp, then I'd rest a bit and then do another set until I couldn't raise myself off the chair at all. Then I'd sleep some more. I kept both revolvers under the pillow.

I wanted to know how things were at the YB but I didn't think it was a good idea to write to Aunt Ava directly. Even if I didn't put a return address on the envelope, somebody at the post office could be keeping an eye on her mail, with instructions to let the sheriff know about any letter that looked suspicious. It wasn't really very likely they'd go to all that trouble but I didn't want to take any chances. It was even less likely, though, that they'd be watching the vaqueros' mail, and after lying low for more than a month I finally wrote a note to Esteban. I asked how things stood and how my aunt was doing and said to tell her I was all right. I didn't tell him where I was living but said to write me back in care of general delivery at the post office on Commerce, which was two blocks from the Nopales.

By then I was already getting around with a cane, and in another week or so I didn't need it anymore. I took my meals at a little Mex café down the street. I went for a stroll every morning in a nearby park, limping less every day. I'd sit on a bench in the sun and read the local papers. Every afternoon I'd check in at the post office. One day Esteban's letter was waiting for me.

He wrote in a scrawl and mostly in Spanish as bad as his English, but with a few English phrasings mixed in, pretty much the way he usually talked. He said the police had questioned him and some of the other vaqueros about me but the boys all said they had no idea where I might have gone, which was of course the truth. There was a warrant out on me for murder, he said, and there was a reward of five hundred dollars for information leading to my capture. He said he could be a rich man if only he knew exactly where I was living. Maybe he was joking and maybe not. And he said that, in case I didn't know it, the señora had sold the ranch.

She had done so only a few days after the funerals of Don Cullen and Don Reuben. And then a week after the sale, she departed on the train from Marfa with only two bags of belongings. She told everyone she was going to live with a cousin in Albuquerque and gave her new address to a few people. But it was common knowledge that when her bookstore friend Mrs. Morgan had tried to contact her shortly after she moved, the Albuquerque post office said there was no such address in town. Where she had truly gone, Esteban wrote, no one could say.

As for Chente, he had been convicted of assault and sentenced to six months in the county jail. It was doubtful he would receive an early release for good behavior, as he was always fighting with the other inmates. The new owner of the YB—now called the Blue Range Ranch—was a kind man named Colfax who had become rich in the oil business but had always wanted to raise horses. Mr. Colfax had kept on all of the hands and retained Esteban as the foreman. Esteban said he was glad the Blue Range would be strictly a horse ranch, and he concluded with the hope that I was safe and in good health and advised me to go with God.

That was that.

And why I lied to Daniela about how I'd come to leave the YB.

• •

After I got Esteban's letter I gave some thought to hitchhiking out into ranch country and trying to get on as a hand somewhere, but the more I thought about it the less the idea appealed to me. Then one morning I woke up knowing I never wanted to work on a ranch again.

Over the next two months I worked at several different jobs in San Antonio and hated them all. I carried a hod for a construction gang, worked with a road-tarring crew, laid sewer pipe on a municipal project, drove a water truck for the city. I didn't stick with any of them for more than a few weeks. I was busting my back for peanuts and choking on the boredom. I was drunk almost every night and getting into bar fights.

One night in an alley behind a saloon I beat the shit out of a tough-talking merchant sailor who had a couple of inches and about thirty pounds on me. He'd been bullying everybody in the bar and they were glad to see me cool him, and my drinks were on the house the rest of the night. Among the spectators was a guy who had a friend who owned a cathouse at the south end of town and was in need of a good bouncer. The last good one who'd worked there had got stabbed in his sleep by a jealous girlfriend, and the two he'd hired since had both got their asses whipped by rough customers. Was I interested in the job? Sure, why not? The next day he took me out to the place, the Bluebonnet Dance Hall, and introduced me to the owner, a Mr. Stanley, and told him about the way I'd handled the sailor. And I got the job.

The place called itself a dance hall and on the ground floor that's what it was. The "dance hostesses" did their whoring on the second floor. I'd check in around five o'clock and usually not leave till three or four in the morning, depending on how much business the joint was turning. I'd sit in a chair at the foot of the stairs to the second floor and keep an eye on things in the dance parlor and I was within easy call of the floorwoman upstairs if any of the girls had trouble with a customer.

The only troublesome guys we had in there during my first weeks on the job were drunks who either couldn't get it up or couldn't get off for some other reason and thought their three dollars bought them all the time they'd need to get their satisfaction. But the house limit was fifteen minutes unless you ponied up another three bucks. If a customer got unreasonable about it the floorwoman would call down for me and I'd go up and persuade the guy to get his clothes on and take his leave. I hardly ever had to get rougher with any of them than an armlock. Only now and then did I have to punch somebody in the gut to put an end to the argument. I carried the Colt under my jacket but Stanley had told me I'd better never pull it unless some customer pulled a piece first. The job required long hours, but it paid well and had the added benefit of a free fuck at the end of the night.

I'd been there about a month when a guy hit one of the girls and the floorwoman called down for me. The guy was bigger than me but looked scared and said he was really sorry and he'd give the girl some money to make up for it and so on. I figured what the hell, the girl wasn't really hurt, why rough him up? I told him to give her twenty bucks and don't come back. Right, right, he said—and the moment I took my eyes off him he caught me with a hell of a sucker punch. He landed another good one before I got my footing and turned the thing around. Like everybody else in the place Stanley heard the commotion and came rushing upstairs and into the room, but by then it was all over. The guy was groaning on the floor, his nose broken and blown up, a front tooth somewhere under the bed. I had a shiner and was tempted to give him a kick in the balls for good measure but didn't do it. But when Stanley saw him he said, "Oh shit." Turned out the guy was some kind of assistant to the mayor, a regular customer who'd been coming to the Bluebonnet once a week for the past several months. He'd been a problem a few times before but not in a long while, and this was the first time he'd ever taken a swing at anybody. Stanley and a couple of the girls helped him up and tidied him somewhat but then the guy started threatening to make plenty of legal trouble for the club. The matter was finally settled when Stanley gave him a wad of money and fired me.

• •

For a week afterward I was in a fury. It was partly because of losing a job with good pay and free women, partly because of losing it the way I did. Still, that wasn't the whole reason for my anger, or even the main part of it. But even if somebody had put a gun to my head I couldn't have explained exactly what it was, and it made me even angrier that I couldn't.

I started taking long walks every night and I always carried both guns. Then one chilly January night I was walking down a sidewalk bordering a large park thick with trees and shrubbery when I took notice of a fancy Spanish restaurant called Domingo's across the street. The place was doing a brisk business and as I stood there it occurred to me how easy it would be to rob it.

The idea got my blood rushing. The cashier's counter was by the front door and out of view of the dining room. Just stick the gun in the cashier's face and make him hand over the money. If anybody came in the door or out of the dining room while I was at it I'd point the piece at them and tell them to stand fast . . . then grab the dough and hustle across the street into the park . . . then pick any one of a dozen paths out to some other street and mix in with the Saturday-night crowds.

The more I thought about it the simpler the plan seemed and the tighter the hold it took on me. But the smart thing was to wait till the supper rush was over with—let the dining crowd thin out, let the till get a little fatter. Another hour would be about right. I went over and sat on a sidewalk bench deeply shadowed by the trees. There were cars parked along the curbs on both sides of the street but I had a clear view of the restaurant doors. I watched the well-dressed patrons come and go. I was charged up and maybe a little nervous but I was *ready*.

Over the next forty minutes, more and more people came out of Domingo's and got in their cars and left. And then a light-colored Buick sedan came slowly down the street and wheeled into a parking spot almost directly across from the restaurant.

I figured them for late-night diners, but after the Buick's engine shut off and its headlights went dark, nobody got out. Against the glow from the streetlight on the corner behind them I could see the hatted silhouettes of four men sitting in the car. They were looking across the street and had to be watching the restaurant, since it was the only place on the block open for business at that hour. I thought maybe they were waiting to pick up somebody and I hoped it wouldn't take long. I was about ready to get to it and I didn't want a car full of witnesses parked in front of the place.

Another twenty minutes or so went by and the guys in the Buick were still waiting. I was getting pretty irked about it. Why didn't one of those guys go inside and tell whoever they were waiting for that they were there? A few more people came out and got in their cars and left. There were only a half-dozen cars still on the street, including the Buick.

The Buick's motor suddenly started up and I thought, *About time.* But then the front and back doors swung open and a guy got out of each one—palookas, both armed, the front guy with a big automatic, the backdoor guy with a sawed-off double-barrel. The night was chilly enough for their breath to show against the light of the corner lamppost. The two men stepped out into the street and the Buick's other back door opened and one more guy got out, this one holding a revolver.

Son of a bitch. I figured they were going to heist the place.

I stood up and put my hand to the Colt at my back. They obviously hadn't seen me sitting in the shadows. I was furious that they were going to beat me out of the score. I thought about shooting out one of their tires and scooting into the park.

The guy behind the wheel was looking across the street and still hadn't seen me either. I followed his gaze and that's when I saw that the gunmen weren't heading for Domingo's but toward three men who had just come out of the restaurant. The three were walking away down the sidewalk and were unaware of the men closing in on them at an angle from behind and holding their weapons low against their legs.

I didn't know I was going to do it until I hollered, "Behind you!"

The three men on the sidewalk all turned around as the shotgunner raised his weapon and cut loose with both barrels and the hat flew off one of the guys on the sidewalk with part of his head still in it. His buddies pulled pistols and one of them took cover behind a Studebaker as the street guy with the automatic started firing. The street guy closest to me was darkly Mexican and was raising his revolver at me when I shot him twice in the face. He fired a wild round and stumbled backward and dropped the piece and went down. The shotgunner had tossed away the sawed-off and was bringing a revolver out of his coat and I shot him in the side of the head and he did a little drunken sidestep and fell. The guy with the automatic was crouched in front of a Model A and replacing the magazine and looking from me to the guy behind the Studebaker who yelled, "Behind *you*!" I spun around as the driver came out of the Buick and fired at me twice—my coatflap tugged and there was a buzz past my ear—before I shot him with both revolvers, shot him and shot him as gunfire banged behind me and he slammed back against the open car door and slid down on his ass and slumped over with his head draining blood on the running board. I was punched hard under the arm and pivoted back around to see the guy by the Model A turning away to fire at the Studebaker guy and then he looked at me again like he was surprised to see me still on my feet. My revolvers snapped on empty chambers. He showed his teeth as he swung the automatic toward me—but then his head jerked to the side and he fell over with a hand clamped to the side of his head. The Studebaker guy—hatless, with curly gray hair—rushed over to him and bent down and shot him in the ear. Then hustled over to the guy I'd shot in the face and whose leg was moving slightly and gave him one in the head too.

That was it. The whole fight didn't take ten seconds. The sudden silence was enormous and there was a gunsmoke haze. Blood was spreading on the sidewalk around what was left of the shotgunned guy's head. Curly's other pal was sprawled on his back with his eyes open and his legs turned funny and his shirtfront shining red. Curly bent over him and dug a set of keys out of his pocket and yelled at me, "Come on if you're coming!"

I ran after him. At the end of the street he got behind the wheel of a yellow Cadillac and the engine fired up as I got in on the passenger side. Before I could close the door the car shot backward and went swaying around the corner and braked sharply, snapping my head back against the seat and slamming my door shut. Then the Caddy leaped forward with the tires screaming.

A few minutes later we flashed past the city limits sign. By then he had asked my name and I'd told him—and he'd introduced himself as Rosario Maceo but said I could call him Rose.

• •

We made Houston before dawn. At the outskirts of the city Rose turned off the main highway. I asked where we were going and he said to see a doctor.

My wound had crusted up pretty good and the bleeding was down to a seep. It still hurt but not as bad as before, maybe because I was slightly crocked from the bottle of rum Rose pulled out from under the seat. He had told me it was the shooter with the automatic who got me—just before Rose nailed him. I'd asked about the two guys on the sidewalk and he said, "Mangan and Lucas. Good men. Hate losing them."

We hadn't said much else on the drive. We'd watched the road steadily zooming under us as we sped through the night, splattering jackrabbits caught in the headlights, listening to whatever music we could pick up on coming-and-going radio stations, mostly Western swing stuff. We stopped at all-night stations to fill the tank. I didn't know where we were going and I didn't care, as long as it was away from San Antonio. The only thing I was sorry to leave behind was the roll of $250 I'd hidden in a baseboard niche under the bed. For most of the ride I just sipped at the rum and kept dozing off.

We drove down a ritzylooking residential street lined with high trees and wide sidewalks. The lawns were big and neatly trimmed, the cars all luxury models. He wheeled into the side driveway of a large two-story and parked deep in the shadows. He helped me out of the car and around to a small side porch and must've pushed a secret button or something because a minute later a light came on in the kitchen and the door opened and a neatly barbered and bespectacled man in a shiny black bathrobe said for us to come in.

His name was Dr. Monroe and he was a whiz. Less than an hour later we were back in the car and I was feeling no pain except for a mild rum headache. According to the doc the bullet had passed through the big muscle that ran along my side and had slightly scraped a rib but damaged nothing but tissue. He cleaned the wound and treated it with sulfa and bandaged it up, then gave me an injection to dull the pain and said to take it easy for a few days. He said any doctor or a good nurse could remove the stitches when they were ready to come out. Rose said, "Hell, they won't be the first I took out."

We stopped at a café overlooking the ship channel and I waited in the car and watched the reddening sky while Rose went in to buy a sack of beignets. He said the place made the best ones in Texas. It was the first time I'd heard the word and it must've shown on my face. As he stepped up to the bakery door he looked back at me and tapped a sign on the window: FRESH BEIGNETS. When he got back to the car he had already finished one and was licking his fingers. I took a look in the sack and saw little thick squares of fried dough covered with powdered sugar. They smelled wonderful. I was still a little dopey from the injection but I was hungry too. The things tasted great.

"It's the same as a doughnut except it's square and don't have a hole in it," Rose said. He took another one from the sack and held it in his mouth while he worked the steering wheel and gearshift and got us rolling again.

"Yeah," I said. "Like a circle's the same as a square except it's round and got no corners."

His smile was outlined with powdered sugar. "Got us a fucken wiseguy."

He'd bought a newspaper from a hawker in front of the bakery and said for me to take a look at the bottom of the front page. The report must've just made it under the edition deadline: SIX SLAIN IN SAN ANTONIO GUN BATTLE. He'd already skimmed it but wanted me to read it to him, so I did. The report quoted several witnesses who came to the door of Domingo's when they heard the gunfire but most of them ducked back out of sight when they saw the gunmen shooting it out in front of the restaurant. Only one patron and a waiter kept on taking peeks at the action from around the door. The patron told police he saw at least a dozen men blazing away at each other, all of them Mexicans, and then some ran away down the street and some drove off in a green Ford touring car. The waiter agreed that it had been about a dozen, but he said only one had run away while another three got in a gray DeSoto to make their getaway. He too was sure all the principals were Mexicans. Police had identified four of the dead as members of a local criminal gang and speculated that the gunfight was the result of a dispute over gambling jurisdictions.

"Eyewitnesses," Rose said. "God love them."

"What was it about?" I said.

"Money," he said. "What else?"

I waited to hear more but that was all he ever said to me about it.

We were on the causeway and I was gawking at Galveston Bay gleaming like pink glass under the low sun when he asked if I wanted a job. I said doing what and he said making sure people didn't fuck with him or his brother or get away with it if they did.

"Let me tell you, kid, I think maybe it's the job for you."

I said maybe it was.

A half-hour later we were in the Club office and he'd introduced me to Sam and Artie and Mrs. Bianco. And then, with just me and him and Sam in the office, he reenacted the gunfight for Sam's benefit, showing how he'd ducked behind the car when he heard me holler a warning and flicking his fingers beside his ears to show what happened to Lucas' head when the double load of buckshot hit him. He waved his arms around as he described the bullets ricocheting off the wall behind him and punching holes in the car windows. He made gunshot noises and slapped his hand to his head or chest when he described somebody getting hit. He mimicked pistols with his thumbs and index fingers as he showed how I stood in the middle of the street shooting right and left and how I whirled around to shoot the guy at the Buick about seven or eight times.

He told Sam it was like watching Billy the Kid in action.

"Only this one's *Jimmy* the Kid!" Sam said—and he slapped me on the back and then hugged me hard.

Watkins was the referee and a club rat named Wagner was working the bell. It rang for round one and Otis and I came out of our corners and touched gloves and fast as a blink he lunged and hit me with a right lead that made the room wobble. I staggered backward and he stayed on top of me, working the jabs hard in my face, each one stinging pretty good, since we weren't using headgear—and then *bam-bam* he drilled me with a left-right to the forehead and under the eye and I slid along the ropes and sat down hard.

The club rats were whooping and hollering and some were yelling for Otis to finish me and some for me to get up, goddammit, get *up*. They were five-deep around the ring. Otis went to a neutral corner and Watkins started the count over me. I got up on one knee, everything a little blurry at the edges. I took the count to eight and stood up.

Otis popped me some more good ones but I clinched him every chance I got—getting boos from the rats. Every time I hugged him, though, Otis showed how seriously he was taking things by giving me shots to the short ribs and awful close to the kidneys. The round seemed to last three days instead of three minutes before Wagner hit the bell. Otis worked his mouthpiece forward with his tongue and pinched it out with the thumb of his glove and grinned at me.

A rat named Hickey was working my corner. He rinsed my mouthpiece and sponged my face and said, "You got him now, Jimmyboy. He's an old man, he's already wearing out."

I wanted to say that if he was wearing out it was from hitting me so much, but figured I'd be wiser to save my breath. My right cheek felt bloated and my ribs were half-numb.

The bell clanged and we got back to it. I was still a little fluttery in the legs. We circled and kept trading jabs and he now and then hooked me to the ribs to remind me that they needed protection too. He made me wish I had four arms. We were pretty close to the end of the round when he got careless and threw a lazy right hook behind a jab and I was able to whip a left over his right and catch him solid just above the jaw. He backpedaled into the ropes and I went at him with both hands and the club rats were howling like Indians but Otis covered up expertly and I couldn't do any more real damage to him before the bell sounded.

"Whooo!" Hickey said, toweling me, giving me water, holding the bucket for me to spit into. "He's all yours, Jimmy—you about crossed his eyes for good with that left. *Wow!*"

What I'd really done was make Otis steaming mad—just like the last time we'd sparred. But this time he had a full round left to exercise his displeasure on me.

He knocked me down four times in the next two minutes. I took an eight-count before getting up again each time. I was up on one knee after the fourth knockdown—hearing the club rats' clamor and Watkins shouting the count as he swung his arm over me—and I looked over and saw Otis grinning at me from the other corner.

He yelled, "Some fun, hey?"

Son of a bitch.

". . . Eight! . . ." Watkins shouted—and I stood up.

Watkins leaned in close like he was checking the laces on my gloves and said just loud enough for me to hear: "Christ, man, enough. It's a minute to go. Stay away from him." He stepped back and waved us at each other.

Otis came at me on his toes and rapped me with three hard jabs and easily dodged my hook. Bastard was *playing* with me, dropping his hands to his waist and juking from side to side like he was daring me to land a punch, smiling around his mouthpiece.

He popped me twice more with the jab and then drew his right hand way back and began whirling it all around like he was winding up a haymaker. He looked over at the rats in the front row and waggled his brows like he was saying Watch *this* now.

He shouldn't have taken his eyes off me. I leaped and grabbed him in a headlock and started punching him in the face as hard and fast as I could.

For a second the rats went mute—and then all them were shrieking "Foul! . . . *Foul!*"

He twisted and pulled and we reeled around the ring every which way but I kept punching and punching, feeling his nose give way, vaguely aware of Watkins trying to pull me off him.

Otis tried to punch me in the balls and I hit him even harder. I forced his head lower and then clubbed him behind the neck and brought my knee up hard in his face. He sailed back into the ropes and flopped down, losing his mouthpiece, his nose pouring blood.

Like any pro fighter who gets knocked almost unconscious, his instinct was to get on his feet fast, to beat the count, his body trying to get off the canvas even while his brain was still bouncing around in his skull. He got to his hands and knees and fell over on his side, wallowing like a drunk, trying again to get up.

Watkins had me in a bearhug from behind, pulling me back from Otis and cussing me. I said to let go but he didn't—maybe he couldn't hear me for all the racket the rats were making. I stomped on his instep and that did the trick. He let out a yelp and hopped over to the ropes to keep from falling.

Our gloves weren't taped, so I clamped one in my armpit and yanked my hand free of it, then pulled off the other glove. Otis was up now and he swayed against the ropes for a second and then his eyes focused on me. Blood was running over his mouth and off his chin.

I raised my taped hands and gestured for him to come at me. For a second I thought he'd do it—but he must've read my eyes, and he wasn't stupid. He spat a mouthful of blood on the canvas between us and stayed put.

"Some fun, hey?" I said.

"Fuck you," he said, his voice thick.

He managed to climb down from the ring without help, then walked stiffly across the gym and into his little office and closed the door.

Watkins was tearful with pain, sitting on the canvas and holding his foot. The rats had shut up and were gawking at me. They backed away as I stepped out between the ropes.

I got a towel from the stack and started for the showers—and caught sight of Rose turning away from the gym door.

• •

When I went to the office a little later, Sam was in the outer room chatting with Mrs. Bianco. He grinned big when he saw me. Mrs. Bianco looked pained.

"Well hell, Kid, I can see why Otis got you a little peeved. You looked in the mirror lately?"

Of course I had. And seen my swollen ears and eyebrows, the large mouse under my right eye.

"I hear you might have a little trouble finding sparring partners from now on," Sam said. He put up his fists and made a bob-and-weave motion, then slapped me on the shoulder. "Jimmy the Kid! By hook or by crook, goddammit, he don't lose."

Mrs. Bianco nodded toward Rose's office and I went on in.

Rose looked up from some papers in front of him. His face had no expression—which meant he was mad as hell and trying to hide it.

"Good thing Otis had better sense than you and walked away," he said. "We don't need headlines about somebody getting crippled in our health club. A health club is supposed to be *good* for your fucken health. Guy gets the shit beat out of him in a health club in front of a bunch of witnesses—especially a guy supposed to be in charge of things—well, word gets around, people say, What the fuck kinda health club is *that*?—know what I mean?"

It wasn't a question so I kept my mouth shut.

"You want to use the gym from now on, you do it at night, when there's nobody else there—except maybe me. And no more sparring, not with nobody. Let's give Otis and the squarejohns a chance to settle their nerves."

"Okay," I said.

"Okay," he said. "Heard anything that might connect to Dallas?"

He always could switch the subject that fast. One thing done with, on to the next.

"Nothing," I said. "I'd say Sam called it right."

"Maybe so. Stick around the Club for another coupla days. If Dallas don't move by then, I got some out-of-town jobs need your attention."

"Just say the word."

Then I thought of Daniela, and the idea of leaving town for a while lacked its usual spark.

I was at the door when he called out, "Say, Kid," and I turned.

"Next time we're in the gym, teach me that move with the knee."

"Sure thing, Don Rosario."

• •

She answered my knock on the Avila's door at exactly six-thirty—and her smile fell away when she saw my face.

"Ay, dios. Qué . . . What happened?" Her hand started for my face and then withdrew uncertainly, as if she were afraid of causing me pain.

"Sparring at the gym," I said, clarifying the word for her by raising my fists and tucking in my chin. "Boxeando. I should've known better than to spar with a pro."

"Pro?"

"Professional." I told her the sparring had gotten a little too intense, that an amateur should never get intense with a pro. I said I had used bad judgment. "It looks worse than it feels," I said.

She gingerly touched the mouse under my eye. When she put a fingertip to my bruised lip I kissed it. Her eyes widened—and then she drew her hand away when Señora Avila called from the kitchen, asking if I was at the door.

The señora came into the room, drying her hands on a dish towel—and then saw me and said, "Ay, *hijo*—pero que te *paso*?"

I had to explain again about the sparring. She shook her head and said men should not fight for fun, that there was already too much real cause for fighting in the world. She asked if I would like something to eat, if my mouth did not hurt too much. I thanked her and said I'd already eaten. I'd seen her husband at the Casa Verde before I left. Gregorio was having his weekly neighborhood poker game in the kitchen, the radio tuned loudly to a Mexican station out of

Houston, the icebox packed with beer, the counter full of bowls of fried chiles and chicharrones. Back during my first weeks in La Colonia, I'd accepted the group's invitation to sit in on the game, but right from the start I sensed the other men's nervousness and I could tell that none of them was playing his best—except for Gregorio, whose best wasn't worth a damn anyway. They weren't raising me when they should've, they weren't calling my bluffs. After an hour of play I made some excuse and took my leave, and although I was invited to the game every week for weeks afterward, I always begged off, and finally they were able not to ask me anymore.

Daniela went to the sofa to fetch the straw bag containing her towel and other things. I was wearing my swim trunks under my pants and my towel was in the car. Just then, Rocha entered from the hallway, his head bandage freshly changed but still held in place by the sillylooking ribbon. He paused when he saw me—his eyes running over my beat-up face—and then busted out laughing.

"Felipe!" Señora Avila chided him for his amusement in my disfigurement. "No es cosa cómica. No seas tan bruto, por amor de dios!"

He just laughed harder. For a second I had an urge to go in there and bust his nose for him, see how funny he thought *that* was. He slumped against the wall and bumped his head slightly and winced and put his hand to the ridiculous bandage but kept on laughing.

And then I just couldn't help it and started laughing along with him.

The women looked at us like we'd lost our minds. Daniela gawked at the señora and the woman shook her head and shrugged and the expressions on their faces made me and Rocha laugh even harder.

Mrs. Avila's aspect became a little anxious. "*Ya,* locos!" she said.

Daniela's eyes on me were large. I waved a hand at her like it was nothing to be concerned about, and I worked to get myself under control. Rocha wiped at his eyes with a dirty bandanna and straightened up. And then we looked at each other and broke up again.

It took another half-minute but we finally got a grip on ourselves. Rocha had to dry his eyes again and he blew his nose and tucked away the bandanna. He looked at me and we grinned but didn't go into another laughing fit. He cleared his throat and asked if I'd like a bottle of beer.

I thanked him but said maybe later. He nodded and raised a hand at me and went off to the kitchen, chuckling low.

Mrs. Avila said we were both crazy as goats and then kissed Daniela on the cheek and said she should have a good time but to be home by ten o'clock. She gave me a tight look of maternal warning and I nodded, which I thought was vague enough to keep from being an outright promise. The señora stood in the doorway and watched us go out to the Terraplane convertible I'd borrowed from the Club. It was a warm night and I'd already put the top down.

The road from Brownsville to Kingsville runs straight north and the sparse traffic moves fast. They make good time to Corpus Christi before being slowed by one stoplight after another. The coastal lowland is a patchwork terrain of swamp and scrubland and grazing pasture, and Gustavo remarks that it looks the same as the gulf country in Mexico. Angel tells him this region was part of Mexico at one time, before the gringos stole it for themselves about ninety years ago. The information comes as outrageous news to Gustavo and he falls to a fit of low cursing of every gringo ever born, be he dead or alive.

They take turns trying to nap in the backseat of the car while the other drives but their sleep is fitful at best and both of them are left unrested and irritated.

At sundown the sky is the color of raw beef. They stop at a roadside café called La Mexicana to have an early supper. Angel orders pork tacos and Gustavo goes for the chicken enchiladas and both of them are greatly disappointed with the food. When they go to pay at the register, Gustavo tells the cashier that the food isn't fit for pigs, but she is an Anglo woman who speaks no Spanish and only stares apprehensively at their hard brown faces.

Then they are on the road again, bearing into the darkness of the newrisen night.

I turned west at the seawall, away from the bright lights of the boulevard's good-time joints. The sky was clear, the stars thick and blazing in the east, dimmer in the west, where the moon was gleaming like a silver egg high above the gulf. She laughed at the pleasure of her hair whipping in the wind and had to keep brushing it from her eyes. The radio was tuned to a big-band station and she swayed to the rhythms of "I Get a Kick Out of You." The Hollywood Dinner Club's big spotlight beam was revolving in the sky ahead of us and off to our right. She said the Avilas had told her all about the Hollywood, even though they themselves had never set foot inside. They had told her it was as luxurious as a palace, that it belonged to the man I worked for.

"Him and his brother," I said. "Would you like to go dancing there sometime? They have swell dance bands."

"Swell?"

"Very good. Excellent."

She slid closer to me on the seat and hooked her arm around my elbow. I felt the light press of her breast against my arm, the touch of her thigh against my leg. "I think that is a swell idea," she said.

I drove almost all the way out to the west end of the island before turning off onto a narrow hardpacked access road that connected to a stretch of beach hardly anyone ever used except for a few daytime fishermen. The Hollywood spotlight was far behind us now and we could no longer see the glow of the city lights. I parked alongside a row of dunes and cut the lights and motor. The tide was in, and we sat in the car, listening to a mild surf lapping along the beach. The gulf was almost placid, its waves low and gentle and gleaming bright under the moon.

"It's beautiful," she said.

"It's the same water you swam in at Veracruz. But like I warned you, girl—it's probably colder right now than what you're used to."

She slapped my shoulder playfully and said, "I am not so afraid of cold water as someone I know." Then slid across the seat and got out of the car.

I stepped out and stripped down to my bathing trunks and tossed my clothes on the car roof. The Mexican Colt was under the driver's seat. When she came around the car she had her dress in one hand and her bag in the other and she placed them both on the hood of the Terraplane.

The bathing suit she wore was a stunner—a black sleek thing that clung to her like a second skin. It rode high on her legs and was held up by a pair of thin straps and was cut so low in the front it exposed the tops of her breasts. She held out her arms and did a model's pirouette and I saw that the suit was backless almost to her waist. If she'd worn that thing on a public beach she would've been arrested for indecent exposure. My dick swelled in my swimsuit.

"It was made in France. I bought it from a catalog but I have not worn it until now. If it shocks you I can put my dress on and swim in that." She could probably read my face in the moonlight. Her voice was full of fun.

"No. It's fine. It's . . . I like it."

She laughed. "I thought perhaps you would."

She reached in the bag and took out a folded cotton bedsheet and handed it to me. "So we don't have to sit on the sand," she said.

As I spread the sheet out on the sand, she ran into the water, her legs flashing, her hair flying. She took long splashing strides until the water was to her thighs and then dove into a swell. She came up about ten yards beyond where she'd gone under, then stood in water as deep as her breasts, her hair plastered to her head and shoulders. She waved to me and yelled, "Come on, pollito—it's not so cold! Don't be afraid to get your feathers wet!"

I ran in. It wasn't as cold as it could've been but was cold enough. I whooped and dove and came up sputtering. I trudged toward her through the waist-deep water and she laughed and began backstroking away.

I dove again and started swimming hard, but every time I paused to look ahead of me I saw that she had put even more distance between us, backstroking smoothly, moving through the water as lightly as a canoe.

I swam on in my clumsy fashion, forcing myself to breathe in rhythm with my strokes. The next time I looked in front of me she was treading water twenty feet away, watching me. I stroked on, then stopped and looked again and couldn't see her. Then heard her laughter and saw that she had moved off to my left.

"What's the matter, Mr. Youngblood? Are you lost?" I could see the whiteness of her teeth. She went into a smooth crawl, heading for open water. I swam after her.

She went out a long way before she finally stopped and turned around to watch me plodding toward her. When I got to within a few feet of her I stopped stroking. We were out farther than I'd ever been before. From way out here the beach was a thin pale strip in front of a vague dark line of dunes.

We treaded water, rising and falling on the mild swells. The moon was slightly behind me, its light on her face, her smile. I slowly sidestroked closer to her until we were within arm's length of each other. Her foot lightly brushed my leg. She reached out and touched my face.

Then her eyes shifted past me and went wide and she said in a whisper, "Ay, *dios* . . ."

I turned to look—and saw a black fin standing high against the light of the moon and cutting toward us like an enormous cleaver.

Twenty yards away . . . fifteen . . .

Daniela grabbed my arm and yanked me to her and swirled us around so that she was between it and me. I tried to get back in front of her but she held me off balance with an arm around my neck, pinning my head against her shoulder. She ordered me to pull my feet up under me as high as I could. She had the physical advantage over me in the water and I couldn't have broken loose of her except with a struggle that wouldn't have helped matters at all, so I drew my feet up and her legs pulled up against mine and she clutched me tightly to her, one arm still around my neck, the other around my chest.

The thing barreled past us, its rush so strong and close that the wash lifted and pushed us aside and I saw the white scars of buckshot and bullets in the monstrous fin. Its wake had a fiery sparkle and the tailfin hissed by like a scythe blade.

Daniela held me fast, turning us so we could see the phosphorescent streaks as it bore away.

Then it swung around and started back.

"Levanta los pies!" she said, nudging my leg—and I pulled my feet back up under me as high as I could. Her legs clamped up around mine and she held us in a tight bobbing tangle of arms and legs as the shark came at us again.

Daniela kicked at it as it bumped us. I saw grooves along the front of its wide flat hammerhead and saw the eye on its outer edge—black as a shotgun muzzle and twice the size. It knocked us aside as lightly as a ball of cork.

The high fin trailed its glimmering fire toward the moonbright horizon and then vanished under the surface.

"Vete!" Daniela said, pushing me off toward the distant beach.

I swam—fighting down the fear that surged at the thought of the thing turning around and coming for us again, this time from underneath and with its jaws wide.

She could've made it back to the beach in half the time it took me, but she stayed at my side, swimming easily and slowly and with hardly a sound, while I stroked as hard as I could, busting up the water and gulping mouthfuls of it and huffing like a bellows. I had no idea how long it was before we were in water shallow enough to stand up in. I hacked out some of the water I'd swallowed and we slogged out of the surf and staggered over to the bedsheet and sprawled onto it.

I lay on my back, panting, staring up at the stars. She hugged my chest and pressed herself against me, her face on my neck, her breath rapid and warm on my skin.

When I was finally able to talk, I said, "Jesus *Christ*!"

"I have never seen a martillo so big."

"*Whooo!* It had to be that Black Tom bastard they tell about. They say it's been around here forever. They say it's eaten more than a dozen men over the years. They say it once ate a goddamn *rowboat*—and the two guys in it."

"Then we must thank God we were not in a . . . goddamn rowboat," she said.

My laughter started me coughing again. I propped myself up on an elbow and got the fit under control.

"What made you think," I said between hard breaths, "of pulling up our legs?"

"My father was a fisherman. He knew very much about sharks. But he said the trick does not always work."

Her eyes were bright and wide, her breasts pumping. I'd nearly pissed at the sight of that monster. And she'd kicked it.

I put my hand on her leg and she lost her smile and for a moment I thought maybe I was pushing things. Then she hooked a hand around my neck and pulled my face down to hers.

We kissed long and hard. Our tongues got into it. I stroked her leg and then moved my hand to her breast and she made a low sound. I pushed the straps off her shoulders and tugged down her top. Her nipples were erect under my fingertips. I put my lips to them, my tongue, and she arched her back and pulled my face harder against her. She slid a hand down my chest and belly and into my trunks and closed it around my erection.

We slipped off our suits. She sucked a deep breath when I entered her. Her legs clamped tight around mine and we rocked and rocked and it couldn't have been a minute before I came and collapsed on her like I'd been clubbed, my face against her neck and hers against mine, both of us gasping like we were trying to inhale each other from under our skins.

After a while we were kissing again, stroking each other's hips and ass. My cock hardened inside her. We started rocking once more, this time more slowly and gently. I had better control now and held myself back until I sensed her getting close—and just as she arched against me and gave a high moan I let myself go.

We held to each other and didn't talk much as the night grew cooler. The moon was a lot closer to the gulf when she whispered that Señora Avila would be worried. We hugged and kissed and the press of her breasts and belly started rousing me again. She laughed low against my ear and then rolled away and stood up and went to retrieve her dress from the car hood, saying we really shouldn't make Señora Avila worry. So I got up and got dressed and put the top up on the Terraplane. We kissed a few times more in the car and then I got us rolling.

It was a little past ten o'clock. She was right that Mrs. Avila would be anxious. She snuggled against me and hugged my arm, her legs folded under her on the car seat, her skirt high on her thighs. Her face was against my shoulder and her damp hair smelled of the sea. We rolled along without talking, just listening to the radio—"Temptation," "Begin the Beguine." She knew "Red Sails in the Sunset" in Spanish and softly sang along with the instrumental.

I supposed there was really no reason to be surprised that she was so bold about sex. Anybody as brave as she'd been with that hammerhead wasn't likely to be afraid of too many things or be one for coyness. Except for whores, though, I'd never met a Mexican girl so sexually direct. Most Mex girls of respectable family made at least a show of being good girls, and most actually stayed virgin till their wedding night. But Daniela was no virgin, and I wondered how she'd lost it, especially since she was hardly more than a kid. But I didn't wonder about it for long—because when you got right down to it, what the hell difference did it make?

• •

The Avila porch light was on, of course, and light showed in all the windows. At the end of the street the Casa Verde was all lit up too, the card game still in progress. I parked in the shadows of an oak in front of the Avila house. We were kissing goodnight when the screendoor screeched and the señora came out to the top step and looked at us with a theatrical hand over her eyes like she was scouting the open sea under a bright sun.

In the darkness of the car, Daniela giggled and held my hand pressed to her breast. She kissed me and said, "I must go."

"Will you have breakfast with me tomorrow?"

"Of course." She put a hand to my face and kissed me again.

"Seven?" I said.

"Yes."

I got out and went around to her side of the car and opened the door for her and she slung her bag over her shoulder and I held her hand as we went up the dirt walkway to the Avila porch, where the señora stood with her arms out to receive the girl.

"Goodnight," she said. "I had a very lovely time."

I raised her hand to my lips.

"Ya, *basta*!" Mrs. Avila said, coming down to put an arm around the girl and pull her away. Daniela said goodnight again and laughed like a child as she allowed Mrs. Avila to steer her around and up the porch steps.

At the door she looked back at me to smile and wave and I raised my hand to her. Then the screendoor slapped shut and the wooden door closed behind it.

• •

I parked the Terraplane next to the rickety fence in front of the Casa Verde, and as I clumped up the porch steps and entered the parlor I heard laughter and radio music and good-natured cursings coming from the kitchen. The house smelled of cigarette smoke and fried chiles. I went to the kitchen doorway and saw Pablo Lopez laughing and pulling in a pot at the table. They were all happily half-drunk. The countertop was littered with empty beer bottles and the sink crammed with greasy plates.

Gregorio looked over at me and said, "Qué tal, joven? Como te va?" Then he frowned slightly and I remembered what my face looked like.

I said everything was fine as could be, and he shrugged and said, "Ya lo creo." I exchanged hellos with the others at the table and they also refrained from remarking on my bruises. All this time as their neighbor and I still made them nervous. I fetched a beer from the ice-box and leaned against the counter and watched Morales form up the deck and begin shuffling.

There was an awkward silence while "Arbolito" played on the radio and then Gregorio asked if I wanted to sit in. The others all nodded and said yes, join us, please, and so forth. I said no, thanks, I was tired and going to bed in a minute. Avila's wife must've told him of Daniela's date with me, but of course he would make no mention of it. I was debating whether to tell them of our adventure with Black Tom when Gregorio asked if I'd seen my telephone message on the slateboard. I hadn't. The only messages I'd ever received at the Casa Verde had been from the office and I hadn't gotten one in so long that I rarely even glanced at the board anymore when I came into the house.

I went down the hall and saw "llamo el clobb—10:06 pm" scrawled on the slate next to the phone. I picked up the earpiece and dialed Rose's number and he answered on the first ring.

"Youngblood," I said.

"Where the fuck *you* been?"

I started to tell him but he said, "Never mind—just get your ass down here."

"What is it?"

"Micks. Now get over here." He hung up.

I figured I'd better be prepared for anything, so I went up to my room and packed a small valise. I put the .380 in the bag and took off my coat and put on the shoulder holster and slipped the Mexican .44 in it and put my coat back on. Then I went back downstairs and put the valise on the table by the phone and went into the kitchen. The game had just broken up and some of them were laughing and counting their money and some were bitching about their rotten luck, and then they all shut up and looked at me.

I told Avila that Daniela was expecting me to take her to breakfast in the morning but something had come up and I might not be able to meet her as I'd said. I said to tell her I didn't know how long I would be away, maybe only until later tomorrow, maybe a few days, but in any case I would call on her as soon as I returned.

"Sí, claro, le daré el mensaje," Avila said, nodding rapidly.

"Okay then," I said.

They'd hit the team that made the nightly cash collection from the joints along the north end of the county—including all the places where Ragsdale had put in the Dallas slots. The two Ghosts had come out of a little club in Dickinson with the next-to-last pickup of the night and had just got in their car in the parking lot when a black Hudson sedan pulled up beside them and the men at the passenger-side windows opened fire with .45 automatics. The Ghost behind the wheel took hits in the head and died in a blink but our other guy—a fellow named Dooley—managed to tumble out the right-side door and run off with the attackers chasing him on foot and still shooting at him and he made it into the woods behind the club and hid in the darkness. He stayed crouched in the bushes and tried not to even breathe. He wouldn't know it until after he was taken to the hospital but he'd been hit three times. He heard the shooters walking along the edge of the woods and cursing. He heard one of them say "Pete's gonna shit." Then he heard them walking away on the parking lot gravel and then somebody yelled something and there were a few more pistol shots and a moment later the Hudson went tearing out of the parking lot.

The last few patrons who'd been in the club would tell the police they heard the shooting and came out and saw two men walking back toward a pair of cars parked side by side. One of the men fired shots over their heads and the patrons all ran back inside and the shooter fired several rounds through the glass front window and they all hit the floor. The owner of the joint had crawled over to the telephone and called the police. What the owner didn't tell the cops was that he also made a call to the Turf Club. After a while one of the patrons had peeked outside and saw that one of the cars was gone but the other car was still there—and then saw another man come staggering from behind the club and into the lot and fall down, but everybody in the club was too scared to go out and help him. Then the cops showed up.

The witnesses had all been smart enough not to spill too much to the police. They all said they'd never seen either of the two victims before. None of them had been sure of the make of car the shooters were in or if there had been another man in the car. Dooley the wounded Ghost feigned unconsciousness to avoid being questioned. Then one of Rose's lawyers showed up ahead of the ambulance and had a private moment with Dooley before the ambulance guys took him away. He got the story from Dooley and told him what to tell the cops when they questioned him in the hospital. The lawyer then had a talk with the sergeant in charge of the investigation. Then he and the sergeant went to the station and chatted with the captain. When the official report was released it detailed a homicide by unknown assailants during the commission of an armed robbery and said the perpetrators stole nothing more than the wallet of the murder victim. The report made no mention of the Maceo name or that the guys in the Hudson had made off with more than two grand of collection cash.

"I figure they been checking us out the last few days," Rose said. "They knew the places where Willie Rags put in those slots and they cased the route. They picked the Dickinson club for the hit because it's on an open stretch of road, not much else around there, not many witnesses passing by. It makes for an easy getaway."

It was nearly eleven-thirty and we were sitting in the office, me and him and Sam. I asked Rose what made him so sure it was the Dallas micks.

"Who else?" Rose said. "They hit the collection on the slots those Dallas fucks think belong to them. It aint coincidence."

"What if the robbers were just anybody and didn't know what route they were hitting?" I said. "And if it *was* Dallas, what would be their point? They couldn't expect the take to cover the worth of the machines they lost."

"Their *point,*" Rose said, "is to try to fuck with our business, to scare the piss out of our customers, make us think it can happen again, make us wonder when and where, maybe get us to reconsider their offer to negotiate. *That's* their fucking point. Or maybe they just wanted to do something to *feel* better about losing their goddamn machines. That would sure as shit be *my* point."

He blew out a hard breath and ran a hand through his hair. He was smoking mad. Outsiders had not only robbed his men, they had done it on his own turf.

"We're not just guessing it was them," Sam said. He slid a photograph across the desk to me. I turned it around and regarded the picture of a beefy, well-dressed blond guy sitting in a circular booth and showing his big white teeth at the camera, a goodlooking woman on either side of him. He was close to handsome even with a small scar over one eye and a nose that had been broken sometime. His eyes were so lightcolored they seemed to have no irises at all.

"That's Healy," Sam said. "*Peter* Healy. Pete Healy. As in 'Pete's gonna shit.' "

I looked up from the picture and Rose was showing that smile of his that had nothing in it that smiles are supposed to have.

"I don't move on just a guess, Kid," he said. "You oughta know that by now. And I aint been sitting on my hands these last few days. While they been checking us out I been checking *them* out. This Healy's got a rep. He's a comer, a hardass. Got his start on the loading docks in New Orleans but the word is he killed a guy and took off to Fort Worth. Got in with the Carlson bunch. Then he moved over to the Burke outfit in Dallas. Went on his own over a year ago and took a gorilla named Parker with him. Parker used to do muscle and clip-work for Burke. Six-four, two-seventy they say, scares everybody shit-less. Healy was already getting a piece of most of the slots in both Tarrant *and* Dallas County. Now he owns *all* the machines up there."

"The Fort Worth and Dallas outfits are afraid he's getting too ambitious," Sam said. "Afraid he might start moving in on their gambling clubs, maybe the cathouses."

"Those Dallas guys are pussies in cowboy hats," Rose said. "Too scared to put the fucker in his place—six feet under."

"Healy keeps beating them to the punch," Sam said. "He popped Lou Morgan, Carlson's main muscle—and I mean *he* did it. Went up to Morgan in some little sandwich joint and boom-boom, two times in the head and walked out cool as could be. Broad daylight, a dozen people in there, and nobody saw a thing. The Parker guy's a piece of work too. He took down two of Burke's biggest palookas in an alley fight. Bit one's nose and ear off. Broke the other one's back."

"It's getting close to a fucken war up there," Rose said. "A month ago one of Healy's biggest joints burned down. Next day three of Burke's best boys vanish. A week later one of them pops up in White Rock Lake. They drag the lake and bring up a car with the other two guys in it. All three had a bullet behind the ear. Persons unknown, the cops said, but the outfits know who it was."

"With so much going on up there," I said, "why would Healy start trouble with us by moving his machines down here?"

"That was Ragsdale's doing," Sam said. "Willie Rags contracted the slots from Healy and told him he was going to put them in Houston, Beaumont, Port Arthur, all over the oil patch. But then he got ambitious. Thought he'd impress Healy by getting some of them into Galveston County."

"So Healy's big mistake was dealing with Ragsdale," I said.

"No, that was only his *first* mistake," Rose said. "His second mistake was thinking the slots still belonged to him. Then he hit my guys . . . *that* was his big fucken mistake."

"I guess I'm off to Dallas," I said.

"I want it done yesterday," Rose said. He took two envelopes out of his top drawer and tossed them to me. One contained expense money, the other a city map of Dallas with exact directions to Healy's office and to his home, and map markings showing the locations of several of his favorite restaurants and bars.

"Parker too," Rose said.

"We talked to the Fort Worth and Dallas outfits an hour ago," Sam said. "We'll be settling our thing with Healy but we'll be doing them a hell of a favor too—Healy out of their hair and their hands clean, nothing to hide from the cops. But they want Parker out too, and to show their appreciation they ponied up a big advance on a contract to buy all their machines from us from now on."

"The least they can do," I said.

"You and your partners will get a bonus on this one," Sam said with a grin. "The least *we* can do."

I stared at Rose. He almost smiled—then looked at his watch.

I got going.

• •

The phone rang and rang before somebody finally picked up. A woman. "Jesus . . . *what*?" she said.

"Sheila?" I said.

There was a moment's hesitation, and then, in barely above a whisper: "Who's this?" One of those who never knew when one beau might call while she was with another.

"Let me talk to LQ," I said.

"*Huh?* Say, who *is* this?" I could tell by her voice she was half in the bag. "You know what time it is? Do I know you?"

"Just put him on the phone, will you, sugar? It's *real* important."

The softer tone and the "sugar" did the trick. "Well . . . he's sleeping pretty hard right now."

"He's passed out, you mean?"

"I don't know if I'd say *that*. Just he's sleeping pretty hard and it'd take a while to wake him, I think. Say, now, don't I *know* you . . . ?"

"How about Brando?"

"Who?"

"Ray."

"Oh . . . Just a minute, I'll go look."

The phone clunked down and then I heard her voice at a distance but couldn't make out what she was saying. After a minute somebody picked up the phone and coughed and said, "Yeah?" Brando.

"It's me. Tell me how to get there. We got work."

He gave me directions to Sheila's house and then said, "Where we headed?"

I gave him a rundown on what happened to our men in Dickinson and what the job was. "I'm on the way to the ferry right now," I said. "See you in about three hours. Be sure the Dodge is gassed."

"It's gassed already. Listen, me and LQ aint got but pistols. If we gonna need—"

"I already saw Richardson and got two Remington pumps with buckshot loads," I said. Richardson was a graybeard who ran a hardware store in town but his real business was guns. He could get you any kind you wanted in almost any quantity. He even made after-hours deals at his home—his attic was an arsenal. He did a lucrative trade with Maceo men.

"Pumps," Brando said. "Outstanding."

"Be ready, both of you."

• •

The Dodge was parked at the curb in front of the house. I pulled up behind it and snapped off the radio in the middle of "Limehouse Blues." It was close to four o'clock. The moon had set behind the pines but there were only a few thin clouds and the stars were thick and bright. There was an old Ford coupe in the driveway. The living room window showed light behind the curtain. I gunned the engine a couple of times and somebody pulled the curtain aside just enough to peek out and then let it fall back. Then the house went dark and the front door opened and LQ and Brando came out with their bags. The women stepped out with them and there was a lot of hugging and kissing and patting of asses while I locked up the Terraplane.

I put my valise in the trunk of the Dodge and got in the backseat. LQ and Brando came over and put their Gladstones in the truck too. There was a smaller bag with the pickup money and LQ jammed it under the front seat.

"You drive," he told Brando, and settled himself by the shotgun window. Brando went around and got behind the wheel and cranked up the motor.

"Too bad that Terraplane seats only two inside," Brando said. "I'd like to drive that honey to Dallas."

"We took that honey to Dallas I'd be driving and you'd be the one riding in the rumble seat," LQ said.

"Drive *this,*" Brando said, jacking his fist. He got us rolling. The radio started blaring "Stardust" and he turned the volume down.

"Goddamn day would have to have a lot more than twenty-four hours in it for you to've picked a lousier time to roust us," LQ said without looking back at me. I could tell by his voice he was still partly drunk.

"Twenty-seven o'clock," Brando said, and chuckled. "Thirty-three o'clock."

"It didn't take you three hours to pack a bag," I said. "While you've been sleeping it off some more I've been driving, so don't cry on my shoulder."

I took off my coat and balled it into a pillow and stretched out on the seat with my back toward them and closed my eyes.

"He don't sound real eager to hear about our good time, does he?" Brando said.

• •

The weather stayed pleasant with only a hint of chill. The day broke cloudless and the air smelled sweet and dry. They hadn't had a good look at my face till the morning light, and they naturally made a bunch of jokes about it—LQ saying it looked like I'd picked a fight with the wrong little girl—before I told them about the sparring match with Otis.

"Hellfire," LQ said, "I never did understand why you done all that boxing anyhow. Playfighting by a bunch of rules. That don't help a man a damn bit when he gets in a for-real fight. How you done *him* is proof of that."

"What I don't get," Brando said, "is why you waited till you got knocked on your ass so many times before you busted him up. First time he floored *me* would've been the last."

We stopped at a roadside café and took a booth in the back corner and all of us ordered coffee and cornbread, eggs and pork chops and grits. The waitress was a trim pretty thing in a tight skirt and we all gave her the once-over and she smiled at our attention.

She'd just walked off to the kitchen window with our orders when Brando said, "Oh man, I can't keep it to myself no more—you *gotta* hear this," and started telling me all about his fun with Cora Jane, the friend that Sheila had gotten for him. Cora Jane had done this to him, he said, she had done that, she had done everything. She had even shown him a couple of tricks he hadn't heard of.

He didn't shut up about Cora Jane till the waitress showed up with our breakfast plates. She fetched the coffeepot and refilled our cups and gave us all another pretty smile and said to just whistle if there was anything else we'd like.

LQ watched her sweetlooking ass walk away and whispered, "I got half a mind to *tell* her what I'd like . . ."

"You got half a mind, period," Brando said, then got back to the subject of Cora Jane. There was no denying he'd had himself a time.

"That Cora Jane sounds like a ball of fire," LQ said. He said Sheila was fun in bed but she liked her booze a little too much. After she'd been drinking a while he got the feeling she didn't really know who she was fucking or really care.

"Hell man," Brando said, "what difference does it make what's going on in her head as long as you get to put it to her?"

"Makes a difference," LQ said.

"You're never satisfied, that's your trouble. You expect too goddamn much."

"What the hell you know about it?" LQ said. "You'd hump a rockpile if you thought a snake was in it."

"Snake *this*."

• •

We got back on the road but took our time. We didn't want to get to Dallas till just about dark. Brando drove while LQ and I sat in the back and went over the maps and the directions to Healy's office and to his home. The routes had been clearly marked on the map in green ink. Because his house was a couple of miles south of downtown and not too far off the highway, we decided we'd check it first, even though it wasn't likely he'd be there at such an early hour. His office was in a downtown building a few blocks west of the city park and close to the railtracks. If we didn't find him there, either, we'd start checking his favorite hangouts.

We stopped at a roadside lunch wagon and bought hamburgers with all the trimmings and bottles of ice-cold Coke and ate the lunch at a picnic table in the shade of a tree. When we got going again, LQ was at the wheel while I went over the maps with Brando.

"What if he aint anywhere we look?" Brando said. "Could be we'll check someplace and he aint there and then we head for another place and he's headed for the place we just checked."

"We're not leaving Dallas till we put him down," I said. "If we don't find him tonight we'll hunt for him again in the morning. If we spot him in daylight we'll tail him till it's dark, then pick our best chance to do it. No daylight hit if we can help it. Too chancy."

"We could end up hunting him for days," Brando said. "What if we find him and he's got ten guys with him?"

"Damn poor odds, all right," LQ said. "To be fair we'd have to let him send for more guys."

His big grin filled the rearview and I gave him one back.

"Ha ha," Brando said. "I'm serious, man. What if we find Healy but the Parker guy's not with him? Or what if we find Parker first? As soon as we do one of them, the other's bound to hear about it and get set for us—or make himself too scarce to find."

"Parker's his main muscle," I said. "Wherever Healy's at, Parker's probably with him."

"One of these days I'd like to have a plan that aint got no prob'ly to it," LQ said.

"Be nice if Healy was home when we got there," Brando said. "And if there wasn't nobody with him but Parker."

"Yeah, that'd be nice, all right," LQ said. "And it'd be nice if they got killed in a car wreck today. Or if they both came down with a case of the blues so bad they shot theirselves and left a little note saying they just couldn't stand it no more and we heard about it on the radio as soon as we got to Dallas. *That'd* be nice."

• •

We passed the city-limit sign at dusk. LQ pulled off onto a side road and stopped the car and Brando got out and poured some Coke in the dust to make enough mud to smear on the license plates. He wiped his hands on a rag and got back in the car and we moved on. By the time we were making our slow way through the streets of Healy's neighborhood and reading the street signs by lamp-post light, the sky was dark and the moon fat and orange and just above the trees.

"It's the next right," LQ said from the backseat.

"I know it," Brando said.

"Don't slow down when we drive by," I said.

"I *know* it."

We made the turn onto Carpenter Street and I counted three houses down on the right. There was a dark-colored Chrysler parked in the driveway of the third house and a pair of men were just then coming out the front door and down the porch steps. One of them was a blond guy holding his hat and adjusting the crown crease with the edge of his hand. The streetlight showed Healy's face clearly—he looked just like his picture. The other guy was so big there was no question who he was. He must've said something funny because Healy laughed as he put on his hat. Parker gave us a glance as we passed by, but you could tell he was checking nothing but the car speed.

"Sweet Jesus," LQ said softly. "You *believe* this luck?"

I turned to look at them through the rear window and saw them getting in the Chrysler, Parker behind the wheel. I told Brando to take a slow right at the next corner, and as we made the turn I saw the Chrysler back out into the street and then head off in the other direction from us. And just-like-that, I had a plan.

"Take a right and floor it, man," I said. "Get us in front of them before they hit the highway."

Brando screeched the Dodge around the corner and gunned it down the street running parallel to Carpenter as I told them what I had in mind. LQ and I grabbed up the shotguns and jacked shells in the chambers. There was hardly any traffic on these residential blocks and we zoomed through three stop signs in a row and almost hit a scooting cat. We barreled up to a T-intersection and Brando had to brake sharp for it and take the turn pretty wide and we just did miss colliding with an oncoming car that went veering off the road.

"Yaaaa-hoooo!" LQ hollered.

We went barreling up the block and there was the Chrysler, coming from our right on Carpenter. Brando wheeled a hard left just in front of their car and Parker had to stomp his brakes to keep from ramming us. We came to a halt at the stop sign at the corner, the highway just another block ahead, and the Chrysler rolled up behind us with its klaxon blaring.

Parker stuck his big head out the window and shouted, *"You stupid shit!* I oughta yank you out of that car and rip your ass in half!"

There was one car coming our way from the direction of the highway and no traffic at all behind the Chrysler.

"Now," I said. LQ stepped out on one side of the car and I got out on the other and we swung up the shotguns. Behind the glare of the Chrysler's headlights Healy was just a dark shape on the other side of the windshield for an instant before the glass exploded in the blast of my Remington. LQ's shotgun boomed at the same time and we pumped fast and fired three more loads apiece and then scooted back into the Dodge. Brando sped us across the intersection and past the car stopped on the other side. Nobody in it could've seen our faces under our hat brims even if they'd tried to, especially not against our headlights' blaze. Hell, all they would remember was the flashing blasts.

Then we were on the highway and headed back south.

"Wooooo!" LQ yelled. "Yall see that big bastard's face when I pointed the pump at him? The surprise of his goddamn life. Half his head went all over the backseat. *Yow!*"

"Piece of cake," Brando said. "Just like I figured."

• •

An hour south of Dallas we stopped at a roadhouse and gorged on barbecue ribs and corn on the cob and shared two pitchers of beer. We were loud and happy and laughing like hell. Everything tasted great, every wisecrack was hilarious. Just being alive was a kind of aching pleasure from way deep inside.

"Listen," LQ said. "There's a place called Miss Jenny's just this side of Waco. Aint all that much out of our way. I hear it's worth every penny. Hell boys, we deserve us a *re*ward."

All I really wanted was to get back to Galveston, but Brando said "Damn right!" and I wasn't about to argue against their fun, so I said, "Why the hell not?"

We took the junction road to the Waco highway and got to Miss Jenny's an hour later. Because it was Sunday night, business was slower than usual and we didn't have to wait long before we got taken care of. I picked out a brownskinned girl that looked part Mexican but it turned out she was another one born and raised in the U.S. who couldn't speak but a few words of Spanish. She was enthusiastic but I had a little trouble finishing up until I closed my eyes and imagined Daniela—and then I came like a shot. But while I was getting dressed I felt even glummer than usual after getting my ashes hauled.

I was the first one back to the parlor. Brando came out a minute later, eager to tell me what a great time he'd had with a six-foot blonde named Queenie. LQ had bought himself two girls and so he took a while longer. He finally emerged from the hallway about a quarter hour later, grinning big and swaggering like a rodeo rider.

"Could be I was wrong about you're never satisfied," Brando said. "You looking plenty satisfied this minute."

"And I'd like to say, Chico, that it's a real pleasure to hear you say something that's correct for a change."

We hit the road again but hadn't gone thirty miles before all of us were yawning, the adrenaline charge was worn off now and our lack of proper sleep the night before was getting to us. So we pulled into a motor court in a burg called Marlin and got rooms for the rest of the night.

We slept late and then had a big breakfast at a café down the road before we got rolling south once more. We swung east at Houston and got to Sheila's house at four-thirty in the afternoon. I got out of the Dodge and tossed my valise into the Terraplane. LQ and Brando had started hinting around about maybe spending a little more time in Orange before heading back to Galveston, but I told them to forget it. They were still holding Friday's collection money and Artie Goldman would be mighty red-assed if it wasn't handed in today. I gave them the rest of the expense money to turn in too.

Where the hell was *I* going, LQ wanted to know.

"Got a date."

"Who with?" Brando said.

"You guys don't know her. Tell you about her next time."

"Well, ex-*cuse* us for asking," LQ said. He nudged Brando with an elbow and said, "Must be he don't want you to know he's took up with your momma."

"Only because the two-dollar line to see *your* momma is so damn long."

I followed them through Port Arthur and Sabine to the coast highway, then down the Bolivar Peninsula to the ferry. While we were crossing the bay we had a smoke at the bow rail and watched a school of porpoises rolling ahead of the ferryboat in the last of the orange sunset. Then we were at the dock and the gate went down and we drove off the boat. LQ and Brando headed for the Club and I turned off toward La Colonia.

I had intended to go to the Casa Verde and get cleaned up before calling on her, but when I saw how dark the Avila place was I pulled over. Their old Ford wasn't in its usual spot alongside the house, so maybe they'd all gone out to eat or something, but even so they would've left the porch light on. The rest of the neighborhood looked and sounded the same as always—porch lights glowing, lights in the windows, faint music from radios, the sporadic laughter of kids.

I went up on the porch and knocked and knocked but got no answer. I tried the door and it was locked. I went around to the back of the house and there the Ford was, where Avila never parked it. The blinds were down in every window but there wasn't a show of light behind any of them. I was about to break a pane in the kitchen door, then thought to try that knob too and the door swung open.

I switched on the kitchen light, then crossed into the dining room and turned on that light. The dining table was turned out of place and a corner of it had hit the wall hard enough to crack the plaster. A couple of dining chairs were on their sides and ants were swarming around the sugar bowl on the floor. The living room was such a jumble of skewed and upset furniture and scattered bedclothes that it took me a moment to see Rocha lying on the sofa—hugging a pillow against his stomach and staring at me, his head bandage gone and his face caked with dried blood.

• •

I took a fast look for her—in the bathroom and in the Avilas' bedroom. The couple was lying facedown on the sagging mattress in a furrow of dark jelled blood. The smell was getting high.

I went back out to Rocha and righted a table lamp and turned it on. Under its light his eyes were bright with pain. The bandage off his head was lying at the foot of the hallway. In addition to the head wounds I'd given him he now had knife cuts on his scalp and face. The worst wound was in his stomach.

"Cómo te parece?" he said in a rasp.

I said it didn't look too bad but he needed a doctor and I'd get him to one. But first I wanted to know where the girl was.

They took her, he said. Two of them, both Mexicans, both big. One with a pencil mustache and the other with a big bandido and a squinteye scar.

Did he know who they were?

Well hell yeah. They had to be the rich fuck's guys.

What rich fuck?

Calveras, who else?

Who was that?

I didn't know about Calveras?

"Dígame," I said.

He said that on the drive from Brownsville she had told him a story she'd already told his aunt and uncle about getting kidnapped down in Veracruz by a rich guy named Calveras. Had a wooden leg and only one eye. Had a hacienda in Durango or Chihuahua, he couldn't remember where she'd said. Las Cadenas, the place was called—after a river it was next to. She'd been a prisoner for months before she escaped and went to hide in Brownsville with Rocha's aunt and uncle, who'd known her since she was little. Rocha thought she might be pulling their leg about the rich guy—she seemed the type to overdramatize things, didn't I think so? But his aunt and uncle believed her, and when she said she was afraid of being so close to the border because Calveras might find her, his uncle Oscar invited her to come to Galveston. Then the Avilas heard her story and they offered her a place to stay. Rocha himself still hadn't believed her, though—not until those pricks showed up last night.

They'd come in the back way. One-thirty, two o'clock. Quiet as cats. Daniela was sleeping on the sofa, he was on the floor. He woke up as one of them was starting to crouch over him and there was just enough light to see the knife. His shotgun was in the closet and might as well have been on the moon. He kicked the guy and they tangled up and Daniela let out a scream that got cut short. They went crashing all around and the guy was cutting at his head and trying for his throat and then stabbed him in the stomach before Rocha locked on the guy's knife arm and got his teeth in his ear. The guy pulled away as the hall light came on behind Rocha and he heard Avila say "Qué *pasa*? Quién *es*?" and that's when he got his look at them—the other guy was holding Daniela from behind with a hand on her mouth. Then the light cut off and a door slammed and Rocha threw a shoulder into the guy and sent him crashing and bolted through the kitchen and out the door. He ran across the yard and tore through the hedge into the neighbor's backyard and fell down, choking bad, then realized he had a piece of ear in his throat and managed to spit it out. He had to keep wiping blood from his eyes but the real pain was in his gut. The neighbor's house was still dark—probably nobody in the neighborhood had heard a thing. He was expecting them to come through the hedge looking for him and he lay still to keep from giving himself away. He had no idea how long he'd been lying there before he heard the Avilas' car start up beside the house and then pull into the backyard. A moment later he heard whispering at the Avila back door but he couldn't make out what was being said. He heard a low cry and one of them cursed and said to shut up and he knew they were taking her. He heard them moving off through the grass. And then he didn't hear anything until a car started up somewhere down the street and drove away.

He didn't know any of the neighbors, didn't know if they could be trusted, so he went back into the Avila house. He found them with their throats cut. There was no telephone but even if there had been he wouldn't have called the police. He'd been a cop himself—which came as news to me—but it wouldn't help him much, since he'd been fired and now had an arrest record for various felonies. He figured the police would find it easier to charge him with killing the Avilas than to believe his story. He'd stretched out on the sofa to ease the pain in his gut and to think things over but he must've passed out. When he came to, he could tell that it was late in the day. His belly hurt bad but the bleeding had slowed down to an ooze. And then he was out again. The next time he opened his eyes, there I was.

Well hell. It wasn't like I didn't know how fast things can change.

What I wanted to know was why the Avilas hadn't told *me* the goddamned truth?

Because she told them not to tell anybody, Rocha said. She came up with the stuff about being orphaned and the Picachos being her godparents, and the Avilas went along with it because she said the truth was too complicated and shameful and didn't matter to anybody around here anyway. Besides, who the hell was I they had to tell the truth to? All they knew about me was I was a pistolero with gringo eyes. They were afraid of me.

She wasn't. Why didn't *she* tell me?

Christ sake, she was a woman—who the hell knew why a woman did anything? He gave a raspy chuckle and said maybe she trusted some guys more than others.

I asked if that was why he'd stayed in Galveston—in some long-shot hope that she'd give *him* a tumble.

He said to go to hell. Maybe she would've, if I hadn't shown up with my goddamn fancy clothes and boots and cars.

I said if he was waiting for me to apologize for spoiling his plans he was going to bleed to death first—and we both grinned. Then his face clenched in pain, and I got busy.

• •

I called Rose from the Casa Verde.

The phone picked up and he said, "Yeah?"

"Youngblood."

"Why the hell aint you here?" He said LQ and Brando had told him about how smooth the Dallas job had gone. He sounded tickled pink.

I said I'd be there but I was with a guy in bad need of a doctor who wouldn't ask a lot of questions or pull the cops into it.

"What? Bullet?"

"Knife in the belly. Bunch of other cuts."

"One of our guys?"

"No, just a friend."

There was a second's silence on the line.

"Warrants?"

"No, but he's Tex-Mex with a record and he'd be an easy fall guy if they connect him to the thing. Double killing. The guys who did it are long gone."

"Cops onto it yet?"

"No. Once the guy's safe I'll phone the cops with an anonymous tip about the bodies."

"Christ, Kid, what the fuck company you keeping? Hold on."

It took about fifteen minutes but it seemed like an hour before he was back on the line and saying my guy was cleared for admission to the hospital and nobody there was going to be asking the wrong questions or calling the cops.

"Just tell the guy at the emergency desk your man's name is Johnny Garcia. They've got him down as a driver for Gulf Vending and he's coming in for an appendectomy. All taken care of. And listen: soon as you drop him off you get your ass over here. We got something here belongs to you."

• •

Up in the Studio Lounge LQ and Brando were at the bar with Sam. They waved me over and I saw Sam say something to the bartender. A bottle of beer and a double shot of tequila were waiting for me when I got to the bar.

LQ and Brando had been drinking since they'd turned in the collection money to Mrs. Bianco and they were loudly happy and slightly buzzed. Sam was in high spirits himself. He clinked his shot glass against mine and said, "Nice going, Kid. Here's to success."

He ordered another round for all of us and said, "Hey, fellas, what do you call a woman who's having her period and owns a crystal ball?"

We looked at each other and shrugged. "We give up," LQ said.

"A bitch who knows everything."

He said for us to come on and we followed him to the office.

Rose was at his desk when we came in. He took three envelopes from a drawer and handed them to Sam and Sam passed them out to us. Each envelope held ten fifty-dollar bills.

"A little something to show our appreciation for a job well done, fellas," Sam said. "Enjoy."

I hadn't told LQ and Brando about the bonus and they were happy as longshot winners. I slipped the envelope into my coat pocket. All I wanted now was to get going.

But then Rose said to me, "So? Who's the guy in the hospital? Friend of yours, you say?"

I'd intended to have a good story to explain Rocha if I had to, a story that wouldn't promote too many questions or involve mention of Daniela. But on the way over from the hospital I'd had other things on my mind. All I could think to say now was, "He's the cousin of a friend. They're damn grateful for what you did." I hoped that would get me off the hook for having to know anything more about the guy. The last thing I wanted was to get into a discussion about any of it.

"Come again?" Rose said. "I pulled strings to help a guy who's not even *your* friend? Hey, Kid, I aint in the habit of doing big-time favors for just anybody."

"I know. Like I said, my friend's grateful. Me too."

"I get it," Sam said. "This friend of yours . . . it's a girl, right?"

If I said no, I'd have to invent some guy on the spot, and I wasn't up to it. "How'd you guess?" I said, smiling big. But now I was going to have to give them some of it.

"When a guy does something for no good reason, there's usually a girl," Sam said.

"It's kind of a rough story," I said.

LQ and Brando had started for the door but paused and gave me a curious look at Rose's mention of some guy in the hospital. On hearing about the girl, they exchanged a look and sat down on the small sofa. Sam lit a cigarette and leaned back in his chair. Rose tapped his fingers on the desktop.

Except for saying they were cousins and that I'd met them at a neighborhood party and taken a shine to them—especially her, I said, waggling my eyebrows to show what a casual thing it had been—I told it pretty much as Rocha had told it to me. Why not? But I didn't clutter it up with a lot of detail. I said it turned out she'd been kidnapped in Mexico by some rich guy and finally got away from him and came to Galveston with Rocha. They were staying with friends of theirs named Avila. Last night a couple of goons who must've been the rich guy's muscle busted into the house and grabbed her. They killed the Avilas—dead witnesses tell no tales—and tried to kill Rocha too but only left him in bad need of a doctor. If I hadn't shown up when I did, he probably wouldn't have made it. Or if Rose hadn't got him in the hospital without the police getting involved.

LQ and Brando were watching me closely.

"I gave the cops a call," I said. "They're probably at the scene right now, but they won't get much. It's a neighborhood where nobody ever sees anything, even if they do. Anyway, I figure those two are over the border by now."

"With the girl," Rose said.

"I guess," I said.

"Some story, Kid," Sam said. "You weren't kidding about rough. You knew the people who got it?"

"Yeah. Nice folk."

"Jeez, tough break for them."

"Goes to show you can't be too careful who you take in under your roof," LQ said. "Come on, Ramon, I could use a drink." They got up and went out.

I started to get up too, but Rose said, "Hold on a sec, Kid," and waved me back down in my chair.

"I better go press the flesh," Sam said. "Make sure everybody's drinking up and staying happy." Then he was gone too.

Rose studied me over the flame of his lighter as he fired up a smoke. "This girl . . . she's kind of special, huh?"

"I wouldn't say that. We went out a coupla times."

"How long you say you know her?"

"Not long. Didn't really get to know her very well."

"How long's not long?"

"Well . . . a couple of days." I grinned to show him how funny I thought it was.

He wasn't buying it. "They say it don't take long, sometimes—to get to know somebody pretty good, I mean."

"Yeah, so I've heard."

I stood up.

"So what you got in mind now?" he said.

"Do a little drinking with LQ and Brando, celebrate the bonus. Thanks a lot, by the way."

"Don't bullshit a bullshitter, Kid. Only reason you aint already on the way to the border is you needed cash."

I had made up my mind to go after her the minute Rocha told me what happened—but I'd wanted to avoid any talk about it. There wasn't anything to talk about.

"I gotta get going," I said.

"Let me tell you something about women, Jimmy."

"I have to go," I said. I felt like I had a snake twisting around inside me.

"A woman's never the reason. It's always something else. Always. The important thing is to know what it really is."

"All I know is, *he's* not gonna decide how it goes."

He stared at me without expression for a second—and then showed that smile that was nothing but teeth.

"Well hell, Kid . . . now you're making sense."

• •

LQ and Brando fell in beside me as I made my way through the Studio crowd and headed for the elevator. LQ had his hands in his pockets and was twirling a toothpick between his teeth. Mr. Nonchalance. Some guy not watching where he was going bumped hard into Brando and said "Hey Jack—" and started to turn. And then he caught Ray's look and shut up and moved on.

We rode down in a packed elevator. When we got out on the street I said I'd see them later and started around to the parking lot to get my valise out of the Terraplane. The train station was close enough to walk to.

They came along behind me, LQ whistling "Happy Days Are Here Again." I asked where they thought they were going.

"Name it," LQ said.

"I got something to tend to that's nothing to do with business. See you guys later."

"Sure enough will, because we're coming," LQ said. "Won't take but a minute to get our bags."

"I just told you it's not a business thing. It doesn't concern you guys."

"Bullshit," Brando said.

"Goddamn it, it's personal, I'm telling you—"

"We're partners," Brando said.

"Business or personal," LQ said around his toothpick. "In sunshine or in rain."

As soon as we got on the move the snake inside me settled down, but it felt coiled and ready. We left Galveston well before dawn, then grabbed the first westbound connection out of Houston. The day broke red behind us as we pulled out of the station. I'd called Rose from the Galveston depot and said LQ and Brando were going with me. He said he'd figured they would be and that their visas would be ready too when we got to the border.

The train made stops at several small stations along the way and finally pulled into San Antonio a little before noon. It stopped there long enough for us to get out and have a café lunch rather than eat in the dining car. It was the first time I'd been to San Antone since the night two years before when Rose and I had gone speeding out of it in the Cadillac, leaving dead men in the street.

We hadn't talked much on the train, every man pretty much keeping to his own thoughts, but once the waitress served us our steak sandwiches and slaw, Brando said, "So how long we got to wait before hearing about this girl?"

I said she was Mexican and her name was Daniela, she was damn pretty and spoke good English. I told about meeting her at the Avilas' after the fight with Rocha but said I'd first seen her on New Year's Eve when she went by in front of us in a beat-to-hell Model T.

"Hellfire, I remember that!" LQ said. "She was a *fine*looking chiquita. You young rascal—you track her down or what?"

"No. Just luck."

Brando wanted to know what chiquita we were talking about, how come he didn't know about her.

"If you'd pull your head out of your ass every once in a while," LQ said, "you might catch some of what's going on."

"Catch *this,*" Brando said.

I told about having breakfast with her at the Steam Whistle and then about our swim in the gulf that night. The part about the hammerhead knocked them for a loop.

"I've heard tell about Black Tom since I was a kid," LQ said, "but I never believed he was no damn twenty-foot long. I *still* don't."

"Well I didn't put a measuring tape on it but it was like a train going by."

"Goddamn, man!" Brando said. "She saved your ass."

"I'm not ashamed to admit it."

LQ said, "She took a kick at that thing, no lie?"

"No lie."

"That's some girl."

"Yeah."

"Then what?"

"I took her home."

"Well now," LQ said, cutting a look at Brando, "what I can't help but wonder is, did you and this ladyfriend have the pleasure of, ah, doing the deed, shall we say?"

"Yeah," Brando said. "That's what I can't help but wonder too."

"None of your goddamn business, either of you."

They grinned right back at me. "Thought so," LQ said.

We got back aboard and the train rolled out of San Antone. For a while we just stared out the window at the changing landscape. The grass thinned out and the trees got scrubbier and there was more dust and rock. The sky enlarged as the country opened up.

Then LQ said, "So what's the plan, Kid? I mean, we just gonna go knock on his door and ask him to hand her over, or what?"

"I'm not *asking* him a damn thing," I said.

They both smiled.

"So? What's the plan then?" LQ said.

"Don't know yet. A guy's meeting us at the border with the kind of information we need for a plan."

"This rich guy," Brando said, "he's bound to have some muscle on the payroll, right? Maybe more guys like the two he sent to snatch her?"

I said I didn't know, but Daniela had told Rocha the place had cattle, so the guy had plenty of ranch hands for sure.

"Cowboys, shit," LQ said. "If all he's got is cowboys, I don't care if he got a hundred. I never met a cowboy any damn good with a gun."

"Jimmy here's a cowboy," Brando said.

"Not since we known him he aint," LQ said.

• •

That afternoon we reached the border at Del Rio. A dapper and neatly barbered Mexican named Lalo Calderón was at the station to greet us. He spoke good English and wore a white suit, dark sunglasses, and a mustache as thin as a line of ink. He smelled strongly of a flowery perfume. My face had healed up pretty well except for the shiner, and he gave it a look but made no remark on it. The only thing Rose had told me about him was that he was "a former associate" and very efficient. He now owned an import company with offices in Del Rio, Laredo, and San Antonio. I figured Rose hadn't told him anything more than necessary about us.

We went into a café and took a table in a front corner by the window and ordered a round of beers. Calderón handed me our passports—mine in the name of Michael Chavez, LQ's and Brando's identifying them as George Thompson and Leon Buscar. He also provided a roadmap with a route marked for us in red ink all the way from Villa Acuña to a small town called Escalón, and a folded sheet of paper with a hand-drawn map of the way from Escalón to La Hacienda de Las Cadenas, a distance noted in pencil as about twenty miles. He said the estate was deeded to one César Calveras Dogal. On another sheet of paper was a diagram of the hacienda itself, with several notations in Spanish.

"What about police?" I said.

"The nearest station of police is in Jiménez. That is fifty miles from Escalón. At Las Cadenas, Calveras is the police."

He gave us directions to Sanchez's filling station across the river in Villa Acuña and said a car would be waiting for us there. He stood up and apologized that he could not stay longer but he had another pressing engagement. He hadn't touched his beer except to toast our health.

"Good luck with your business, gentlemen."

He went out and crossed the street to an idling Chrysler waiting at the curb and got into the backseat and the car took him away.

"You get a good whiff of that fella?" Brando said. "About like a whorehouse parlor."

• •

It was an altogether different smell when we walked over the bridge and caught the Rio Grande's ripe stink of shit and dead things.

"Fall in there and you're like to die of poisoning or some godawful disease before you can even drown," LQ said.

The town was a tangle of rutted dirt streets flanking a large plaza. Dogs and chickens dodged rattling burro carts and honking jalopies and grinding trucks. We went past an open marketplace full of hagglers and snarling with flies, hung with the butchered carcasses of calves and pigs and what Brando was absolutely sure was a dog. One stall held a row of skinned cowheads. The air was hazed with the smoke of cooking fires. Street vendors hawked sticks of meatstrips roasted on charcoal braziers. The sidewalks were full of squatting old women beggars in black rebozos.

"We damn sure aint in Galveston no more," LQ said. "Sweet Baby Jesus, *look* at this goddamn place."

"Wish all I had to do was look at it and not smell it," Brando said.

The Sanchez filling station consisted of a small tin-roofed garage and two gasoline pumps. The ground all around the building was black and pungent with drained motor oil, littered with torn tires and rusted car frames and half-gutted engine blocks. Sanchez was a little guy in filthy overalls. I told him my name was Chavez and he said yes, yes, he had been expecting us. We followed him around to the back of the garage and there stood a black Hudson sedan. Gleaming from a fresh washing, it was the cleanest-looking thing in town.

Sanchez beckoned us to the rear of the car, saying, "Hay una sorpresa para ustedes en el portaequipaje."

He worked the key in the trunk lock and took a squinting look all around, then raised the lid and gestured grandly into the trunk. It contained a pair of lever-action Winchester ten-gauge shotguns and a huge rifle of a sort I'd never seen.

"Son of a bitch," LQ said. "That's a BAR." He took out the weapon—and Sanchez had another nervous look around.

A Browning Automatic Rifle, LQ said, U.S. Army issue, .30-06 caliber, with a magazine holding twenty rounds. He said he'd fired one many a time during his army days. He detached the loaded magazine and showed us how the weapon's action operated, then snapped the magazine back in place and worked the slide to chamber a round and then set the safety.

"I'll tell you what," he said, patting the rifle, "this here's about half of any plan a man will ever need."

There was also a shoulder-strap canvas packet holding five more loaded BAR magazines and a couple of cartons of ten-gauge shells.

I asked Sanchez who provided the weapons. He didn't know, but Don Lalo had instructed him to be sure to show it to us. I told LQ and Brando what Sanchez said and LQ wondered how come Calderone would do us such a kindness.

"Rose is how come," I said.

• •

We went into a restaurant and had chicken enchiladas and beer and fought off the flies while we ate our supper and studied the roadmap. La Hacienda de Las Cadenas wasn't on the map but its approximate locale had been marked with an *X* and we figured its distance from Villa Acuña at roughly 400 road miles. The only town of size on our route was Monclova, which lay almost due south about 200 miles. The map showed only a few scattered placenames along the way—all of them little villages, the waiter had told us, and none with electricity. At Monclova we'd turn west into what looked like even rougher country.

"It's nothing but desert for at least a hundred miles to either side of the damn road," Brando said.

"I bet this here says 'Middle of Nowhere,' " LQ said, tapping his finger on a blank portion of the map labeled BOLSON DE MAPIMÍ. Back on the YB I'd always heard that the Mapimí was one of the meanest deserts anywhere, but I didn't see any reason to mention it just now. The last fifty miles or so of our route would take us through the south end of it.

We then studied the diagram of the rectangular hacienda compound. It was enclosed by high walls and marked as 250 yards deep and a quarter-mile wide, its length running east-west. Its only entryway was a double-doored gate in the center of the south wall. Directly under the gate description was a penciled note in Spanish saying that the gate was always open and posted with an armed guard. The driveway into the compound ran straight for about seventy-five yards to a big courtyard. The casa grande was on the far side of the courtyard and faced south toward the gate. Another notation said the servants' quarters were on the lower floor, the family's rooms on the upper. There were various patios and small gardens all about the house, and a large garden directly behind it. Just past the big garden were a corral and a riding track, and, beyond them, a mesquite thicket that ran the length of the compound's rear wall. An unbroken row of tiny penciled squares along the west wall was labeled as the peon living quarters. Over against the east wall, adjacent to the woods, a small square indicated the stable. A square at the southeast corner of the compound was the garage. Between them was the vaquero bunkhouse.

The way I saw it, everything depended on getting past the gate. If they were able to shut us out, the whole business could get pretty bitchy. Once we were inside the compound, all we had to do was get to the house, get Daniela, and then get out again.

"Sounds so damn simple," LQ said, "I can see why you were ready to do it by yourself."

"Unless the guy's got a bunch of pistoleros, I figure there *won't* be that much to it," I said.

"That's the thing," Brando said. "What if he does have a bunch of pistoleros?"

"They might be smart enough not to argue with a BAR."

"And if they aint smart enough?"

"Then we'll play it any way we have to."

They stared at me. Then Brando said, "*That's* the plan?"

"You don't have to have any part of it, either of you. You can cross back over the bridge and catch a train to Galveston."

"You say that again I'm liable to take you up on it," LQ said.

"You don't have to have—"

"Go to hell, wiseguy," LQ said.

"If anybody's got a better plan," I said, "I'm ready to hear it—as long as it doesn't mean waiting. I'm not waiting."

Brando blew out a breath and threw up his hands.

"The best plans are always simple," I said. "Everybody knows that."

"In that case," LQ said, "we got us the greatest goddamn plan in the world."

• •

We took rooms in what was said to be the best of the hotels in town and went to bed early so we could get going before daybreak. But when we met downstairs at dawn LQ and Brando were red-eyed and full of complaints about the lumpy beds and the light of the full moon blazing in through the gauzy curtains and the ranchero music that blared incessantly through much of the night from the cantina across the street. It didn't help their mood much when I said I'd had a pretty good night's rest myself.

I said that just to needle them. The truth was, I dreamt all night, one dream after another—of being out in the deepwater sea with a giant shark circling around me; of Reuben lying in the dust with a terrible stomach wound and calling for me to help him; of Daniela standing naked on a brightly lit platform while a crowd of men in the surrounding darkness bids to buy her. And of Rodolfo Fierro, sitting in a high-backed chair on an elevated platform, dressed in a fine black suit and cloak and wearing a Montana hat at a cocky angle, his legs stretched out in front of him and crossed at the ankles and his coatflap fallen aside to expose a holster holding a Colt .44 with ivory grips of carved Mexican eagles. He was staring down at several long rows of clearly terrified men while a voice speaking in Spanish delivered verdicts of death. Then he looked over their heads at me, and in English I said, Hey Daddy . . . and he smiled . . .

• •

We put a five-gallon can of drinking water on the floor by the backseat and three cans of gasoline into the trunk and got on our way before daybreak. The sun rose out of the flatlands and shone red on the mountains to the west just under the setting silver moon. The sky was clear except for the dust we raised behind us on the packed dirt road.

The countryside reminded me of the YB Ranch—cactus of every kind and mesquite trees and creosote scrub, mesas and mountains on every horizon. But it was alien territory to LQ and different even to Brando, who came from a part of Texas with geography a lot tamer than this region of brute rock ground and thorns on damned near everything.

Now and then we'd see a small cross—sometimes a cluster of crosses—stuck in the ground alongside the road and we came to find out they had been placed by the families of people killed at those spots in motor vehicle accidents.

Two hours after leaving Villa Acuña we reached the junction road from the border town of Piedras Negras. There had been a rainstorm a day or so earlier and truck traffic had made a washboard of the road surface. The car jarred hard and sometimes jerked to one side or the other and Brando cursed and fought the wheel. There were plenty of stations within range of our radio, most of them playing ranchero music, which LQ and I liked but Brando had had enough of, and he searched the dial till he found one out of Eagle Pass broadcasting Texas string-band stuff.

As the morning grew warmer, pale dust devils rose in the open country and went whirling toward the dark ranges in the distance. Around midmorning we came to a ferry crossing at a river the color of caramel. The ferry was a rope rig and could carry only three cars at a time. There were four cars ahead of us, so we had to wait. There were three small crosses at the edge of the riverbank. LQ and Brando napped under a tree and I skipped rocks on the water until it was our turn to cross.

• •

We got to Monclova in the early afternoon and gassed the car at a filling station. I got directions from the attendant to get to the westbound road. Brando wanted to have a beer before moving on, so we parked around the corner from the main plaza and went into a cantina.

The place was cool and dim and a radio was playing mariachi music. Besides us the only other patrons were two guys at a table against the wall and another three standing together at the far end of the bar and laughing with the cantinero. You could tell by their clothes they were vaqueros—and by their laughter and gestures that they were drunk.

The cantinero came over and looked at each of us in turn, then asked Brando, "Qué quieren de tomar?"

"Cerveza," Brando said with his gringo accent. He looked at me and said, "Tell him I want the coldest one in the joint."

"Tres cervezas," I said. "Bien frías."

The cantinero stared at my eyes and then gave Brando another look before going to fetch the beer. He set the bottles in front of us and went back to his friends at the end of the bar and whispered something to them. They turned to look at us. One of them, the biggest, came down the bar, puffing a cigarillo.

"Buenas tardes."

"Buenas tardes," I said.

He asked to know where we were from, and I told him.

"Ah, Tejas," he said. He looked at LQ and said that a blond gringo certainly had a good reason for not speaking Spanish. Then looked at me again and said anybody who looked Mexican and could speak Spanish as well as I did could be forgiven for having gringo eyes. But what he was curious about, he said, turning to Brando, was why a guy who looked so fucking Mexican couldn't speak Spanish well enough to ask for a cold beer.

"Eres un pinche pocho, verdad?"

The vaquero was looking for a fight but he badly underestimated Brando's readiness to give it to him. The insult was barely off the guy's tongue before Ray brought his knee up into his balls and hit him in the mouth with the bottle of beer. Glass shattered and beer sprayed and the vaquero went down on his ass and over on his side, drawing his knees up and clutching his crotch. He puked through his broken teeth.

The cantinero started to sidestep down the bar but LQ already had the .380 in his hand and waggled it at him, and the barman brought his hands up in view and stepped away from the counter. The two at the end of the bar stood gawking. The pair at the table were beaming at the entertainment.

LQ put up his pistol and leaned over the bar to peer into the shelf under it and came up with a cutoff single-barrel sixteen-gauge. The cantinero looked apologetic. LQ opened the breech and took out the shell and flung it across the room, then stood the shotgun against the front of the bar.

"Let's get a move on," I said.

"Gimme another beer," Brando said to the cantinero. "For the busted one."

"Mándame?"

"Dale otra cerveza," I said.

He went to the cooler and fetched three beers to the bar.

"Put them in a bag," Brando said.

"Cómo?"

"Ponlas en una bolsa," I said.

He looked around and found a paper sack and put the bottles in it. Brando picked it up and carried it out under his arm.

LQ and I paused at the door and eyeballed everybody in the room. I didn't think any of them was likely to discuss us with the police. We went out the door and down the street to the car. Brando already had the engine running. We got in and he drove us off nice and easy and I gave him the directions out of town.

When we got on the open road, I opened the beers and passed them around and we took a few pulls without talking until LQ said, "You getting awful thin-skinned, aint you, Ramon? All the fella called you was a phony Mexican."

He leaned so that Brando couldn't see his face in the rearview and he gave me a wink.

"Correct me if I'm wrong, Jimmy," LQ said, "but aint that what pocho means—a phony Mex? A Mexican who talks and acts American?"

"Pretty much," I said.

Brando kept his eyes on the road, steering with one hand and holding his beer with the other, but he was still pretty tight about the whole business—you could see it in his jaw and how he was gripping the wheel.

"I mean, you're all the time saying you *aint* Mexican, no matter how much you look it, always saying how you were born in the States and all," LQ said. "Seems to me he was saying the same thing. So what's there to get blackassed about?"

"It's how he said it," Brando said.

"How he said it? Goddamn, you bust up a man 'cause you don't like *how* he says something? Woooo, you even thinner in the skin than I thought."

"Go fuck yourself," Brando said.

"Ah, Ramon," LQ said with the usual big sigh, "if only I could. I'd be doing it with—"

"You'd be doing it with a dumb-ass redneck nobody but you can stand," Ray said.

I smiled out at the road.

"Well golly gee, aint we in a mood?"

"Mood *this,*" Brando said—then caught sight of LQ's grin in the mirror and couldn't restrain his own.

Pretty soon they were talking about how they couldn't wait to see Sheila and Cora Ann again and how much the girls would like it if they took them some Mexican sandals, maybe a sombrero.

"Hell, Kid," LQ said to me, "you and your chiquita—we oughta call her Danny—you and Danny ought to come over and join us for a backyard barbecue or something."

"Damn right," Brando said. "I think we oughta do it as soon as we get back home."

"Sounds good to me," I said.

• •

We didn't see anything but desert for the next hour and a half and then came to a wide spot in the road taken up with a few weathered shacks and a one-pump filling station and a tiny café with an open wall and a pair of bench tables. The guy who filled our tank said there wasn't so much as another hut, never mind a place to get gas or a bite to eat, between there and Escalón, 165 miles away. We went to the café and had pork tacos and beer, then got back in the Hudson and drove on.

We were pushing deep into nowhere, just like it looked on the map, and the road got worse. It was full of cracks and potholes and the Hudson sometimes thumped into one so hard it was a wonder we didn't blow a tire. The gas-pump guy had said we were lucky to be making this drive in the good weather of the year, that the heat of summer was unbearable, but even now you could see heat waves where the highway met the horizon.

We rolled through a vast pale desert of scraggly brush and rocky outcrops and long red mesas. Far to the southwest black thunderheads sparked with silent lightning and dragged purple veils of rain over the jagged ranges on the horizon. We saw no other living thing but a pair of vultures circling high over the sunlit wasteland to the north.

"Jesus," Brando said. "Where the *hell* are we?"

"I believe we took a wrong turn and come to the moon," LQ said. He reached over to the front seat and got the hand-drawn map from beside me and sat back and opened it.

"According to this," he said, "that hacienda place is straight thataway"—he pointed south—"about thirty–forty miles."

"I know it," I said. "But there's no way to get there except by way of the Escalón road—and that's . . . what . . . twice as long, all told?"

"At least that, according to this map. Fella sure lives out of the way, don't he? Say, what's this here, where the river runs out?"

LQ leaned over the seat to point out the little clump of penciled tufts labeled "ciénaga" just north of the hacienda.

"Sort of a swamp," I said. "This close to the desert it's probably just a mud patch."

I didn't say much for a while after that—just smoked and stared out at the passing landscape. I couldn't have explained it, but there was something about this country that pulled at me. In some inexplicable way it felt like a place I'd once known but had forgotten all about.

The sun was almost down to the ridge of distant mountains in the west and glaring hard against the windshield when the road angled off to southward. The map showed the angle and we calculated that we were less than forty miles from Escalón.

And then, shortly after dark, the road ended at a junction with another highway and we were there.

Escalón was nothing but a tiny railstation and a small rocky cemetery and a dozen scattered houses along a single dirt street. No motor vehicles. No telephone or even a telegraph line.

The road ran north to Jiménez and south to Torreón, which lay even farther away. The fat creamy moon had just risen over the black mountains. A light wind kicked up and carried the smell of charcoal cooking. A dog barked and barked but hung back in the shadows beside the depot. The station door was open and showed soft yellow light. A man in a rail agent's cap stepped into the doorway and peered out at us.

"Cállate," he said, and the dog shut up and slunk off. "Buenas noches, señores. Les puedo ayudar?"

I told Brando to keep a lookout and LQ and I went into the station. The agent stepped aside for us and then went around behind the narrow counter. In the light of a pair of kerosene lanterns I saw that his face was badly scarred, as if it had been torn open in several places and then badly sutured. His left arm had been ruined too and he held it at an awkward twist.

"Christ amighty, amigo," LQ said, "you look like you been in a hatchet fight and everybody had a hatchet but you."

"Perdóname, señor," the clerk said. "No hablo inglés." His face twisted even more awfully and I supposed he was smiling in apology for his inability to speak English.

I told him my friend didn't speak Spanish, and he gestured with his good arm in a manner to imply that life was full of complications.

I took out the map of the hacienda and spread it open on the counter between us. I asked if he could vouch for its accuracy, if there were any local roads that the map did not show.

He bent over it and considered for a minute and then said it looked correct to him.

So the road a couple of miles south was the only one connecting the Hacienda de Las Cadenas to the Jiménez-Torreón highway?

"Sí," he said. "Es el único camino." He asked if we were new employees of Don César. "O no más son amigos de el?"

There was no way he could warn Calveras of our coming and so I said no, we weren't the man's employees or his friends, either. I handed the map to LQ. "It's jake. Just the one road."

"Ah, pues, son enemigos," the clerk said. He put his hand to a scarred cheek and smiled his awful smile. "Espero que lo castigan bastante bien. Mejor si lo matan."

"What's he yammering about?" LQ said.

"He hopes we kick Calveras' ass but he'd be happier if we killed him. I don't think he cares much for the man."

"Bastard probably give him that face. Ask him does he know how many guns the place got."

I asked, and he said, "De pistoleros? No estoy seguro. Como una dozena, yo creo."

"He say a *dozen*?" LQ said.

"Maybe a dozen, he's not sure."

"Y cuantos son ustedes?"

"Tres."

"Tres?" His ruined mouth twisted and he shook his head.

"Go to hell, Jack," LQ said as we started for the door. "Odds like that, the sumbitch best send for more guys."

• •

The road was about as wide as a big truck and went snaking through high dense brush and tall stands of mesquite trees. The hacienda's pasturelands were somewhere far to the east. We drove without headlights and very slowly, raising no dust, making our way by the small patches of moonlight that filtered through the trees. We'd been on the move for the better part of an hour when we went around a long curve through the heavy scrub and saw the lights of the hacienda in the distance ahead.

When we figured we were within a mile of the place, LQ and I got out of the car. He carried the BAR and the shoulder bag of extra magazines; I had one of the shotguns and one coat pocket full of extra shells for it, the other pocket full of .44 cartridges. The road was still closely bounded and deeply shadowed by brush and mesquite. I headed up the road with LQ ten yards behind me and Brando easing the Hudson along behind LQ, far enough back that I couldn't hear the motor.

About eighty yards from the compound the trees and taller brush abruptly ended. LQ came up beside me and we crouched in the road's last portion of darkness. We had a clear view of the compound gate and the guard posted there, but between us and the compound it was all moonlit open ground and there was no shadow at all on the long front wall. Brando was still in the car, about thirty yards behind us.

The wooden gate was tall and double-doored, the left door open inward, the right one shut. The guard sat in a straightback chair in front of the closed door. We could see the red flarings of his cigarette and it looked like there was some kind of long gun propped against the gate beside him. The wall was about twelve feet high and we could see the glitter of the broken bottles cemented along the top of it, a safeguard common to every walled residence, large or small, we'd seen in Mexico. The open gate door was dimly yellow with light from the courtyard within.

We talked it over in a whisper and came up with a plan. I went back down the road to tell it to Brando and then stood on the running board as he very gingerly brought the Hudson up to about fifteen yards from the shadowed end of the road and stopped. We could see LQ's crouched silhouette up ahead.

"Keep your eye on me," I told Brando, then I hustled back up to LQ.

"Okay," LQ said, handing me his hat and the BAR. "Here goes nothing." He slipped into the brush to the right of the road and vanished. I slung the BAR over one shoulder, the shotgun over the other.

It took nearly half an hour for him to move around to the east side of the compound. I kept watching the far end of the front wall and finally saw his blond head poke out from behind it.

The guard was sitting with his back to him. He'd been chain-smoking and he lit another cigarette as LQ started toward him, walking steadily and sticking close to the wall, his shadow short and leaning a little ahead of him. If the guard turned around and saw him coming LQ would probably have to shoot him—and the ones inside might get the gate shut on us.

LQ was almost to him when the guard jerked around in his chair—maybe he heard LQ's footsteps. He jumped up and spun around to grab for the long gun but then LQ was on him, clubbing at him with his pistol. I heard the guy hollering—and figured they sure as hell heard him inside—and then LQ had him down and shut him up.

I was already running for the gate and beckoning Brando to come on. I heard the Hudson roaring behind me and I looked back as it shot out into the moonlight and swerved around in a tight circle and Brando gunned it back into the narrow mouth of the road and braked hard—the car now facing back the way we came and blocking the mouth of the road. The door flew open and Brando came on the run, shotgun in hand.

LQ was standing in the open gate pointing the .380 at somebody inside and yelling, "Put it down, man, put it down!" A pistolshot sounded from the courtyard and the round ricocheted off the stone wall. LQ crouched beside the closed door and opened fire with the .380, snapping off three or four rounds in a row, the muzzle flashing yellow, then took cover behind the door.

I ran up and gave LQ his hat and the BAR and whipped the shotgun off my shoulder. Somebody inside was crying in pain and praying to the Holy Mother.

"Map's got it right," LQ said. "Driveway goes straight to a pool fountain some seventy–eighty yards off and the house is just the other side of it."

Brando ran up, grinning big. *"Woooo."*

There was a lot of shouting in the compound, mostly unintelligible, some of it demanding to know what was going on, some of it informing that Julio had been shot and needed help. Somebody ordering somebody to shut the fucking gate and somebody yelling back for *him* to shut the fucking gate.

LQ peeked around the open door and jerked his head back quick as several pistols fired and bullets whacked the thick wood.

"There's a bunch coming from the right," he said. "Let's do it if we're gonna do it."

I told him to cover us from the gate—we didn't want them shutting the door and trapping us inside. "Keep behind me, Ray—straight for the house. I'll go upstairs, you hold the front door. Shoot anything you aint sure of."

I slapped LQ on the shoulder and said, "Do it."

He stood up and leaned around the door and fired a long sweeping burst of the BAR, the rifle pumping out rounds in *bam-bam-bam* fashion, flaring bright and cracking loud. I'd never heard one before and it was pretty impressive.

Brando and I ran up the driveway. It was wide and cobbled and flanked on either side by torchlights and low hedges, stone benches, various statues. The diagram hadn't mentioned all the trees on the place. The courtyard was straight ahead, a circular stone fountain in the middle of it with some kind of sculpture spouting water in the center of the pool. The house just beyond it was blazing with light. From the shadowy area off to our right voices shouted, "Allí van! Por allá! Allí van!"

I ran in a crouch as gunshots cracked. A bullet struck a statue close to my head and stone fragments pecked my cheek. Rounds hummed through the hedges. Then LQ's BAR was hammering again and there was screaming and it sounded like LQ shot up an entire magazine before he stopped firing. There were anguished cries, shriekings for help.

The courtyard hedge was higher than the one along the driveway and as I ran around the fountain a man came rushing out of a hedge pathway with a pistol in his hand and seemed astonished to see me. I blasted him in the chest with the ten-gauge and he flew backward into the hedge and hung there in a bloody tangle.

"Right side!" Brando yelled, and I turned and saw two more with rifles coming out of the other hedge. Brando's shotgun took half the head off one of them. The other fired at me from the hip and I heard the bullet pass me. I gave him a load in the belly and he bounced off the base of a horse statue and left a red mess on the stone.

The BAR was rapping again and there was more screaming—and then Brando cried out. I turned and saw him on the ground, clutching his side and cussing a blue streak.

Two guys came out of the hedge on the other side of the fountain and I fired at them and one spun around and went down and the other ducked behind the fountain. Brando sat up and pulled his revolver and the guy never knew Ray was there until he peeked around that side of the fountain and his hair jumped when Brando shot him in the head.

"Go on, go on!" Brando yelled.

I started for the house and spotted a man looking down from the balcony—a guy with long white hair and a black eyepatch. I raised the shotgun and he darted away just as I blew fragments off the stone rail where he'd been standing. I thought I heard a woman scream up there. Daniela.

The shotgun lever seized and I flung the weapon away and drew the Mexican Colt and ran up the front steps. A man in an apron and gripping a meat cleaver came at me from a side door—brave but stupid. I shot him and he fell down, blood spurting from his neck. I ran into the main parlor and damn near shot a pair of terrified maids hugging tight to each other.

I raced up the wide stairway, taking the steps two at a time, but as I reached the middle landing a large man suddenly appeared at the top of the stairs and shot at me and my right foot kicked out from under me and I fell sideways on the steps. His next bullet gouged a hole in the carpet under my nose. Then we fired at the same time and my cheek burned and he flinched and his gun hand drooped. He started to raise the revolver again and I shot him in the chest and he discharged a round into the wall and dropped the gun and came tumbling down the steps to the landing and lay on his back without moving.

I sat up and checked my foot and saw that the heel of my boot had been shot off. I raised my other foot and whacked the heel with the Colt barrel a half-dozen times before it broke off. I wiped blood from my right cheek, then stood up and looked down at the guy and saw that he was still alive and staring at me. He had a pencil mustache and a bandaged ear.

"Te doy un recuerdo de Felipe Rocha," I said. He opened his mouth to speak but never got it out before I shot him in the eye.

I reloaded the Colt and went on up to the top landing, moving warily now. I heard the BAR again—and then froze at the sound of a submachine gun, firing rounds faster than LQ's Browning ever could. It was a long burst.

A tommy gun. Jesus.

The tommy and the Browning fired at the same time, long bursts . . . and then nothing. I stood waiting, and there came a few pistolshots, and then no more gunfire. Nothing but the muted crying and wailing of wounded men and terrified women.

But Daniela was somewhere up *here*—and the thing to do right now was find her.

The first room I tried was an empty bedroom. In the next one a young maid was huddled in a corner and crying.

"Donde está Daniela Zarate?"

Gone, she said. The patrón took her—just a few minutes ago. There was a private stairway in his chambers.

I grabbed her and shoved her into the hall and told her to show me the way to Calveras' room. She looked down the hall and her eyes went large and I stepped out into the hall and pointed the Colt at a guy dressed like some dandy from another age. He wore a sharp little beard in the old gachupín style and his hair was tied back in a ponytail. He'd been about to descend the staircase but now put his hands up slightly and said he wished me no harm and was surrendering without conditions. He lowered his hands to his side and turned the palms outward in a show of capitulation and asked how he could be of service. I asked where the patrón's chambers were. He pointed past me and even as I turned to look I sensed my mistake and I whirled back around to see him raising a pocket revolver and we both fired. I hit him in the heart and he dropped like a puppet with its strings cut.

I felt a burning in the muscle between my neck and shoulder and found that he'd nicked me through it. It burned but the blood flow wasn't too bad. I stuffed a handkerchief against it up under my shirt and coat. The maid was pressed back against the wall with her hands at her mouth.

"Enséñame la escalera," I said, and she led me to the patrón's chambers and showed me the secret stairway. It was a narrow winding thing, tight as a corkscrew. I followed it down to a little door that opened into a patio at the rear corner of the house, next to a narrow driveway that curved around from the courtyard.

There was only one way out of the compound—so if LQ was still holding the gate, Calveras was still inside the walls. I hustled back around to the driveway in front of the house, the Colt in my hand. The wailing was louder out here. LQ had done plenty of damage with the Browning. A group of house servants caught sight of me and ran back into the casa grande. The courtyard was deserted, the bodies already removed except for the dead guy in the hedge. Brando was gone too, but the torchlight was sufficient to show the dark bloodstains where he'd fallen.

As I hurried down the drive, others saw me coming and fled into the darkness to either side of the hedges. They did the smart thing. I was ready to shoot anybody who even looked at me wrong. The moaning and crying was scattered in the darkness to my left, but much of it was concentrated over where a cast of light showed above the trees. According to the hacienda map the bunkhouse was over there, and I supposed that was where the wounded had been taken, the dead too, probably. I wondered if Brando was among them—and figured I'd know soon enough.

I could see the gate up ahead. Somebody was sitting there with his back against the open door. If it wasn't LQ I hoped it was somebody dead or too shot-up to shoot me.

The west side of the compound, where the worker quarters were, was all dark. As soon as the shooting started, the peons had probably shut their doors and blown out their lamps. They didn't need to know what was going on to know it was no business of theirs.

The torchlights were bright on me, but even as I got closer to the gate I still couldn't make out who was sitting there in the shadows. And now I noticed that the open gate-door was slightly askew, its lower hinge twisted almost free of the wall. Then LQ's voice said, "Who goes there, friend or foe?"—and he chuckled.

"How you doing, man?"

"Could be worse. Where's Ray?"

"I don't know. I saw him get hit but I don't know how bad. I thought he might've come back here."

"Nah he aint," he said. "Think he's dead?"

"I don't know."

"I think we done for of all of them who wanted to make a fight of it. I'd say the rest are just waiting for us to go away."

He had the BAR across his lap. The .380 and an extra magazine for it were on the ground beside him. He was hatless and coatless and both his shirtsleeves had been ripped off and I could see he'd used them to bandage his left arm.

I squatted beside him and lit a cigarette and handed it to him. "How bad?"

"I got the bleeding pretty well stopped. Armbone's busted." His voice was tight with pain. "You find her?"

"No. But I saw him, and a maid said he's got her. As long as we're on the gate, he's not taking her anywhere. Soon as it's light I'll start looking."

"Ah hell, Jimmy, he's gone, man. I can't say if she was with him, but if you didn't find her she mighta been with—"

I grabbed his good arm. "What the hell you talking about, he's gone . . . if she was *with* him? . . . *When?*"

"Hey, man." He jerked his arm and I let go of it.

"Fucken Cadillac. Who else it gonna be but him? It come tearing out of that hedge. I give it a burst, but this gorilla leans out the window and opens up on me with a goddamn *Thompson*. I about shit. I hunkered down outside the wall and *wham,* they clip the door and go skidding by with a fender peeled back and the bastard gave me some more of the tommy gun and nailed me in the arm. But I sureshit nailed him better. The Caddy had to cut a sharp turn on account of we blocked the road and the shooter come tumbling out. That's him yonder. I put a coupla .380s in his head to be sure he wasn't just resting up."

He was pointing at a big man lying a dozen yards beyond the gate, faceup, his arms flung out, his legs in an awkward twist. The tommy gun lay close by.

"I couldn't see in the car all that good," LQ said, "but I guess she mighta been in there."

She was—I knew she was. She would've told him I was coming. She would've kicked at him and said James Rudolph Youngblood was coming. As soon as he heard the shooting he would've known who it was and he would've taken her with him. I stood up, telling myself to stay cool, to *think*.

"We blocked the only road. Where'd he go?"

"Thataway, around the corner." He waved toward the east end of the compound wall.

The moon was high and bright as a gaslamp. My wound burned and I checked it with my fingertips. It was swollen but the bloodflow had slowed to nothing and was already clotting. I went over to the dead guy. He had a big droopy mustache and there was enough moonlight to show the white scar at the edge of his eye. More good news for Rocha.

Then I remembered the river. The map showed a river running past the hacienda a couple of miles east of it, running all the way out to the ciénaga. I picked up the Thompson and went back to LQ.

"I'm betting there's a road that goes over to the river. From there he'll try to make it to the Monclova road."

"Shitfire," LQ said. "There's nothing between here and there but desert, all rocky ground for . . . what'd we figure, forty miles? He aint making it to that road, not without a pair of wings."

I detached the tommy gun's magazine and checked the load, then snapped it back in place and handed LQ the weapon and he tested a one-hand grip on it, bracing the butt against his hip and swinging the muzzle from side to side. He grinned and cradled the gun under his arm.

"I'm gonna go get her."

"That's why we come," he said.

"Got enough smokes?"

"Yep. Could do with some handy water."

I went over to the Hudson and had to duck under the dash and hot-wire the ignition, since Brando had the keys. I cranked up the engine and backed the car around and drove up beside the gate. I took the water can out of the back and filled a couple of empty beer bottles for myself and jammed them between the backseat and the door so they wouldn't spill, then set the rest of the can next to LQ, together with a tin cup.

"Be back soon as I can," I said.

"Good Lord willing, I expect I'll be here."

• •

I drove to the northeast rim of the bluff behind the compound and got out of the car. From there I could scan the country to the north for miles—a pale wasteland under the blazing white moon. To the northeast I could also see the lower portion of the river, extending into the distance like a wrinkled silver ribbon and ending at a dark patch of ground that had to be the ciénaga.

And then I saw something else—a small and barely visible cloud of dust moving slowly north alongside the river. It was them. He had his lights off. Me too. We didn't need headlights anyway, not under that moon.

I hopped back into the car and wheeled it around and eased it along the dense growth of brush and mesquites at the edge of the open ground, gunning the engine, searching for the road to the river. And then I found it. It wasn't a road so much as a rocky trail rutted by cartwheels. It went winding through the scrub and was so narrow that mesquite branches scraped both sides of the car. I had to take it easy over the rough ground—but even as slow as I was going, the Hudson swayed and bobbed like a boat on choppy waters.

Finally the scrub thinned out and shortened and the river came into view again, much closer now and shining bright under the moon. It was shallow and packed with sandbars. A few yards from the bank the trail turned north, and it was still rough going. Even at fifteen miles an hour the car bounced and swayed and the steering wheel jerked every which way. Now I was raising some dust too, and I wondered if he'd seen it.

I'd gone downriver about three miles when a front tire blew like a pistolshot. The Hudson pulled hard to the right but I wrenched it straight and kept going, the tire flopping. The river narrowed steadily. Then the ground gradually began to smooth out under the Hudson and the terrain began to darken and get grassy. I'd arrived at the end of the river, at the south end of the muddy ciénaga.

I stopped the car and got out to look things over. A cool north breeze had picked up and it pushed the stink of the mudpit into my face. The ground was slick under my heel-less boots. If I'd driven any farther north I would've bogged down in the muck.

He couldn't have crossed the river anywhere along the way. To get past the ciénaga he had to go around it to the west. There were no tracks on the smooth ground around me, so he must've angled over in that direction before coming this close to the mud. I got back in the car and followed the edge of the mudpit to westward.

In less than a quarter mile I came on the Caddy's tracks where they came up from the south and I could tell from the shape of them that he'd blown at least one tire on each side. The moon eased around to my right from behind me as I followed the tracks along the curving rim of the ciénaga to northward. Then the Caddy's tracks angled away from the mudpit and I knew we were past it. The ground was hard and rough again. The Hudson jolted and pitched.

I drove on, the Hudson's shadow slowly contracting against the left side of the car.

And then there the Cadillac was, not a half mile ahead. In the distance it looked like a bug on a dirty tablecloth. It took a moment for me to realize that it wasn't moving. I drew the Mexican Colt from my pants and set it beside me.

I closed in very slowly, then stopped about thirty yards from the Caddy. I didn't know how he was armed. If he had a rifle he probably would've used it before letting me get that close. Then again, maybe he was trying to get me in so close that he couldn't miss. If he wanted to bargain I was willing: give her to me and we'd be quits. I was pretty sure I'd mean it.

I eased the Hudson forward, ready to wheel it sideways and take cover behind it if he opened fire. Twenty yards from the Caddy I stopped again. It was slumped forward on two front flats. I pulled up to within ten yards. Then closer. And then I was idling right behind it. The interior of the Caddy was too dark for me to see anything in there.

I put the Hudson in neutral and opened my door wide and waited a minute. Nothing from the Caddy. I had the Colt cocked in my hand. Then I switched on my headlights—if he'd been looking back at me, he'd have been blinded in that moment—and I slid out of the Hudson and ran in a crouch up beside the driver's door and jumped up and stuck the Colt in the window, all set to blow his brains out.

He wasn't there.

But she was—slumped against the passenger door—and in the same moment that I saw her I realized what a clear target I made in the shine of my headlights. I dropped down and scurried back to the Hudson and reached in and switched off the lights.

I went around to the Cadillac's passenger side and tucked the Colt in my pants and eased the door open and caught her as she started to fall. Her eyes were closed and she groaned softly and her breath was warm on my face. She moaned louder as I eased her over on the seat and got in beside her. And I felt the blood.

I examined her by the light of the moon. Her elbow was smashed and her lower right arm was slick with blood. Her right side was sopped—blood oozing from a bullet hole just under her arm and from two more, close together, between the ribs and hip.

There was nothing to do about wounds like that. Not in our circumstance. I went back to the Hudson and got one of the bottles I'd filled with water. Some of it had spilled in all the bouncing around but there was still plenty. I put the water to her lips and maybe she sipped some of it but mostly it just ran out of her mouth. I wiped the dribble from her chin and set the bottle on the floor.

I put my hand to her cheek and said her name. I asked her to open her eyes and look at me, to say something, but she didn't. I held her and crooned to her. I stroked her hair and spoke to her of everything that came to mind. I told her how beautiful she was, how wonderfully brave. I told her how my heart did a little flip the first time I'd seen her. I tried to sing "Red Sails in the Sunset" but forgot the words in both English and Spanish and told her I was sorry. I described the moon and said she really ought to take a look at it and I laughed for both of us at my attempt to trick her into opening her eyes. I talked to her until the sky turned gray at the rim of the mountains. Then I leaned down to retrieve the bottle of water to see if she might drink a little more and when I turned back to her she was dead.

He hadn't done it, not wounds like that, not on the side away from him. I didn't have to take the bullets out and see them to know they were .30–06 rounds from a BAR.

The Cadillac motor wouldn't turn over. Maybe LQ had hit the oil pan and all the oil leaked out and the engine had finally seized.

I gently laid her on her side and told her I'd be back.

Then I went and got in the Hudson and set out into the deeper desert.

• •

The sun was half-risen behind the jagged mountains and looking like a great raw wound when I spotted him a half mile ahead. At first I took him for another greasewood shrub and then understood what I was looking at. He was lying huddled on his side and the possibility that he was dead made my gut go tight.

I stopped the car ten feet from him and blew the klaxon and he stirred slightly. Praise Jesus.

I got out and walked up to him. His hat had fallen off and I saw the black strap of his eyepatch tight against the back of his head. His lank white hair hung over his face. His breathing was raspy but there were no obvious wounds on him, no bloodstains I could see. His coatflap hung down straight with the weight of something heavy in the pocket and I reached down and relieved him of a .38 revolver and slung it out into the scrub. A portion of his wooden leg was visible between the hem of his pantleg and the top of his lowcut Spanish boot. I gave it a hard kick.

He flinched and groaned. I said for him to look at me.

"Mírame, viejo," I said. "Mírame bien."

He struggled to push himself up on an elbow, grunting hard, and he finally managed to sit up. He brushed the hair from his eyes and turned his face up to me, sand clinging to his eyepatch, his good eye baggy and bloodshot.

The sun had just risen over the mountains behind him and it blazed full on my face. I was squinting against its glare. I told him again to have a good look at me, that I was the last thing he was going to see in this world. His eye fixed on me hard.

I pulled down my hat brim to shade my eyes and I took out the Colt. I put the muzzle against his forehead and cocked the hammer.

And the son of a bitch laughed.

Laughed and asked if I was a hallucination. "O eres un espanto?" he said—and laughed even harder, as if the possibility that I was a ghost was the funniest thing in the world.

All these years, he said, all these miserable years gone by and here I was again, threatening his life once more. Well, go ahead and shoot, he said—he was no more afraid of me now than he had been back then.

My finger quivered on the trigger. If he had gone insane he couldn't appreciate the moment. Then what satisfaction could there be?

He laughed again and said, No, no, of *course* I wasn't him. How could I be *him,* all these years later? I was just one more of his brute kind. There was no end to our kind. Our mongrel breed had robbed him of everything once before, and now, even *now,* we would rob from him yet again? We would have the girl too? Well, fuck the lot of us. Did I think he was afraid? He spat on my boots. *That* was how afraid he was. Go ahead, he said . . . *shoot.*

I saw the lie in his eyes. He *was* afraid. He was afraid I wouldn't shoot him. He wanted to die but didn't have the balls to shoot himself. Jesus. Who knew what the hell anybody was like under the skin?

I knew that to let him go on living would be greater punishment than to put a quick end to his misery. But it would also be punishment for all the people he would continue to make miserable as long as he was alive.

Or as long as he was able.

I put a hand on his shoulder and smiled at him and tucked the Colt away under my coatflap. His eye went wide with alarm as if he knew what was coming and he tried to break away but I seized a fistful of his hair and held his head fast as I brought out the icepick. He screeched and shut his eye tight and I swiped the tip of the pick through the pinched eyelid and a thin jet of bloody fluid caught the sunlight for one sparking instant—and then his hand was over his eye and blood was running between his fingers and he was screaming.

I left him there, screaming and screaming, staggering around in his darkness under the glaring white sun.

I carried her to the Hudson and then cut the seat-covers out of the Cadillac and used them for a shroud. I replaced the flat tire with the spare and then followed our earlier tracks as I drove back around to the south side of the mudpit. That's where I buried her. I dug the grave with the tire jack and my hands, working shirtless. It was a long process even in that soft earth. My shoulder wound opened again and blood streaked my chest. When the hole was finally deep enough, I gently laid her in it. And then I covered her up.

I was slow and careful driving back and the tires held up all the way. The sun was directly overhead when I emerged from the scrub trail and pulled up to the compound gate. LQ and Brando were sitting in ladderback chairs in the shade of the gate archway, staring at me. I turned off the motor and got out of the car.

LQ's left arm had been splinted and freshly bandaged and it was cradled in a clean white sling. He held the tommy gun under his good arm. Brando had the BAR slung on his shoulder and wore no visible bandage but he grimaced and pressed a hand to his side as he stood up.

"Thought you might be dead," he said.

"Thought you might be," I said.

LQ gestured at my bloody shirt. "You bad?"

"No. Who fixed you guys up?"

"Bunch of peons," Brando said. "Took me over to a hut and bandaged me pretty good. Then we come out here and found this peckerwood still alive and they patched him too."

"Where're they now?"

"Went home, I guess." He gestured toward the peon

housing on the other side of the compound. "They talked a whole bunch but I never got a word of it."

"From what I could make out, it was mostly bitching about Calveras," LQ said. "What a son of a bitch he was and how they hoped he never come back and so on."

"Well, he aint coming back," I said.

"Glad to hear it," LQ said. "Where's—"

"She aint coming back either."

They stared at me for a second. "Shit," Brando said. "I'm sorry, Jimmy."

"*He* do her?" LQ said. His eyes gave away what he was really asking. I figured he'd been thinking things over, his mind replaying the exchange of gunfire with the guy in the car.

"Yeah. He did."

He rubbed his eyes with his fingertips and let out a long breath.

Brando put his hand on my good shoulder. "Listen, Jimmy. What say we quit this goddamn country and go home?"

"Let's do it," LQ said.

"Let's," I said.

• •

Late that night we were back in Villa Acuña. Sanchez's filling station was closed, and we left the Hudson parked in the rear of it. The car looked a lot less snappy than it had two days ago. LQ wanted to take the Thompson with us, but I said we'd never be able to smuggle it past the border guards, and we left it in the car trunk with the BAR.

A norther had kicked up and steadily strengthened. It gusted hard and cold. We turned up our collars and hugged our coats to us and squinted against the blowing sand. We held tight to our hats as we crossed the bridge. LQ yelled, "So long, Mexico!" and spat over the railing—but just then the wind turned and slung the spit on his hat. He cussed a blue streak and Brando laughed.

They slept as the train rocked through the night. I sipped coffee and stared out at the moonlit landscape, catching sight of a lone coyote now and then, a solitary tumbleweed bounding alongside the tracks. The country regained grass and hills and trees. Brando had cleaned out my wound with tequila and bandaged it with a clean cloth he got from somewhere, but the shoulder had stiffened through the day and the ache of it ran deep under the muscle, down to the bone.

We went through San Antonio, chugged through Seguin, Luling, Columbus, and still I couldn't sleep.

The day broke gray and very cold and the trees were shaking in the wind. In Houston we changed trains. And then we were over Galveston Bay and at last I fell asleep for the few minutes it took to arrive at the station.

We stepped down from the coach and here came Big Sam through the crowd, smiling his movie star smile—then making a face of sympathy at the sight of LQ's armsling. He shook our hands and said he was happy to see us all back.

Rose was waiting at the station's front doors.

"Welcome home, Kid."

I nodded.

He smiled—and then led the way out, checking his watch as he went, because there were things to tend to, as always. Deals to close, payments to pick up, promises to collect on, warnings to deliver, accounts to settle . . .